CHEROKEE SABRE

CHEROKEE SABRE

Jamison Roberts

sabre
press

This book is a work of fiction. Names, characters, events, locales, and incidents are either the products of the author's imagination or used in a fictitious manner. Any resemblance to actual persons, living or dead, or actual events is purely coincidental.

Published by Sabre Press

Tulsa, OK

Library of Congress Control Number: 2020911751

ISBN: 978-1-7353068-0-3

Arrowhead
Cavern

Exhibition
Hall

Shrine

Jordan's
Gallery

Zayne

CHAPTER 1

Brilliant columns of light danced through green-tinted liquid as the sun broke the water's surface. A strange object caught a hint of bright light as it made its way through the cool, clean water. The way it fluttered back and forth, the object appeared and behaved almost like prey. She had flushed out and snagged a few choice morsels earlier, but this new quarry would pass nearby.

An occasional flick of her fins allowed her to maintain her position as she hovered above the rock-strewn riverbed. Concealed by green aquatic plants, she waited eagerly to ambush the unwary meal. Its movement wasn't as smooth as she might have expected, a bit jerky. Was it wounded? Regardless, it was one of the most tempting things she'd encountered all day. Normally, she preferred to chase her prey, thrilled by an active hunt, however she couldn't let such an easy prize just pass her by.

Her eyes tracked the object's motion as it glided closer. Instinct impressed upon her a desire to wait for the right moment to strike the unsuspecting prey.

So close. The meal was almost even with her.

Almost there, just a bit more.

Her gaze followed its movement as it swam past. The food

would be hers; her patience would soon pay off.

Now!

With a powerful stroke of her tail, she darted forward, striking the object from behind with all the strength she possessed. As she spread her jaw open as wide as possible, the powerful suction she created drew the meal into her mouth.

Confusion rushed through her as she realized something was wrong. The object was much too hard, and its taste was unnatural. Unknown flavors and textures overwhelmed her taste buds. As soon as she'd inhaled the meal, she tried to purge it. At that moment, she felt a sharp tug. Startled, she realized she hadn't been able to expel the thing completely. Another sudden jerk propelled her through the water. Raw fear surged through her. Her quarry had lodged itself inside her lip. Not only that, the thing continued to drag her. Her mind reeled; it shouldn't have been possible. The prey had way too much power behind it.

She whipped her tail back and forth, fighting to escape. No matter how hard she tried, she could not free herself. Pulled forward yet again, she knew something was very wrong; the force wouldn't stop. She made another attempt to spit the food out, but it was stuck. Baffled, she had never encountered anything similar to this small prey dragging her through the water.

A vague nightmare resurfaced from when she was younger. She'd come across another odd bit of food. It had looked different, however. That object had the appearance and mannerisms of an injured worm. Although also easy to catch, there had been a similar unnatural tang, and she'd experienced the same uncontrollable pull. Ripped from the water and unable to breathe, she'd experienced a horrible stinging sensation as the air began to dry out her gills. Some enormous creature had pried the worm from her lip, all the while making strange, loud noises. There had been bright lights, then, just when she had almost given up all hope, she'd been slipped back into the cool liquid of her natural environment.

She suddenly realized the severity of her peril. Frantic, she started to put up a proper fight. She used all her power attempting to escape. It didn't work; she couldn't get free. She was being pulled, dragged in a direction she somehow knew she didn't want to go.

Steve Pascall
6:27 pm

The boat rocked with the gentle flow of the river. It amazed Steve how the motion always seemed to calm him, to make his problems just drift away. The fiberglass hull, with its red reflective paint, caught the sun just right, making a splendid pattern on the water's surface.

For years he'd scrimped and saved for the bass boat he'd always wanted. It wasn't until his recent promotion that Steve could finally afford it. Not his first boat, but the best he'd ever owned. At almost nineteen feet long, his new bass boat wasn't the biggest out there or the nicest, but it was his. Steve smiled at the thought of his first boat; an old, forest green, aluminum jon boat. They were just so different; any comparison between the two vessels wouldn't have been fair.

Steve glanced down at the large outboard motor; at two hundred horsepower, it was more than he would ever need. Powerful enough for him to cruise across any lake at nearly seventy miles per hour once the boat was on plane. Steve marveled at the process of the hydrodynamic lift produced, which allowed the craft to rise to the plane. As the speed increased, the craft's bow lifted from the water, which lessened the hull's contact with the liquid, thus reducing its drag significantly and allowing the boat to reach faster speeds.

A sharp tug on his line yanked his mind back to the task at hand. He lifted the tip of the seven-foot-long, graphite, casting rod, and twisted the reel's handle several times. Steve liked the feel of the new Abu Garcia Ambassadeur in his hands. Its double bearings, gear ratio, and drag all felt just right. Steadily turning the ergonomically designed handle, he attempted to apply just enough pressure to let the fish wear itself out.

You mustn't rush these things.

"You got one!" Gabriel exclaimed, bouncing up and down.

Steve gazed down at his son and delighted at the expression of joy brightening his small face at the appearance of the day's first fish. The expression mirrored the wonder and excitement he remembered feeling when he was the boy's age.

They'd started late; it hadn't been until after six that evening when they'd put the boat in the water. His son had been ecstatic to accompany him on the trip. Gabriel's eyes had gone wide when he learned he'd be able to go camping and fishing with his dad and uncle. Steve supposed at eight years old everything seemed exciting.

"Yeah, I think it's a big one too," Steve beamed.

He was grateful for the opportunity to have this father/son bonding time. Steve hadn't been close enough to his own father and refused to make the same mistake with Gabriel. It wasn't easy being a single dad, and Steve wanted to do his best. He'd found his son an old rod and reel at a flea market the month before. The rod was nothing special. However, the reel, an old Zebco Model 33, just like his uncle had taught him to fish with, was still in excellent condition. Someone had taken great care of it.

He glanced at his Lowrance depth/fish finder to check the riverbed's depth beneath his hull. *Five feet, still safe.* Just to be sure, he lowered his foot onto the pedal of the trolling motor for a second. He heard the satisfying hum as the small, powerful motor kicked in. Steve had positioned the boat in one of the calmer sections of the river, out of the main current, and needed to keep the boat away from the bank.

The line jerked back and forth as the fish fought. A few more gentle turns of the handle brought in the slack.

Steve was glad he'd used one of his old Swimmin' Minnows. The lure was one of his favorites. With its natural swimming motion and paint job of light shades of green and white, it had a realistic look. He had various lures to choose from in his turquoise, metal, pocket tackle box. Just like the old tackle box his uncle had always carried.

It seemed the fish was beginning to tire. *Not long now.* All he had to do was keep up the gentle pressure and slowly reel it in.

His focus shifted skyward, and Steve scanned the heavens. It was a beautiful day. There was just the barest hint of clouds in the bright, clear blue sky. The cool, clean water of the river contrasted the multiple colors of green, brown, and gray present on the shore.

As he pulled the fish alongside the boat, Steve lifted the tip of the rod and finished reeling the enormous fish to the starboard bow. The largemouth bass appeared to be one of the biggest he had ever caught. It had to be at least five pounds, surely not a record but still a splendid catch.

Steve had known people his entire life who couldn't wait to get out of Oklahoma. He'd never understood, never wanted to leave. With fifty-eight lakes and over one hundred and seventy species of fish, why would you ever want to? It was crazy.

Once the bass was at the edge of the boat, he stooped and, making sure to keep the line taut, he slipped a thumb into the fish's mouth. As he squeezed the fish's lower lip, between thumb and forefinger, the fish thrashed around, continuing its fight.

"Wow, that is a big one!" his son exclaimed as Steve lifted the bass over the gunwale.

"Grab the camera out of my bag and take a picture," he instructed.

While Gabriel dug through the bag, Steve realized the fish might even be a little bigger than he'd first thought. He leaned the rod into the crook of his arm. Steve flipped his multi-tool open and pried the hook from the fish's mouth with its pliers. He watched Gabriel pull the camera from the bag and its case. His son's caution with electronics impressed him, besides the boy seemed to know as much about the devices as he did.

"Say cheese!"

"Cheese," Steve replied. A smile lit his face a moment before the flash did. "Take another, just in case."

After the second flash went off, he set the rod carefully on the boat. He bent down to open the live well and lowered the fish inside. The fish would taste great. Steve was all for catch and release with younger fish, but he didn't see a point in depriving himself of such a treat.

"Let me see," Steve beamed as he reached out for the camera.

The camera's performance impressed him. Even in automatic mode, it took crystal clear photos. In order to capture the scene, the camera had adjusted automatically for light exposure and color. On the screen, he stood below the light blue sky in his fishing jacket. His light brown hair peeked out from beneath his 'Red Bird' ball cap, catching the light. He could clearly make out his bronze, B.A.S.S. belt buckle at his waist. The river water had a clear blue color to it, from natural springs found in much of the surrounding area of Oklahoma. A plump bass in one hand and a Falcon rod in the other, behind him, a majestic view of some limestone cliffs.

"Wow, this is great!" Steve praised.

He didn't notice that the second picture had a small crack, absent from the first, which ran vertically all the way to the top of the cliff.

CHAPTER 2

Sam Pascall
6:33 pm

As he pulled the handle, Sam Pascall felt the latch click on the rear door of his dark blue, GMC SUV. With little effort, he swung the door up over his head. The vehicle sat in the grass near the edge of a narrow dirt road. The clear blue of the river peeked through the canopy to the west, further down the lane. Sam stretched his neck, gazing past the multiple species of trees that lined the sides of the road in either direction. His brother had directed them to the spot and described a clearing somewhere close by. Through the thick trees, he couldn't make out much, but he thought he glimpsed it.

Sam reached in to grab his backpack and swung the stylish, black bag over a muscular shoulder. As he grabbed the handle of his worn tent, a rumbling shook the ground beneath him. Back snapping straight, Sam barely avoided hitting his head on the open door as he swung around and stepped away from the car. Eyes searching the landscape, Sam peered around and caught sight of several plumes of dust billow from the dirt road not far away.

"Wow, did you just feel that?" Sam exclaimed. He peered

over his shoulder, eyeing his three companions. "Did anyone else feel that?"

"Was it an earthquake?" His girlfriend, June Moon, showed only a vague interest. Stretched into the rear of the vehicle, June rummaged through the bags. Sam's eyes traveled down her willowy body. He was a lucky man; June was such a beauty. Strong cheekbones and jaw; straight, black hair flowed over the front of each shoulder, divided into two braids. Sam's eyes followed the curve of her back down to her waist. Her shirt rode up, revealing her naturally tanned skin, common to Native Americans, and exposed two cute dimples on the small of her back right above—

"Ahem."

At the sudden cough, Sam's eyes shot to her face. As June eyed him over her shoulder, an impish smile lit up her face. She raised an eyebrow coyly, maintaining eye contact for a moment longer, before tearing her eyes away. Sam felt the muscles on one side of his face lift into a smirk, he knew she enjoyed gazing into his blue eyes. While he watched, June pulled another of the tents from the vehicle and propped it against the bumper.

Sam gave his head a shake to clear it, before he replied, "Yeah, I think it was." He'd almost fallen into her strikingly gorgeous, brown eyes. Attention shifted back to the task at hand; Sam leaned his tent against the car next to the other. He dropped the pack from his shoulder and laid it on the ground. Sam moved next to June and reached for the final tent. "I wish we'd invested in some better tents. You know they have some that are smaller and easier to set up," he complained, focused on the well-used tents.

"As infrequently as we go camping, it's easier just to borrow our family's old tents," June mused, "and cheaper." June was almost always, sometimes maddeningly, the voice of reason.

"They've been happening more often of late," Jim blurted. His statement brought a few blank stares from the group. Sam wondered what the hell that had to do with tents. The confusion on their faces seemed to convince Jim he needed to elaborate. "Earthquakes have been occurring more often," he explained.

Now Sam understood, Jim hadn't gotten a chance to weigh in, so he had brought the discussion back around to the previous topic. Jim was always keen to put his two cents in, no matter the discussion.

"There weren't always so many earthquakes in Oklahoma," Hannah complained as she shoved a bag to her boyfriend. She slipped a hair tie from her wrist as she reached back to pull her dirty blonde hair into a ponytail. "My grampa says it's drilling for oil that causes them."

While she spoke, Sam scanned the other couple. Hannah couldn't have been more than five feet tall. A lifetime of gymnastics and sports had molded her body. She had broad shoulders and a small waist. She wore a tight pair of jeans. A white, V-neck top, likely a few sizes too small, ended just below her belly button and showed off her flat stomach and well-defined obliques. From the look of her tan, she'd soaked up rays most of the summer.

By contrast, Jim stood three or four inches over six feet. Slim yet muscular, he wore a tight green polo shirt and a pair of khaki pants. He wore his gelled hair in a part on one side. A pair of rectangular black glasses perched atop his nose; a neatly trimmed beard covered the lower half of his face. Jim stuck out his chest and brought his arms around to meet behind his back. His sternum popped loudly. Sam winced, *that couldn't be healthy.*

"Or Natural Gas," Jim added as he stretched an arm across his chest and popped his shoulder. He reached down to pull some bug spray from the bag and spritzed his tanned skin. Jim offered the spray to the others. With no takers, he shrugged and stuck the bottle back into his bag.

"When is your brother going to get here?" June asked as she twisted to meet Sam's gaze.

"He's already here. They got here earlier, to put the boat in," he replied. Sam slung his backpack over his shoulder and snatched up a tent with his other hand. "I'm supposed to meet them near the river at twilight," he concluded.

"They?" Jim asked, looking at June in confusion.

"His brother and nephew," June replied as she and Sam

ventured into the tree line.

Mighty old Oak and Hickory trees sprinkled the landscape around them. The forest floor, covered in dead leaves and branches, was dusted with young saplings and wild brush. Still more varieties of trees filled in the rest. Through gaps in the tree cover, Sam barely spotted the clearing where they decided to set up camp. It was about a hundred yards from the dirt road and an equal distance to the river.

They advanced toward the clearing, winding around any obstacles. Behind them, Jim and Hannah followed, lugging a cooler between them. The crunch of leaves and crack of limbs pierced through the quiet of the woods. Before long, the tree cover lessened enough for them to see the entire meadow.

"Your nephew is here?" Jim sputtered as they caught up. "How old is he?" he asked.

"Gabriel's eight years old," Sam replied with a look over his shoulder. Confused by the tone of Jim's voice, he gazed back at Hannah. "We told Hannah they were coming. Didn't she tell you?" Sam queried.

"Ha, of course, I told him, but he never listens to me," she complained.

"I do so," Jim shot back, annoyance in his tone, "what are we going to do with an eight-year-old tagging along. I mean, there are certain things I expected from this trip." Jim sat his side of the cooler down as they reached the center of the clearing and looked at Hannah. "Or, at least, hoped for. I brought this as well," he finished as he pulled a small bag out of his pocket.

"No need to worry. He's a good kid. Besides, he'll be asleep by 9:00; 9:30 tops," June said as she cleared the ground of any branches or rocks. "You just have to be quiet is all. Which, I gather, might be harder for some than others," she jested with a glance at her roommate, Hannah. Sam smirked; June had mentioned that sometimes when Hannah and Jim were intimate, she tended to be a tad noisy.

"Besides, you can surely go a few hours without getting high," Hannah said, neck and cheeks flushed red. She either hadn't heard June's last comment or purposefully ignored it, not deigning to respond. Sam thought it was probably the latter. She moved over to help as he lay out the first tent.

"I guess," Jim grumbled. Still put out by the turn of events, he shuffled over to Hannah and Sam to help with the tents.

Steve Pascall
8:22 pm

The sun was low on the horizon and dropping behind the hills to the west as Steve inched his boat toward the shore. Sam waited for them by an old wooden dock. The aroma of burnt logs filled Steve's nostrils as he pulled his boat alongside the platform. He tossed one end of a rope to Sam, who pulled it taut so Steve and Gabriel could climb from the boat.

"Uncle Sam!" Gabriel exclaimed, running over to hug him.

Sam kneeled to take his nephew into his arms and smiled. "Hey, buddy!"

As Sam helped by tying the boat to the dock, Steve could tell Gabriel was tired after several hours in the boat. With the boy's short brown hair and freckled face, Steve was astounded by the similarities between himself and his son. Steve still couldn't get over how fast his son was growing. Gabriel was almost up to his chest.

"Come on, we have everything set up," Sam encouraged. As Steve ducked down to pluck the fish out of the live well, Sam reached over and locked the fishing poles into one of the boat's storage compartments.

The hill sloped up from the river at a gentle grade as they headed toward the camp. As he walked along the narrow path, Steve noticed a thin layer of brown leaves partially covered the trail. The leaves on a few of the trees had also just started to turn. It was almost time for the beautiful fall colors. It was a wonderful time for fishing.

"Did you have fun today?" Sam asked Gabriel. He sidestepped some brush as he led them through the woods.

"Yeah, Dad caught the biggest fish though. None of mine

were even big enough to keep," Gabriel replied in a resigned tone as he hopped on, then over a fallen tree.

"You gotta give them time to grow," Sam put in. He dodged a set of large stones that sprung from the soil. "You're almost big enough to keep," he said with a wink.

Gabriel scrunched up his nose as he gave his uncle a withering look. "Whatever!"

Before long, Steve was greeted by the warm glow of a raging campfire. Spaced out around the fire were three tents, one set a little further away from the other two. Hannah and Jim roasted hot dogs over the flames. A few feet from them a portable gas grill sat waiting, ready for use. June lounged, curled in a lawn chair not far from the fire, reading a novel in the dim light.

Steve still didn't know how he felt about Jim and Hannah, he had been around them several times that summer but still hadn't decided. He'd hung out with his brother more often since his marriage had imploded. It might not have been so bad, but his ex-wife had gotten most of their friends in the divorce. *Fairweather friends, the lot of them,* he accused. He let out a deep sigh. That wasn't quite fair; most of them had been her friends, to begin with. He glanced over to his brother's girlfriend. June, on the other hand; she was great. She was always so kind to Gabriel.

His eyes swept over the clearing and took in the campsite. Steve indicated the tent furthest away with a nod as he asked, "Is that ours?" He sat the fish down on an old cutting board.

"Yeah, I thought you might want some space when the little man's bedtime comes around," Sam answered. Sam pulled a fillet knife from his bag and tossed it over.

"I'm not tired," Gabriel protested. "Daddy said I could stay up longer tonight."

"But not too late," Steve said distractedly, eyeing the knife intently. About nine inches long, the wooden handle protruded from a decorative leather sheath. Steve rubbed his thumb over the fish carved into the handle before pulling the knife from the leather. On the blade, he could just barely see cursive writing etched in the metal. "Where did you get this?" Steve asked, still studying the knife.

"Found it at Mom's house," Sam explained dismissively.

Steve looked up at his little brother. "This belonged to Uncle Ben. I've been looking for this," he said.

"Oh, well, now you found it," Sam observed with a shrug.

"Where was it?" he asked.

Sam met his eyes. With a smirk, he replied, "In the knife drawer, where else?"

"Huh," Steve grunted as he and Sam began cleaning the fish for dinner.

Sam Pascall
9:13 pm

After everyone had eaten dinner, Sam reached over to the cooler and dragged it toward him. Sam undid the clasp and opened the lid. The ice inside had mostly melted, leaving the cool beers floating just under the surface. The chilly water licked his hand as he pulled a beer from the cooler. Sam turned to the others. "Anyone need another?"

"Here," Jim called; hand raised.

A muffled shriek floated through the trees and snatched their attention as it pierced the night air. Sam's head snapped to the east, toward the source of the cry.

"What was that?" Gabriel yelped.

Sam's eyes strafed the tree line for a second. Much of it was indistinct in the low light, but there was no sign of movement. With the cry, an old story flashed into his mind.

"Probably a bobcat," Gabriel's father assured.

"Bobcat's scream?" the boy asked warily.

"Yeah, they're screamers," Hannah chimed in.

"They're not the only ones," June quipped, bringing a blush to the other girl.

"What else screams?" Gabriel asked.

Sam shot June a look of mock warning. "Owls, owls scream too," he blurted.

13

After a moment without any further sounds, Sam returned his attention to Jim, then tossed the can across to him.

Sam plucked another can from the icy water. "Anyone else?" he asked, holding it up as he looked at each person in turn. Hannah was still nursing hers. Steve shook his head as their eyes met. June had switched to pop after her first beer. With a shrug, Sam settled back into his seat next to his girlfriend, stretching an arm around her shoulders. They hadn't brought enough lawn chairs, so June had spread a blanket on the ground in front of a log, a few feet away from the fire.

The fish his brother had caught had been excellent, and you can hardly beat a flame-kissed hot dog. With the warmth of the fire in front of him, a full belly, and June snuggled beside him, Sam was content.

"Has anyone ever heard the legend of the Wampus Cat?" He took a long drink. As the bitter liquid assaulted his tastebuds, he watched the others shake their heads.

"Ok, so long ago there was this Indian bride," he began.

"Native American," Hannah interrupted.

"What?" Sam asked with narrowed eyes, surprised that Hannah had interrupted him.

"Native American, not Indian," she replied.

Jim broke into a grin. "Yeah man, you gotta be PC these days," he joked.

"Shut up!" Hannah grumbled with a roll of her eyes.

"Can I continue?" Sam chided. There was a slight pause before he went on. "Long ago there was this beautiful Indian bride," he began again, breaking into a smile at the look on Hannah's face as he ignored her correction, "who was resentful that her husband and the men of her tribe would always hunt while she had to stay home. Curious, yet aware that women weren't allowed, she decided to follow her husband and the other hunters secretly as they set out on a long hunt. She concealed herself under the skin of a wild cat, and she spied on the men as they performed magic and told sacred stories."

"The laws of the tribe had forbidden women from hearing the sacred stories and seeing their magic. When the woman was found, the men were furious. To punish her, the shaman bound her in the wild cat's skin, transforming her into a monster. It is said she was half-wildcat, half-human, cursed to wander the woods forever. Apparently, she likes to stalk campfires, sometimes stealing food but sometimes attacking unwary campers."

"Are there really wild animals out here?" Gabriel asked his father, eyes wide, fear written on his face.

His father gave Sam a menacing glare before he let out a bark of laughter. "No Gabriel, there's nothing to worry about. Uncle Sam is just trying to scare us."

"Well, it's working," the boy muttered to a general round of laughter.

CHAPTER 3

10:45 pm

As she crept through the woods, the smell of cooked meat and burnt logs flooded into her nostrils. She parted her jaws to let the air drift past the roof of her mouth and into her lungs. Other scents were unfamiliar to her, some sweet and cloying, others sour and bitter. The night was cool and dark, the stars shone in the clear sky, and the moon was full and bright. The moon looked closer than she remembered, massive. Confusion and hunger overwhelmed her. She had no clue how long she'd slept. From the painful emptiness in her belly, she could tell it had been ages since she had eaten. Too long. She was starving, ravenous.

The fading light of the fire filtered through her slit pupils and struck her retinas. Strange, bright colored tents dotted the clearing, filled with the enticing smell of people. It had been so long. She'd been stuck for so long. Confined. Caged. Imprisoned in the cave, trapped inside the rock until the earth itself had shaken. The deep rumble from below had torn the final pieces of her stone prison asunder, releasing her.

Soft laughter and whispers floated from one tent. There was a sudden cry of alarm as she spooked a nighthawk from its nest.

16

In an instant, she dropped to the ground and the voices ceased. There was movement inside the tent.

"What is it, Sam?" A female voice said.

Not understanding these strange words, she nestled lower to the ground.

"Did you hear that?" the man asked as the tent flap opened and a head peeked out.

"What?" the woman asked.

"I think it was a bird," he replied, slurring his words a bit as he crawled clumsily out of the tent. In the moonlight, the man appeared to have light, straw-colored hair. He was tall and very pale. "Come on, June, let's see what spooked him. Come on." The young man reached his hand into the tent to pull the young woman out. The young woman had rich tanned skin just like she had once possessed. The young woman's hair was dark, separated into two long braids.

"Are you sure this is a good idea?" she sassed, joining him outside the tent.

"Why not? It was just a bird," he assured, leading her away from camp.

After the two disappeared into the woods, she rose from the earth, prowled forward, and stalked her prey.

Steve Pascall
10:57 pm

An odd sound greeted Steve as he drifted awake. It was some kind of wet crunching. He rolled over in his sleeping bag and squeezed his eyes shut. He attempted to drift off again; daylight would be there before he knew it, and they were in for a long day. There were more odd sucking sounds. *Squelches*, his sleep fogged mind announced. Had the sound woken him? What were they doing? Whoever it was, whatever they were doing, Steve wished they would cut it out. Right before Gabriel had gone to bed, Sam chose to tell that scary story. Steve could have throttled him for that. After that, Sam and his friends had started to drink more. When Steve had called it quits, after only two beers, they had still been going strong.

Steve heard that strange sound again. What was it? Rubbing his eyes, he tried to place it. This time it had been more of a squelching, sucking, gnawing thing. He struggled to sit up, groggily wondering what the sound was. Beside him, his son still slept. Steve was thankful for that, at least. Careful not to wake his son, Steve unzipped the tent and crawled out, curious to see what they were doing out there.

Steve scanned the camp; the fire was only embers now, and aside from that odd sound, all else seemed quiet. Steve crept toward his brother's tent. In the moonlight, he noticed the flaps unzipped and wide open. A peek inside as he bent over, confirmed it was empty. Steve wondered where his brother had gone.

"Huh," he grunted softly.

From across the way, he heard the odd sound again. Steve crept for the other tent. As he approached the second tent, he heard movement inside. Had Sam and June joined the others in their tent? God, if he found all four of them in there together, he didn't know what he'd do.

The tent was closed, zipped to the top. But something wasn't right. He pulled out a small pocket flashlight and switched it on. Steve circled to the far side of the tent. As he came around the side, his bare foot swept across some loose stones, scattering them. The noise and movement inside the tent ceased. Steve's heart raced. Pointing the beam of light toward the tent, he was shocked to see the entire backside of the tent was shredded open. Inside, a massive shadowy shape turned his way.

Sam Pascall
11:03 pm

On the way back to the camp, Sam paused and pulled June in closer to him. He was disappointed they hadn't been able to find the source of the noise, but it had been fun to explore the woods at night with his beautiful girlfriend. Sam had known there was nothing to be worried about.

"Sam, I'm tired, let's go back to bed," June pleaded. "We've already been out here fifteen minutes. It's getting chilly." Sam stroked her cheek. The wind coming off the river and the lake, further to the south, made the air cooler than usual for late August.

"Ok hon," Sam conceded. "You go ahead. I need to get something from the car," he said. Sam took his girlfriend into his arms and kissed her softly. "I'll be there soon."

June gave him a tired smile and replied, "Don't take too long. It's cold out here." She headed toward camp. June glanced back over her shoulder, a mischievous smile on her lips. "I may need you to warm me," she purred.

Using a small flashlight, Sam picked his way through the forest. The night was quiet and eerie, yet exhilarating.

As he approached the car, Sam heard an ear-piercing wail. His breath caught as he spun toward its source. He took off running toward the camp as fast as he could. What was it? What could it be? Sam heard another scream and put on more speed.

Dashing into the clearing, Sam's eyes flew over the campsite, scouring the area. He spotted a small flashlight lying on the ground near Hannah and Jim's tent. Tossing caution aside, Sam bolted around the tent and traced the beam of light with his eyes. The back of his friend's tent was torn open, the inside a bloody mess. When he shot a look back toward the flashlight, he noticed someone lying, rigid on the ground. Sprawled between the tent and the tree line, the body was still. Too still.

"Oh my God, no," he muttered. Steve. His brother lay there, bloody. Still. Dead. Sam stumbled toward his brother's body, dropping to a knee. He gazed slack-jawed down at the corpse. His brother was dead. Steve was dead. How could Steve be dead? What would he do? What would happen to—

Sam's eyes widened. *Gabriel*, the thought burst into his head, *where is Gabriel.*

"Gabriel. Gabriel, where are you?" he yelled, searching for his nephew. Another scream rent the night air, louder and more terrified. Sam stood and whirled toward the sound; he saw a massive shape slink away. Some kind of animal appeared to be dragging something through the brush. Sam started toward the shape and heard yet another shriek. This one ceased mid-scream and was followed by a horrible gurgling sob.

Oh God, Oh GOD! June.

Sam stopped and looked around in panic. He ran toward his brother's tent.

Empty.

Empty!

Where's Gabriel, he thought again, *where could he be?* He heard a sound behind him and spun. *Oh, thank God.*

Gabriel stood next to Sam's tent, unmoving. He darted for his nephew, collapsing to his knees in front of the boy. Grabbing the boy's shoulders, Sam scanned his nephew for any sign of injury. Then enveloped him into a tight hug. There was blood on his shirt and pants, but the boy seemed unhurt. Still clinging to him, Sam rose to his feet, lifting Gabriel with him. Cradling his nephew against his chest, Sam glanced back to where he'd seen the shape. The animal. Not knowing for certain if June was alive or dead, he let out a sob and scrambled for the SUV, Gabriel in his arms.

CHAPTER 4

Fredrick Delacroix
7:33 am

Fredrick Delacroix pulled up next to a navy-blue cruiser similar to his. It too had Cherokee County Sheriff written in bold letters along its side. Illuminated by the red of his brake lights, a white coroner's van was reflected in his rear-view mirror. His eyes flicked over to focus on his reflection. Fredrick's gaze traveled over his fresh buzz cut and down to his face. Deep honey-colored eyes stared back at him and took in his almond skin tone.

Damn, I look good! He thought, smiling in the mirror. Fredrick stroked the thin stubble on his chin before reaching for the door handle. He hadn't had time to shave, and he hoped no one would mention it.

Fredrick opened the door and made a thorough scan of the ground to choose his footing before he slid from his cruiser. Eyeing the waterlogged dirt road, he tried to avoid the larger accumulations of water and mud. His shoes sank a quarter inch into the soil; nothing he could do about that. Fredrick pulled his crisp, navy-blue uniform shirt down at the waist, then ran his hand along its back to make sure it was properly tucked. Beneath the fabric, his fingers skimmed the stiff material of his bulletproof vest. As he adjusted his duty belt, he passed a black truck splattered with both fresh and dried mud, Game Warden stenciled in gray on the front fender. Even in the soft morning light, the large, blue Oklahoma Department of Wildlife Conservation decal popped against its cool black paint. Pressing down with his left hand, Fredrick made sure his service weapon was snugged in its holster.

Once he stepped off the road, he let each foot slide along in the damp grass to remove the worst of the muck. Fredrick gazed across the landscape. Down the road, near the river, was a thin layer of fog fading in the morning light. In front of him, small trees spread out densely on either side of a vague trail. As he followed the path through the woods, the vegetation along its edges showed indications of fresh trampling.

A clearing, about the size of a football field, appeared through the thinning trees. Yellow crime scene tape popped against the greens and browns of the surrounding vegetation. A couple of hundred feet into the clearing stood a royal blue, four-person tent with a thick yellow stripe around it. His eyes shifted to a circle of heavy stones filled with ash and burnt wood. Beyond the campfire stood a cluster of men and women blocking his view of the rest of the area.

Fredrick ducked under the police tape and strode up to his colleagues. Glancing to the east, he squinted into the brightening light on the horizon as sunlight broke through the tree cover.

"Hey boss, what have we got?" Fredrick asked.

"Glad you made it, Freddie. Sorry to call you in on your day off, but we need all the help we can get," the sheriff replied as Fredrick gave a slight nod, faintly gritting his teeth. *Freddie?! My name is Fredrick. Why do so many people have trouble understanding that?* He struggled against the urge to correct his boss; it wasn't worth the hassle, nevertheless it grated on his nerves. *Still, would it be so hard to*—with a sigh he shook his head, banishing the thoughts. No reason to brood over it.

A glance at his watch prompted him to calculate his coming overtime. Now, there was something to consider.

With a flick of the wrist, the sheriff motioned for Fredrick to follow as he stepped away from the group. "Well, it's not good. It looks to be an animal attack. We have three bodies and another missing, presumed dead. If that wasn't enough, a small thunderstorm rolled through a few hours ago, compromising much of the evidence and destroying any scent trail the search dogs could have used. The cell phone coverage out here is spotty, too. So…" he trailed off.

Fredrick let out a grunt as he continued to follow the sheriff. Two occupied body bags lay in the grass beside a crimson tent. The sheriff flipped a page back to peruse his notebook and his eyes reabsorbed the information.

"These two are James Epps, age 22, and Hannah Maitland, age 19," he said, motioning toward each of the body bags in turn. "And over there." The sheriff indicated a third black, heavy plastic body bag. "We have one Steve Pascall, age 28." Between the tent and the tree line, a coroner's assistant zipped the final bag closed. "All three were mauled," he concluded.

As he circled the red-domed tent, Fredrick noticed the vinyl material torn open along the back. Bending over to investigate the interior of the tent, Fredrick saw a substantial amount of blood on the slate gray floor and a tangy copper-like smell invaded his nostrils. He brought his hand up to cover his nose with his right index finger.

"What was it? Do we know?" Fredrick asked, running his eyes along the ragged edges of one split in the fabric. Whatever it was had been powerful.

"We suspect a mountain lion," he replied, "but the O.D.W.C. isn't sure. Unfortunately, we haven't been able to find any clear prints." Fredrick knew the Oklahoma Department of Wildlife Conservation investigated animal attacks this far from civilization.

Fredrick stepped back, nodding. "What do you need me to do?" he asked as one of the body bags was spirited away.

"We need to find the missing student." The sheriff glanced at his notebook. "A Ms. June Moon. The valley is a little more than a square mile in diameter. We've already searched the woods three hundred yards in each direction, so now, we will send some smaller groups out to look. Each group will have to use their portable transceivers. We'll relay any relevant data via the car radios."

Alan Harris
8:51 am

Alan Harris hiked toward the cliffs along the southern edge of the valley. Harris wasn't happy with the assignment. He knew the O.D.W.C. investigated dozens of mountain lion sightings each year, of which they confirmed less than thirty. However, it wasn't the possible wild goose chase that he objected to. He'd been involved with plenty of those in his career, including a time when he'd been forced to chase an actual flock of wild geese.

Those drunken idiots had gotten themselves killed, and now he might have to kill this poor animal. If there was one thing about the job he hated, it was these types of situations. They were a nightmare. Harris couldn't fathom why those immature city kids had decided to set up camp in such a remote place. They hadn't even created a proper camp, nor had they buried their trash. They'd left empty beer cans spread around. The campfire had been right in the middle of the three tents. The scent would have been too enticing for the animal to resist. Of course, Harris was glad the little boy had escaped unhurt, but this incident shouldn't have occurred at all.

Harris had worked for the Department of Wildlife Conservation in Oklahoma for close to twenty years. In that time, he'd only seen a handful of wild animal attacks. The majority of his job comprised enforcing fishing and hunting laws. Harris had read somewhere that big cat attacks in Africa and Asia often left little evidence. Those were lions and tigers, maybe a leopard or jaguar in the Amazon. There had been so few mountain lion attacks, so few fatal, he couldn't be sure what to expect.

Harris looked behind him toward Vasiliy Bodnar, the police

detective assigned to be his partner during the search. Vasiliy was a lanky man in his mid-forties with sharp features and a thick accent. Dressed in a long-sleeve, gray shirt and dark jeans, he carried a black tactical shotgun with a pistol grip strapped over his shoulder. His badge hung on a chain around his neck. Tramping through the woods in a pair of mud-spattered black Oxfords, he wasn't outfitted for this kind of search.

Harris lifted his tan ball cap and wiped the sweat from his balding head. As he plodded along over the damp terrain, Harris wished he had kept up with his workouts. Under his beige uniform shirt and green pants, he carried seventy-five extra pounds. Maybe a hundred, if he was being honest with himself. Harris knew his tall frame distributed the weight well enough, but he'd still just had to start using the next notch in his belt. At least, the ground ahead of them wasn't too uneven.

The forests in the area were composed mostly of several species of oak and hickory trees. There were also swaths of evergreens, pine, and cedar, running through the area. Here and there was the occasional persimmon, cottonwood, sycamore, and elm. He'd even noticed a few examples of Oklahoma's state tree, the redbud, scattered about.

The forest's undergrowth varied widely in density as they progressed. Some areas packed so full of trees and saplings, brush and briar, they could barely wade through. While in others, the mature trees had grown so large as to block out the sun, leaving the ground vegetation unable to thrive. Those were the easiest to charge through. In general, the undergrowth's thickness ranged somewhere between the two extremes.

Rock outcrops also swelled from the soil, sprouting like plants. The partially buried boulders could be a nuisance; however, the real hazard came from the multitude of smaller stones. One wrong step could mean a sprained ankle or twisted knee.

Harris spotted a set of prints in the damp mud. A quick scan of the area revealed nothing of note, so he squatted down to examine the prints. While wet silt distorted the edges of the prints, they appeared to be from a mountain lion. The animal seemed to be roaming in a characteristic overstep gait. If he was tracking a mountain lion, it was likely the one responsible for the deaths. Mountain lions are highly territorial, so he doubted there would be more than one in the area. However, the whole situation made little sense to him. Mountain lion attacks are very rare, and there were never multiple victims. What else could have attacked the campers though?

Fredrick Delacroix
9:26 am

When Fredrick Delacroix had pulled his cruiser through the line of vehicles early that morning, he thought he'd been prepared. He was wrong, very wrong. Nothing could have prepared him for that nightmare. Fredrick had never seen anything like it.

The young sheriff's deputy had been to all manner of crime scenes. The worst had probably been two years before, when a young mother had overdosed, leaving her four-year-old daughter alone for five days before anyone had come looking. The house had reeked of decay and the poor child was dirty and underfed.

However, the pure savage brutality of what he'd seen of this attack was staggering. He was thankful he hadn't arrived earlier. He had been able to avoid much of the carnage.

Fredrick's eyes drifted up from the hand-sketched map clutched in his right hand. He closed his eyes for a second and took a deep breath. The fresh scent of the forest filled his nose as he let his eyes flutter open. Ahead of him, Officer Hernandez's black ponytail draped through the back of her beige cap and caught the light as it bobbed back and forth. She wore olive colored cargo pants and a khaki polo shirt with an embroidered shield on the left breast. Hernandez appeared to be almost a foot shorter than his six-foot-three inches and slender. She looked to be at least half Hispanic. Latin American? His shoulders rose in a slight shrug. The thirty-year-old game warden carried an old bolt action Remington rifle over her shoulder. Hand snugged against the weapon's strap, pulling it taut, Hernandez led them through their search grid.

Fredrick had never been involved in a search with a dangerous animal like a mountain lion around. He had his share of encounters with dogs, which he knew could be dangerous; however, mountain lions were totally foreign. Hernandez seemed competent at her job, so Fredrick was more than willing to let her take the lead.

He hadn't even gotten her first name; she'd just introduced herself as Hernandez.

Fredrick cast his eyes downward to survey the map again. Lined on three sides by limestone cliffs, the valley was approximately one and a half square miles. To the west of the scene, the river ran along the edge of the valley. A dirt road came up from the southwest, followed the riverbank, then meandered north and east, ending several hundred yards east of the campsite. Fredrick and Hernandez were assigned to search an area northeast of the campsite, along the northern cliffs. He followed the game warden northeast, all the while keeping an eye out for the poor Moon girl.

Before long, Fredrick found himself following the ridgeline along the northern edge of the valley, walking along the side of a gully. To his left, the ground sloped down toward a dry creek bed at a forty-degree angle. The slope into the gully was strewn with rock outcrops as well as gigantic boulders. On the far side of the creek bed, the ground leveled out for about a dozen feet before meeting the rock face of the limestone cliffs, which rose approximately sixty feet.

Fredrick paused at the edge of the gully to scan the area. A section of the cliff face where the limestone had split drew his attention. About three feet wide, the fissure started five feet from the valley floor and ran up another five or so feet. Right below the crevice sat a massive boulder. It almost appeared to be an improvised staircase up to the cave.

"I'll check that," he volunteered, pointing at the opening.

"Ok," Hernandez replied.

Fredrick moved to the edge of the slope. It had to be at least twenty feet down to the creek bed. The moist soil along the incline shifted as he started down. On his way into the gully, Fredrick used several boulders to help slow his descent. He slid the last few feet, miraculously keeping his balance. Once he reached the ground, Fredrick took a few steps forward. He chose a flat rock and dragged his foot along its edge to scrape the mud from his shoes. He heard something behind him and turned to see Hernandez following him, half walking, half sliding down the incline. Boots now covered in mud, Hernandez took her place beside him and pulled the old rifle from her shoulder. She settled the butt into her armpit, pointing the barrel at the ground, ready to whip it up if she needed. Catching his eye, she nodded.

Left hand resting on his service piece, Fredrick crept up the worn tiers of the boulder toward the opening in the cliff's side. As he approached the gap in the rock, Fredrick pulled his small, powerful flashlight from its pocket, then glanced down at his companion. The game warden looked on as he turned to study the cave mouth.

Just inside the fissure, a narrow tunnel in the rock ran a few yards before it curved out of sight. He stepped up into the crevice and ventured into the passage. At the end of the passage, Fredrick shifted his flashlight to illuminate the inside of the small chamber. He scrutinized the room while panning the light. On the far side of the cave, he saw another gaping fissure. Along the wall to his right, he noticed what seemed to be a carved design. The cave floor was also strewn with what at first appeared to be debris. To his surprise, Fredrick spotted some Native American artifacts among the objects. A second scan revealed quite a few artifacts. He recognized the arrowheads, spearheads, and a few other weapons right away. There were even a few statues. But there were also some things he couldn't identify.

As he took a few steps forward, Fredrick glanced down. The prints his feet made in the loose earth made him pause. He scanned the floor for other prints, human or animal. Due to the lack of prints, fresh or otherwise, Fredrick realized nothing had been in the cave for years. Fredrick decided to call his discovery in. He shone the light on the artifacts again. He realized he'd better not disturb anything else; you never knew what those science types would consider important.

Fredrick squinted as he stepped from the cave and the bright, warm sunlight hit his face. Hernandez was scanning the trees in front of the cave. With a pivot, she twisted to gaze at him over her shoulder.

"Any sign?" she asked.

Fredrick shook his head as he bounded down from atop the boulder.

"No," he responded as he got closer to her, "but there were some Native American artifacts."

"Really?" she questioned, looking interested.

"Yeah, there were quite a few," he replied. "There was also a carving on one wall."

"Fascinating," she responded.

Fredrick had noticed she wasn't much of a talker. He didn't mind.

Once he joined Hernandez, they hastened to continue the search.

Alan Harris
12:38 pm

Harris scanned his surroundings as he crept through the woods. A shape appeared about a hundred meters away under some dense brush. He paused mid-step and dropped to one knee. In a crouch, he brought his rifle up. Harris tilted his head to rest his cheek on the rifle's stock. He took a deep breath, eye on the object in the high-powered scope. He felt his pant leg grow damp as it drew moisture from the groundcover. Peering past the crosshairs, a mountain lion came into crisp focus. The animal appeared to be tearing into something; he couldn't tell what.

Harris slowly exhaled and inched his finger toward the trigger, then paused. He still wasn't keen to take the shot.

Perhaps it wasn't too late to go another way. If he could somehow prove that this animal hadn't been involved, he wouldn't have to take the shot.

It was eating. The bodies at the campsite had shown signs of being fed upon. The mountain lion shouldn't still be eating if it had recently fed, should it? Harris tilted his rifle to focus on the animal's meal. What if this mountain lion hadn't been a part of the massacre? Could there be more in the area?

As his eye focused on the animal's meal, he let out a deep sigh. Fingers well-defined in the scope, the object the mountain lion gnawed on was a human arm. That sealed it. Harris reacquired his target. Finger tight on the trigger, he emptied his lungs and gently squeezed. The rifle bucked against his shoulder as he saw a small hole appear in the mountain lion's torso. Straight through its heart. It spooked and ran a few strides before it collapsed.

He wished he could have used a tranquilizer gun, but unlike the movies, these animals were too robust to be affected in a timely manner. In the several minutes it took for the tranquilizer to take effect, the mountain lion would become agitated. It might have gotten away, or worse, attacked someone else. Mountain lions are quick, powerful predators. Harris hated it, but he couldn't have taken the risk.

He slipped through the trees toward the spot where the mountain lion had been. Harris scanned the area as he approached and realized that he hadn't found the whole body. His eyes swept over the severed arm as he passed, marking the spot. His gaze locked onto the trail of fresh blood, and he followed the final route the big cat had taken. It took him a minute to follow the path. As the carcass came into view, he scanned the animal but saw no movement; it was no longer breathing.

Once sure the animal had passed, Harris turned and backtracked to the victim's arm. Harris reached over; using the side of his hand, he swept brush and moist dirt from what remained of the arm. With its long slender fingers and naturally tanned skin, it appeared to be the arm from a young native woman.

Harris and Bodnar spent several minutes looking under the nearby brush for the rest of the young woman before Harris pulled his hand-held radio from its slot and switched it on. Button depressed; he spoke into it. "This is Officer Harris with the ODWC. The mountain lion is dead. I repeat, the mountain lion is dead. We have also found what appears to be the left arm of a young woman."

"Acknowledged," the radio squawked its reply. "Please secure the animal's body, as well as the arm."

"What about the rest of the body?" Harris asked. "It might still be nearby."

"Come on back, we'll recall the teams and refocus the search on that entire area."

"10-4, Harris out." As he slipped the radio back into its slot, Harris turned to Bodnar. "Let's bag it up."

CHAPTER 5

Jamie Long
2:05 pm

Jamie Long pushed open the door to the women's volleyball locker room. The University had just completed its renovation of the space. A massive green rug, complete with the hawk head logo above the school's initials, NSU, sat in the middle of the new faux, dark wood floors. Around the room, dark wood cubbies lined the walls. Each niche had a built-in seat with matching green cushions. Printed above each cubby, on a plastic rectangle in the team color, was the team logo, player name, and player number.

Jamie spotted her number and angled over to her cubby. Once she slipped her practice jersey over her head, clad in a sports bra and volleyball shorts, she let her mind review the day's practice. While it had mostly been basic drills and team-building skills, it had gone well. The new assistant coach brought so much energy to the team. Her hopes were high for this year's volleyball team. She and her teammates seemed to work effectively together. Her first year had been a rebuilding year, and though they hadn't disgraced themselves, they hadn't excelled either. Sophomore year had been much better. Still, come November,

Jamie expected great things.

Her sports scholarship was a godsend. She'd still intended to go to college, but she preferred not to be upside down in debt after she graduated. She had gotten decent grades in high school, but she hadn't done well enough for a full ride.

Volleyball had been more of a hobby, to begin with. In middle school, she'd been invited to a summer youth camp called Falls Creek. There had been a sand volleyball tournament every week. Being tall for her age, the other campers begged her to join. She'd been reluctant at first, but by the end of the week, she'd fallen in love with the game.

Unfortunately, her middle school hadn't had a volleyball team, so she hadn't been able to play as often as she would've liked. She had talked the youth minister into building a sand volleyball court at the church and played as often as she could. But she'd been forced to wait for high school to join an actual team. By the time she started high school, she'd sprouted to six feet tall. With her height and experience, she made varsity as a sophomore.

She still wasn't much into the whole church thing, but she had continued to go to the camp through high school, mostly for the volleyball. She'd even considered being a sponsor for the last couple of years.

Church camp had also introduced her to another of her passions. From exploring the areas around Falls Creek and Turner Falls while at the camp, Jamie had fallen in love with geology and paleontology. She'd learned that the area was unique; tens of millions of years of geologic history were visible at a glance. For decades students had come from all around to study the various rock strata.

As she slipped her shorts down toned legs, she heard her phone ring. Jamie tugged her shorts off and tossed them into the cubby. She reached for her bag, unzipped the side pocket, and pulled the phone out.

She brought the phone to her ear and answered, "Hello."

"Jamie?" a female voice asked, "Jamie Long?"

"Uh yeah, this is Jamie," she glanced at the caller ID, then asked, "Who's this?"

"This is Cassie Byrne. I got your number from Professor Stone," the voice responded.

"How can I help you, Cassie?" Jamie asked. She had no idea why the professor's TA would call her.

"The professor wants you to meet with him in about an hour, if you can."

Jamie shot a glance at the time. "I can do an hour." She still needed to shower, but that wouldn't take long. "What's this about?"

"I'm not sure, something about a cave. I just got a text asking me to invite you," Cassie replied. "Shall I tell him you'll be there?"

"Yeah, no problem. I'll be there," Jamie replied.

"Good, see you then," Cassie said, then hung up.

"Huh," Jamie breathed. She stuck her phone into its pocket and grabbed her towel, wondering what that was all about.

Jordan Adler
2:12 pm

It was quiet in the library. The smell of old leather permeated the room, and the air conditioning made it comfortably cool. Jordan Adler sat at a small, wood laminate table, a large white column in front of her. As she stroked the close-cropped edge of her pixie cut, she could feel the rough, gray Berber carpet beneath her bare feet. She studied the news story on her tablet. Jordan reread the heading of the article.

Mountain Lion Attack?

Saturday morning, the small community of Welling, Oklahoma was rocked with the news of an animal attack. Three students attending the nearby Northeastern State University and a friend were killed in an apparent animal attack.

Hannah Maitland (age 19), June Moon (age 20), James Epps (age 22), and Steve Pascall (age 28) were camping together with Pascall's young son, and brother (Sam age 21).

Jordan straightened the sleeve of her t-shirt, the white material smooth between her fingers. Again, she skipped down to the part that had sparked her interest.

"The poor boy saw it all," says a source in the sheriff's office. "It appears Ms. Moon and her boyfriend (Sam Pascall) were away from the camp when the attack began."

"The boy was so scared, traumatized in truth, he claims it was not a mountain lion, but some kind of monster," officials say. "The boy's uncle (Sam Pascall) did not actually see the attack. However, the Oklahoma Department of Wildlife Conservation admitted that it was likely a mountain lion."

Poor kid, she mused.

Her grandfather popped unbidden into her mind. She remembered the first time Grandpa Joe had taken her along her parent's property in search of arrowheads, she'd been six. He'd told Jordan that Indians had inhabited the area for many thousands of years. Grandpa Joe used to tell her stories of Native American myths. Many of them had evil spirits that harmed people.

The tales of skin changers, switching back and forth between man and beast, used to freak her out. For a while, even the family livestock had frightened her. She wouldn't go near any of the animals. Grandpa Joe had assured her that the animals were exactly what they seemed. He'd told her that if skin changers had ever existed, the magic had been lost long before he'd been born, else he would have turned himself into an eagle to soar through the clouds.

Jordan's mother had always insisted the moment Grandpa Joe came into their lives had been a blessing, Jordan tended to agree. She loved her Grandpa Joe. Jordan's biological grandfather had skipped out on his family after her mother was born. Her grandmother had met and married Joe not long after. He had helped raise Jordan's mother and her Uncle Lewis.

Grandpa Joe appeared to be a full blood Indian. She knew he was part Cherokee, but when she was little, Jordan never could get him to tell her what other tribes he belonged to. He would often say he was half Osage, half Chickasaw or else half Choctaw, half Comanche, or one of a dozen other tribes. She had asked her grandmother about it once and had been told Grandpa Joe wasn't sure himself. The only thing he was sure of was that his mother had been half Cherokee.

Jordan tapped the power button to put the tablet to sleep and moved it to the side of the table. She focused her attention back on her book. Her assignment was to read three chapters by Monday, but it had to be the most boring novel she'd ever read. Why had she decided to take British Lit? *Oh right, because Dr. Walker teaches it.*

A sudden noise trilled beneath the table, startling her. Upon realizing she'd forgotten to put her phone on silent, Jordan shot a hand into her pocket and snatched the device. She slid her thumb across the touch screen as she extracted the phone to connect the call.

As she brought the phone to her ear, Jordan peered around to see if anyone had been disturbed. "Hello," she whispered.

"Is this a bad time?" she heard a man say. Jordan glanced at the caller ID. Professor Stone, her favorite teacher. She grinned.

"No, I'm in the library," she murmured, "just a second." Jordan slipped the tablet and book into her bag. She slid her feet into the flip-flops under the table. Jordan stood and hefted her bag over her shoulder. On her way to the exit, Jordan dropped the CliffsNotes onto the return cart. She'd just have to try again later.

"Hey Professor, what's going on?" she asked once she left

the library.

"I have a project you might be interested in."

"Oh?" she asked. Her pulse sped up and a sensation of warmth spread through her body. Jordan had to fight to maintain her composure. "What is it?"

"I'm planning to do an archaeological survey of a nearby cave system. Come to my office in an hour and we'll talk about it more," he replied.

OMG! Really! Tingles of excitement shot down her spine and her breath quickened. *Keep it together, keep it together.* She hadn't had many opportunities to do real archaeology.

"Ok, I'll be there," she answered with a nervous glance at the time on her phone.

Dr. Theodore Stone
2:54 pm

Professor Theodore Stone sat behind his L-shaped desk, resting his ample girth in the comfortable office chair. He gazed solemnly at the framed picture of his family that sat on his desk. Stone stood next to his beautiful wife as she held their young daughter in her arms. It was the last photo he had of his family. His wife had died in a car wreck three months later, leaving him to raise a little girl on his own. It hadn't been easy at times, but so far, he thought he'd done a good job.

Behind him, along the length of the wall, stood a floor to ceiling bookshelf, overflowing with books. On the floor in front of the bookshelf were stacks of books piled waist-high at the outer edges. One shelf held his published books. They weren't exactly bestsellers, but he had received critical acclaim from colleagues in his field.

As Stone studied the list of names on his desk, he reviewed his choices for the upcoming cave expedition. He'd strived to assemble a team that could work together. He was well aware of how stubborn academics could be, having spent his adult life in the profession. Stone intended to give some of his more promising students a chance for hands-on experience.

Cassie Byrne bustled into the office. "Hey Professor, what more can you tell me about this cave?" she inquired as she plopped down into a seat in front of his desk. Stone was glad she had chosen to ask him to be her doctoral advisor. She was a gifted young woman. Smart, disciplined, ambitious, all admirable traits. Though she could be a little controlling.

"We don't know much. I got a call from the sheriff's department not long ago," Professor Stone stated. "Did you happen to hear about the animal attack, somewhere southeast near Lake Tenkiller?"

"Yeah," she answered. "It's so awful. I knew one of the students that died."

"I agree, it is a shame," Stone empathized. "During the search, one of the teams found a variety of Native American artifacts inside an isolated cave."

"Really?" She inquired, eyes widening a bit. "What kind? Do you know?"

"No." Stone gave his head a slow shake. "The University, with the encouragement of the Tribe, has requested that I put together a team to go assess the find," Stone continued. "I would be honored if you and Henry Blake were to join me. It is also my intention to invite a few undergraduates."

Cassie's eyes sparkled with interest. "That sounds great, who did you have in mind?" she asked.

He glanced down and scanned his list once again, "I was thinking about Jamie Long, Jordan Adler, and Michael Redfern. Did you get ahold of Ms. Long?"

She nodded. "I did, she said, she'll be here."

"Good, thank you for that. What do you think?"

Cassie gave a slight shrug. "Jamie is an excellent student, but I got the impression she's more interested in paleontology than archaeology."

"Yes, that is true. However, there is a lot of overlap between the two disciplines. Besides, Ms. Long has also studied geology and has ample experience with caving. What about the others?" Stone inquired.

Cassie nodded. "Well, Michael can be a little arrogant, but he is the top of the class. I hardly know Jordan; do you think she's ready?"

"Do you know how we met?" Stone asked. When Cassie shook her head, he continued. "I was doing the college fair at the Tahlequah High School a few years ago. Up comes this young student with a box of arrowheads. She grew up on a farm along the river, you see, and was always exploring. She even had pictures and a map with the locations of some sites marked."

"Really," Cassie replied, nodding in approval.

There was a light knock as the door creaked open.

Henry Blake stuck his head into the room. "Hey Doc," he greeted as he leaned into the room. "You wanted to see me?"

"Henry, come in, come in." Stone beamed as he rose out of his chair a bit and waved the boy inside. "Take a seat. I take it you got my message?"

"Yeah, you said someone found a cave painting?" Henry asked, dropping into the chair beside Cassie.

"Indeed, it's so exciting," Professor Stone enthused. "In an isolated valley along the Illinois River, a sheriff's deputy found a cave with several native artifacts and at least one painting or carving. We're not sure exactly what's there. Lucky for us, the young man prudently chose not to disturb the site too much. The tribal council was intrigued, to say the least, and asked the University to plan a survey to evaluate the site."

"You want me to come along?" Henry asked, interested.

"Yes, of course, Cassie has agreed to come along as well. We have some work to do to be ready by next Friday."

CHAPTER 6

Vasiliy Bodnar
3:56 pm

Detective Vasiliy Bodnar fought through the undergrowth as he struggled back through the woods. He was nearing the area where the mountain lion had been killed. At least, he hoped so. It was his intention to scour the area further. There was a decent chance the body of the young Moon girl was close by. It was worth a shot.

Once the animal had been killed, Bodnar and Harris had loaded the mountain lion, along with the severed arm, into a large animal body bag and lugged it back to the vehicles. Upon hearing the news of the animal's death, a call had gone out, beckoning all the teams to return. By the time Bodnar and Harris had hauled the animal's corpse to the rally point, most of the other teams had already arrived. Crowded around the vehicles were many more people than he'd seen hours earlier. As the hours had slipped by with no sign of the missing girl, more search and rescue personnel and volunteers had been brought in to join the search.

Milling around the vehicles, representatives from different departments compared notes on the search and what little they'd found. Due to the rain, much of the evidence had washed away. According to one of the sheriff's deputies, the dogs they'd brought in hadn't been too useful. They'd seemed confused and terrified for some reason. That same deputy had found a cave of Indian, or rather, Native American artifacts. That was the most interesting discovery, aside from the mountain lion gnawing on the severed arm.

The sheriff intended to make sure they had the responsible animal, so he'd sent the mountain lion's corpse with one of the coroners to get a necropsy. With the discovery of the arm, the lead searchers had come up with a revised plan. As they prepared to continue, some personnel had been given new search areas, while others were asked to begin a grid search. Harris, after a conversation with his fellow game warden, had informed Bodnar he would be leaving. Bodnar had been disappointed at Harris's decision to leave, but the game warden had seemed upset after killing the animal.

Bodnar stumbled, shot out an arm to catch himself on a nearby tree, then let out a deep sigh. With the vegetation and the uneven ground, his progress through the forest was slow. Much slower than he would have liked. At least he didn't have mud to contend with any longer; most of the moisture had evaporated during the day. But Harris had seemed to know an easier way to travel through the woods. Possibly something to do with the lay of the land. Bodnar wasn't as comfortable in the woods as urban areas. Transferring from Brooklyn to Tahlequah might not have been his best move. It was a shame Harris had left early.

Before long, Bodnar came to an immense, flat outcrop jutting from the ground. On the far edge of the enormous stone, the ground fell away, leaving a steep drop-off. He hopped up onto the boulder and sidled to the ledge. As Bodnar leaned over the edge, he studied the landscape ten feet below. Under thick brush and mostly covered with dead leaves and broken branches, Bodnar barely made out the body of a young woman lying on her back.

His eyes scanned the outcrop for an easy way down. Not immediately seeing one, it took Bodnar several minutes to find a safe path down to the body. He strode over and knelt beside her. Bodnar didn't want to disturb any evidence there might be on or around the body. It appeared to be an animal attack, but that call wasn't his to make. The sheriff would likely want the medical examiner and perhaps the crime scene unit to inspect the body.

Scrub brush and hair obscured her face. Gone was the left arm, torn off at the shoulder, and the stomach was ripped out. Bodnar knew this was the body of June Moon, but he needed to make a positive identification before they could call off the search. Bodnar moved his eyes toward her feet to study the inside of her left ankle. There, just above the ankle, he saw the small tattoo her boyfriend had told them about; it read NDN.

3:58 pm

What were all these people doing here? Did they want revenge for the ones she'd killed? Were they members of the same tribe? How big could the tribe be?

The night before hadn't gone as planned. She'd just been so hungry. Drawn to the smell of cooking meat, she had only thought to take one, maybe two, of the humans. The small one wouldn't have been worth her time; too skinny, not much meat. After the couple had wandered off into the woods, she'd considered taking them, but figured sleeping prey would be easier, quicker, in her starved and weakened condition.

Even then, she had planned on only the two in the odd dwelling. It hadn't been until the third bumbled up to the back of the dwelling, to see her eating, that, with one decisive blow, she'd struck him down as well. She'd returned to her meal, oblivious of the first two humans she'd seen. They'd slipped her mind until the girl, too, had come across her in the middle of devouring her prey.

She'd dragged the screaming young girl away, having to silence her near the edge of the clearing when the man arrived. She might have killed him too if he hadn't taken the young one and fled. She had dragged her final kill through the woods, no sense in letting the meat go to waste, and hid the girl under some brush closer to her lair. By the time she'd returned to get the rest of her meal, other humans were there. More than before. She might have been able to take them, but she didn't want to risk it. Besides, she didn't know what kind of weapons they had. There were no spears or bows, but they had to have been armed with something.

What were those strange, smooth objects they'd arrived in? At first, she thought they might be hairless animals of some sort. She remembered animals larger even than the unfamiliar objects; mammoth, ground sloth, and mastodon. But then the humans had stepped out of them. They were hollow? Were they some sort of mobile dwelling? So loud. And the brightness of the lights. What magic was that?

Sated for the moment, she hung back to watch the new arrivals. She might have underestimated them if they could wield such magic. She'd watched as they split up to search the area, talking to each other in an indecipherable language. The longer she waited, the more of the strange objects arrived and the more people filed out. Once it occurred to her that they were looking for the meal she'd dragged off, she set about obscuring her trail.

When she'd finally returned for her saved meal, she found it too to be missing. Marks on the ground revealed the path in which her kill had been dragged. Furious, her nostrils told her a smaller cousin of what she had become was involved. She'd already lost her meal to her smaller cousin, yet they were still roaming through her woods.

Myranda Hernandez
4:12 pm

It had been a long day, hell, a long week. Myranda Hernandez looked forward to her upcoming vacation. On Monday, she planned to pay a surprise visit to her father's relatives in Mexico. She hadn't seen them in a couple of years and wanted to catch up. Family was important, or so her father always told her. In her heart, Myranda knew he was right, but it was hard to keep up, especially with them being so far away. Her career kept her busy as well. However, she was determined to make the effort.

After her colleague, Harris, had killed the cougar and found the severed arm, she'd been reassigned to search a different area. Hernandez knew that he hated to kill animals, knew that Harris became a game warden more for the conservation aspect of the job. So, with the animal dead, she'd told him she'd make arrangements to catch a ride with someone else if he wanted to take off. *I still need to do that.* She'd forgotten about it earlier. *It would be just my luck to be left out here and have to hike back into town.* She let out a slight chuckle.

They still hadn't found the missing girl. Myranda knew they might not find her, but she still wanted to try for the girl's family. Truth was, Myranda was surprised the cougar had left any of the bodies. Cougars prefer to cover their kills with debris, coming back to eat until the meat is gone or spoiled. She supposed the young man might have scared it off. But after killing four adults, it seemed odd to leave him and the boy alive. Hell, it was all odd. At least the animal was dead. As soon as she'd heard, a whole mess of trepidation she hadn't known she'd been carrying had just evaporated. The situation had spooked her more than she realized.

Myranda Hernandez fixated on her muddy black boots as she plodded through the thick brush. Rock outcrops sprouted from the soil; in the last hundred yards, their number had gone through a gradual increase. She'd become more vigilant of them since her tumble. Hernandez glanced at the tear in her light green uniform pants and noticed the bloody scrape along her tan skin. It wasn't too bad, but she would have to patch it up as soon as she got home. Hernandez shot a look at her watch; still hours until dusk. She tightened the hand around her rifle strap, snugging the weapon against her back, and scanned the area again.

Myranda Hernandez had wanted to be a game warden since the eighth grade. It wasn't easy, but it was worth the effort. To be a game warden, she'd needed to learn all about wilderness survival, and Oklahoma wildlife regulations and laws—

A sudden noise behind her prompted Hernandez to whip her body around. Eyes scanning the forest, she spotted a squirrel bolt along the forest floor then scurry up a tree. Hernandez smirked, chuckled, and then sighed. Evidently, she was still a little anxious, despite the knowledge that the animal was dead. She took a deep breath to calm her nerves as she let her gaze follow the squirrel. Hernandez caught another noise behind her, this one seamed louder. Calmer now, she took her time to react. No hurry. As she started to turn back, she felt a massive weight land on her shoulders, slamming her down. Hernandez turned her head. Confused, she tried to see what had hit her. Her heart pounded and dread flooded her veins. There was a pressure on the back of her neck, then deep pain as teeth pierced her skin. With a quick twisting motion, her body went numb.

Her eyes went wide as an overwhelming panic filled her mind. She was paralyzed, her lungs had stopped working. She couldn't breathe. As the black crept along the edges of her vision, she saw a massive tawny paw step into her sightline. Then two, then three. Four, then five?

CHAPTER 7

Fredrick Delacroix
10:39 am

Sitting at his desk Tuesday morning, Fredrick Delacroix studied a preliminary copy of the weekend's incident report. The events outlined in the report appeared straightforward. The attack had occurred just before midnight on Friday. Aside from that game warden—*What was his name?* His eyes flicked to that section of the report and scanned through the data to find the man's name. *Harris, Alan Harris. That's right.*

In addition to Harris finding the Moon girl's severed arm, lying near the dead animal, the necropsy of the mountain lion had shown human remains in the cat's stomach. Another man, a detective Bodnar, had even discovered the rest of the young woman's remains not far from where they'd discovered the arm.

So, why do I have the feeling I'm missing something? He just couldn't put his finger on the problem.

If it had been up to him, Fredrick would have put a rush on the lab work. That might have put an ease to the tension slowly bubbling in his gut. Samples of the remains found inside the cat's digestive tract had been sent to the lab for DNA matching. However, since the case seemed to be resolved, Fredrick knew the results of the DNA test might take weeks to return. While he wasn't pleased with the wait, he understood there were other priorities for the lab's time.

Still, there was something. He just couldn't shake off a rising wave of unease.

When the searchers gathered, after the animal had been shot, Fredrick had informed his boss of his discovery of a cave containing Native American relics. The sheriff had requested that he liaise with the local tribes and suggested that Fredrick might want to notify them before he returned to the search. As the cave's discovery had been made in Cherokee County, whose county seat, Tahlequah, is also the capital of the Cherokee Nation; he'd made a cursory report to the Cherokee Nation, informing them of the cave's existence.

The tribe had been thrilled with the discovery and had made arrangements for an archaeology professor from Northeastern State University, Theodore Stone, to survey the site. The plan was for Professor Stone, along with a group of students, to head out to the area the next weekend and have a look around.

When Fredrick returned to his office the day after the attack, the tribe had put him in contact with Professor Stone. Fredrick had sent along a copy of his map, as well as the exact coordinates of the cave he'd saved to his GPS. Over the past few days, the professor had swamped Fredrick's inbox with questions as well as requests for any details he could recall.

While the constant inquiries were beginning to get on Fredrick's nerves, he wanted to be sure the area was safe for them.

Allen Harris
1:53 pm

Harris hoped Myranda Hernandez was having a pleasant time on her vacation in Mexico. She deserved it. He didn't know how wise her idea of a surprise visit had been, but he guessed every family was different. Though upset after killing the mountain lion, Harris still felt bad about leaving her to finish the search without him. It didn't seem very professional. Yet, she had been the one to make the offer. She was a good game warden, and she cared for the animals.

If someone had asked him Saturday morning, he would have wagered a mountain lion wasn't responsible for the attacks. There were just too many inconsistencies, too much separation from a mountain lion's normal behavior. A mountain lion shouldn't have attacked so many people at once. Under normal circumstances, it would have been more likely to just take the young boy. The bodies should have been removed from the area and hidden. Maybe it had been rabid? He would have to get them to test for that. Or maybe a brain tumor or some other illness?

But Harris had no doubt it had been involved; after all, he had been the one to find the animal. It had been with the missing girl's arm, had been feeding on it. He glanced at the report. The body, found not far away by Bodnar, was buried under loose brush and vegetation. There were even mountain lion prints around the area. All the clues pointed to the mountain lion.

There was still something about the situation that just didn't quite make sense. But no matter how hard he tried, Harris couldn't see what it was.

CHAPTER 8

Zayne Stone
Friday, August 31st
7:33 am

Soft hues of orange and pink burst across the sky with the dawn light. Cheek snuggled into the chair's soft gray fabric, Zayne Stone gazed from the passenger window of the van. It was a little chilly, heading into Labor Day weekend. She had decided to remain in the vehicle; seventy-two degrees was just a bit too cold for her shorts and designer tee.

Zayne's eyes drifted to her father. She hadn't seen him this excited in a long time. He'd been planning this trip all week, ever since he'd heard about the cave. Her dad was almost hopping around as his students helped him pack the van. Surprisingly, he had taken her out of school for the day to join him. Zayne liked the idea of a four-day weekend, even if she had to look through some smelly old cave.

Her dad was super nice and super short. Aside from Zayne, he was the shortest one there, barely reaching five feet. His hair needed a trim. Her dad was bald on top with a scruffy ring of hair, a style one of her friends called a power donut. Every time she heard that, it made her giggle. Her dad needed to lose some weight too, but he just wasn't interested in diets or exercise. It worried her sometimes. He kind of reminded her of that actor Danny DeVito, except he was Cherokee.

Cassie, her father's teaching assistant, seemed to be the one in charge at the moment. For the last twenty minutes, Cassie oversaw the others as they loaded the van. She stood there, looking like she'd just rolled out of bed, telling everyone what to do. Dressed in an old, sleeveless t-shirt, with no makeup, and her hair pulled into a ponytail, Cassie wasn't even trying to look good. She did anyway, which made it even worse. Zayne liked the way Cassie's lime green top went with her pink jeans. She'd never thought to mix the two colors. Perhaps she'd ask Cassie for some style tips.

Zayne yawned, exhausted, she'd woken up so early that morning. She kind of wanted to take a nap, but she knew she wouldn't be able to. Instead, Zayne skipped to another song on her phone. Only one earbud in, she absentmindedly fiddled with the other while she bobbed her foot to the music. Her dad was always telling her not to spend too much time on the thing. After all, as he liked to remind her, he didn't have one when he was her age. How did people even get along without smartphones?

Zayne's eyes shifted over to Henry Blake as he hefted one of the molded plastic cases. He was so cute. Henry had these deep, light blue eyes and a short stylish haircut. He was thin, but she could see his muscular arms peeking out from beneath his tight shirt sleeves. He was so funny too and always made her laugh. Too bad he was so old, 28 was ancient.

Jordan Adler opened the sliding passenger door and set her bag on the seat. With her cute, short pixie cut hair, and in long tan cargo shorts, with a plain white t-shirt and bulky blue shoes, Jordan looked and dressed like a boy. Zayne hadn't known what to make of Jordan when she first met her. She hadn't ever known anyone quite like her. Zayne wasn't sure why she dressed that way and was too afraid to ask. Jordan was easygoing and kind, though, so she might ask during the trip. Surely, she wouldn't get upset.

"Hi Jordan," she bubbled.

"Hey Zayne," Jordan responded warmly. "How are you today?"

"I'm ok," she grinned.

As Jordan moved back over to join the others loading the van, Zayne slipped back to the seat beside Jordan's bag. She hoped Jordan wouldn't mind.

Through the open door, Zayne saw a tall, heavy young man, she didn't know. He had greasy brown hair, which looked like it hadn't been washed in years, pulled back into a small ponytail. An unkempt beard covered his face. He wore a black t-shirt of some band; its graphic had faded away from many wash cycles. She watched him as he carried a heavy molded plastic case, with the words 'archaeology dept' stenciled on the lid, to the back of the van. Cassie had called him Michael, so she supposed that was his name.

Jamie Long played volleyball and was one of the tallest girls Zayne had ever seen. She was so beautiful. Her heart-shaped face was framed by long, black hair. Her hazel eyes and thick black eyebrows easily drew the eye. Jamie had naturally tanned, olive skin and an athletic yet curvy body. She appeared to have a more Mediterranean coloring. Maybe Greek or Italian. Zayne wasn't sure. She'd seen Jamie play volleyball but had never met her. She was looking forward to it.

Jordan climbed into the seat beside Zayne, followed by Henry. As the others filed into the van, Zayne peered back to watch the last bags being loaded. They had taken the two rear seats out of the van to make room for equipment and supplies.

Everyone also had a massive backpack. Cassie and Henry had come over to their house the night before to help Dad pack. Zayne had even helped. Dad, Cassie, and Henry each had their own backpacks, and the college had provided packs for the rest of the students. To even out the loads, they'd split the nonperishable food and cookware among packs. Each pack also contained a sleeping bag, a foam pad, and a tent which left just enough room for their clothes.

Cassie opened the driver's door and climbed in. She spun to face them and surveyed the full van. Zayne's dad was the last one in as he boosted himself into the passenger seat.

"Are we ready?" Professor Stone asked in anticipation. He glanced from face to face around the group.

"Yeah, I think so," Cassie responded with a turn of the key. The engine roared to life as Henry Blake tugged the door shut.

Zayne put her right leg under her as she turned in her seat to face Jordan.

"Oh my gosh, did I tell you about—"

Henry Blake
8:37 am

Henry let out a contented sigh; the drive had only taken about thirty-five minutes. Jordan had listened to Zayne tell a long-winded story about some boy. At least, he thought it was about a boy; he'd zoned her out some. It amazed Henry that Jordan could be so attentive to the young girl. Jordan seemed to be able to tolerate almost anyone and truly care about what they said. Without a doubt, he lacked that particular gift.

The van entered a turnaround at the end of the dirt road and swung around. Cassie pulled the van off the side of the road and coasted to a stop. On the way in, they'd passed the police tape that still marked the scene of last weekend's incident.

Henry grasped the handle, heaved the van door open, and hopped down to the dirt road. He stretched stiff muscles while dreading what came next. They now had to slog through the woods with their supplies and bags. He watched the others exit the van. Probably not the team he would have picked, but not bad.

Henry couldn't understand why the professor brought his 11-year-old daughter. Not that he didn't like her; she was a good kid, maybe a little talkative and giggly. He just thought she would get in the way, be a distraction.

Henry opened the back door and grabbed his backpack. He swung it over his shoulders. At the thought of distractions, he glanced at Jamie Long, the six-foot-one-inch volleyball player.

She was truly stunning, and she always seemed to dress to draw attention, with short shorts and tight shirts. He'd have to be careful; he didn't want to be that guy, the TA known to date students. Even if he wasn't directly involved in her education.

"Do you have the map?" he asked Cassie as she stepped up beside him. Cassie was a fantastic student and teacher's assistant but could be a little bossy. She, and by extension, everyone else around her, were cursed by her type-A personality.

"Of course!" she chided. Her annoyed expression conveyed her true feelings for such a silly question. She held up a clipboard with copies of the map secured to it. "I made several copies, just in case." He just grinned at her. He liked to push her buttons, and she knew that. Realizing she had walked into that one, she rolled her eyes and sighed.

The map was hand drawn, with the cave's location marked by the sheriff's deputy who'd discovered the cave. Cassie pulled a few copies from her clipboard and handed them around.

"It's going to be a bit of a hike to get there," Cassie pointed out. "I looked at the satellite images of the valley and marked a few areas that could be used for our campsite."

"As long as we don't camp where those people died," Jamie put in as she hefted her backpack onto her shoulders. "Are we sure it's safe?" she asked with a look at everyone and no one.

"Oh yes, yes, they killed the animal responsible," Stone assured. "They even did a necropsy to make sure. They found remains of the victims in its stomach."

"What's a necropsy?" Zayne asked with interest.

"Oh, it's what they call an animal autopsy," Stone explained. He turned back to Cassie and asked, "How far to the cave? I would like to drop off the majority of the supplies at the cave."

"Let's see." She consulted her map, which was filled with notations. "The cave is about a mile from here, maybe a little further…"

Cassie's voice faded as Henry walked away from the group. Jordan stood at the edge of the dirt road and gazed in the direction of the clearing where the students had died almost a week before. Jordan must have heard him approach. As he neared, she glanced back over her shoulder at him.

"Did you know any of them?" he asked.

"Not really. I'd seen a couple of them around. Different circles, you know?" Jordan breathed.

"Yeah."

"Did you hear what the little boy said happened?" After a shake of the head, she continued, "He said it was some kind of monster, not a mountain lion."

"Really?" he asked. Henry heard soft footsteps approach, he glanced back and noticed Zayne sidling up to them.

"Yeah," she went on, "though I suppose it was just seeing his dad die and all. Maybe it was easier to blame a big scary monster."

He nodded slowly. Jordan's analysis sounded reasonable.

"Hey, Zayne, you promise you'll protect me?" he asked, turning to her.

"No need to worry," she squeaked, her face flushing a pinkish hue. She let out a cough. "I'll take care of you."

Henry grunted as Jordan's elbow slammed into his ribs. He gave her a reproachful look. It wasn't like he was making fun of the girl; she had a crush; it was cute.

"Hey, guys, come over here and grab your bags," Cassie called from the rear of the van.

"Yes mother," Henry roared back as they strode over.

Cassie Byrne
8:53 am

Cassie Byrne waved the group toward the back doors. As she knew Henry liked to think he was funny, she chose to ignore his comment. Professor Stone, in his colossal backpack, stood beside her, bouncing on the balls of his feet and rubbing his hands together. Professor Stone was always passionate about his work; however, she couldn't recall seeing him so animated.

Jordan and Zayne were the last to grab their backpacks from the van.

"Ok, listen up," Cassie said. "We don't know where we'll be setting up camp. There might be enough room by the cave, but I doubt it. We have a lot of supplies that we need to bring with us. So, we're heading to the cave first, then we'll decide where to set up. We need each of you to grab as much as possible from the back of the van. We'll have to come back for the rest later."

From previous digs, she knew the importance of having ample supplies. Cassie had been to many dig sites in several countries. One of the most interesting was Petra, the ancient city carved into the sandstone cliffs of Jordan. Established along trade routes, the city was purported to have gained much of its wealth as a major trading center. The main entrance to the city was a canyon three-quarters of a mile long. Construction of the ancient city had begun some twenty-four hundred years ago.

Cassie had also been blessed to be chosen for a small dig at Lascaux a few years before. Cut into the limestone hills of Southern France, the Lascaux cave system contains over six hundred prehistoric cave paintings. Along with the paintings, there are roughly fourteen hundred engraved images that depict many types of animals and shapes. Estimated to be between twenty to thirty thousand years old, the artwork is more than ten times older than Petra. The beautiful Paleolithic cave paintings had been breathtaking.

Cassie grabbed a camera case and slung the strap over her shoulder. She lifted a bulky cooler and started toward the cave. The ground inside the woods was strewn with decomposing leaves and scrub brush. To begin with, she'd decided to follow an old, well-used game trail. Minutes into the journey, she could already sense her arm and back muscles begin to strain against the load as she made her way toward the cave.

CHAPTER 9

Henry Blake
9:58 am

As they reached the level ground in front of the cave, Henry Blake set down a pair of massive molded plastic cases. His back and arms ached as he shrugged off a bulky duffle bag, followed by his pack. Perhaps it hadn't been the best idea to lug so much through the forest at once. Henry hadn't even considered how difficult the terrain would be when he'd decided to overburden himself. And the last stretch down the hillside, over and around the mossy boulders, had been tough. He was still trying to catch his breath.

With a glance around, he could tell Cassie had been right. The area here wasn't spacious enough for a proper campsite. Besides, just because the creek bed was dry now didn't mean it wouldn't flood if it rained.

"I would like one of the canopy tents set up here to use as the headquarters and to store the supplies," Professor Stone huffed. He indicated a level area above the creek bed, flush with the cliff as he tried to catch his breath. "Henry, I believe you will find them both in one of your bags. Would you and Jamie be so kind as to set that up for me?"

"Sure," he huffed, with a slow nod of his head. Henry looked over toward Jamie and saw her nod at him. "We can take care of that."

"Good, good." Stone turned to Cassie. "I would like you and Jordan to search to the east and southeast for a suitable area spacious enough to make camp. Michael and I will explore to the west."

"What about me?" Zayne asked. "What should I do?"

"Why don't you stay here with us?" Jamie asked. "I need someone to help me do the heavy lifting while Henry sits around on his ass. Besides, someone has to be in charge," she continued while she grinned at Henry.

"Very funny," Henry grumbled, then broke into a slight smile.

Stone gave them each a grateful look.

"Let's meet back here in say…" Stone glanced down at his watch. "I think forty-five minutes should do," he finished as he looked around the group.

"Come on, Cassie." Jordan turned to the east. "I bet we find a better campsite."

"I think you're right," Cassie replied, following. "According to the satellite images…" Her voice faded away as they made their way up the hill, into the woods. Cassie had a tendency of being too literal and often failed to grasp people's jokes.

"Good," Professor Stone said and spun west. "Let's go, Michael."

Jamie helped Henry pull one of the bulky tents from its bag as the professor and Michael walked away to scout their area.

"Zayne, why don't you take the instructions?" Jamie asked before she handed the booklet to the adolescent girl. "Henry and I are yours to command."

Jordan Adler
10:07 am

As she walked alongside Cassie Byrne, Jordan scanned the

moderately wooded forest for a suitable clearing. She was aware Cassie had a great deal of experience with archaeological digs, so she would be a great person to learn from. Jordan had been on a few small digs around the country, but her family wasn't wealthy like Cassie's. She couldn't afford to go all over the world. Jordan had seen rich kids come and go, who thought Daddy's money could get them anything, including grades. Cassie wasn't like that. She might be rich, but Cassie worked hard to get her education. Jordan respected that.

"So, Cassie," she started, "what exactly are we looking for in a campsite?"

"You haven't ever been camping?" Cassie asked, eyes widening a bit.

"Plenty of times," Jordan replied, "but mostly around the farm. Along the river too, or at the lake, but never like this. I wasn't the one to pick the campsites either."

"Oh, well, it's a good question," Cassie responded. "The most important thing to look for is a source of fresh water. We've brought enough bottled water with us to last all four days we're going to be here for this survey. However, it's a long hike back to the van and there are more supplies to get, so carrying cases of bottled water through the woods, over this terrain, is not ideal. We also need to think about future trips. Having an area picked out for next time would be ideal. If there is a next time."

"Uh-huh," Jordan muttered as she stepped over a fallen tree. Her eyes scanned the area. "What else?"

"Well, we're going to need a large, relatively level area. Natural shade would be good to have, and we should avoid any game trails. We don't want to wake up surrounded by angry deer," Cassie said, pausing a moment to laugh at her own joke. "We're far enough away from the cliffs, but if we were closer, falling rocks could be a concern."

"What about predators?" Jordan asked with some trepidation. "Do we have anything to worry about? There weren't any in the valley around our farm."

Cassie gave her a sympathetic look. "We don't think so, but

we will take precautions. What happened last Saturday is rare, virtually unheard of. Mountain lions are territorial, so there shouldn't be any more in the area. Black bears have also been reported to be in the area, but in general, they live in higher elevations. Black bears tend to avoid confrontations with people. As long as we take precautions, we should be safe."

"Bear bags?" Jordan asked.

"Well that could work, but there are easier ways," Cassie responded. She scanned the map, then glanced to check her compass heading. "The coolers we brought are bear-proof. We'll keep them away from camp and padlock them at night, just in case. We should also bury our trash and waste."

"Black Bears don't normally attack people though, do they?" Jordan asked.

"No, usually they'll just steal food," Cassie replied.

As they walked along, Jordan noticed the woods starting to thin. She saw an expanse of green grassland emerge through the thinning trees. Striding into the middle of the clearing, Jordan scanned the area. The meadow looked to be a little more than an acre, with two massive oak trees casting shade over most of the northeastern half of the area. Along the southwest corner of the clearing ran a small, spring-fed creek no more than a few feet wide.

"Wow," Jordan breathed in awe. "It's perfect."

"Yeah," Cassie agreed, "come on, let's go back and get the others."

Jamie Long
9:58 am

Jamie Long pulled the tent cord taut in order to hammer the final stake into the ground. The tent had gone up quickly with Zayne's expert instruction. It seemed she might have helped her dad with tents before. Spinning as she stood, Jamie caught Henry's eyes dart away from her butt. Her lip curled up a bit at the edge of her mouth. Guys were always so obvious.

Jamie noticed guys glancing abruptly away from her often. For the most part, she liked the looks she got. There was a certain amount of exhilaration that came from drawing attention. Some didn't even try to be subtle though, they just stood and leered at her. It made her skin crawl; it was so creepy. Michael Redfern was like that. She couldn't stand him.

At least Henry always attempted to maintain eye contact, which she respected. As she preferred to dress in tight-fitting clothes, Jamie was well aware it required considerable effort. The attention was more of a byproduct, anyway; her primary goal was to feel good about herself. Besides, her mom had told her, "If you got it, flaunt it. You're not always going to look this good."

"So, we've got the tent up, now what?" Jamie asked, rubbing the back of her neck. "Do you know which supplies the professor wants to leave here? We could move that stuff into the tent."

"Good call," Henry replied as he walked over and kneeled by the pile of supplies. Henry sorted through the pile and pulled two heavy, molded plastic cases out. He handed both to Jamie. "Here, take these two." Henry pulled another case from the pile as she hefted the cases and turned toward the tent. "Zayne, you take this one."

"Ok," Zayne said. With a glance over her shoulder, Jamie noticed that Zayne was struggling to lift the hefty case, nevertheless, she looked determined to prove she could handle it.

As Jamie exited the tent to get another load, she noticed Henry had piled everybody's hiking backpacks a few feet away, which left a much smaller stack. He carried two of the remaining bags into the tent.

They moved everything in just a few minutes. Jamie suspected the professor might want a few of the items at the campsite, but it was a good start.

Henry Blake
10:43 am

Henry sat on a small boulder beside the cliff, eyeing the terrain as he waited for the second of the teams to get back. The jaunt through the woods, laden with supplies and equipment, had been exhausting.

A rustle from the woods, several minutes earlier, had heralded Cassie and Jordan's return. The two shapes emerged from the trees atop the gully's rim. As they'd made their way down the slope to join them, Henry could tell they were excited. Both had been smiling. Once they'd reached him, he'd inquired about their search. They hadn't been very forthcoming with the information but had admitted to finding a suitable campsite. He hadn't felt like trying to coax any more details from them.

He gazed toward the younger of his companions; maybe he'd been wrong about Zayne. So far, she was pulling her own weight. She hadn't complained once. He didn't have much experience with kids her age, so he couldn't be sure if her attitude was typical or atypical. Either way, it was a pleasant surprise.

After a while, Henry noticed another sound coming from the west. He turned to see Professor Stone and Michael Redfern walking along the dry creek bed toward the group. As they approached, the looks they wore on their faces weren't as positive as the girls had been.

"How did your scouting go?" Stone inquired as he studied Cassie and Jordan.

"Wonderful," Jordan replied. "It has everything we need, right Cassie? Water, shade, space," Cassie nodded along until Jordan finished, "and a view." At the last statement, she shot Jordan a quizzical look but refrained from comment. "It's perfect."

"Good, good. We found an area that could have worked, but it doesn't have a water source. Shall we head that way?" Stone responded. He checked his watch before walking over to grab his bag. "I want to have the camp set up and be back here ready to do the preliminary survey of the cave by noon. Everyone, come over and grab your packs."

Henry moved over, with the others, to grab his pack. Stone held Cassie and Jordan's packs up for them. After the girls grabbed their bags, Dr. Stone darted toward the newly constructed supply tent.

"We need some items from in here as well," he called back. "Come on everybody, gather round."

CHAPTER 10

Dr. Theodore Stone
11:00 am

As his eyes drifted up toward the clear blue sky, Professor Stone felt the cool air hit the thin layer of perspiration on his bald head. He liked this time of the year; the scorching summer temperatures were shifting, getting cooler. And the leaves were about to change colors.

Ahead of him, his daughter talked animatedly with Jamie. Stone liked how his students included Zayne, made her feel like part of the group. He knew some of them put up with her a little reluctantly, but some seemed to enjoy Zayne's company. He'd known parents who brought their kids along just to evade paying for childcare. Stone could have opted to let his Zayne stay with family for the weekend, but he wanted his daughter to experience this.

Ahead, a small meadow devoid of trees caught his attention. As they came to the clearing, Stone took it in and formed a plan for the camp. Jordan was right, it was perfect.

"We'll need to gather the food and cookware from each of our bags. I would like to set up the other canopy tent over by the creek to use as a kitchen area. Cassie, would you please oversee that?" Stone asked with a glance to her.

"I'll see to it," Cassie nodded.

"Good, good." His eyes shifted, scanning the gear his students carried. "Somewhere in one of these cases is a folding table."

"I'll find it," she assured.

Stone smiled in gratitude. "Thank you. I'd like us to set up our tents over there," he said, pointing across the clearing, "under those trees. Now, each of the tents can sleep two people. Would anyone like to share a tent?"

Michael Redfern turned toward Jamie, eyes bright. "Do you wanna—?"

"No," Jamie blurted. "Definitely not!"

At the rebuke, his eyes darted to Jordan standing behind her. "No," Jordan spat out with a shudder. Professor Stone noticed the venomous expression that spread across her face.

"Come on man, seriously? Don't be a creep," Henry sighed, as Michael took a step back.

"I wasn't—" Michael sputtered; his mind worked behind his eyes. "I was only going to ask if she wanted to—oh, never mind," he groaned. Michael shrugged before he strode off across the clearing to pick his spot.

Stone watched the girls give each other an exasperated look; apparently, they didn't believe him. When he'd proposed sharing tents, he hadn't even considered co-ed pairings. On reassessment, there always seemed to be a certain amount of bed-hopping among the students. He was glad Zayne wouldn't be exposed to that on this trip. He'd have to be more specific in the future.

Zayne crept toward the girls. "Um, I was wondering," she murmured, "if I could stay with one of you guys? I don't want to be a bother though. So, it's ok if you don't want me to. I just..." Zayne trailed off.

"Of course," Jamie blurted, "You can stay with any of us." She shot a glance at the other two for confirmation. "Right?"

"Yeah," Cassie agreed with a shrug, Jordan nodded along.

"Are you sure? You don't mind?" Zayne's bubbled.

Jordan took Zayne's arm in hers and led her across the field. "Hon, it's absolutely no bother," Jordan assured her.

Michael Redfern
11:17 am

After he placed his tent out on its footprint, Michael Redfern glared over toward Jamie. He felt his anger begin to boil. How dare she look at him with so much disgust? So, what if he intended to ask her to share a tent? The way she'd dressed, she was almost begging for attention. His eyes followed her well-toned legs all the way up to that marvelous ass. As Jamie turned to the side, he took in her tight stomach and natural, full, C-cup breasts, under that skintight shirt. Attempting to calm himself down, Michael took a deep breath, then slowly exhaled while shifting his attention back to the task at hand. It was her loss.

As he started to connect the color-coded poles, Michael heard a laugh across the way. A glance toward the sound revealed Henry joking around with Cassie while he assisted erecting the canopy tent. Henry thought he was so much better than everyone else, just because he was pretty. So, what if he had stylish hair, large muscles, or a strong jawline? He wasn't anything special. Michael couldn't stand Henry; he was just a dumb jock. And Cassie, well she wouldn't be his top choice for a hookup, but she looked alright. If she would just put a little effort into make-up and clothes, she could look pretty. It was a shame.

The frame took shape as he stabbed the poles into the grommets on the canvas tent floor. He shifted his attention to Jordan and Zayne, fooling around as they tried to set up a tent. He felt a bit of anger boil up again; everyone but him was goofing around.

And Jordan, Jordan had the nerve to give him that disgusted look, and the repulsed tone she'd used. He hadn't even intended to ask her, anyway; his eyes had just drifted toward her after Jamie had shut him down. Jordan was probably gay anyway. She certainly dressed butch enough. She looked like a 12-year-old boy. That must be it. There was no way he would ever even try to get with her. He was certainly not into little boys.

Michael angrily clipped the tent body to the frame, applying more force than was necessary. Then he set about securing the tent into the ground.

Henry Blake
11:45 am

Finished with his tent, Henry walked toward the professor. Professor Stone was just finishing his tent, attaching the rain fly. Henry scanned the area to see the rest of the group were either putting the finishing touches on their tents or had already finished.

"What now, professor?" Henry asked, trying to sound nonchalant. He was beyond ready to inspect the cave, but tried not to let his excitement be too visible. He knew the professor had experience with cave digs and was eager to learn from him.

Stone took a moment to survey the site before he responded as if thinking out loud. "Well, the campsite is pretty much set up. There are a few things we still need to do. We'll need to build a fire pit, we also need to dig a latrine, and we have more supplies to get from the van." Stone paused at seeing the look of disappointment in Henry's eyes. He broke into a smile as he continued, "but we can do all that later. I'm ready to get a look at the cave as well. Did you happen to notice whether the case with the portable work lights was among those at the cave site?"

"Sorry Doc, I don't know. I don't remember seeing it, but I can't be sure. I didn't open any of them," he responded.

Stone gave a slight nod, his eyes losing focus. Henry scanned the area again. He noticed the girls standing together, watching their conversation, before looking back to the professor.

Eyes snapping back into focus, Stone said, "We'll just have to see what we need to do once we get to the cave. I brought some extra flashlights if we need them." He dropped to one knee near his pack. Stone rummaged through the bag for a moment before bringing up a canvas bag. "Why don't you make sure everyone is ready? We'll head to the cave in five minutes," Stone concluded with a check of the time.

"All right, Doc, will do," Henry replied. He turned and strode toward the group of girls, smiling brightly. "Y'all ready?" Henry asked.

"Yeah," they chorused.

A glance around failed to reveal Michael. "Does anyone know where Michael went?" he inquired.

"He went into the woods over there," Zayne said, pointing to the north, "a few minutes ago. Want me to help you find him?"

"No, you guys stay here," Henry grinned. "I'll be back soon."

On his way towards the woods, he realized he'd unquestionably misjudged Zayne. She might talk a lot, but she was a hard worker, always willing to pitch in. Henry thought he knew why Michael had gone into the woods alone, though. Zayne didn't need to see that.

Sure enough, as he walked along, he caught the acrid odor of urine, not far away. Michael stepped out from behind an old tree, zipping up his pants.

"What's up," Michael greeted. "I can't even take a piss without a search party coming for me? Or did you come to scold me again?"

"We're about ready to head to the cave," Henry shot back. He considered making a scathing reply but decided not to bother. "Four minutes." Henry turned back to the camp. He hadn't known Michael could be so bitter. In class, he'd always been amiable enough.

He barely heard Michael's muttered, "Thanks."

CHAPTER 11

Jordan Adler
12:00 pm

Jordan Adler took the last bite of her sandwich and crammed the empty baggy into her pants pocket. Finished with her light lunch, she was ready to check out the cave. Truth was, she had been ready ever since she'd heard about it the previous weekend. Upon reaching the tent by the cave, Cassie had slipped inside and returned with an insulated canvas bag. While she'd passed the sandwiches around, Professor Stone conducted a search through their gear, looking for something. He stopped his search after he'd found a rather bulky camera bag.

Jordan heard the click when Stone attached an expensive-looking lens onto an older model Canon SLR camera body. He then inserted the battery and flicked the switch to on.

"Jordan, come here please," he said as he manipulated a few settings. Jordan scurried into the tent. He gazed up into her eyes and continued, "I would like you to take the camera and use it to document everything, and I mean everything. I would like pictures of the cave from before we set foot inside until we leave. You'll enter first, just enough to see the whole cavern and take pictures of the walls, floor, and ceiling. After that, you must photograph every artifact in its original position."

"Ok Professor," she said once he placed the camera into her hands. Jordan slid the strap over her head and snugged it around her neck before exiting the tent. Once outside, Jordan slipped the lens cap off, letting it hang from the camera by the thin cord. As she brought the viewfinder up to her eye, Jordan heard Stone pull something else from the bag. Jordan held the shutter-release button halfway down, to let the automatic focus do its job, before snapping a few pictures of the cave mouth.

She turned back around as she heard the professor speak again. "Michael, would you please take this," he said as he passed Michael a similar, yet newer looking camera with a powerful light attached to the top. "You'll use this to get HD video of everything. Same instructions as Jordan, except that you'll be second into the cave."

"Got it, professor," Michael responded.

Stone stood straight and turned to the others, "Jamie and Zayne, I'd like you to draw a detailed sketch of the inside of the cave. Please include the shape of the walls and the location of the artifacts. There are some clipboards and paper in that case over there."

Both moved over to grab a clipboard.

"Jordan, if you will?" He asked, motioning to the cave.

Jordan approached the massive boulder that lay beneath the cave entrance. It had three distinct tiers, which from the front looked almost like stairs. She stepped onto the first tier, careful not to slip on the worn face of the rock.

"Jamie, can you hold this for a second," she asked while slipping the camera from around her neck. Jordan worried she would fall and break the camera or crack the lens against the rock. Wouldn't that look just great in front of all these more experienced students?

Jamie moved forward as she replied, "Sure, no problem." After grabbing the offered camera, she took a step back.

Unencumbered by the camera, Jordan felt more comfortable as she quickly scaled the remaining two tiers. As she crouched down, Jamie stepped forward and returned the camera.

"Thank you," Jordan said.

"No problem."

Jordan spun toward the fissure in the rock and stepped up into the tight crack. Standing inside the cave mouth, Jordan snapped another picture. Then she glided along the passage, around the bend.

Only a tiny amount of sunlight made its way into the chamber. She could barely make out the far walls. There were footprints in the loose dirt as she looked down. She used them as she moved forward. Jordan stopped a step into the cave and started taking pictures; walls, floor, and ceiling. She zoomed in as far as she could on the artifacts and the carved image.

Finished with her initial pictures, she headed out to let Michael in to get the video.

Dr. Theodore Stone
12:05 pm

Stone's students had helped him erect two folding tables, one snugged against the north side of the tent and the other to the east, along its rear. Stone knelt, rummaging through the containers stashed under the two narrow plastic tables. As Jordan's voice drifted through the thin canvas, Professor Stone took a second to glance up and peer out one of the windows built into the tent's side.

Good, that was good. Jordan was finished.

While his students continued to chat a few feet away, his attention shifted back to one of the large, molded plastic cases; inside was a lightweight portable generator and a solar panel used to charge it. He closed and latched the lid, then moved it to one side. That would return with them to camp. Aside from sorting through their gear, Stone was also making a mental list of the supplies they still needed to get from the van before that evening. He hefted one of the molded plastic cases, letting it thump down on the table, then snapped it open and glanced inside. His eyes roved over the interior.

"Uh, Professor," Michael called from the cave entrance. Stone brought his head up. "Professor, there's not enough illumination in here for video, even with this light you gave me. I got the video you wanted, but it's too grainy."

"I suspected it would be," Stone confessed. He strode forward, pausing to pick up a case he'd stashed by the tent's entrance. "I'm going to have to put in some of these work lights regardless, and I wanted a record of the site before I did that. Come on down."

"Ok, Professor," Michael said before hopping down from the boulder.

Professor Stone set the case down as he approached the entrance and turned to Henry. "Henry, would you be so kind as to help me with this?" he asked, indicating the case beside him.

"Sure Doc," he replied. As Henry stepped forward, Stone turned and scurried to the top of the boulder. Once at the top, he pulled his headband flashlight out of a pants pocket and stretched the elastic over his bald head. Stone bent down as Henry passed the case up to him.

Stone lugged the case into the cleft within the rock. With his free hand, he reached up to turn his light on. Following the cone of light illuminating the ground in front of him, Stone shuffled through the narrow tunnel. As he reached the first room, he took in the earthy smell of the cave. Stone surveyed the area slowly, marking the points of interest in his mind. He noticed that only the right side of the room seemed to hold anything of note; the artifacts and carving. Still, he'd try to keep the group's impact on the site to a minimum. There could be important details that weren't immediately noticeable.

Stone retreated a step and deposited the case outside the room. He crouched to snap the latches open and lifted the lid. Inside were six rechargeable portable work lights. Stone pulled the first one out and scooted to the end of the tunnel where it widened into the first chamber.

He noticed the only footprints in the room were indistinct and was glad the students had thought to use them. Stone had forgotten to remind them to be careful where they stepped. In the dark, it would have been easy to step on something important.

Stone scanned the area to the left, just inside the room. In front of him, bedrock lay under a very thin layer of dirt and debris. Stone looked for anything of note as he swept an eight square inch spot with the side of his hand. He cleared the negligible buildup of loose gravel and dirt. Nothing significant stood out, so he sat the light on the spot and turned it on. Light burst through the cave.

Now able to see better, Stone realized that most of the loose dirt was in a small area in front of the passage. The rest of the cave floor was either covered in dried mud and dirt, or else had veins of bedrock peeking from beneath the hard-packed earth. He scoured the room, on the lookout for anything. He performed the same procedure to place two more lights on the left side of the room, and two on the right. He placed one along the left wall and another straight across from the cave opening, then one in both corners on the right.

Cassie Byrne
12:45 pm

Cassie gazed around the well-lit cave as she bent down to wipe the dirt from her knees. After Stone set up the portable work lights, Michael reshot the video. As soon as Michael had finished, Professor Stone had bid them all follow him into the cave. He'd requested they spread out, each assigned to search an area of the chamber on hands and knees.

The professor stood on the opposite side of the chamber, staring down at the artifacts. Cassie snaked across the room to join him.

"You're finished with your section?" Stone asked as she approached.

"Yes, nothing new," Cassie informed.

Standing next to the professor, Cassie took her first thorough look at the collection of objects.

"In truth, I would have been surprised if there had been. The way the objects are laid out on the exposed bedrock, like this, appears almost ceremonial in nature," Stone remarked.

Spread throughout the 4 by 4ft square, were knives made of bone and stone, as well as a few examples of stone and metal axe blades, a tomahawk, stone and wooden clubs, even a remarkable club made from jawbone. The metal surfaces were pitted with rust, and several of the wooden handles had rotted away with age. Arrowheads, large and small, ancient to modern, dusted the area. Aside from the varying styles of arrowheads, spearheads, and other Native American weapons represented, there were effigies, statues, and carvings on an assortment of mediums.

Over the next several minutes, the remaining students completed their search grids, then drifted over to congregate around the professor. Aside from the original group of artifacts, nothing of note had been found in the room.

"Wow, that's a big arrowhead!" Zayne exclaimed, pointing at one item as she joined them.

Stone appraised the indicated object. "That is not just any arrowhead, darling," he stated. "It is a Clovis point. They are more than thirteen thousand years old. Look at the roughly leaf-shaped point, the edges are flaked on each side."

"What's that?" Zayne asked.

"Hmm?" Stone replied, looking at his young daughter.

"Flaked," Zayne said, "what does that mean?"

"Oh, the ancient native peoples would use hard, oval-shaped stones to chip off small pieces of the rock, forming the object into the desired shape," her dad explained. "See these shallow grooves at the base," he shifted a finger to indicate the area, "they're called flutes and were used to attach the tip to a spear or knife handle."

"Oh," she replied.

Stone pointed at another object. "That is a Folsom point. The Folsom point is similar to a Clovis point in some regards, for example, they have the same bifacial flaking and similar leaf shape. However, they are very different in others, the Folsom point is much smaller, and see how the flutes go almost all the way up. It's about nine thousand years old."

"Are all these things so old?" Zayne asked excitedly.

"No, see that." Stone indicated a turtle shell with designs carved on it. "It appears to be from the Caddoan-Mississippian culture."

"It's maybe a thousand to twelve hundred years old," Cassie put in. "That looks like a Chunkey player, doesn't it?" Cassie asked, pointing to a small stone effigy.

"It appears to be, yes," Stone agreed.

"He's not that fat," Henry said.

"Chunkey, the game," Cassie said with a roll of her eyes. "It's also known as tchung-kee or the hoop and stick game."

"Oh yeah," Zayne said, "with the disc and the spears." She shot Henry a confused look. "You've never heard of Chunkey?"

"Of course, he has," Cassie sighed, "he was just trying to be funny." Cassie put the most emphasis on the word, trying. "It's in the curriculum of your father's Native American history class."

"What is it," Jamie asked. Her eyes drifted down and away. "I haven't taken that class yet," she sheepishly added.

"Traditionally, it was a two-player game, where a stone disc was rolled down a pitch. The players would then throw spears, trying to get as close to the disc as possible," Cassie explained. After a pause, she pointed to another object. "That's a metal hunting knife; that can't be more than a couple hundred years old, can it?" She asked.

"Indeed," Stone agreed, "this appears to be some kind of shrine."

"Its focus, or rather its theme, seems to be centered around hunting or hunters," Jordan put in. "The arrowheads, the shell carving, the effigy, even the carving in the cave wall."

Cassie had come to that realization too. She glanced at the carving once more. It appeared to be a man holding a spear, ready to throw.

Zayne Stone
1:20 pm

As Zayne sat cross-legged on a hard-stone section of the cave floor, she continued to draw the objects lying in front of her. Jamie sat beside her, also sketching the items. Her father and the others had started to call it a shrine. She wanted to try as hard as she could to make her sketch as accurate as possible. Zayne wished she had paid closer attention to her dad when he'd talked to her about this stuff. It was quite interesting. She had a hard time wrapping her mind around the fact that some of these items were over ten thousand years old. At only 11, Zayne couldn't fathom anything being so ancient.

Her dad had asked Cassie and Henry to accompany him outside, to grab something. In all the excitement, she'd forgotten what. A flash illuminated the room every few seconds; a constant reminder that Jordan and Michael were both still capturing images of the shrine. Jordan had already taken loads of pictures.

Zayne looked up toward the entrance as she heard someone enter the cavern. Her dad carried a small plastic storage box, about the size of a shoebox, with plastic bags inside. As her father came up behind her, Zayne stretched her neck to look up at him.

"That's wonderful, hon," he said, peering over her shoulder to examine her sketch.

"Thanks, Dad," Jamie quipped beside her, not looking up.

"Yours is good too, sweetheart," Stone replied light-heartedly, patting Jamie's head. Zayne giggled at the look of amusement that lit her dad's face. He leaned over to study her drawing more thoroughly. "Both of you take your time."

CHAPTER 12

Jordan Adler
3:58 pm

Professor Stone knelt on the cold rock of the cave floor; knees covered by some old carpet layers knee pads. Jordan watched as he took meticulous notes about each object. Face inches away, Stone's eyes traced over each item in turn. Every so often he would rock back and reach over for his clipboard. With the board pressed firmly to his thighs, he would scribble something on the paper before he set the clipboard aside and leaned forward again.

When Stone finished jotting a note on the final object, he stashed the pen in his shirt pocket, grabbed his notes, and struggled up to his feet. Clipboard clutched in his left hand, Stone twisted his wrist and gazed down at his watch. He extended each finger on his right hand one at a time, counting.

"Ok, we still have several hours before evenfall." Stone turned to peer longingly toward the passage that led further into the cave system. He let a sigh slip from his lips and spun back toward the group. "However, we don't have enough time to explore any further into the caves today. Why don't I take Zayne and Jordan with me to the campsite while the rest of you go to the van and grab the remaining supplies."

"Ok Doc, we'll take care of it," Henry agreed.

Everybody filed toward the exit. On his way out, Professor Stone stooped down and pulled something from behind the light at the cave entrance. "Jordan, would you kindly round up the batteries from the lights?" he asked, then tossed her the item.

She reached out and caught the bag hurtling toward her. "Yeah, sure," she nodded. Jordan turned back. As she circled the cave, she popped out the batteries from each work light and stored them in the small canvas bag.

As she neared the final work light, Jordan pressed the button on her headband. She'd left the light nearest the cave's entrance for last. Jordan took a moment to scan the cave once more before kneeling beside the light. Once she pulled the batteries out, the cave plunged into darkness, save for her small headlamp.

The bright afternoon sun hit her eyes as she exited the cave, momentarily blinding her. Jordan turned her head and blinked her eyes to let them readjust to the daylight. Jordan hopped down from the boulder and strolled over to the supply tent. Zayne and her father were inside, looking through one of the supply containers.

"Professor, here are the batteries." She offered him the bag.

"Good, good, can you hold on to that for now?" Stone asked, not looking at her. "We will take them to the campsite and charge them tonight." Stone turned his head to his daughter. "Zayne, would you grab the charger from that case?" he asked, pointing.

"Sure, Daddy," Zayne said, strolling across the tent. Each latch opened with a snap and she pulled the lid up. From the container, Zayne pulled a square plastic charger. "Is this it?" she asked.

"Yeah, hand it to me, if you please." Stone took the charger from his daughter and placed it into the open case in front of him. Jordan stepped forward. As she peeked inside, she saw it was the one that contained the portable generator. Stone turned to Jordan. "Ok, go ahead and put the batteries in here. I'd like you to carry this case to the campsite as well."

"All right, Professor, anything else?" Jordan asked. She placed the batteries in, then closed and secured the lid.

Stone swept his eyes through the tent. "No, that's all," he replied, "Zayne?" He offered a small bag to his daughter. As soon as she grabbed it, Stone shuffled to another container. "I'll take this one." He paused for another quick survey of the tent. "Let's head to the campsite," he finished with a nod.

Jordan picked her way up the rock-strewn slope, lugging the bulky plastic case. Beside her, Zayne stepped up onto a boulder, even with the top of the hill. Zayne glanced back and stared toward the cave entrance.

"That was neat," Zayne exclaimed. She brought her head around and beamed at Jordan.

"It was," she agreed.

Zayne whipped her head around toward her father, who was walking a little way ahead of them. "Hey, Dad, are we going to explore the rest of the cave?" Zayne called out.

"That depends," Stone huffed. The big man was out of breath.

"On what?" Zayne asked after a lengthy pause.

"Hmm?" Stone murmured distractedly, his mind far away.

"What does it depend on?"

"Oh, well, we'll have to see. There are several factors that could limit how far we can explore. Such as, how active the cave is, the gradient of the cave floor, and the general layout of the cave," he explained.

"Why?"

"Well, if the cave is still active, which means it has water flowing through it, it can be treacherous. We lack the equipment or experience we'd need to explore flooded caves. Likewise, if the cave system is too steep, we may have trouble getting from room to room. We must also be on the lookout for hidden pits or crevasses." Stone looked back at his daughter. "Did you see the groove worn into the rock floor in the middle of the cave we were in?"

"Yeah, what does it mean?" Zayne seemed eager to learn.

"Well, it appears to indicate that water used to flow through there—"

"And as it did, it wore down the rock over the years to make the groove." Jordan slipped back into the dialogue.

"Correct," Stone beamed. He paused and spun to face them. "And if I had to guess. I would say, at some point in the distant past, an underground creek flowed down through these hills from the cliffs above, ending at the entrance to our cave."

"Not still?" Zayne piped in.

"I do not believe so, no. It was too dry in there. Though, there may still be some flow from time to time," he finished, then spun around.

Zayne Stone
4:27 pm

As she hefted another rock, Zayne let out a grunt. "How many more do we need?"

"I doubt we'll need many more. Take that back to camp," Jordan replied.

After they'd returned to the campsite, Zayne set out with Jordan to collect rocks for a fire pit. Zayne's father wanted them to search for larger rocks. They'd found all the stones they could want, about two hundred yards southwest of the camp, along an old natural drainage ditch. Its flow, only present during rainfall, left a trail of large, smooth rocks.

Zayne was having such a wonderful time on this trip; she hadn't dreamed it would be so fun. She'd been to a few dig sites with her dad, but this trip was by far the best. Was it her age? She'd turned eleven just two months ago. At eleven, she had to be more mature than she'd been at ten. Could that be it?

Zayne lugged the rock as she clumped back toward her dad. He was arranging the stones for the fire pit, in the midst of making a circle about three feet in diameter. He'd placed three of the bigger rocks in the middle of the circle, about a foot and a half apart. Balanced on the middle rocks, a foot off the ground, was a circular cooking grate.

"Do you need many more?" She asked. Head cocked to the side, she studied the structure in the middle. Zayne had never seen a campfire that looked like that.

With a glance, her dad nodded. "No, I would like you to gather some firewood," he answered.

"Do we have an axe?" Zayne asked eagerly, eyes wide.

"No, it looks like the axe is still in the van. We are also waiting to dig the latrine. The others ought to bring the shovel as well." Stone frowned at the disappointment blossoming on her cute face. "What is it, Zayne?"

"I wanted to use the axe." She gave him her best puppy dog eyes.

"Maybe later," Stone chuckled. "But for right now, gather up as much dry wood as you can find."

She let out an exasperated sigh and spun around. "Fine," she grumbled. As she shuffled away, Zayne shot a quick grin over her shoulder, just to let her dad know she wasn't really upset.

Michael Redfern
5:03 pm

Michael huffed and grunted as he struggled through the woods. He reached up and grasped a low-hanging branch, snapping it in half with a loud crack. There were too many trees. At least they were getting closer to the parking area. Finally.

It wasn't fair. An hour each way; why did 'he' have to go back to the van? Jordan and Stone's daughter got to just sit around the campsite with the professor, while he had to hike two miles through a freaking forest, half of which he'd be lugging tons of equipment.

To make things worse, that fool Henry was flirting away with both girls. Unsatisfied with only one girl, Henry had to try to take both. Hell, he'd probably try to get with the others, the queer and the little brat back at camp, before long.

Michael kicked a stone, sending it flying over a slight ledge to his right.

They were just suck-ups, all of them, trying to make him look bad to the professor. Michael had known about most of the items in the cave and would have proven it if he'd been given half a chance. Why hadn't the professor asked him any questions?

The van sat in shadow as it came into view ahead. Cassie slipped a hand in her pocket and proceeded to dig around, searching for the keys. *She better not have forgotten them*, Michael groused. With his luck, they'd probably try to make him go back for them if she had. *No, no, definitely not*, he wouldn't do it. They couldn't make him.

"Here," Henry said. "Doc gave them to me." Henry pulled the keys from his pocket and tossed them through the air.

As the keys smacked into her hands, Cassie fumbled at them for a second before she got a secure grip. Cassie extended an arm and pressed the button twice; the alarm gave off two loud chirps as the doors were unlocked.

Jamie strolled to the back door and pulled it open. "What all do we need?" Jamie asked, looking over to Cassie and Henry. Michael rolled his eyes, annoyed at being left out again. Michael grunted and ambled around to the front of the van. He slipped his phone from his pocket to check it. At the rear of the van, he caught snippets of Cassie's indistinct instructions.

Michael lost himself in the device for a few minutes; until the sound of footsteps scraping against the loose gravel brought his attention back around. As he turned, Michael saw Cassie ambling toward him, a duffel snugged around one shoulder. What did she want?

"Michael, we're ready," she said.

"Oh, hey Cassie, I'll just be a minute," he responded, giving her a slight smile. "I've got my map." *Can't you leave me alone for a few minutes?* "I'll catch up with you guys."

"Alright, there's only a couple bags left. Grab them if you will," Cassie replied as she held the keys out to Michael. "Here are the keys, don't forget to lock it."

"Sure, no problem," Michael agreed. After taking the offered keys, he returned his attention to the phone.

After he finished browsing his social media accounts, Michael trudged around to the rear door. He scanned the nearly empty cargo area. Along with two enormous canvas bags, and a molded plastic container, the only items remaining were several cases of bottled water pushed up against the back seat. Michael shoved the gear aside and vaulted into the back of the van, then crawled toward the water bottles, thirsty. A sudden pain shot from his knee.

"Argh," he yelled. After plopping back, he reached up and flicked on the overhead light. With the light on, he was better able to see the bloody scrape he'd received from one of the seat anchors. "Damn-it," he sighed.

Michael stabbed his fingers through the thin layer of plastic covering the case of water and ripped it open, then tugged a bottle of water through the plastic. With a flick of the wrist, he twisted the cap off. Michael brought the bottle to his lips to take a deep drink. He slid toward the closest door and wrenched it open. Michael crawled out the side door and grabbed its handle. While he spun, he dragged the door shut.

After returning to the back doors, Michael yanked the bags out of the van, tossing them to the ground. He slammed the doors, then reached into his pocket. There was a loud chirp as he pressed the lock button. Michael reached down and scooped the bags from the ground, draping one over a shoulder.

If he'd looked back as he strode away, he might have noticed the dome light was still illuminated.

Jamie Long
5:58 pm

As Jamie approached the clearing, she caught a whiff of cooking meat. It appeared as if the other group had been busy. Smelled as if they'd been busy, anyway. Jamie inhaled the aroma. It smelled so good; she was so hungry. Lunch had been too light.

Upon entering the field, she glanced around. Her eyes

scanned the area, taking in what they'd accomplished. Built from large smooth stones, the campfire was the most notable addition. Jordan and the professor were at the campfire, busy cooking something. Upon noticing dinner wasn't quite ready, Jamie veered toward the kitchen area. It too had been rearranged. She shrugged off her burden, easing the bags to the ground beside the canopy tent. Even in her shape, there was a burning in the muscles across her shoulders. After the two trips loaded with supplies, she feared she'd be sore the next day.

That task completed; Jamie strode toward her tent. Once inside, she zipped it halfway and slipped out of her clothes. She ripped her pack open and stared inside, trying to decide what she wanted to wear. After reexamining her options, Jamie changed into a cropped hoodie and a pair of loose nylon shorts. As she exited the tent, Jamie ran her hands along the smooth skin of her stomach, where the bottom of the hoodie met her exposed midriff.

She gazed around the campsite. Not far from the tents, but out of the tree's shadow, someone had set up a makeshift charging station. A portable generator, hooked up to a solar panel, sat on a plastic tarp. A camera battery sat in its cradle, red light slowly blinking. Beside that was another charger, this one had four batteries coated in a blue plastic material. She wondered which piece of equipment they belonged to.

With a glance at her phone, Jamie realized she'd have to charge it soon, as well. It was already down to fifty percent. Occasionally, her phone seemed to connect to the cell network, and she'd receive her messages. Throughout the day, she'd gotten bursts of text messages, some having been sent hours before. Jamie didn't really mind being away from her social media accounts; sometimes you just need a break from all that.

Standing there, lost in thought, she noticed someone glide in her direction. She peered to her left and saw Henry drifting toward her, shovel in hand.

"Jamie," he said in greeting, giving her a polite nod.

"Henry." Jamie pushed a loose strand of hair behind her ear and gave him her most brilliant smile.

Henry slowed his stride, eyes brightening at the sight of her smile. Henry moved past her and spun to keep her in sight. Jamie trailed him with her eyes, rotating her body to follow. "I'm heading to dig a latrine," he said, shifting the shovel to indicate it as he walked backwards. "Do you wanna help?"

Jamie crinkled her nose in mock disgust. "You want me to help you dig a poop pit?" Henry knit his brow. The embarrassed confusion traveling across his face told her he was trying to frame a response. Jamie winked, then broke into another dazzling smile. "I'm just kidding. I need to talk to the professor, though."

"Ok, well," he wavered, trying to get his mind back on track. "I'll be over there if you want to join me." He shot a thumb over his shoulder, pointing vaguely to the east before spinning back around.

After a moment, Jamie turned away from Henry. The professor knelt outside the kitchen tent, sorting through the new supplies. As she angled that way, Jamie stole a look at Henry, considering him. She couldn't deny; he was cute.

CHAPTER 13

Jordan Adler
6:15 pm

The campfire's smoke billowed to the east, riding on the wind. Perched atop the flames, a skillet sat on a metal cooking grate. Sizzling inside the cast iron frying pan was a mixture of ground beef and noodles. Jordan's two jobs were to keep the fire going and watch their dinner, make sure it didn't burn. She and Zayne had been joined by Cassie a few minutes before. The three of them stood by the cookfire.

Jordan glanced at the older woman, letting her face show the hint of a frown. If her hunch was correct, Cassie had only joined them to make sure she didn't mess up their dinner. Jordan could do without anyone watching over her shoulder. So far, Cassie's tendency to assess everyone's work hadn't flared up.

"Where are we going to sit?" Zayne blurted.

"Around the fire," Cassie said.

Jordan pulled her eyes away from the skillet to find the younger girl. She spent a moment peering at Zayne's face. Zayne's complexion matched her father's, creamy brown skin that spoke to their shared native heritage. Almond-shaped eyes sparked with curiosity, accented by a spray of freckles across the bridge of her nose. Shoulder-length ebony hair fell past high cheekbones and a pointed chin. Jordan returned her gaze to the fire. That was a good question. Jordan didn't really want to sit on the ground.

"No, I mean, what are we going to sit on," Zayne explained patiently.

"I think there are a few tarps or a blanket we could use to sit on," Cassie offered.

Zayne scrunched her nose. "You're not supposed to sit on the ground around a campfire. We're camping, not having a picnic."

Jordan used the spatula to stir the meal. "What do you want to use," Jordan asked, meeting the girl's eyes again.

Zayne's eyes moved to the stones around the fire, then past Jordan and into the woods behind her. "We could use a log from a fallen tree," Zayne exclaimed. "That would be neat." She turned to Cassie, "Can we do that?"

Cassie nodded. "That could work," she agreed.

Jordan could tell Cassie hadn't recognized Zayne's subtle plea for assistance.

"How bout this, Zayne," Jordan offered, "why don't we wait until after the food is finished, then I'll help you?"

"What does she need help with?" Jamie asked, walking up.

"Jordan's going to help me get a log to sit on," Zayne beamed.

"How about I help, and we can get one big enough for all three of us?" Jamie suggested.

"What about the boys," Zayne wondered, "and Cassie?"

"The boys can find their own seats…" Jamie trailed off as she shot a questioning look at Cassie.

"Don't worry about me. I'll just use a blanket," Cassie paused and looked at the cooking meal. "Why don't you three go ahead and let me finish supper."

"Are you sure?" Jordan asked half-heartedly, already offering Cassie the spatula.

"Yeah, go on."

Zayne Stone
6:23 pm

Zayne was thrilled. Here she was with these two older girls, young women really, and they'd agreed with her. Not only had they liked her idea to use a log to sit on, but they were also helping her find one. If only Henry had joined them, it would have been perfect. Then again, she might be more reluctant to talk in front of him. And God, she hoped no one else noticed the blush that rose to her cheeks every time he spoke to her. That would be mortifying!

"So, Zayne, how are you enjoying the trip thus far?" Jamie asked.

"Oh, it's great! I had no idea archaeology could be so fun. Is it always like this? I don't remember the other times being this fun. I wish I would have known. Now I want to join Dad on other digs. Do you think Dad will let me?"

Zayne glanced at her companions as they halted, and she stopped talking upon seeing the bemused looks on the young women's faces. She felt a hint of a blush rise to her face. She'd done it again. Zayne knew when she got excited, she had a tendency to ramble. It was something she was working on.

"Let's head this way," Jamie suggested. The tall girl carried the axe over her shoulder as their little group trekked through the woods. They still hadn't found what they were looking for. There had been a few fallen trees, but they'd been all rotted out or too small.

"Are you both going to be archaeologists like Dad?"

"I am," Jordan confirmed.

"Not me," Jamie countered, "I will be a paleontologist."

"Really! Dinosaurs? But why are you here?" Zayne exclaimed, pleased she'd limited herself to two questions.

Jamie chuckled. "Yes, dinosaurs, but also much more. Written in the fossil record are countless species of plant and animal from long before dinosaurs. Paleontologists and archaeologists have many similarities and often work together."

"Look there," Jordan called.

She was pointing to a large grayish-white tree ahead. Half of the tree drooped to the ground on one side, broken where the tree had forked as it grew. Eager to see if it would work, Zayne followed the girls as they strode over.

"It looks recent," Jordan commented as she examined the break. "What do you think?"

Jamie brought the axe off her shoulder. "Step back, let me see," Jamie urged.

Once Zayne and Jordan had stepped aside, Jamie shot a glance at them to make sure they were clear. She swung the axe around, lifted it above her head, and brought it down hard on a section of the splintered wood. The axe head sank deep into the softened wood. Another few strikes left that whole fork laying on the ground.

"It should do," Jamie agreed.

It was another fifteen minutes effort, taking turns with the axe, for them to have a section of tree four feet long.

"Zayne, why don't you carry the axe while Jordan and I carry the log," Jamie offered.

Cassie Byrne
8:57 pm

Cassie ran her hand along the cooler's edges before checking to make sure the clasps were secured. Cassie snapped padlocks in place in the slots on either side. She swept her light over the cooler. Made of molded plastic, it contained a thick layer of insulation that would keep their food cool the entire weekend.

The evening had been, overall, uneventful. Henry had been in rare form all night, cracking his stupid jokes. Cassie suppressed a smile at the thought, and a muted snort burst from her nostrils. When Jordan and Jamie had appeared from the forest, hauling that log between them, Henry had feigned being upset, asking why they hadn't brought enough to share with the class. Cassie broke into a reluctant smile; he could be such a child sometimes. Henry had continued his mock complaints, only stopping when an axe-wielding Zayne had offered to help him get his own.

During supper, their discovery and its significance dominated most of the conversation. It was an interesting find. The sheer volume of distinct cultures and periods represented was unique. Cassie couldn't recall a similar site; artifacts from across the centuries, ending up in one place like that. Amazing.

There had also been a sense of enthusiasm about the exploration planned in the coming days, as well as speculation about what might be found. There was no way to predict the surprises the cave had in store for them. Zayne had inquired about possible treasure, turning a few heads. Zayne's father dashed her hopes about finding any gold or silver. While it was technically possible, Stone explained that they had little chance to find anything of much intrinsic value.

He'd gone on to explain different smelting and metalworking methods used by pre-Columbian cultures. Cassie had already known much of the information, but she'd enjoyed the look of intense interest on Zayne's face as she learned.

Stone had summarized how the South American cultures of the Andean regions had used gold and copper as status symbols for thousands of years. Some three to four thousand years ago, well before they'd discovered smelting techniques, a process of heating and cold hammering had been used to shape the naturally occurring material. Additional evidence from Bolivia suggested that copper smelting began two thousand years ago. But it wasn't until the Incas that metal was put to more functional use.

His description of the use of tumbaga in Central America piqued Cassie's curiosity. She found the alloy of gold and copper most interesting. According to the professor, the alloy's melting point was lower than either of the individual metals. Harder than copper, tumbaga remained malleable after being shaped. The metal could then be treated with citric acid to remove the copper from the outer layer, leaving pure gold on the surface.

Cassie glanced over to the tents; most of the others had already gone to bed. She'd appointed herself to double-check everything before turning in. It was just easier that way; quicker.

In the tree line across the field, Cassie spotted movement. Her breath caught as she shifted to get a better view. Henry appeared from the woods, flashlight beam preceding him, probably returning from the latrine. It was only Henry. She let the air slip from her lungs while her eyes followed him to his tent. Cassie hadn't been aware she'd been so uneasy. The deaths, the week before, seemed to have affected her more than she'd realized.

Cassie rechecked the tent to make sure she'd put away all the food. You couldn't be too careful. She didn't want any critters making a mess of their camp in the middle of the night. Assured everything was put away, Cassie turned and strode toward the fire pit. There weren't any visible embers.

After dinner, they'd sat around the campfire for another hour, talking while the fire dwindled and died. Henry had then drowned the fire with a bucket of water they'd placed nearby, ready in case of emergencies. Next, he'd smothered it with dirt, mixing the ashes and soil.

Cassie bent down and placed a hand against the earth to make certain it was cool to the touch.

Jordan Adler
9:04 pm

Jordan lay in her tent. Next to her, Zayne fidgeted in her sleeping bag. Rolling around, trying to get comfortable, the sound of Zayne's clothes rubbing against the canvas of the cheap sleeping bag was like strings of explosions. Outside, the cadence of crickets and jar flies pulsed through the night air. Sounds of life active all around her. Her mind raced with the discovery of the artifacts. What did they mean? Were there more? What awaited them tomorrow? Excitement built for their exploration the next day.

Jordan sighed; at this rate, her mind wouldn't let her get much sleep. She used to have trouble sleeping, even having to take sleeping pills for a long while, until she developed a weird technique to calm her mind. To quiet her brain of extraneous thoughts. She'd never told anyone about it. It would have been too difficult to explain. Besides, it seemed odd even to her. Jordan squeezed her eyes shut and took a deep breath.

She began to push everything from her mind, visualizing an image of the inside of her skull. Her mind, no less active, merely associated the interior of her skull to an archaeological find, and the active bits of her brain as the layers of mud and earth packed atop it. Now came the oddest bit. She would picture a trowel. Her goal was to use the tool to uncover the bone beneath. Starting with one of the more active sections of her mind, she would use the trowel to scrape away layers of mud until the area had quieted. As if she were uncovering a precious discovery, Jordan would continue in sections, bit by bit, some areas needing more attention than others, until she realized her thoughts were much less frenzied. She would then make up a narrative in her mind, concentrating on creating that story until she drifted off.

The Beast
9:43 pm

She crept through the trees, circling the clearing. Nostrils flexing, she took in a deep lungful of the cool night air. More people. More. There were new intruders in her forest. She could smell them. Why were they here? The scents mingled in the night air, making it hard to pinpoint how many there were, but she could tell it wasn't more than ten. Days had passed since the last set of interlopers disappeared. Why had these new strangers invaded her forest?

Part of her just wanted to rip them to shreds, to teach them not to trespass in her forest. But that might not be the best idea. Still fresh in her memory was what had happened only days before. After her last encounter, so many people had been so quick to appear. Would members of this new group's tribe come searching for them if they disappeared? She could only assume they would. Attacking them was out, for now.

Still, she was drawn to have a look. To check out their camp. The smell of cooking meat was, again, so very enticing. Luckily for them, she had recently fed. In the dim light from the waning gibbous moon, she could clearly make out the camp.

She stopped circling and slipped between the trees, into the clearing. The first structure she came to was full of enticing smells. The aroma of meat, grain, and fruit filled the space. Unable to spot any food, however, she moved on. She passed the remains of their cookfire as she slunk toward the group of shelters.

She prowled around and between their artificial dwellings, taking in every detail. The tents were similar to those of the week before. Flimsy. It would be simple for her to rip right through them. Did they really expect those thin layers of material to keep them safe? Did they even have predators left to worry about?

Light escaped from one of the fragile dwellings. Not from fire; this light was somehow eerie and unnatural. It reminded her of the moon. From the vehicles the week before, she knew they had somehow harnessed the power of the sun. But now the moon? Was that possible? Also drifting from the dwelling's thin skin were muted voices. There couldn't be that many people in there, could there? She stalked up to the dwelling and inhaled the scent of it. Her nose confirmed the smell of one, maybe two humans. A musk of body odor encroached, along with some odd smells she'd encountered the week before.

She failed to notice a low chuffing sound escape from her throat as she continued to prowl around the camp.

CHAPTER 14

Zayne Stone
Saturday, September 1st
7:29 am

Muted voices and sounds of activity drifted through thin canvas walls, pulling Zayne out of her slumber. Diffused morning light assaulted her eyelids as she rolled over. She opened her eyes to see she was alone in the tent. Zayne pulled her bedroll tighter around her shoulders. She'd had trouble falling asleep the night before, and she could have sworn there'd been something lurking around outside her tent. In the middle of the night, she woke Jordan up to go with her to pee. She was so embarrassed that she'd done that. She had felt like such a child. Surprisingly, Jordan hadn't seemed to mind in the least, escorting a scared, silly little girl to the toilet at three in the morning.

The night had been colder than Zayne would have guessed. Even with the hoodie, she'd borrowed from Jamie, the chill forced Zayne to cuddle up in her sleeping bag. She brought her hand out of the sleeping bag and reached for her phone. Zayne tilted it toward her to check the time; the large digital letters read 7:31. She let out a soft groan before worming her way out of the bag. Zayne crawled on her knees over to her pack. She pried the bag open and reached inside. She rummaged around for a pair of long pants and pulled her favorite jeans from the bag. Zayne turned to make sure the tent was zipped. The cold prickled against her bare skin as she slipped her pajama pants off. Shivering in the chilled air, Zayne yanked her jeans on. Due to the lower temperature, she decided to leave the oversized hoodie on.

She unzipped the tent and crawled out. Yawning, Zayne got to her feet. She stretched as she took in the scene around her. Across the clearing, standing over a small fire, her father was busy making coffee. At the kitchen tent, Henry and Cassie were setting out food for the group's breakfast. Jamie, balancing a roll of toilet paper, was talking animatedly to Jordan, as they came out of the woods and ambled toward the tents.

There was a hollowness in her stomach as Zayne trudged across the field toward the food tent. As she stepped from the shadows cast by the huge trees, the morning sun warmed the back of her shirt. The morning dew spritzed up and dampened her sneakers.

Henry smiled when he caught sight of her. "Good morning, sleepyhead."

Zayne felt the familiar flush rise at his words, and her heart quickened.

"Good morning, Zayne," Cassie greeted her warmly. "How d'you sleep?"

Wiping the sleep out of her right eye, Zayne perused the food being laid out. "Not very well," she replied, choosing a fruit tart. "I kept hearing noises outside."

"Was it a monster?" Henry asked in a spooky voice, waving his fingers in front of her face, like an idiot.

"No!" Zayne shot back indignantly, scrunching her nose. She turned to grab a bottled water, then peered back over her shoulder. "It sounded like someone was wandering around, is all."

Zayne spun away and strode off toward the firepit. She plopped down on their log. Her eyes swept over the ash in the pit. Zayne ripped the foil wrapping open and started eating.

Her gaze shifted to the forest, and Zayne let the sounds of the camp flow past her as she slowly woke up. After a while, she noticed she was holding an empty wrapper. When she glanced around, she realized almost everyone was getting ready. Zayne took another quick sip of her water, then screwed the cap on and stood up.

She bolted toward her tent, stuffing the wrapper in her pocket. By the time she'd changed into her own shirt, everyone else was ready. They were all standing around the kitchen tent, cleaning up breakfast as she strode up.

After fishing the empty wrapper from her pocket, Zayne tossed it in the small trash bag before joining the group.

Henry Blake
8:03 am

Shadows shifted across the cave walls in a preternatural dance, raising goosebumps on Henry's arms. Michael Redfern had reclaimed the video camera he'd used the previous day, its powerful beam mixing with a single work light to cast silhouettes of the group on the walls behind them. Michael filmed the group as they milled around the chamber, waiting for Professor Stone. Henry couldn't help but notice that Michael was paying more attention to the girls than was absolutely necessary. Henry glanced at the time; he wished the professor would hurry up.

Stone was outside arranging the new supplies in the tent. During the fifteen-minute trek to the cave, each team member had been burdened with various necessities the professor believed essential for that day. Stone had presented Henry with a bulky, nylon bag and asked him to lead the team members into the cave and hand out the contents.

Henry opened the bag and peeked inside. The bag held lightweight, polycarbonate caving helmets equipped with an LED headlamp for each of them. His exploration of the bag had drawn the attention of a few of his fellow students. It was as good a time as any. He plucked one helmet from the bag and tossed it across the room. Jamie snatched it from the air as it flew at her. Henry tossed another of the helmets toward Cassie, who almost dropped it. At her near fumble, he thought better of throwing any more of them.

"Come on, everyone put on your pretzel," Henry said, passing out the helmets.

"That's not how you say it," Cassie said in exasperation.

"I know," he replied with a grin. Henry grabbed a final helmet before tossing the empty bag on the floor near the entrance. He secured the strap of his helmet under his chin as he peered around.

His eyes fell on Zayne's confused expression as she studied the label stamped on her helmet. "Mine says Petzl," she murmured, shooting a curious a look at Jamie.

"It's just one of Henry's poor attempts at humor," Jamie responded, giving the young girl a slight shake of the head.

When Zayne shifted her gaze toward him, Henry gave her a goofy grin and a wink, triggering a touch of crimson to rush up to her face.

He spun, flicked on his light, and ambled away.

From the opening to the next passage, Henry spotted a long, thin fissure along the cave wall. He moved deeper into the passage to investigate the jagged opening. Right away, Henry realized he could never squeeze inside. Henry craned his head to illuminate the entire space.

"Doc, look at this," Henry called, "there's another passage."

Jamie moved up beside him to examine the formation. "It looks as if the stone shifted along a fault, creating a narrow passage."

"I think you're right, my dear," Stone said, looking at Jamie. "I suppose we ought to see where it leads."

"Only someone tiny can fit in here," Henry sighed, looking back at the group and focusing on Jordan. His eyes drifted to her small chest, then swept down her legs. Five-foot three inches and slender, Jordan might be able to squeeze through.

"I'll do it," Zayne volunteered, raising her hand. "I'll see where it goes."

"No," several people said at once.

"I'll go," Jordan said, giving the young girl a comforting smile. "Aside from Zayne, I'm the smallest."

Jordan Adler
8:14 am

Jordan peered through the dark passage. Jamie, standing to her left, planned to stay at the entrance of the rift while Jordan explored. The cleft in the rock was tiny, just large enough for her to fit through. Jordan reached up to tighten the strap on her helmet, then flipped on the light. The chill of the cave all around her made her grateful she'd worn long pants.

As Jordan squeezed into the small crack in the cave wall, rock pressed in on each side of her. The sound of her cargo pants brushing against the rock filled the narrow space. Jordan took a deep breath, trying to calm her nerves. She hadn't ever been too claustrophobic, however, the idea of getting stuck under a mountain of rock was beginning to terrify her.

Jordan followed the small headlamp beam with her eyes as she crept along the dark rift. The passage ahead of her had a slight cant to it. She took small, careful steps, hearing tiny rocks and gravel scrape the stone floor beneath her boots. The passage narrowed as it veered to the right. As she reached the turn, Jordan struggled to squeeze herself past the corner; the rock was closing in tighter on her chest.

Just at the point when Jordan feared she'd have to turn around, the passage widened out again. Jordan paused, taking deep breaths as she studied her surroundings. Jordan could breathe easier; she didn't have to squirm through anymore.

"Can you hear me?" She called back to Jamie.

"Is something wrong?" Jamie snapped.

"No, I'm fine," Jordan assured. "The passage has widened considerably. I just wanted you to know that I'm going to search further ahead."

"Ok," Jamie confirmed. "Maybe I could squeeze through."

"I wouldn't try," Jordan responded, a slight smile sliding across her lips. "I barely wriggled my way through, and I'm not nearly as blessed as you are. You know, up top." Light laughter drifted through the tunnel.

Jordan studied the walls for any sign of danger or instability. She'd also need to keep an eye out for holes in the floor. It would suck if she was swallowed by the earth. Not seeing any obvious danger ahead of her, she probed forward.

The passage continued to widen as she moved forward, opening into a small, beautiful chamber. Or, as Jamie might call it, a grotto. The far wall looked like a massive curtain, stalactites hung from the ceiling on either side and flowed down the right wall. Several thick stalagmites rose from the floor. On the left side of the chamber, a worn groove in the floor separated two of the largest formations. A stream had, at some point, flowed from a small opening between the stalagmites, down a slight grade across the room, then through a diagonal shaft in the curtain wall and into the next chamber.

Crouching, Jordan peered down the small passage, which ended in a drop-off. Without a clear view of what came next, Jordan considered the wisdom of continuing. She couldn't risk being unable to retrace her steps or getting stuck. Jordan got down to her belly and wriggled down the smooth incline toward the drop-off. She peeked over the edge. It was a few feet to the cave floor.

She pushed herself back into the tunnel and decided to go for it. Jordan twisted herself around and slid feet first down the incline. On her way down, the smooth stone cooled her belly. First her feet, then her legs slipped over the edge. Waist balancing on the ledge, she put her hands to either side and lowered herself.

As her feet struck the floor, an echo filled the cave. Gazing around, she surveyed the area. It was a cavern, bigger by far than the rest of the cave she'd seen. Illuminated by her headlamp, odd shapes caught her eye. Stepping deeper into the chamber, Jordan's light swept over ancient artwork filling the walls.

Dr. Theodore Stone
8:32 am

Professor Stone swept his eyes down from the domed rock ceiling and along rough stone walls lit by Michael's beam. Stone stood at the rear of the chamber, eyes following an old channel worn into the stone, just visible under the thin layer of dust and dirt that covered most of the floor. Small boulders lay scattered along the length of the room, as if a giant had tossed them about like dice. This room was at least twice the size of the first chamber. Zayne and his pupils had split up to help him search the chamber for any artifacts. So far, they'd come up empty. Nor were there any visible signs of human activity. He couldn't say for sure, but a more thorough check might be in the cards at a later date.

Stone's eyes settled on his daughter; he was still surprised that Zayne volunteered to go into that small, dark tunnel alone. He hadn't felt quite as comfortable allowing Jordan to follow the rift passage as he'd let on. Caves could quickly become dangerous for the unwary. Stone had told the whole group to watch their step, both for dangers and signs of human presence; to literally not set a foot down without watching it touch the ground. He'd also told Jordan not to stray too far or too deep into the cave system.

Though he'd asked Jamie to stay behind with Jordan for safety, Stone still half-expected Jamie to run up in a panic and inform him Jordan was hurt or else stuck.

Jordan Adler
8:42 am

It had taken Jordan a little longer than she expected to get back to the others. While the hole back into the previous chamber was only a few feet from the cave floor, it was at an odd angle. She'd had to shift a large rock over to give her a boost up. By the time she'd squeezed herself back around the corner and into

Jamie's sight, Jordan could tell the other girl had been getting worried. As they caught each other's eye, the look of concern on Jamie's face melted away.

"Where have you been?" Jamie scolded in a tone equal parts of anger and relief. Jordan watched as Jamie brought her hand up, thumb and index finger almost touching. "I was this close to calling the National Guard," she only half-joked.

"Sorry, I got a little... distracted," Jordan evaded, trying to sound as contrite as possible without feeling it. "Go get the others, will you? I need to share what I found."

"Distracted? Distracted! That's it? That's all I get?" Jamie asked, throwing her hands up and letting out a sigh. The twinkle in her eye betrayed her true feelings.

"I need a moment to catch my breath, a little fresh air. I'll be outside, near the opening," Jordan smirked.

"Fine, keep your secrets," Jamie retorted, a smile creeping across her face before turning to walk off.

Jordan watched Jamie head deeper into the cave system. Once Jamie disappeared from view, Jordan spun toward the cave entrance and made for the clean, fresh air outside.

Dr. Theodore Stone
8:49 am

As Professor Stone approached Jordan outside the cave, he took in her appearance. She sat on a boulder across from the entrance and drank from a bottle of water. Though Jamie had assured him Jordan hadn't been injured, Stone's eyes raked the young woman, scanning for any sign of blood or injury. Jordan's caving helmet lay on the rock next to her, stone dust covered her face and clothes, her short, honey brown hair appeared the only clean part of her.

"Jamie said you found something?" Stone asked.

The young lady beamed. "After I squeezed through the tunnel, it opened up into this tiny gallery. In truth, it was breathtaking. Through a hole worn into the rock, I found a chamber full of these ancient paintings."

"How old?" Henry asked, entranced.

"I'm not sure." Jordan took another sip. "But I did see a very good likeness of a mammoth. There were more too, a lot more." Jordan leaned back on her hands to stretch out on the boulder. She'd settled the water bottle on the stone, in the crook of her thumb and index finger.

"Truthfully?" Stone asked, looking at Jordan with a mixture of hope and apprehension. It wouldn't be like her to make something like this up, but if she were right, this could be the find of a lifetime.

She absentmindedly fiddled with the water bottle, spinning it clockwise in small increments. "Yeah, it is amazing." Jordan beamed up at him.

Michael peered up from the viewfinder. "How did they get in there?" Holding the camera steady, capturing the conversation for posterity, Michael wore a skeptical expression. "They couldn't have all been as small as you."

"No, there's another way into the chamber. I'd assume there's a way through the cave." She answered. "I'd be willing to find out."

"Anyway, the rift appears rather recent, geologically speaking," Jamie put in.

"It's a maze in there. It might take a while to find another path," Cassie cautioned.

"I can help!" Zayne proclaimed. "I can go with Jordan? It is safe, right? Please?" she pleaded, eyes bouncing from her father to Jordan and back again.

"What do you say?" Stone asked Jordan.

She gave a slight shrug. "It'd be okay with me. I've yet to see anything concerning. And I won't let her go anywhere I haven't gone first. But it's up to you."

He shifted his eyes away from the group to focus on the cliff face. Stone wondered what he should do. So far, what they'd seen of the cave system was fairly level, but he knew that could change rapidly and drastically.

"Jordan, come over here with me," Jamie said thoughtfully,

motioning toward the supply tent. "I have an idea." Stone heard their footsteps as they retreated.

He turned back to his daughter and took her hand as he knelt in front of her. He conceded, "Fine, you can go with Jordan—"

"Really?!! You mean it?" Zayne exclaimed.

Stone raised a hand to silence the girl. "But you must be careful. Stay within sight of each other. You mustn't wander off."

"Thank you, Daddy!" Zayne wrapped her arms around him in a tight hug. "Thank you, thank you!"

CHAPTER 15

David Richardson
8:54 am

As he crested the hill, David Richardson let his eyes drift along the valley in front of him. Beautiful. To make sure it was out of sight, David hid their truck behind some foliage along a disused spur of the county road to the north. From there it had been about a half-mile hike to the edge of the valley. Geographically separated from the surrounding area, the valley was a chore to enter. But the mixture of tree ages and heights, along with the varying types of ground cover, provided an ample selection of places to set up.

David and Stanley Richardson, brothers out of Nowata, loved to hunt. In truth, they enjoyed it so much, they often wouldn't let pesky little things like seasons or limits stop them. They preferred bow hunting, as it was quieter, and therefore easier to avoid notice. In their opinion, bow hunting required more skill than using a rifle. David knew no better feeling than bringing down a brawny buck with an arrow through the heart after luring it to within forty yards or so. His brother, Stanley, seemed to prefer the skill and precise aim involved when hunting smaller game. Neither brother cared much for trophies, as they might bring unwanted questions or attention.

Behind him, Stanley's head swiveled around as he took in his surroundings. Slung on cords around his belt were a few squirrels they'd already taken. David's younger brother tended to be more on the heavy side and stood a few inches taller, a fact that always rankled him. Thick long beard covering his face, he might have been mistaken for bigfoot at a glance.

Clad head to toe in forest camo, David and Stanley had forgone the safety of bright orange vests or hats, in favor of invisibility. Outside of the public hunting areas, and not looking to draw attention to themselves, they'd figured it wasn't necessary. Each carrying their compound bows, a small pack with essentials, and a stand, they planned to stay for a few days. They hadn't brought much food, preferring to eat what they'd killed themselves.

They both relished a challenge, so when they heard about a cougar attacking people near Lake Tenkiller they'd started packing their gear before the news report had finished. Even after the reports of the animal's death, they continued planning. There had been disappointment for sure, but where there was one, there could be more. They'd been looking for something to do for Labor Day weekend anyway, so they might as well have a look around. If they were lucky, they might even bag one of the black bears said to roam the area. It didn't matter, they'd find something to kill, that was for sure.

CHAPTER 16

Jordan Adler
9:14 am

Worming her way back through the narrow tunnel, Jordan carried two work lights in a canvas bag. She hoped they could find an easier way to the chamber of cave art. Jordan wasn't sure if the passage could be widened safely, or if they'd even be allowed to do so. Regardless, it would be nice to not be required to squeeze through any longer.

Behind her, Zayne was having an easier time navigating the tunnel. The eleven-year-old was beaming with excitement, thrilled to be included. The professor was wary of letting his daughter explore the cave to be sure, but he must have trusted Jordan implicitly; she wouldn't disappoint him. Even then, it wasn't as if they were blindly wandering through the cave. They would stay in sight of the chamber of artwork.

Upon reaching the small gallery made up of natural cave formations, Jordan strode straight for the smooth shaft that lead into the next area. As she squatted, she aimed her light through the opening and peered down the incline.

"Oooh, that's neat," Zayne marveled.

Zayne was gawking at the natural decorations "I know, it's

wonderful, isn't it?" Jordan asked. "Do you know how they're formed?"

"Water, right?" Zayne responded without taking her eyes from the formations, "dripping or something."

"Yeah, exactly, small amounts of water flow through cracks in the limestone. Over the years, they can form all kinds of wondrous deposits. This room has a wide variety of formations, such as the stalactites formed on the ceiling," Jordan expounded. Seeing that Zayne's attention was intently focused on her, Jordan started to point out the formations. "See those long, thin pieces hanging from the ceiling, they're called soda straws. Stalagmites are the formations on the cave floor. As the water drips from the ceiling, layers of silt accumulate on the ground, allowing the structures to take shape. Where a stalactite and a stalagmite meet like this," Jordan said, pointing, "that's called a column. Along the wall, those wavy sheets are called curtains or drapes."

"What are they made of?" Zayne asked.

"I'm not sure. I think it is mostly calcium carbonate."

Zayne eyed her suspiciously. "How do you know all this?"

"You got me." Jordan broke into a smile. "After your father told me about the artifacts, I did some research on caves. But if you're really interested, Jamie knows a lot more about cave formations than I do," Jordan replied.

"She won't mind?" Zayne asked, looking somewhat reluctant.

"I doubt it," Jordan assured with a smile. "She likes to talk about geology."

"I'll think about asking her," Zayne allowed, her face scrunched in concentration.

"Come on, the next chamber is even better," Jordan encouraged.

As she knew what to expect, Jordan thrust herself down the incline, rolling to her stomach about halfway along. She felt her legs drop over the edge and pushed herself from the small tunnel, landing on her feet on the large stone.

"Jordan?" Zayne's voice quavered. In the light of her

headlamp, Jordan saw Zayne crouched down, peeking through the tunnel.

"It'll be ok, just push yourself down the incline. I've got you," Jordan coaxed in her most reassuring tone.

Dr. Theodore Stone
9:19 am

From the first chamber, where the artifacts had been discovered, Stone led the group through the fissure in the opposite wall. About a quarter of the way through the tunnel to the next room, the small pressure crack, Jordan and Zayne had squeezed through, led off to the right. Stone guided the group past that, around a corner to the left. Through the tunnel, another slight jog to the left led into the chamber they had explored earlier. Having already inspected the chamber, he moved quicker than he might have otherwise dared. He knew there weren't any visible signs or evidence that they needed to be careful in preserving. After making their way to the back of the room, Stone slowed as he approached the far tunnel. The next passage looked short and led up a slight incline into the next chamber.

As he turned back to the group, Stone boomed, "From here on we will go at a slower pace. We must assume that ancient peoples came through here on their way to explore the rest of the cave system. We don't know what to expect in the coming areas, but I don't want us to trample anything of historical significance in our haste to move forward," Stone paused. He glanced into the gloomy tunnel ahead and cocked his head to the side. The light on his helmet illuminated the path. "I want everyone looking for the smallest sign. Be on the lookout for footprints and claw marks, as well as any other artifacts. I also want you to be aware of animal or plant species or any delicate cave formations. We don't want it said that we destroyed the ecosystem or ascetic appeal of the cave. Understood?"

Stone nodded at the chorus of "Yes, Professor," he received from most present. He had to suppress a smile at Henry's cheerful "Sure, Doc." Even though he was a bit of a smartass, Henry was an outstanding student, very committed to learning. Stone wished he had more like him.

"Ms. Long, if you would join me up here, I could use your experience in the geology of caves," Stone said, motioning for her to come forward.

He saw her eyes widen; a slight look of surprise swept across her face. As quick as it appeared, the look of surprise vanished, changed to one of determination as she stepped forward to join him. Stone enjoyed having his students show their interests where possible.

"Of course, Professor, I'd be happy to help," Jamie stated, a hint of pride coming through her voice.

Jamie beside him, Stone shuffled up the slight incline into the next chamber.

Jordan Adler
9:24 am

While they followed the illumination from their headlamps, Jordan and Zayne picked their way through the massive cavern that contained the paintings. A wide opening halfway along the north side of the chamber led deeper into the cave system.

"Wow," Zayne breathed.

Jordan looked back toward the young girl. Zayne had stopped in the middle of the room, her light sweeping the walls as she took it all in. Jordan smiled at the look of awe on Zayne's face. "Amazing, isn't it?" Jordan asked.

"Yeah," she replied, studying the paintings.

"Come on," Jordan encouraged.

"How are we going to find a way to the others?" Zayne asked.

"Jamie came up with a plan that might work. She suggested we aim the work lights back into the deeper parts of the cave to flood it with light," Jordan explained. "While we stay here, everyone else will come through the cave the other way.

Hopefully, the light will penetrate the darkness enough to lead them through to us."

As she entered the passage, Jordan swept her headlamp around. Once she reached the far entrance to the tunnel, Jordan dropped to one knee and placed one of the powerful lights at its opening.

Jamie Long
9:26 am

Jamie stood at the tunnel mouth, studying the newest chamber. The cavern had to be spacious enough to hold a basketball court and its ceiling at least twenty-five to thirty feet high. Along the ceiling were a few lonely cave formations. The floor had a wide, shallow dry streambed coming from one tunnel. The streambed split not far from the passage; one fork once flowed along the wall into the chamber they'd just explored, and the other ran diagonally across the room into one of the other tunnels. The cavern was strewn with small- and medium-sized rocks. The floor also had a few huge stalagmites, and several smaller ones spread around. One stalagmite was the size of a dining room table, standing right in the crook where the creek bed split. It had no corresponding stalactite above it. From where she stood, Jamie could see at least four tunnels leading out, including the one they'd just come through.

"Ok, I want everybody to turn off your lights," Jamie said.

"Why?" Cassie questioned.

"I had Zayne and Jordan take two work lights. They're going to put them in the tunnel facing the cave's interior and hopefully, we'll be able to see the light. After that, all we'd need to do is follow it," Jamie explained.

"Excellent reasoning," Stone mused. "Ok everyone, lights off."

As the headlamps switched off, one after another, the cave became darker and darker. Finally, only Professor Stone's lamp was lit. He looked around at each of them, then Stone reached up and extinguished his light. With a final click, the cavern fell into darkness.

Unsurprised by how dark the cave became; Jamie wasn't quite ready for it either. Even knowing the sun couldn't penetrate this deep into the cave system, the complete darkness still took her breath away. Jamie blinked her eyes while she waited for her pupils to dilate. As her eyes slowly adjusted to the darkness, she caught sight of an area across from the group that was ever so much lighter than the rest of the cave.

"Professor, do you see that," she breathed.

"Where my dear?" Stone replied.

"Straight across from us," Michael announced.

"Yeah," Henry put in, "it does seem brighter in that tunnel."

"I think we ought to take a look," Stone suggested. "Everyone, switch your lights back on."

Michael's beam was the first to pierce the darkness. As the headlamps burst to life one by one, Jamie squinted into the sudden light and waited for her eyesight to readapt. Professor Stone scanned the floor ahead before moving toward the tunnel they had decided to explore. Stone led them along the dry creek on the north side of the cavern until they came to the edge.

"Try to step where I step," Stone declared, then stepped from the creek bed, onto the loose gravel of the cave floor. From there, the group was forced to dodge the various rocks strewn about the floor as they angled toward the passage. The professor would glance back often to make sure the group was following his footsteps as he led them into the next tunnel.

Stone paused the group as they reached a point where the tunnel split in two. Peering around him, Jamie could see a small amount of light reflecting off the stone walls in one corridor. Stone gazed along the second passage for a moment before nodding and turning into the illuminated passage. As Stone led the group further through the tunnel, the way started getting brighter.

Once they exited the tunnel, they came into another small room filled with speleothems of all kinds. Across the ceiling were stalactites, large and small. Various sizes of stalagmites grew from the floor as well as columns where the two types of formations joined. Along the walls, the flowstone made beautiful wavy shapes. It was by far the most active room in the cave system she'd seen yet.

From where they stood, they saw a wide, illuminated tunnel to their left. Careful not to trample any of the formations, Jamie followed the professor through the room. As they entered the lit tunnel, Jordan came into view, standing at the opposite end of the passage.

CHAPTER 17

Henry Blake
9:44 am

Henry Blake stood in front of the rock wall, his eyes panning from painting to painting, taking it all in. The walls of the chamber were smooth, almost appearing as if they'd been shaped; carved or sanded down. He was unsure if they might have formed like that, or if the Paleo-Indian artists were responsible. Around him, the others stood silently, each lost in their own thoughts, nobody willing to break the silence.

The chamber was magnificent. Unlike anything he'd ever seen. Animals of all sorts were represented on the walls. Many of the paintings were images of lone animals, while others involved some form of hunting. Henry wondered if the art was religious in nature, possibly giving honor or appreciation to the animals that had provided for the tribe. He would have given almost anything to know.

Henry shifted his attention and stepped forward, eyes locked on one image. It appeared to be a depiction of a massive, long-horned bison. Painted in mostly red and yellow ochre, with black highlights, the detail of the animal was extraordinary.

Above that was a scene of some elephantine species being

hunted. The animal stood on its hind legs, rearing up, trunk high in the air, ready to bring massive forelegs down on its foe. A Paleo-Indian stood not far in front, holding a spear as if ready to pierce the animal's thick hide. Henry squinted and leaned forward for a closer look. It might have been a mastodon. The animal's body appeared longer and lower than that of one of the other mammoth pictures, and its face was also longer. Also absent from the image were the domed head and a fatty deposit on its back, common to mammoths.

Henry's eyes shifted to another image, this one—

"Is that a camel?" a small voice blurted, shattering the silence. Henry whipped his head toward the sound and caught Zayne pointing at one painting. "If this is so old, how come there's a camel? There aren't—weren't camels in America, were there?" Zayne asked, not pausing for an answer. "And there's a horse. Horses didn't come to America until the Spanish, right?" Zayne looked back toward her father.

"It's either not that old or else very, very old," Professor Stone remarked distractedly as he continued studying the artwork.

"How so?" Michael inquired as he stepped back, shifting his position to capture the whole group in his viewfinder.

"The fossil record shows that North America did have various species of megafauna that went extinct near the end of the last ice age," Jamie put in.

"Megafauna?" Zayne asked.

Eyes following the conversation, Henry massaged the crick in his neck.

"Megafauna are animals that weigh more than, say, ninety to a hundred pounds, a lot of which—"

"So, my dog is megafauna?" Zayne cut in.

Jamie, apparently stunned by the interruption or, more likely, the odd question, knit her brows together as she cocked her head and gazed at Zayne. Henry had a tough time keeping the laughter from bubbling from his throat. His hand rose to cover his mouth as he tried to pass it off as a cough. By the look of consternation on Jordan's face, he wasn't sure how successful he was at covering his mirth.

After a lengthy pause, Jamie took in a shallow breath. "Um, I guess? Technically, I'd say you're right, but we don't really think of them that way..." her voice trailed off, eyes moving back and forth, lost in thought.

"You were saying?" Jordan coaxed.

As her gaze shot over to Jordan, Jamie looked blank. "Hm?" Jaime breathed.

"You were saying something about the megafauna," Jordan prompted. At Jamie's blank stare she went on, "How a lot of them did something—"

"Oh, right," Jamie went on, "a lot of them went extinct at the end of the last ice age."

"You already said that," Michael smirked.

"Oh," Jamie sighed and gave a brief lift of her shoulders. "I forgot what I was going to say," Jamie admitted sheepishly.

"No worries, my dear, happens to the best of us," Stone consoled, patting her shoulder. He turned to the others. "Jamie is quite right. The fossil record shows many of these animals disappeared about ten to twelve thousand years ago. The modern Native Americans wouldn't have known the details of these animals. Some of these species weren't even discovered," Professor Stone paused, turned to the wall, and stepped forward, "or rather, rediscovered until the early nineteen-hundreds."

Professor Stone reached out, and ever so gently brushed a finger along one shape. "This is a stockoceros, if I'm not mistaken, a type of antelope. See how all four horns are close to the same length." The professor lightly tapped the image twice before turning to his students. "This wasn't even discovered until the nineteen forties. If I had to guess, I'd say all the artwork I've seen so far has every indication of being genuine. It will require more study, of course, but, well, yeah..." he trailed off.

"Congratulations Jordan, you're going to be famous," Henry boomed, cuffing her on the back. The force of the blow knocked Jordan a step forward. "Sorry," he chuckled. As he turned away, Henry could have sworn he caught a resentful look flash across Michael's face.

"Henry, be careful," Jordan chided with a smile. "You're likely to hurt someone. Besides, I was just the only one tiny enough to fit through the crack."

Cassie Byrne
10:10 am

"Look at this," Cassie said, studying a series of drawings. "Professor, can you come here a moment?"

She'd followed the paintings around the room, stopping every once in a while to have a closer look at one. The paintings were extensive, covering the chamber. Most of the artwork was similar. She wondered what they represented. Cassie knew some people believed that cave paintings had been created by shamans and were somehow meant to capture the essence of the animal, while others thought the young men of the tribe were responsible as a sort of bravado. However, she tended to agree with Henri Breuil, who suggested the images could have been created as a way to make them easier to hunt, or in some way increase their numbers; a sort of hunting magic.

Cassie stood in one corner of the chamber. In front of her was an uneven portion of the wall. A section of stone jutted out from the wall, forming a wide trapezoidal-shaped area, facing back into the cave. The paintings in front of her differed from the others, they seemed to depict a narrative.

"What have you found?" Stone asked, his voice coming from right beside her. Cassie jumped, startled that he'd approached so close without her knowledge. "I'm sorry, my dear," Stone soothed, gripping her shoulder. "I didn't intend to spook you."

"Oh, it's okay Professor, I wasn't paying attention. What does this look like to you?" Cassie inquired, pointing at one section of the wall.

"Well, let's see," Stone murmured, bending closer to study the area she'd indicated. He cocked his head to the side as he followed the glyphs, his hand hovering just above each in turn.

Stone studied the illustrations for several minutes. "Huh," Stone uttered, knitting his brow together. "The pictures in this whole section are atypical of the rest."

"How so?" Michael asked.

Cassie jumped again, not realizing he was there. When had he joined them?

"This seems to be a myth of some kind," Stone explained.

"A myth? Most of the paintings are remarkably lifelike," Michael said with interest. "Why add a myth here."

"Indeed, it doesn't match the rest of the cave. The creature depicted here is obviously mythical," Stone murmured, running a finger under the beast. Cassie shifted her gaze to follow his finger. To her, it appeared to be some massive cat with six legs. "Aside from that; of all the illustrations in this chamber, this series of pictures alone appear to form a narrative," Stone elaborated.

"What kind of story?" Jamie asked with interest.

Forehead creased, Cassie glanced over at Jamie, squinting at her. Where had she come from? Cassie realized she must have been engrossed in deciphering the primitive pictures. Three people had, more or less, snuck up on her. Cassie was usually much more observant; she prided herself on being so, in fact.

Cassie heard footsteps and turned to see Henry stride over. On the other side of the cavern, she saw Jordan making a sketch of one of the drawings. Zayne seemed to be wandering around, perusing various paintings.

Henry craned his neck. "Come on, kiddies gather 'round. It's story-time," he called, projecting his voice toward Jordan on the far wall.

"Let's see," Stone said, looking at the first drawing, "There was a young woman—"

"No, that's not how you start a story," Zayne said, shooting her father a smile. "You have to start with 'once upon a time.'"

"Actually, Cherokee stories were often introduced by saying 'This is what the old men told me when I was a boy.'" A pout slipped across Zayne's face. The professor beamed and gave her a warm look. "Very well, my dear. Once upon a time…"

CHAPTER 18
Truth Behind the Legend

She crept to avoid making any noise; she had to watch her step, be careful not to tread on any twigs or branches. Snugged across her shoulders was a heavy animal pelt, a gift from her father many years before. It was difficult to keep pace with her brother and the other hunters, as they glided through the forest.

It wasn't fair; it wasn't right. For as long as she could remember, from the time she could pick up a spear, she'd been as good a hunter and tracker as her brother. Their father had forbidden her from learning how, which only encouraged her to become even more determined to learn. She'd watched and listened as they taught the young men. She had become superb at stalking and snuck away to practice whenever possible.

That morning, the men of the tribe set out on a special hunt. A secret hunt. Tired of being left behind, the young girl followed them. By staying downwind and skulking, she managed to pursue them all day without being spotted. As the men made camp that night, she tugged her animal skin tighter around her shoulders and hunkered down behind a boulder to wait. Concealed, she peered around the stone's edge, watching and listening into the night as the hunters told sacred stories and used magic.

She was amazed and furious that these secrets were kept from her and the other women of the tribe. She was so angry, so betrayed, she failed to realize the danger she'd blundered into. A massive predator was closing in, having caught the scent of the hunters and their campfire. As it slunk nearer, the skin she wore caught its attention as well. It stalked in to investigate, prowling ever closer. The cat was only a few yards away before she heard anything. Surprised and afraid, she whirled to see a looming predator. She stumbled backwards and trod on a dead branch.

Snap!

Surprised anything could have gotten so close, the hunters fell silent and rose from the campfire. Weapons in hand, they made their way to investigate the noise. Upon seeing the hunters bearing down on it, weapons ready, the big cat bolted into the underbrush. Relieved the danger was past, the young woman turned and thanked the hunters with a sincere smile. The smile which lit her face died as she saw their expressions of fury and outrage.

Women were forbidden from witnessing the tribe's magic and sacred stories. This young girl had snuck up to their camp and spied on them. The hunters seized the young girl and held her as her brother was forced to tie her up. They sent a runner to get the tribe's remaining elders, including the ancient medicine man.

The rest of that long night, the young girl cried and pleaded with the hunters for forgiveness and promised never to follow them again. She swore not to say a word about what she'd seen or heard. The hunters paid her no mind, furious at the young girl for spying on their most closely guarded secrets. Even the young girl's brother had no sympathy for her, feeling betrayed and embarrassed. By the time the medicine man made it to the camp early the next morning, she'd given up her pleading and sat curled under her giant cat pelt.

The ancient medicine man sat and listened to the story.

Grim expression plastered on his face, he turned to the young girl. "It is forbidden for women to view our tribe's sacred magic or hear our sacred stories. Why have you followed the hunters and witnessed the sacred mysteries women have no right to see?" Hurt and furious the young girl tried to explain, insisted she was only curious, and all the while withheld admitting to the jealousy she'd endured at being left out.

After hearing the tale and her reasons, the old medicine man spoke with the other elders for a long time. They discussed the young girl's fate, several arguing to put her to death, while others were more lenient, suggesting she only be exiled. All were agreed, however, that the punishment needed to be severe in order to deter anyone else from ever repeating her sins.

Finished speaking with the elders, the medicine man separated from the group and returned to the girl. An air of weary sadness etched in his lined face as he considered her fate. The ancient medicine man knew she must be punished, and he needed to make an example of her. Seeing the great sabre-toothed cat pelt she wore, and understanding she longed to be a hunter and tracker, the medicine man bound her in the skin of the great beast. Her body transformed into that of a large sabre-toothed cat.

As punishment, and to mark her as unnatural, she also grew an extra pair of legs, separating her forever from the other beasts of the land.

Panicked at the change and fearful of the hunters who had been her tribe, the feline bolted away from the camp.

As the tribe made preparations for the journey home, the young girl's brother, having still loved his sister despite everything, decided to go off on his own for a while. With the blessing of the elders, he separated from the group, intent on journeying to one of the tribe's sacred caves to mourn and pray.

Scared and confused, hurt and angry, the young girl, now an unnatural beast, found herself getting hungry. With her new sense of smell and keen eyesight, along with her knowledge of tracking animals while human, she quickly found her first meal. She spotted a powerfully built deer grazing in a field and slunk nearer to him. From downwind, she approached as she stalked her prey. She prowled through the long grass until she was almost upon the deer; she sprung. Her two massive canines sunk into the neck of the animal. The sweet taste of warm blood flooded into her mouth. With one quick twist of her powerful jaws, the deer's struggling came to an abrupt halt.

The ecstasy in that first taste of blood was unlike anything she'd ever experienced. She knew then what she was made for. Tearing into the creature's stomach, she ate.

During the journey home, having done such powerful magic, and being of such an advanced age, the medicine man grew ill. Before the next full moon, he'd succumbed. Because of the circumstances and manner of the medicine man's death, his son and grandson blamed the young girl. Had she not followed them, or seen and heard what she should not have, the medicine man would still be alive.

A small group of hunters set off to find the beast, seeking to kill her for revenge. Among the party were the medicine man's son and grandson, as well as three friends from the tribe. The hunters easily followed prints and signs the immense cat made after she'd run away. Before long, they'd come upon her most recent kill. The carcass of a large, four-horned antelope lay eviscerated on the ground, most of its internal organs missing.

Still bitter from the betrayal of her tribe, she was surprised to catch the scent of them. She watched from a hilltop not far away, astonished that, after everything else, she was being hunted. Furious, she brooded over the injustice of it. Not only was she denied a place with the hunters because of her sex, but she was also transformed into this great, ugly, bloodthirsty beast.

And now they were hunting her.

Her!

There were just five of them, the fools. Did they not realize how powerful she had become? Did they not understand the magic coursing through her? She took solace that her brother was not among them.

While two of the hunters knelt, examining her kill, the others looked about for tracks and other signs. Upon finding her tracks, they stalked her. The group crept away from the kill toward a hill covered in long, yellowing grass. At all times, they kept the beast upwind of their progress.

However, the hunter's underestimation of her was their undoing. As they climbed the hill, following the tracks, they didn't notice the tides of fortune shift away from them. They were now the ones being stalked. Having found the animal so easily, they'd lost objectivity.

In the blink of an eye one of their number, the rearmost, was gone. Snatched and dragged away without a sound, a broken neck just like her other prey; the men in front of him did not even notice. The next man managed a pained gargle as she ripped his throat out. The remaining three men whirled and saw two of their number were missing.

The beast crouched down, staying low in the grass. One man, always blessed with more courage than common sense, more brave than smart, rushed toward her. As he sprinted forward, he lowered his spear when he saw her massive shape appear before him. The giant cat pounced, knocking the breath from his lungs as he fell to the ground on his back. The sabre-toothed beast landed with her massive middle set of paws on top of his chest. Using her forepaws to hold his head still, she bent toward him. He watched paralyzed, eyes wide with fear, as the cat lowered its jaws over his face and tore into his flesh.

Now, only the son and grandson of the old medicine man remained alive. Their spears lowered as they inched toward the enormous cat. The beast, her weight set on four legs, bent her torso up, raising one powerful set of forelegs. The cat, dark red blood dripping from her jaws, tracked the men as they separated. The men circled to either side of her, weary of her extra set of claws. As one, learned from years of practice, both men thrust their spears at her. She snapped into action. Darting to her left, she dodged one spear completely, swatting at its owner with a powerful forepaw. As she attacked one, the other man's spear grazed her ribs, drawing a copious amount of blood. The younger of the two men fell, his spear broken, a deep gash across his chest where her claws raked him.

The cat let out a furious roar as she spun toward the last man. The hunter's gaze fell upon his son, lying on the ground, coughing up blood.

While in the caves, the young man took his time to depict the fate of his sister on the cave wall, hoping that it would stop the same thing from happening again. With loving care, he portrayed the story scene by scene, ending with the beast she became, a punishment for her crimes.

Once the young girl's brother returned to the village, he found a horror he could not have imagined. Every man, woman, and child, gone. Fled, or else dead. Blood stained the ground; some beast had torn apart many of the tribe. He didn't know why this occurred, but he somehow knew the beast who was once his sister was responsible.

The massive cat waited nearby. After she'd returned to her home, she'd destroyed the village and scattered its people. Her people. Many of the fools chose to fight her. Their sacrifice had been pointless. How dare they send such fools to hunt her down? Had turning her into a beast not been punishment enough? The sabre-tooth hadn't found her brother, and she feared she might have to deal with him.

When her brother eventually returned, he seemed distraught and outraged by what she'd done to the village. Didn't he understand she was just protecting herself? Couldn't he understand that they had deserved it? He stayed long enough to prepare their sacred rights. Her brother lay the bodies out, as was their custom, giving their flesh back to nature.

After the preparations, he packed what supplies he needed and fled back to his cave. Sick with grief over the loss of his sister and horrified of what she'd done, he determined to stop her. Once there, he knew he had to come up with some way to stop the beast, his sister. A precarious strategy started to build in his mind.

The young man knew of a secret spot not far away. It was

dangerous, forbidden for any to go. Many years before, the medicine man told him a story of an underground pool hidden within a cave. But the pool wasn't filled with water, nothing that entered the pool could survive. Any animal that ventured into the pool became stuck and could not get free. A young boy once followed an animal into the cave and found it stuck. Not realizing the danger, or thinking himself light enough, the young boy had approached the animal, and he too became stuck. Several days later his tribe found him and the animal dead, sinking into the pool.

It would be risky. As he knew he was unlikely to survive, the young man added to his sister's story, even going so far as to add his plan, hoping that somehow the illustrations would help him succeed. The young man then made his way toward the hidden cave, wondering if his sister would really hunt him down. When the boy reached the forbidden cave, he found its opening was unstable. Ignoring the danger, he made his way inside.

Curious about what her brother was doing, she followed him, never getting too close.

As the cat pursued her brother into the cave, she smelled something very strange. The beast made her way down into the cave and found her brother standing, spear raised, on a ledge in front of a hidden pool, dark and strange. Disappointed that her brother decided to take up arms against her, not knowing it was a trap, the big cat rushed toward her brother and pounced. She was quick and skillful enough to miss the spear as she plowed into her brother, slashing at him. They both toppled off the side of the ledge. As she landed on her side in the dark sludgy pool, the cat noticed that the liquid wasn't deep and had an odd texture.

When she tried to regain her feet, she found she was stuck. She roared in anger as she struggled.

Her brother drew her focus; she noticed the depth of his injuries. He lay on the stone floor not far away, just at the edge of the pool. As she watched, he slowly bled out, tears flowing down his face.

CHAPTER 19

Jordan Adler
10:27 am

"This story," Jordan said as Stone finished, "Grandpa Joe told me a story similar to this. Surely, you've heard it?" she asked, looking at Professor Stone.

"Yes, this story is very much like that of the Wampus Cat," Stone mused. Jordan watched as his eyes darted back and forth.

"That's a Cherokee legend, isn't it?" Henry muttered, looking confused.

"Indeed, it is," Stone answered absentmindedly, still focused on the illustrations.

"Well," Henry said. He paused and screwed up his face. "Why is it here?"

Zayne's brows crinkled. "What do you mean?"

"Well, shouldn't this be in North Carolina or Tennessee?" Henry questioned.

"Why?" Zayne looked thoroughly confused.

"You've learned about the Trail of Tears, right?" Henry inquired.

"Of course," Zayne said indignantly. "When the U.S. government took away our land, forcing us to, and—and—"

Her eyes brightened. "Oh, now I understand. The Cherokee people came from the east. So if this is here, how come they have the story there too?"

"Exactly, my dear," Stone said, coming out of his reverie. "Being an oral legend, we can't be sure when, or where, it started."

"Once the Cherokees settled the area, someone may have found this cave and the story might have filtered back to the tribe members who remained in the area," Cassie speculated.

"Or, theoretically, the legend could have started here and spread through oral retellings," Stone put in. "There are stories of skin changers all throughout Native American myths."

"Do you think there's any way to find out?" Jamie asked.

"There would be no way to know, not conclusively anyway," Cassie demurred.

"I would like to have someone at the college examine their records, maybe the tribal records too," Stone returned. "I intend to invite more people to come out and examine the caves, anyway."

"Are you going to call The Odd Couple?" Henry's lip curled up at the side.

"My dear boy, I've asked you not to call them that," Stone reminded reproachfully. "It's not kind. However, I do intend to call Mr. and Ms. Abbey."

"Oh, come on Professor, they don't mind," Henry countered.

Allen and Amy Abbey were grad students and superb researchers. Jordan met the siblings through the professor and had taken to them straight away. Sporting the most amazing, eclectic clothes, they prided themselves on being odd. Always willing to assist their friends, they wouldn't do all the work but were happy to point the way for simple projects. The more difficult projects might cost a pizza for their assistance in the search. Between them, using digital and physical libraries, they could find just about any information you sought. Whether it be from old newspapers, official documents, or rare books, the Abbey's were thorough.

"That may be, but all the same, I'd rather you didn't," Stone persisted.

"Alright Professor, if you insist," Henry groused, shifting his eyes down. Jordan got the distinct impression Henry's acquiesce was feigned.

Jamie Long
10:31 am

Jamie had followed the tale with rapt attention. She'd never been filled with this kind of wonder by archaeology before. Jamie realized this discovery might have changed things for her. While she was still more interested in fossils, she—

"Now, I want us all to leave," Stone snapped. "I don't want to contaminate the site."

"What do you mean—"

"Contaminate—"

"Why—"

Raising his hands to quell the uproar, Stone elaborated, "We need to rethink this whole situation. If this site is as important as I believe it to be, I need some time to consider how I want us to proceed. Rest assured, we are not abandoning the dig. Now, I want everybody out of this cavern."

Stone shooed them from the room amid mutters and moans.

As they exited the room, Stone caught Jamie's arm. "Hold up for a minute, everyone. Jamie, could I please have a minute of your time."

"Of course, Professor."

"The nature of archaeology is one of destruction." Stone winced at the word. "Destruction is the wrong word; disruption may be more appropriate. Just the act of looking below the surface disrupts the site. That's why we must be meticulous in our site management and note-taking. Keeping that in mind, I want our disruption of the cave system kept to a minimum."

Jamie nodded slowly, unsure of the direction of the conversation. Had she made a mistake somehow? Was this a rebuke? She couldn't remember messing up.

"I would like you to mark a safe path through the cave for us to follow. I meant to do it on the way in, but in all the excitement..." Stone dug through one pocket and produced two thick pieces of chalk. "You may choose someone to help you. Be on the lookout for any important marks or prints on the cave floor, as well as any sign of the cave's ecosystem. You know more than the others what to look for and what areas to avoid. I'd like us to refrain from damaging any of the formations as well." Stone offered her the chalk.

Throughout his explanation, Jamie felt a growing swell of pride envelop her. The professor trusted her enough for such an important assignment. "I understand Professor Stone," Jamie marveled, feeling herself glowing.

"Who would you like to help you?" he asked.

Jamie looked over the group standing around waiting for them. There was one person who appeared more eager at the prospect of the assignment. "How about Zayne?"

"Are you sure?" Stone asked, eyes widening.

"Yeah, we make a good team," Jamie responded, tucking a lock of hair behind her ear.

"As you wish," Stone agreed with a shrug.

Stone turned to the others. "The rest of you please make your way out of the caves, if you would. I'll join you in a few minutes." Stone pivoted away, then whipped back. "Oh, and please be careful. I would like you to try to use the same route we used on the way in. Henry, Cassie, would either of you be so kind as to show Jordan the path?"

"Come on superstar," Henry wrapped an arm around the smaller girl's shoulder and steered her toward the exit, "you'll need tips about how to handle your new fame."

Cassie met the professor's gaze, then rolled her eyes and walked away.

Jamie couldn't help but smile. Even Michael's dour scowl couldn't bring her down.

"On our way in, I counted at least four passages we've yet to search." Stone pointed to one on the opposite end of the chamber. "It might be necessary to know where they lead, so you have permission to follow each passage until you reach the next chamber, but I'd ask you to stray no further. I'd urge you to keep mostly to the areas we've already explored."

"Yes Professor," she agreed.

"Remember to study the floor before marking out the best route. We don't want to destroy any trails the artists might have used or any delicate features of the cave. Oh, and I'd also ask you to refrain from re-entering the chamber of artwork."

"I understand."

From helping the professor lead the group through before, she already knew some areas to avoid. For the most part, she would stick to the old streambeds, though now dry, centuries of flowing water had, more than likely, already wiped anything of import. They'd still check, of course.

"Zayne, honey, you stick with Jamie, and do exactly as she says."

"Ok, Daddy."

Professor Stone gave his daughter a hug before he turned and strode away.

CHAPTER 20

Allen Abbey
10:47 am

Allen Abbey sat in his sister's sanctum sanctorum, watching as she played her favorite video game. Amy loved Skyrim. If asked, he couldn't have said for sure how many times she'd played it through, he suspected she couldn't either.

Their father had purchased a decent house for them, which was the least he could do after being absent most of their lives. The four-bedroom house was a perfect fit for their needs. They had set aside the biggest bedroom for Amy's home office.

Allen shifted in the comfortable armchair and returned his focus to his sister. Amy Abbey was five feet four inches tall, about a hundred and four pounds, and absolutely terrified of the outside world. She rarely left the house. On the rare occasions she did, she'd avoid crowds like the plague. It wasn't uncommon for her to refuse to leave the vehicle or to plead for him to take her home without getting what she'd wanted. She'd never learned how to drive; Allen was her personal driver. He didn't mind; he loved his sister, and he'd do anything for her.

Her fears began in high school, getting progressively worse. By the time she'd started college, they both figured online courses would be the best option. Amy was brilliant and there were some teachers, like Professor Stone, who understood her fears, allowing Amy to take some classes from home.

Allen and Amy often entertained small groups of their friends from college, having dinner parties or movie nights. Amy could handle groups of four or five and was quite popular for someone that never left the house.

Allen, on the other hand, knew he was an extravert, maybe too much so.

Nah!

Allen had thrived as he began college, always making new friends. Some made jokes or snide remarks about his sister. They didn't stay around for long; neither of the Abbey's wanted that kind of negativity in their lives.

Beside him, his phone went off, alerting him to an incoming call. Languidly looking over, Allen checked the caller ID.

"Who is it?" Amy asked distractedly.

"It's Professor Stone," he replied and heard Amy's game go silent. Allen swiped his thumb across the screen, answered it, and then pressed the speaker function. "Hello?"

"Allen, this is Theodore Stone, is Amy with you?" he said.

"I'm here, Professor," Amy called.

"Good, good. I have a favor to ask if I could," Stone said. "I need a bit of research done. Are you two interested in helping?"

Amy stood and moved closer to her brother. She plopped down on the edge of her futon, curling her feet underneath her. Amy leaned toward the phone.

"What do you want us to search for?" She inquired with interest.

"I want you to look into the Cherokee myth of the Wampus Cat or catawampus. I'd also like for you to check any local mention of cave art or paintings," Stone responded.

"I take it your cave survey has proved fruitful?" Allen coaxed.

The Abbeys listened as Professor Stone shared what his team had already found. After the explanation, the professor swore them to secrecy.

Dr. Theodore Stone
10:51 am

With the swipe of his thumb, Stone disconnected the call and sighed. *That went well.* He could always count on the Abbeys. With them looking into both the cave and the legend, Stone had one less thing to worry about. Zayne was safe with Jamie, and the rest of his students were—

Professor Stone stopped pacing and peered around the clearing. *Two by the mess tent, one coming back from the latrine, and the fourth, the fourth…* Scanning the clearing again, Stone craned his neck, trying to raise his sightline as much as his 5-foot frame would allow. *Ah, there she is.* Jordan must have been hidden behind one of the boys. She'd also changed out of her dust-coated clothes, into a pair of cargo pants and a gray and blue t-shirt. Prudent.

With all his charges accounted for, Stone went back to his uneven pacing. Drifting around the generator in the middle of the clearing, his eyes returned to his cell. The number in the top corner read 27%, he'd have to charge it soon. Attention focused; he noticed a segment of the next icon disappear. That left only a single bar. Reception in the valley was terrible. Throughout his call to the Abbeys, his cell service teetered between one and two bars.

Stone still needed to decide which colleague he wanted to invite to share his discovery. It would have to be someone he trusted. If he wasn't careful, word would get out, triggering waves of opportunists and media to roll in and flood the site.

The students.

At the thought, Stone whipped his head up and glanced over to the shape which had been drifting by in his peripheral vision. "Cassie." Good, he could count on Cassie.

The young woman angled toward him. "Yes Professor?"

"For the time being, I'd like you, and the rest of the students to refrain from discussing our find with anyone. Do you know if anyone has shared news of the discovery?"

"Surely not, Professor. Besides…"

When Cassie nodded down at the generator, Stone followed her gaze. Three phones lay on the tarp, plugged into the device. He'd been pacing around the thing, and he hadn't even noticed.

"Good, good," Stone sighed. That was good. It could have been a disaster. "To whom do they belong."

"Well, that's mine, and there's Henry's." She indicated each in turn. "I don't recognize the other."

"Would you please convey my request to the others?"

"Of course, Professor," Cassie assured.

"Thank you, my dear," he replied.

As Cassie turned and strode away, Stone returned his attention to his task. He scrolled through his contacts. One name immediately jumped out at him. Of course, Dr. Miriam Segan head of Archaeology at the University of Arkansas. Why hadn't he thought of her earlier? His lapses were a testament to the importance of the site.

After another moment's reflection, Stone selected her name and pressed the call icon.

CHAPTER 21

David Richardson
11:11 am

David Richardson's focus slid down the shaft, from the fletching to the arrowhead. Bowstring taut, he tracked a deer in his sights. David took a deep breath and slowly relaxed his arm to let the string slacken. Deer wasn't what he'd come for.

David stood on the metal grate of his tree stand above a well-used game trail; from there he hoped to spot any predators. Positioned so he could see in both directions, his stand was set up in a gnarled tree, canted away from the trail. He focused most of his attention on an area upwind, the direction he thought the animals would most likely come from. The position he'd chosen left David enough room to easily draw his bow. The other side of the trail was a bust, one scent of him and any animal approaching would spook. A major factor in picking this spot was a perfectly formed mountain lion footprint nearby. From his spot in the tree, David had seen several small predators, as well as plenty of prey animals. He had seen nothing good enough to sacrifice his position.

He and his brother split up earlier, each having their own

plan. David wondered how his brother was faring. Stanley had intended to use the squirrels they'd already caught to set as bait. They'd made a bet about which method would catch them the biggest game.

Both being bullheaded, they often argued about the best ways to hunt. Sometimes their debates ended in shoving, or occasionally, punches. David smiled; no matter how heated the conversation, they would always end the night with a cold beer and the day's ESPN highlights.

Lost in thought, focusing on the trail ahead, David was surprised to hear a slight rustling come from behind him. Careful not to make any sudden movements, he shifted his stance, bringing his whole body around. Whatever movement there had been, came to a halt as he'd turned. Craning his neck, David narrowed his eyes and scanned the underbrush, searching for the source of the noise. Save for the game trail, undergrowth pervaded the surrounding woods in all directions. Ferns, saplings, and shrubs peppered the ground.

He couldn't catch sight of what had made the noise. When a gentle gust of wind brushed David's back, he realized the movement had come from downwind. Couldn't it smell him? His nose had just begun to catch the odor of bacteria attacking the sweat accumulated under his arms. The trek into the valley left him a little damper than he would have liked. Could his scent remover be better than he'd realized? Perhaps the animal had smelled him and was just curious about the source.

Either way, it didn't matter; something, some animal, had been creeping toward him. He strained his eyes and searched for any sign of movement. David waited for several long minutes, scanning the woods the whole time. He had yet to spot the source of the noise. Had it been the wind? Try as he might, he just couldn't see anything.

David let out a disgusted huff and twisted back around to his previous vantage point. All that time wasted on nothing. Though he kept an ear out for movement, he resumed his watch of the trail.

Stanley Richardson
11:27 am

Feet braced on a lightweight aluminum stand; Stanley Richardson shifted his bulk, resting it lower into his tree saddle. Unlike a normal stand, the saddle put him behind the tree's trunk but positioned him in such a way that he could clearly peer around both sides. Slight pressure applied by either foot would swing him in the opposite direction. The addition of another step on the far side of the tree allowed him to shift easily around the trunk, giving him a 360° view from his perch.

The whole system was new to him. Like his brother, Stanley had learned to hunt in a traditional tree stand. He'd always wanted to try a tree saddle, but he didn't have enough disposable income to invest in a whole new system without knowing if he would like it. The professionally made saddles were expensive. It wasn't until a friend of one of his hunting buddies died in a hunting mishap that he got the chance.

The kid had been eighteen or nineteen, an avid hunter by the age of nine. Stanley thought it was nine, maybe ten. He shook his head; it didn't matter. After the incident, his brother and he went to pay their respects to the kid's mother. She was grateful for the kind words they'd shared, as well as the fond memories, bogus as they were. The brothers had gently steered the conversation toward the topic of hunting equipment. They were always looking for good deals.

After expressing doubts about knowing what to do with all her son's things. David had subtly hinted that they might like to buy some of his stuff. He'd done it in such a way that when she'd offered to sell some of the items, she'd thought it was her idea. Stanley was envious of his brother's ability to manipulate people. Either the woman didn't know what she had, or she wanted to get rid of it. Stanley acquired the entire system for a hundred dollars, less than a fourth of what it was worth.

Stanley pressed down with his right foot, which caused him to shift to his left. The rig was simple once you got the hang of it. He'd had to practice the set up a few times in his backyard.

He could just imagine making it all the way out into the woods, only then to try to figure out how to set the whole contraption up.

Stanley shifted his focus to the lure he had set up in the small clearing. His tree stood downwind of the clearing, right at its edge. With the tree between himself and the bait, he was well enough concealed from any animal wandering close by. He waited for the right animal to show up, wouldn't know his target until he saw it. With the cougar supposedly dead, you never could trust the news anymore, he didn't know exactly what he was hunting.

The bet with his brother and his choice to use the squirrels as bait had limited his options to predators or scavengers. If he were lucky, a bear might wander through. He doubted it, but you never really knew. There were foxes and raccoons around, though they were smaller than he might have liked. A wild hog could be his best bet, or he might see a bobcat.

With his mind drifting, it took him a bit longer to notice a rustling behind him. When he twisted around, the movement stopped. Stanley pushed one foot into the trunk, shifting himself slowly around the tree. He came to a stop and rested his weight on a step opposite his small stand. Now able to see the area, he scanned the woods, searching for the source of the noise.

On the other side of some dense brush, Stanley caught the barest hint of movement and discoloration. It could have been an animal, maybe a bobcat, burrowing behind the cover. Stanley pulled out his range finder and measured the distance. About thirty yards. He checked the wind speed and direction. That was odd; whatever the noise had been, it came from downwind. Was it an animal? Stanley shrugged his doubts away and waited patiently for the animal to show itself. What else could it be?

As he waited, Stanley wondered if he'd been mistaken. Perhaps it wasn't an animal after all. The forest around him had gone silent. It was unnerving. After several minutes, the object moved slightly. Ok, so it was an animal, but why was it huddled there, unmoving? It had to have gotten his scent, but instead of bolting, it just burrowed into the foliage.

Stanley watched and waited for a long time, ready to bring his bow up and take the shot.

After a while, the animal rose to its feet and started to slink away. While the animal's effort to keep itself obscured was, for the most part, successful, Stanley did catch a better glimpse of the animal's hide. Whatever it was, it was big. And it was moving away from him. Stanley didn't like it, but if he didn't take the shot soon, he'd lose his chance. He attached his mechanical release to the string and pulled it back, resting it and his hand against the anchor points he memorized long ago. Upper body forming a T, he felt the contact at nose, lip, and ear. He pivoted his whole upper body, so it kept its form, and squinted through the peep sight, aiming at the animal. He took a deep breath and let it out. His finger rested on the trigger; the arrow was ready to fly. He considered the shot again. It wouldn't be as clean as he would have liked, but he felt he had to take the chance.

Stanley took in another half breath, then slowly let it out as he pulled his elbow back. The finger resting on the trigger engaged the caliper release, which loosed the arrow. There was a sudden movement from the animal in front of him. Stanley watched as the arrow sailed through the air and grazed its intended target.

"Damn-it," he cursed under his breath.

The projectile gouging the animal resulted in it moving into view. Stanley's eyes shot open in surprise as he finally got an unobstructed view of the animal.

David Richardson
11:44 am

A faint shriek yanked David's mind back to awareness. He shot a look in the direction the cry had originated. *Stanley*, it was his brother Stanley. It had to be. David spun on the stand, then swung his lineman belt around the trunk to attach it to his harness. Secured now by two separate lines, David reached up to disconnect his safety rope. As he was about to shift his weight to the first step, his eyes fell upon his pack. He might need that, and he couldn't forget his bow. He snatched his haul line and snapped it to the carabiner on his bag. David plucked his bow off the branch, looped the line around it, and let it down. The nylon cord burned as the equipment's weight dragged the haul line through his hands. He then swung around to the first step and started his climb down the tree.

He tried to focus on his journey as he lowered himself down the succession of steps. His mind, however, spun as he worried about his brother. What had happened to his brother? What could have possibly made Stanley scream like that? There had been such a mix of pain and terror in the cry. Had he fallen out of the tree? From the beginning, David hadn't liked the look of Stanley's new tree harness. Why couldn't he have continued using the tried-and-true methods their father had taught them?

Before he knew it, David's boots slammed into the soil. He released the connection to his lineman's belt, then dove for his equipment and ripped both items from the rope. Bow in a tight grip, David slipped his pack over a shoulder, turned, and raced to the area his brother had gone.

As he darted between and around the trees and foliage, he kept an eye out for Stanley. Where was his little brother? David watched his feet strike the ground as he ran. He sped through the woods, legs propelling him as fast as he could pump them.

Once he reached the spot where he'd separated from his brother, he shot to the east. David ran for another minute before sliding to a stop. Where had he gone from there? Where was his brother?

"Stanley!" he called before darting around another tree. He whipped his head around, eyes open for any sign. "Stanley," he cried again.

As he opened his mouth for a third shout, he heard a pained cry from the southeast. He darted once again toward his brother. Rushing to the source of the yell, he smashed through the woods making all kinds of noise. Twigs snapped and leaves crunched beneath his feet. David left broken branches and trampled brush in his wake.

He broke into the clearing at a sprint, jerking his head around. He spotted his brother lying on the ground next to a tree on the far side. Covered in blood, his brother was gaping at him wide-eyed. Oh, God. What had happened? Stanley held one hand to a gash in his chest, applying pressure to the wound, the other extending weakly in David's direction. David advanced toward his brother, taking shambling steps.

His eyes scanned the scene, trying to understand what had happened. Stanley's face had paled; blood gushed from the wound in his chest. Too much blood, he was losing too much blood. If David didn't do something quick, his brother would bleed out. Agony clung to Stanley's face, and his eyes shone with tears as David looked on. His brother's mouth moved as he tried to form words. Tried to speak.

As he got closer, David noticed Stanley's finger extended, pointing at him. He was asking for help. His little brother was begging for him to help. "It's okay, little brother, I'm here. Everything's going to be alright," he croaked, failing miserably to convince even himself.

Stanley gave a slight shake of the head and a gurgle escaped his lips as he jabbed the finger at David. No, that wasn't right. Stanley wasn't pointing at him; he was pointing somewhere to his left. David's eyebrow shot up. What was Stanley pointing at? His eyes were round with panic. It was almost as if Stanley were trying to tell David there was something behind him. Stanley couldn't be trying to play a joke now, could he?

David stopped again. He was about to spin around to see where Stanley was pointing when he felt a massive impact. Something huge had hit him. He fell so quickly that he just barely extended his hands in front of him when he hit the ground. There was a pain in both wrists from the impact and his chin slammed into the hard-packed earth. David's vision went fuzzy as a fresh pain exploded in his neck. Had he broken his goddamn spine? David's eyes shot again to his brother. The last thing he saw, as his vision faded, were the tears flowing down his brother's face. In his final thought, David wondered why his brother was so sad. Stanley was the one who was hurt so badly.

CHAPTER 22

Jamie Long
11:50 am

J amie had to admit, she enjoyed Zayne's company. The young
girl had a refreshing quality of wide-eyed enthusiasm about
her. She was always helpful, did whatever you asked.

After they'd sketched out a rough outline of where they
wanted the paths to go, she and Zayne set about marking them.
They'd put at least one of the powerful work lights into each
chamber to make the job easier. The professor brought a supply
of orange survey flags similar to the ones used by gas companies.
Each flag was made of heavy, flexible plastic material wrapped
around a metal wire. They also had a number of small reflective
discs, about the size of coasters, to use where there wasn't
enough soil to place the wires.

A major perk of the job was that she and Zayne were the first
to see more of the cave system.

Though more difficult to negotiate, they'd found another
route to get from the entrance to the art gallery. Earlier explorers
would have likely used the easiest path. Etched along the ancient
route could be valuable clues about the humans and animals
who'd used the cave system. If it hadn't been for the worn creek

beds, she might have chosen the more difficult path.

After retreating out into the sunlight for a quick break, she glanced at her phone.

Not quite noon.

Jamie tried to keep a picture of the cave system in her mind; it was difficult. At the supply tent, Jamie grabbed a clipboard, a couple of sheets of paper, and a pencil. "Zayne, do you want to help me sketch the cave?"

"Sure, I'll help, but why?" Zayne asked with genuine curiosity.

"With so many chambers, I just think we might need a rough sketch. It might help us, or others in further exploration," Jamie explained.

"It's our cave," Zayne asserted, a frown darkening her features, "we should be the ones to explore it first."

"I agree with you, but we might not get a choice in the matter," Jamie said.

"Why not?" Zayne asked.

"Well, it is an important find. While your dad is in charge, for now, the tribe might want to change that." As she saw the outrage flow across Zayne's cute face, Jamie hurriedly continued, "Which they almost certainly wouldn't do. They were the ones that asked him out here in the first place."

"They better not," Zayne warned. "I haven't seen him this excited in a long time, and you know him, he gets excited about everything."

"He does have a certain amount of enthusiasm about his work, doesn't he?" Jamie asked, curling her lip into a slight smile. "So, you want to help?"

"Sure," Zayne said.

Jamie drew a line across the bottom of the sheet. Tapping at it with her pencil, she began, "This is the cliff face." She shifted the pencil to the left corner and used the eraser to make a slight gap in the line. "Here's the entrance," Jamie elaborated. From the entrance, she drew a corridor leading into the first room. "The artifact room," she said. A tunnel ran north from the top of the artifact room and curved around. Before the curve, Jamie drew a thin line, splitting off to the right.

"That's where me and Jordan went," Zayne interrupted.

"Exactly, what does the small room Jordan found look like? Can you draw it for me?" Jamie asked as she slid the clipboard toward Zayne.

"Umm-hmm," she murmured, taking the pencil. Zayne extended the narrow lines a bit before pausing. She scrunched her eyes shut. Zayne's concentration was evident in the way she extended her tongue, curling it up over the corner of her lip. She drew a shape that resembled an upside-down bowling pin. Zayne picked the tip of the pencil up, cocked her head to the side, and gave a confident nod. "That's close, I think," Zayne said as she handed the clipboard back to Jamie. "You should see it, it's so pretty."

"I intend to," Jamie replied, studying the drawing. Connected to Zayne's drawing, Jamie drew an enormous cavern, running at an angle to the northeast all the way out to the right side of the page. "That is the chamber with all the cave art."

Jamie moved the pencil back to the beginning of Jordan's passage. Above the narrow line was the curve in the tunnel. She extended it around to the left where it widened out a bit, then curved south, then narrowed as it curved to the left again. The tunnel connecting the first two chambers ended up looking like the top of a shepherd's crook. The second chamber stretched north to south in a rectangular shape.

"We should name them!" Zayne blurted.

"Huh?" Jamie said smartly.

"You know, like the tourist caves. They name all their rooms," she explained.

"If you want to, we can," Jamie said, shrugging as she smiled at the younger girl's enthusiasm.

"Ok, the first one can be the Shrine, like Dad was saying yesterday, right?" Zayne paused, looking at Jamie. She nodded, prompting the girl to continue. "And the room with the art can be the Exhibition Hall," Zayne finished smiling, seaming proud of herself for being so clever.

"Yeah, those are wonderful names. What about this one?"

She said, tapping the second chamber.

Zayne crinkled her nose as she bunched her lips and brought them to the corner of her mouth. "I'm not sure," she mused, "but this can be Jordan's Gallery." Zayne tapped the bowling pin shape she'd drawn.

"I think she'd like that," Jamie agreed. She jotted the names down, leaving the second chamber blank for the moment. At the top of the second room, she drew a brief passage running into the next chamber to the northeast. About half as long as the previous room, this chamber slanted up to the right. Four passages connected it to the rest of the system, forming a hub of sorts. If she remembered correctly, it spread wider in the middle, tapering into a point, almost like an arrowhead. "This could be the Arrowhead Cavern," Jamie offered, looking at Zayne.

"Ohh, I like that," Zayne agreed with a nod.

A tunnel led to the right from the Arrowhead's southern corner to a smaller chamber shaped like a waving flag. Above that, an oblong room connected to the Exhibition Hall. From the oblong room, a tunnel snaked up to the left and diverged into two passages. One corridor ran back down connecting to the tip of the Arrowhead, while the other led up and to the right, into a large unexplored chamber.

Above the Arrowhead, Jamie lightly sketched a tunnel and the opening to an enormous cavern. They'd only glanced inside earlier, not inspecting it long enough for a proper rendering.

The Beast
11:59 am

Blinding rage swept over her as she stalked toward the cave. They had hurt her. Those two stupid men had come into her valley and hurt her. Though already fading, pain like she hadn't felt in a very long time, pulsed from her haunch where the arrow had grazed her.

When the intruders had first shown up, she'd been curious.

And why not? These people were so different from her tribe. All the new people were. The week before, she'd been so hungry, she hadn't taken time to indulge in her curiosity. She'd prowled around this new group, through their camp, trying to understand them. Trying to see what they wanted. After watching them most of the night, she'd followed them that morning and had been surprised to see them enter that cave. It was the same cave her brother retreated to all those years before. What was its significance?

After a while, she'd gotten tired of watching the cave, waiting atop the hill that overlooked its entrance. She'd been there for ages. She had decided to leave them to their labors, whatever they might be. Stalking through the forest, she'd encountered those two men. She felt her anger boil. They'd hurt her. In her home, her woods. How dare they?

Having taken care of the two men, she wanted the other group gone as well, needed them gone. Banished from her valley. She didn't know if they were part of the same tribe, but it didn't matter. They had to go. And she would make them leave one way or another, no matter the cost.

CHAPTER 23

Jamie Long
12:13 pm

The colossal cavern just north of the Arrowhead was the biggest they'd come across by far. Even lit by one of the strong floodlights, the edges of the room were indistinct shadows. By Jamie's estimation, all the other chambers may have been able to fit inside. Cut into one side of the cavern's wall, an opening stretched twenty to thirty feet wide. Beyond it was the first genuine evidence of an uneven level within the cave. What she'd seen of the rest of the system had been relatively level due to a higher rate of fracturing in the limestone.

She shifted her attention back to the pit. Peering over the ledge, Jamie chucked another stone down and heard an echoing clank as it bounced off the rock below. The rock face, having been eroded, fell vertically about five feet and was followed by a steep, inclined rock shelf, maybe fifteen feet long. The way the gap had formed made it impossible to see the bottom from where she stood. Jamie presumed it went further into the cave system and was curious where it led.

The trench plunged into darkness as Jamie flipped her headlamp off. She gazed into the black pit. Jamie was eager to venture further into the cave system. What stopped her wasn't the lack of permission, though. She didn't have the equipment she would need to explore safely. As she glanced back at her young companion, Jamie got a strong hunch that the young girl would want to join her. Jamie was loath to put Zayne in danger either.

Nestled between a boulder and the cave wall, Zayne sat near the chamber's entrance, sketching the cavern for the map they'd created. To avoid glare on her page as she sketched, Zayne had switched her headlamp down to its lowest setting. As she turned back to the pit, Jamie broke into a half-smile; the young girl had been a great helper for the last several hours.

Chilly air prickled against her arms and stomach. Jamie let her fingertips brush the exposed skin. She'd shucked her zip-up hoodie after it got a bit too warm for her liking, stowing it next to Zayne. Sporting a turquoise tank top with her beige pants, Jamie relished the cool, damp air.

A sharp intake of breath split the quiet of the cavern. Concerned, Jamie spun around to face Zayne. Her eyes went wide in astonishment. Muscles taut and bulging, an enormous feline form slunk straight toward Jamie. In the cave's gloom, she couldn't quite make it out. On instinct Jamie drew a foot back, intending to step away. She froze as her heel tottered on the ledge behind her. Jamie brought the foot forward as she turned to glance over her shoulder. She was trapped.

Jamie eyed the creature, squinting to get a better look. *Had two mountain lions attacked the camp last weekend?*

Something was wrong. Something didn't fit. The creature was different; it was too big. Her next thought, a lion escaped from a zoo or a circus. Why hadn't they been warned? Someone should have told them. There should have been an announcement. As the animal prowled closer, its fur was illuminated by the spotlight. A fresh wave of confusion slammed into Jamie. Its coat wasn't a uniform tawny color common to lions or mountain lions. Mixed in along its hide were black-trimmed spots.

Emanating from deep within its throat, a low growl pulled

her focus to the creature's mouth. Jamie's eyes went wide at the sight before her. The creature's jaw hung open, wider than she would have thought possible. And there, protruding from its wide-open mouth, were two impossibly long, deadly fangs. Each tooth looked to be almost a foot long.

Omg, she thought, *it's a sabre-tooth tiger! No, that's crazy. It can't be, there must be some other explanation.* No matter how hard she thought, she couldn't seem to come up with one. Each theory that flashed through her mind made little sense. Cloning? Genetic aberration? Evolutionary throwback?

She tried to push that train of thought from her mind as her eyes flicked over to her companion. The young girl had risen to her feet and stood stock still, not moving an inch.

"Zayne!" Jamie screamed. "Run!"

Jamie's gaze snapped back to the animal in front of her, and she tried again.

"Zayne, you need to run."

This time the girl gave her the slightest shake of the head. Jamie couldn't blame her for being petrified, she too was stricken with terror. The giant beast prowled closer. Jamie slowly tried to inch away. Her movement brought more low growling from the animal. As she carefully edged along the side of the ledge, Jamie moved her eyes between the girl and the tunnel opening. She suddenly realized that the boulder must have hidden Zayne from the beast's attention. The thing turned its body to follow Jamie's slow movement. With an unexpected lunge, the cat bounded to the side. Though still in front of her, it had circled further to her other side and stood head-on with the ledge.

It let out a deep growl, warning her to stop moving. She complied.

For the first time since it appeared, she'd caught a glimpse of the animal's profile. That wasn't possible. It shouldn't be possible. The beast had six legs. Six. Jamie let her eyes scan the beast. Her brain tried to process what she observed. Too many legs. Had it mutated?

"Zayne, sweetie, I want you to run and get help," Jamie

murmured in her most soothing voice. "Can you do that for me?"

Finally, her words seemed to get past Zayne's frozen mind. Zayne shifted her foot, which caused the gravel beneath her shoe to make a slight scraping sound. The animal shifted its attention as it caught the sound and started to turn toward the noise.

"Here," Jamie shouted, drawing the animal's attention back solely on her. As it probed forward, the cat settled lower on its haunches, further separating its rear legs.

The beast was about fifteen feet away when it suddenly lunged. It shifted its upper torso back and brought both of its front legs off the ground. Still propelling itself forward on four legs, it swiped at her with one of its forelegs. Jamie lunged back, tucking in her belly and bowing her body away, as the sabre-tooth's paw came rushing toward her. She rocked back on her heels and brought her hands out, trying to keep her balance. Its claws swept across her abdomen, inciting a sudden blossom of pain before she toppled off the ledge.

CHAPTER 24

Michael Redfern
12:24 pm

Stretched out on his sleeping bag, Michael reached into his jar and slipped a pickle from its juice. He brought the snack up to his mouth and bit into it. Crunch. The sour juice filled his mouth as the aroma flooded his nostrils. Michael let his eyes glide over the tent's canvas walls while his mind drifted. He'd never thought he'd be part of such a monumental discovery so early in his career. Hell, before it had even started. With a little luck, he could use the discovery to catapult his career. He was an integral member of the expedition, after all. And they had all found the cave paintings together, hadn't they?

Michael grunted. He'd already have to share the credit with the professor and four fellow students, which was bad enough. But with Stone intent on bringing more people out to clamber for a piece of their discovery, he'd have to work fast or else be forgotten. Like with Howard Carter's discovery of King Tutankhamun's tomb, nobody would remember the team's names, only the leader.

Michael would need to speak with his father. With his father's business ties to the University's board of directors,

Michael thought there was a good chance of getting his name out, associating himself with the discovery. Perhaps he could even swing getting the caves named after him. Redfern Caverns would be a great name, much better than some alternatives. For instance, Stone Caves would sound horribly redundant.

Adler Caves popped into his mind.

That odd girl's claim was better than anyone else's. Even that dumb lug Henry had suggested that Jordan could take credit for the whole discovery. While she did technically find the cavern, it shouldn't truly count. There was no way he'd let her take the credit just because she's anorexic.

No, Redfern Caverns was a much better name, and he was entitled to just as much credit as anyone else. They'd just need to get the brand out there first.

The Beast
12:30 pm

Intruders. Her lips twisted in a snarl.

She lay nestled into the brush, downwind of her prey. From her vantage point atop a rise, she could make out the whole camp. Two of the intruders were visible, sitting in the shade beside the shelters. From the smell drifting on the wind, there were at least two others in the small dwellings. Another had ventured into the woods, not long before, carrying an odd white bundle. She considered taking that one first. Surely, after she killed one or two of their number, they would flee. They would learn that the valley belonged to her.

Coils of bitter defeat knotted her chest. She'd missed her prey earlier. She'd failed. Not once, but twice. She had crept through the caves, surprised them. Her heart had been racing as the tall girl spotted her. She'd sensed the fear as pheromones filled the cavern. Being so focused on the tall girl, she hadn't realized there was another behind her. Just when she'd been close to achieving her goal, it all went wrong. The one plummeted from a ledge to get away from her. She couldn't blame herself for that; scared prey often acts irrationally. But the little one, she should have caught the child as it fled through the caves.

Astonishment still coursed through her from what she'd discovered in the cavern after her failed pursuit. Art from ages past. Her tribe's artwork. She'd never before realized such works of beauty could exist. Anger boiled in her gut once again; it was just another example of what the tribe had withheld from her.

Discovering that the trespassers had invaded her people's sacred temple, made her more determined to chase them off. This time she would catch someone. Drive the group away in terror. If they knew her power, her ferocity, they'd never return, never trespass in her valley ever again.

Cassie Byrne
12:35 pm

Shadow engulfed Cassie as she stepped from the bright mid-day sun into the kitchen tent. Cassie's eyes roamed the pavilion's interior. The space looked the same as it had earlier in the day.

After they'd straggled back to camp, the professor had made a few calls, requested they refrain from advertising their discovery, and then retreated into his tent. For the last couple of hours, she and her fellow students had been idle. A few minutes before, the professor's head had popped from his tent and he'd requested she begin to prepare lunch for the group. That comical interruption had prompted her to wrap up her conversation with Henry.

Henry had been sure to make a couple of obligatory 'women in the kitchen' jokes.

Though still a bit annoyed, Cassie smiled slightly; the jokes had been quite funny.

Footsteps alerted Cassie to Jordan's presence right before she appeared. "Henry caught me on the way back into the camp and sent me over to help," Jordan said, reaching for a bottle of alcohol hand sanitizer. She squirted a dab on her palm, passed the bottle to Cassie, then rubbed her hands together.

"Sent you?" Cassie sanitized her own hands.

"He told me, as a woman, my place was in the kitchen," Jordan replied, one corner of her mouth curling into a lopsided smile.

Cassie's brows furrowed. "That didn't upset you?"

"Nah. Why should it? It was just a joke," Jordan replied languidly, shrugging her shoulders.

"And what is Henry doing while the womenfolk are in the kitchen?"

Jordan shrugged again. "He said he'd be over in a minute to help."

Cassie kneeled to reach for the cooler, then opened it with a slight pop. Cassie rummaged around for a moment before grabbing a package of lunchmeat. As she stood up, she caught sight of Henry walking toward them.

"Have you guys seen Michael?" Henry said.

"I think he's in his tent," Jordan said.

"I figured," Henry paused to glance at the tents, and sighed. "I didn't want to interrupt him. He's probably trying to figure out a way for us to disappear in the caves so he can take the credit," Henry joked.

"Oh, he's not that bad," Cassie said with an expression of consternation. "He surely wouldn't hurt any of us."

"Maybe not. No, but I doubt he'd lift a finger to save us either," Jordan quipped as she pulled out a package of flour tortillas.

Henry's eyes squinted slightly. "What are those for?" he asked, nodding at the tortillas in Jordan's hands. "I thought we were going to have sandwiches."

"We are," Jordan replied. At the continued look of bewilderment on Henry's face, she went on, "What? Don't you think it's easier than hauling around a few loaves of bread."

"I guess," Henry shrugged.

In her peripheral vision, Cassie detected a sudden movement across the field. As her eyes roved over their collection of tents, Professor Stone emerged from his tent and began to amble toward them. Had that swift movement been the professor? What else could it have been? On his way over, Stone paused for a moment to connect his phone to its charger. Cassie allowed her attention to return to her companions.

"… but is it still even a sandwich?" he asked wryly.

"Technically, it is a wrap," Cassie chimed in.

Jordan rolled her eyes. "Fine, would you like a wrap?" she mocked.

Henry's mouth split into a wide grin. "Sure, I'd love one."

Jordan shoved the package of tortillas at him, smirking. "Good, make me one too."

For a moment, his mouth went slack, then he grinned even wider as he replied, "Yes ma'am."

"Good to see everyone getting along," Stone beamed.

"Hey Professor, did Henry ask you what to do if your dishwasher stops working?" Jordan asked, lip curling.

"Oh god, not you too!" Cassie moaned.

Stone's forehead crinkled a bit, showing his confusion at the odd question. "I suppose you'd get just a new one."

Jordan thumped Henry on the shoulder, smiling. "There's the best answer I've ever heard," she laughed.

Cassie rolled her eyes at the two. Still, she couldn't help but let a smile slip across her face at the professor's confused expression.

On the far side of the camp, another rapid movement caught her attention. Her eyes raked the shelters before focusing on an oddly shaped shadow that had appeared on her tent. No, that wasn't right. Cassie's brain tried to make sense of the shape. As there was nothing to cast it, the discoloration couldn't be a shadow. Rather, it appeared to be the diffused profile of an object visible through the thin canvas of her tent. Whatever it was, it was moving. Only slightly, but still moving. Cassie rose on her tiptoes. Squinting against the brightness of the day, she shaded her eyes with a hand and searched for the shape's source. Whatever it was shifted. Was it Michael? Was he goofing off?

"What is it, my dear?" Stone asked.

At the hint of concern in his voice, Cassie's eyes flicked to his for a moment, then back. Attention laser-focused, she continued looking for movement. "I think I see something," Cassie replied vaguely, shifting a step to the side. Her palms slid down her pant legs to remove the dampness from her hands. When had her hands started sweating?

"What is it?" Jordan inquired. She sounded curious but unconcerned. How could she be unconcerned?

"It is probably just an animal," Henry reassured.

"I think it was an animal," Cassie moaned back. "A big animal." A chill raced down her spine. A cascade of goosebumps triggered the hairs on her arms to stand at attention. Fear. Fear washed over her. Why was she afraid? Even without understanding its cause, Cassie knew her fear was justified.

Henry took a step toward the tents. "They have problems with boar around here. Could it be a boar?" Through her peripheral vision, she read his body language, he was also unconcerned. Cassie couldn't understand how they weren't afraid.

Just as he moved his right foot forward to take another step, a sleek shape slid from behind her tent, freezing Henry in mid-stride. He would have looked almost comical, leg held there in the air, if it hadn't been for the look of sheer terror on his face.

As the thing let out a low menacing growl, Cassie focused back on the beast. A smilodon. *Oh my God, it's a smilodon,* Cassie thought, eyes widening in disbelief. A smilodon was slinking directly toward them.

A part of her brain absentmindedly attempted to quantify the images her eyes were sending. Two massive canines protruded from the creature's short, broad muzzle, well past its lower jaw. From studying the fossil record, she knew that each canine was at least eleven inches in length. The animal's coat was thicker than she would have imagined, the hair longer. It had a beautiful pattern of irregularly shaped spots, the inside consisting of a darker brown than the rest of its hide, a black border encased each spot.

The creature shifted its direction, presenting more of its profile. Cassie's eyes swept its outline. The animal's muscular shoulders rose approximately three and a half feet off the ground; maybe a bit more. Her eyes widened. Shoulders. It had too many shoulders. Cassie dropped her eyes lower. There were too many legs as well. Her mind raced, trying to comprehend what she was seeing. The sabre-tooth had not four, but six legs. Behind its powerful forelegs was a second pair. It couldn't have six legs. It just wasn't possible. No mammal on earth had six legs.

Cassie scanned the rest of the beast. 'Beast' was the most appropriate description she could come up with at that moment. It was massive, bigger than any lion she'd ever seen. Though it was hard to tell from across the field, the length of the animal, from its nose to its unusually short tail, was about seven feet.

A movement to her left interrupted her thoughts. When Henry fell back a step, he almost literally fell back. The heel of his right foot caught on the ground, which made him stumble. He steadied himself on one pole of their kitchen tent. Henry's sudden clumsy movement made the sabre-toothed creature focus its attention on him. As it bent both sets of muscular forelegs, it lowered its body to spread out its weight. The smilodon-beast let out a deafening roar. It adjusted its stance, tightening its haunches, preparing to pounce.

One of the phones rang, drawing the beast's attention. There was a sudden flurry of movement as it leapt toward the shrill ringing sound. Not understanding the source of the noise, the creature swiped one of its massive paws across the line of phones, ending the piercing sound. From the corner of her eye, Cassie watched Henry, apparently seeing an opportunity, spin on his heel and bolt into the woods. Jordan and Professor Stone stood near her, gaping at the creature. She couldn't tell if their lack of reaction meant they hadn't noticed Henry's flight, or if they were just preoccupied with the massive, prehistoric, six-legged creature. Either way, it didn't matter.

The creature shifted its stance, inspecting the area. It prodded at the generator. After a moment, the beast brought its paw back down, slashing once again. A shower of sparks erupted from the generator, which caused the beast to leap back with a yowl as the low hum the machine emitted tapered off, then died.

A loud snarl came from the beast as it studied the wreckage. The large cat sniffed at the smoke rising from the useless generator. It batted at the machine cautiously with a paw. With no reaction, the beast swung a foreleg more forcefully, swiping at the device again. Bored with the momentary distraction, the creature slowly turned its attention back to the group.

Cassie saw something twirling through the air. The small green object landed right behind the animal. The slight impact behind it caused the cat to spin in place and search for the source. The beast brought its paw forward and batted at the small object a couple of times. *Is that a pickle?* Cassie wondered in confusion.

"Here kitty, kitty, kitty."

At that odd utterance, Cassie's eyes snapped to the far side of the campsite. Her eyes panned across the tents, scanning the area for the source of the voice. Cassie craned her neck but could not see anyone.

After a moment, a figure swung out from the space between Cassie and Henry's tents. The man came to a stop in the aisle, feet set shoulder length apart, an axe loosely held across his body. Michael stood resolute, eyes wide, a panicked expression etched on his face.

The beast brought its front two legs off the ground and craned its upper body around as it peered back at them once more. Then the beast's attention returned to Michael, and it dropped its forelegs to the ground. Now focused solely on Michael, the creature edged forward.

Why wasn't he running? He should run. They should all be running.

Cassie opened her mouth to tell him, to shout at him, but nothing came out.

As the beast stalked toward him, Michael gripped the base of the axe tighter with his left hand, his right grasping it beneath the head. Almost in slow motion, Michael pivoted his upper body to the right and brought the tool around. Axe head behind him, he lifted both arms. With the axe poised over his right shoulder; Michael was prepared to strike. The cat bounded toward him. Michael waited until the beast was only a few feet away before bringing the axe down. As the axe swung over his shoulder, he slid his right hand down the shaft until it met the left.

Concentration on his face, Michael put all the power he could into the downward swing. As the axe head sailed closer to the animal, it pounced.

The axe glanced off the beast's hide, drawing blood. The thing hit Michael full in the chest; the impact whipped his body back and slammed him into the ground with bone-jarring force. Air burst from his lungs in a pained gasp, audible despite the beast's furious roar. The axe cartwheeled away, end over end, tumbling across the grass. It tilted over and came to rest, contrasted against the green field.

Professor Stone grabbed her arm and yanked her away from the scene. Cassie kept her eyes locked on Michael as Stone dragged her the first few stumbling steps. The sabre-tooth crouched over his chest; feet planted on either side of the young man. From her vantage point, all she could see of Michael were his jerking legs. Bare feet twitching.

She felt her gorge rise.

Blood.

So much blood.

Cassie doubled over as her breakfast came up.

Another jerk on her arm from the professor brought her attention to him. "Cassie! Come on!" Stone yelled, tugging her arm again. "Cassie! Run!" She glanced over at him, seeing Jordan being pulled along on his other side. Terror and sorrow were written on the other girl's features as tears flowed down her cheeks.

CHAPTER 25

Zayne Stone
12:46 pm

Coarse bark irritated Zayne's skin through the cotton of her t-shirt, making her fidget. When she lifted her head to peer around, her dark locks flowed over her face, obscuring the view of her hiding spot. Curled into a ball, Zayne cowered in a crevice between two massive boulders. Wedged into the gap, a stout tree bathed her whole body in shadow. Zayne couldn't stop shaking as the events of the last hour swam in her mind.

Zayne had been trying to get the shape of the room just right. She knew it would be okay if it was a little off, but she wanted to do her best. Surrounded by college students, several on the way to becoming doctors, Zayne felt the desire to impress them. And why not? Besides, they really seemed to like her. Dad had so much to do, any little thing would help him. Zayne wanted her father to be proud of her.

There had been a soft shuffling coming from the next room, but Zayne hadn't thought much of it. She'd figured it was probably her dad or one of his students. When something slipped into her peripheral vision, curiosity drew her gaze. The gasp escaped her lips before she realized it would happen. Zayne was well aware that her sudden inhalation could have easily been her undoing.

But Jamie had saved her.

Though inadvertent, Jamie's movement had reclaimed the beast's attention.

The monster had just begun its slow turn toward Zayne when Jamie swung around. Gravel scraped into the bedrock and caused a harsh grating sound to erupt from beneath Jamie's boots. The beast abandoned its spin and returned its attention solely to Jamie. The expression on Jamie's face, the horror, Zayne didn't know if she would ever be able to forget that look.

Squeezing her eyes shut, Zayne drove the heels of her palms into her eye sockets. Through the cool presence of her silky hair, dampness leaked from her tear ducts, soaking her hands.

She'd been too scared to move, petrified in place. Jamie had begged her to get help, begged her. But she'd just stood there, eyes wide, following the monster's movement. Jordan mentioned something about a monster the day before, but Zayne hadn't been paying attention. She'd been too busy crushing on Henry. Now Jamie was dead, and it was all her fault.

It was only after Jamie fell from the ledge that Zayne overcame her paralysis. The beast slunk to the ledge and peered into the chasm. Turning on the spot, gravel rasped loudly under her feet and had almost made her fall. She'd bolted toward the tunnel to the next room. As Zayne flew into the Arrowhead Cavern, she'd whipped her head around to peer over her shoulder. Through the opening at the other end of the tunnel, Zayne caught sight of the monster. It hadn't moved. It had, however, shifted its gaze toward her. She'd made a split-second decision to not go directly for the entrance. She had bolted to her left.

Zayne brought her hands away from her face. At least she'd done that right. Even if she made it out before the creature, the thing would have surely caught up to her not long after. With both thumbs, she parted her hair, sweeping it behind her ears. Zayne wiped her damp palms against her pants.

As Zayne had reached the tip of the arrowhead, the loping

gait of the creature filled the cave behind her. She'd rounded the corner where the tunnel snaked to the right. Rocks blurred by as she rushed along, the beat of the creature's footsteps behind her, continuing to get closer. She broke into the next chamber and took another left, aiming for the Exhibition Hall. When Zayne bolted into the chamber filled with art, she'd skidded on some loose rocks and almost fallen again. Eyes locked on her target, Zayne had sprinted as fast as she could for the end of the room; she was the second-fastest girl in her class after all.

She shuddered. That soft thump, thump; the noise the beast's paws had made as it chased her. Even now, she couldn't purge it from her mind.

She'd bounded on the large rock and up into the time-worn hole. Years of training on playgrounds allowed her to scramble quickly up through the tunnel. As she scurried toward the top of the incline, she'd looked down to see the massive creature scrabbling to follow. Its claws raked the sides of the tunnel, trying to gain purchase as it squeezed in after her.

That may have been when her bladder let go, she couldn't be sure. Tears flowed again and her cheeks reddened, she'd wet herself like a toddler. But that face, that huge head, the predatory gleam in its eye. Zayne shivered as she wrapped her arms around herself and tried to regain control.

The beast's jaw had opened impossibly wide, and those teeth were so very long. It was exactly like the story her father had read from the cave wall. Luckily, the creature was too massive and its angle of entry too awkward to squeeze easily into the inclined tunnel. As she'd pulled herself the rest of the way into Jordan's Gallery, Zayne hadn't let that slow her. She'd made for the exit. Where the thin tunnel started, she'd run smack into the wall, knocking the breath from her lungs. It hadn't slowed her either. Shimmying along, she'd made short work of the passage. After slipping from the fracture in the wall, she'd run through the Shrine, then out of the tunnel into the sun. And that was where she'd messed up. Panicked, dazed and shocked, she'd gone the wrong way.

"Idiot," Zayne blurted, striking her forehead with the heel of her hand. "Stupid, Stupid, Stupid."

Zayne had gotten herself lost in the woods. She had no clue how to get back to camp, to warn the others. If she was honest with herself, she was still way too scared to try. Zayne took slow, deep breaths as she leaned her head back against the tree. Tears seeped through her tightly squeezed eyes and down her cheeks.

Zayne heard an indistinct rustling somewhere to her right, off in the distance. Eyes snapping open wide, she cowered lower into her hiding spot. When she heard the sound yet again, she brought her knees up to her chest and wrapped her arms tightly around her legs. Head tucked down, resting on her knees, she waited, dreading the sound. And dreading even more what would follow. She concentrated as hard as possible on the sound, trying to discern its origin, afraid she already knew. As the source of the noise neared, she recognized what had to be slow footsteps moving her way through the groundcover.

As her breath and heart rate quickened, she squeezed her eyes shut, waiting for the beast to find her. Zayne waited for the inevitable pain. It would get her this time. It would kill her. Tears leaked from the corners of her eyes as she tried to push back the racking sobs, threatening to burst from her throat. She was so lost in her panic; she didn't notice the deer calmly wander past.

CHAPTER 26

Dr. Theodore Stone
12:54 pm

S tone stood rigid, eyes focused toward the camp where he'd last seen Michael and the beast. His ears strained to hear anything. That poor, brave, stupid boy. He'd distracted the sabre-toothed cat. The beast. Whatever it had been. Allowed the rest of the group to flee. Part of Stone had longed to do something, anything. Michael was his responsibility after all. His student.

Following the lay of the land, he and the two young women had run southwest along the creek bank. He wasn't sure exactly how far they'd gone before Cassie stumbled, sprawling onto the soft grass along the bank. As she rose back up to her hands and knees, she'd thrown up again. Cassie had then rolled to her side and thumped down on her butt. She'd scooted away from her sick, pushing at the ground weakly with her legs until her back came to rest against a nearby tree trunk. Then Cassie brought her knees to her chest and curled in on herself. Tears streamed down her face as she wept.

He'd frozen.

Unsure of what to do.

Stone knew that if he had tried to confront the beast, he would have likely died as well. The young man made the choice to let them escape. Though Stone couldn't be sure the young man had known what would happen. In their late teens and early twenties, college students didn't always recognize their own limitations. Their own mortality. Regardless, Stone couldn't allow the young man's sacrifice to be in vain. He had other students to worry about. And Zayne. *Oh God, Zayne.* He'd momentarily forgotten about her. His own daughter.

Stone jerked his neck around and peered to the north, the direction of the cave. Stone rubbed a palm across his smooth scalp. Grasping the dome of his head tightly, Stone squeezed his eyes shut, trying to concentrate.

He noticed voices beside him. A murmured conversation. How long had they been talking? Were they talking to him? Stone attempted to shift focus to them.

Jordan sat on the ground next to Cassie, cradling the older girl in her arms, trying to comfort her. She softly rubbed Cassie's back with one hand, murmuring soothing words. He didn't know how long they'd been there. Stone chided himself for freezing again. If the beast had been pursuing them, it would have caught them by now, they would have been dead.

After a moment, Jordan looked up at him. "That was the Wampus Cat. It is different from the legends," Jordan breathed, hints of wonder and terror in her voice. "The body, the head; that was a sabre-tooth. It's just like the paintings on the walls."

"But how? It's just a story, isn't it?" Cassie implored in a whisper, panic edging back onto her face. Her breath came in quick gasps, verging on hyperventilation.

"Shh…" Jordan soothed as she stroked Cassie's back. "Deep breaths," she whispered into Cassie's ear. Cassie squeezed her eyes shut and followed Jordan's instructions. Stone could hear her trying to control her breathing, inhaling and exhaling at a more controlled cadence.

"There are more things in Heaven and Earth…" Stone murmured quietly.

"Pardon?" Jordan asked, a blank look on her face.

"Shakespeare," Cassie mumbled, nodding, "Hamlet."

Stone crouched down in front of the girls, then looked each of them directly in the eye. "We need to get help. I want you two to take the van and get help."

"Alone?" Cassie said.

"What about you?" Jordan inquired. "Aren't you coming with us?"

Stone slowly shook his head. "I need to find the others. Zayne, Jamie, and Henry are out there somewhere. I've led my daughter and my students into a treacherous situation," Stone explained.

"We'll go with you," Jordan offered.

"No! Absolutely not," Stone countered resolutely.

"We can help," Jordan protested. Her statement was followed by a reluctant nod from Cassie.

"I'm not putting you two in any more danger than I have to. Please, go get help," Stone insisted. "I need you to stay together."

Henry Blake
1:02 pm

As Henry slowly came to his senses, he found himself lying down, huddled in a depression behind a fallen tree. Moisture soaked into his clothes from the soft, damp earth. Henry considered his situation as he slowly sat up. As he patted his pockets, it took Henry a moment to remember his phone had been charging. Henry forced his mind to focus as he studied his surroundings. His back against the trunk, the ferns in front of him concealed him from any prying eyes.

Henry couldn't believe what he'd done. Sure, he hadn't been expecting a giant prehistoric cat/monster to pop up out of nowhere, but still. He'd panicked. Just run. Henry wouldn't have thought himself one to panic like that. Henry had run, flat out, until he could hardly stand.

The moment had come. Fight or flight. He'd flown.

He felt shame and guilt pressing in his chest, like a vise around his heart. Oh God, why had he done that? He hoped the others were ok. What must they think of him? He'd never figured himself for a coward. He always thought he would be levelheaded in a crisis.

Henry got to his knees and peeked over the tree trunk. He scanned the area, looking for any sign of the beast. Not seeing any evidence one way or another, he settled back down on the ground, head resting against the tree. Henry closed his eyes and pinched the bridge of his nose.

Henry had to do something. He knew he couldn't stay hidden. Would it even be safe to head back to camp? What were his other options? Henry didn't have a key to the van, so that wasn't an option; besides, he couldn't abandon the others like that—again. Running was one thing, but taking the only vehicle, that was something else entirely. He might be able to hike out of the valley, try to go get help. *The cave.* He could go to the cave and look for Jamie and Zayne. That might be his best bet.

Henry slammed his fist down. The impact forming a small divot in the soft earth. He couldn't pick the safest course for just himself. He had to think of the others. It might be crazy, but he had to go back to check the camp, at least see if there was anything he could do. If he was careful, he might be ok.

Who was he kidding? There was a very slim chance any of them would survive. Still, he knew he had to try.

He peeked over the trunk again and looked for any sign of movement. Henry spotted a couple of squirrels chasing each other in the lower branches of an oak nearby. That was a good sign, right? Wouldn't they run away if a predator was around?

Henry slowly heaved himself to his feet. The squirrels froze as they caught sight of him, bringing their game to a sudden halt, then bolted away. He lifted an eyebrow as he tilted his head. That answered his question.

Henry spun in place, trying to recall which way he'd come. The forest was alien, Henry couldn't recall any of it. Which way should he go? Not recognizing any landmarks right away, he glanced to the sky. The sun appeared to be almost directly overhead. That made sense; it had been lunchtime, after all. But that wouldn't help him find his way back to camp. It appeared as if the sun was canted a bit in one direction. But he couldn't be sure, nor could he just wait around until he was.

How else?

In his heightened emotional state, it took him longer than it should have to remember that moss grows predominantly on the north side of trees. Henry scanned the nearby woods, eyes shooting from tree to tree, he looked for moss. Unfortunately, he seemed to be in a dense area of the forest, filled with moss. Henry decided to wander a bit and try to get his bearings. He knew he'd come to a recognizable area sooner or later.

CHAPTER 27

Dr. Theodore Stone
1:08 pm

Theodore Stone, professor of Archaeology and Native American Studies, was stumped. Never in his wildest dreams had he conceived of anything like this happening. He'd heard ancient legends of various Native tribes all his life, he'd grown up with them, studied them. But he had never, not for a moment, thought of them as real. They were just stories, some having a moral or lesson, many not even containing that much.

If this is real, what else is real? Skin-walkers, Wendigos, Sasquatch?

Stone shook his head, dispelling all extraneous thoughts. He brought his focus back to the present moment. *Those are questions for later. For now, I have a job to do.* Stone had to get the rest of his students home, safe.

Michael Redfern was dead. He'd never lost a student on a dig. There had never been a situation coming close to death. A few sprained ankles, a couple of broken bones, were the worst injuries anyone on his teams received. A guide had once been bitten by a rattlesnake, but that had been the man's own fault, he'd been trying to wrangle the serpent. Stone had been livid at finding out about the man's sideline.

Stone's remaining students and his daughter were scattered around the area. Zayne was safe with Jamie in the caves. At least, he prayed she was. *She must be.* Henry was God knew where; scared and alone. Stone hoped Cassie and Jordan could make it safely back to the van. If the creature was anything like a current big cat, it wouldn't need to make another kill for a while. Stone didn't know if sabre-toothed cats were into surplus killing. The equation he'd been forming in his mind changed when he remembered the thing had, presumably, once been human. Hopefully, it wouldn't go after them just for the fun of it. There was no telling though.

Was that what happened to the campers last weekend? The authorities had assumed that the young man scared the animal off. Stone didn't see the creature being scared off easily.

Stone plodded up a tree-covered slope. Eyes darting around once again, he checked for any sign of the beast. *The beast.* He shook his head again. He couldn't dwell on that. *There lay madness.* Stone forced his mind to focus on his feet, something he could control. *Right foot, left foot, repeat. And again.*

His left hand swept across the coarse bark of a small tree. He ran his palm along the trunk. His eyes closed for a moment. Stone brought the hand up and ran his fingertips through dampness accumulating on his cheek. As he rubbed the moisture between thumb and finger, he wondered how long he'd been weeping. There was no telling.

Stone crested the hill. Between the trees, he caught sight of the steep limestone cliffs in the distance. Mind in turmoil as it was, he hadn't realized he'd come so far. Stone put on some speed as he trotted down the hill, reaching out only occasionally to steady himself on a tree trunk.

The closer he got to the cave, the more frightened he became. The more frightened he became, the faster he traveled. As he reached the rise of the next hill, he was jogging. By the time he started climbing the final hill, he had been running, as fast as he could, for several minutes.

A stitch in his side and his breath ragged, Stone slowed his pace as he crested the hill. The grade of the final stretch down into the gully was steeper than it had been for a while. It wouldn't do for him to fall and break a leg. That was all he needed. Stone wove down the hill, between the large boulders, sliding a couple of times. He turned west to follow the old, dry creek bed in front of the cliff. After skirting alongside the cliff face for a while, it wound around a slight turn and their supply tent came into view.

Stone jogged over to the tent and shot a fleeting glance inside. Nothing seemed to be too disturbed. Stone ducked inside and grabbed a helmet. He slipped from the tent, glanced around once again, then zipped to the cave opening, and climbed onto the boulder. As Stone stepped from the passage into the first chamber, he only did a cursory inspection, only pausing long enough to see if Zayne or Jamie were present. He continued through the second and into the third chamber, also giving them the briefest of looks. Thankful for the work lights the girls had set up in each room, he absently noted the trail they'd marked. Stone paused after his scan of the third chamber; unknown to him, the girls had started calling it the Arrowhead Cavern.

There is no need to panic yet.

The chamber had passages leading in three additional directions. Stone chose to see what was in the chamber directly to his right. He hadn't been that way yet, so he moved to the opening. As he stepped out of the passage, he gazed around. Empty. Across from him was another opening. Stone rushed through the room and leaned in, taking a quick peek. Stone recognized the chamber on the other side of the brief passage. It led to the room with all the artwork.

"Zayne!" Stone bellowed, "Jamie!"

Not getting a reply, Stone backtracked to the third chamber. Again, unsure which way to go, Stone proceeded diagonally across the room into another passage. He stepped into a massive cavern, lit rather poorly by a single work light. A cursory scan of the cave failed to produce either of the girls, so he spun around and traveled back through the passage into the previous room. It was getting more difficult for him to stay calm.

Including his trip in, he'd now checked three of the four

tunnels. With only one direction left, Stone went into the final passage. He swept past the split which led toward the art room, instead opting to go straight, to check out a chamber directly ahead of him. Light from one of the spots illuminated the chamber. Due to a lack of footprints in the soil, he knew the girls hadn't ventured further into the chamber than the work light.

Stone spun and raced back along the tunnel. Then turned left at the split and hastened through the next room and into the vast chamber full of artwork. Unlike his last trip into the room, he didn't even glance at any of the art. His heart fell upon seeing the room was empty too. He took slow, deep breaths, trying to calm himself. Stone strode across the room to the narrow passage Jordan had described. Intending to study it later, he'd only given it a cursory glance before.

Stone looked up into the small, angled passage. "Zayne!" he yelled, "Jamie." His hand brushed against a rough spot etched into the stone. When his gaze drifted down to his fingers, his eyes widened considerably. There were angry gouges in the rock where an animal had clawed at the walls, trying to gain purchase.

CHAPTER 28

Henry Blake
1:14 pm

Henry Blake rushed east through the thick woods, attempting to avoid any extraneous noise on his way back to camp. He didn't know where the animal was, nor did he fancy being mauled by a prehistoric predator.

His original plan to use the moss hadn't panned out. The moss in the valley was apparently unreliable. Thinking he'd been going east, Henry wandered into a small clearing with an unobstructed view of the sky. While in the clearing, he'd studied the sky and realized he had in fact been going north for the last several minutes. Armed with his new information, Henry had again attempted to venture east toward the campsite.

Henry halted and dropped into a crouch. Hand resting against a tree, he concentrated on the sounds around him. Wind blew through the tree limbs, causing the leaves to emit a slight rustle. He'd heard something else. Something foreign to the environment. In the stillness of the wood, he caught another sound drifting towards him. Straining his ears, he caught a high-pitched keening moan, just barely audible. It wasn't the same sound that had stopped him. Henry straightened. Creeping toward the sound, he focused on it and tried to figure out its source. Surely, it wasn't the beast. Could it be an animal? What animal made that kind of noise.

Eyes surveying the area, Henry could see the woods had thinned somewhat around him. There were plenty of trees, but they were larger and spread further apart. The forest floor wasn't flat. Rather, the terrain spread out in gentle waves, not even high enough for him to consider hills. Maybe mounds? Dotting the area, several car-sized, moss-covered boulders sprouted from the ground.

Edging toward the sound, he strained to make it out. His eyes widened when he heard a slight sniff. Someone was weeping! It was the sound of someone trying to suppress their sobs. It had to be one of the girls. Someone had gotten away. The entire world slowed. Ignoring his new caution, Henry rushed forward. *Someone is here! I'm not alone!* It seemed to take forever to find her, hours or days. His mind told him it couldn't have been more than a few seconds, but that made little sense.

At some point, one of the massive boulders had split in two, forming a gap. A huge, double trunked oak tree had grown in the split between the rocks. Henry found Zayne, huddled on the ground, curled into a ball. She'd wedged herself amid the boulders and tree. As he crouched down level with Zayne, Henry caught the strong, pungent odor of urine coming from her. Zayne was making the barely audible whining sound. Her breathing erratic, she was doing her best to keep the noise to a minimum.

He might have been able to reach into the gap and pull her out, but he didn't like the idea. As it was, it took several minutes of soothing murmured words for Zayne to even look up at him. When she did, there was an unfocused panic in the girl's eyes that almost broke his heart. Something must have traumatized the girl. Henry looked around. Where was Jamie? He knew Jamie wouldn't have left the young girl alone. Not intentionally, anyway.

Henry continued quietly talking to her, trying to soothe her frayed nerves. He was almost positive she didn't understand

172

him, didn't know him. Suddenly her eyes cleared, just a bit. It was apparently enough for her to recognize him.

"He-Henry?" Zayne asked in a whisper. The panic in Zayne's eyes turned to confusion as her brows knit.

He gave her his best smile. "Yeah, it's me, Zayne. It's Henry."

"Wh-where's Daddy?" she whimpered. "I want my daddy."

"I'm not sure where he is," Henry said as calm as possible. *He's probably dead. They're all probably dead.* "We got separated." *I ran away like a coward. I left them to die.*

"Oh," she moaned, her lower lip started to quiver.

"I'm sure he's alright. I'm sure everyone is ok," he consoled.

Zayne slowly shook her head. "Jamie's dead."

Her statement hit him like a punch to the gut. Henry felt the air go out of him. "Are you sure?" he implored. *No, No, NO!*

"There was a cat," Zayne explained. "I saw the blood, then she fell."

Henry squeezed his eyes shut for a moment and took a deep breath. "Ok," pausing, he took another deep breath. Henry let it out in a sigh. "Ok, we need to get out of here. We need to get to safety."

Zayne's eyes widened slightly, obviously not keen to venture out of her hidey-hole.

Henry gave her a warm smile as he extended his hand toward her, palm up. "I'll keep you safe. I promise."

Zayne slowly reached out and took his hand.

CHAPTER 29

Jordan Adler
1:18 pm

Foot catching on an exposed tree root, Jordan stumbled and fell to the ground. As her left knee plowed into the hard-packed earth, she reached out with both hands to steady herself and felt her palms press against the cool ground. The impact slammed her jaw shut with a bone-jarring force, and her teeth grazed the edge of her tongue. A metallic taste flooded her mouth as warm blood leaked from the small cut. She cursed herself for her inattention. All she needed was a broken ankle. That would certainly help their current situation.

She'd been looking over her shoulder for the umpteenth time, painfully aware of the creature somewhere behind them. She couldn't wrap her mind around what she'd just seen. She'd never witnessed someone die before. *God, it was so awful. Poor Michael.* And all that blood.

A wave of nausea rolled over her, brought on by thoughts of Michael surging back into her mind, mixed with the nasty copper taste filling her mouth. As hard as she tried, she couldn't seem to force her mind to stop relating the taste which inundated her mouth, with Michael's blood. Jordan spat, trying to rid herself of the awful metallic tang assaulting her taste buds.

Jordan's gaze focused on Cassie, paused in her flight not far away. Though the other girl was waiting for Jordan to regain her feet, the look contorting Cassie's face showed that she was clearly impatient. Jordan leaned forward, pushing both hands into the ground as she used her legs to lift herself back to her feet. Feeling a curious wetness on her left palm, she twisted her wrist to check the sensation. The edges of her hand were dirty and there was a dead leaf stuck to her palm. Jordan flicked the leaf away using her other hand. She then checked her right palm; it too was dirty. Using her pants, Jordan wiped the dirt away.

"Jordan! Come on! Let's go!" Cassie finally blurted.

Jordan's eyes snapped back to the other girl. Fear, disconnected feeling, she realized her mind was showing signs of psychological shock. Why was it just hitting her now? Was it just hitting her? Jordan closed her eyes and pushed all thoughts from her mind.

After a moment, she pried her eyes open and nodded toward Cassie.

"Sorry, I..." Jordan trailed off, furrowing her eyebrows, unsure how to explain.

Cassie merely nodded, then jerked her head to the side to indicate her desire to keep moving. Cassie started toward the van at a healthy pace, forcing Jordan to catch up.

Realizing she could follow Cassie to the van, allowed Jordan to focus more of her mind on the situation. She'd been running through the woods in a panic, only vaguely aware of the way she needed to go. She couldn't allow herself to do that again. She couldn't allow herself to lose focus. It was a stressful situation, a very stressful situation, but she'd need to keep a cool head.

Eyes focused on Cassie's feet in front of her, Jordan reviewed their current situation. A sabre-toothed monster had attacked them. Jordan pushed aside all the impossibilities connected to that simple statement. Somehow, someway, a prehistoric predator had attacked and killed a member of their group. She wouldn't go so far as to call him a friend. Michael had been such a know-it-all. He was always trying to show how smart he was and seemed to enjoy getting in arguments. Maybe she hadn't given him a fair chance. He had saved them after all. Laid down his life for theirs.

CHAPTER 30

Henry Blake
1:24 pm

Henry knew they were nearing the campsite. It was around here somewhere. Coming a different way, the trees took on unfamiliar shapes and patterns. There had been a few he thought he'd recognized, only to discover he was mistaken. He'd led Zayne further north and east than needed, so they'd been forced to shift direction.

Maybe he should have led them to the cave first. From there, the journey to the clearing would have been simple. *The beast.* The beast might have still been there. Had it attacked the camp first, or the caves? There was no way to know.

Was anyone there?

Either way was a gamble, but he thought there was a better chance of people being at camp. Surely, they would have all headed for the van after the thing attacked. *If they're still alive. Shut up! Stop it. Of course, they're ok. Yeah, and Elvis is still alive, and Jimmy Hoffa just went on a long vacation.*

Henry sighed and tried to push the morose thoughts from his head.

After a while, the clearing materialized through the trees and they caught sight of the campsite. Zayne's hand slipped from his as she gasped and rushed forward, bolting past the last few trees.

Henry shot after her. "Zayne!" He called. "Zayne, hold on." He vaguely registered that they were entering the clearing from the north, about midway. Just enough to congratulate himself. So, a little further east than they'd needed, but not bad.

Zayne rounded the northern line of tents and slid to a stop in front of the aisle, which allowed Henry to catch up with her. Wide eyes taking in the destruction, her back stiffened as she let out a gasp. Focused on the girl, Henry hadn't immediately taken in the scene. He shifted his attention to follow her gaze.

The tents were set up in two rows of three, with an aisle in between. The two tents furthest away were torn open, their canvas skin shredded into tatters. Jamie and Michael's tents. Had Michael still been inside? His eyes came to rest on a large swath of red at the edge of the aisle, near the first and second tents on the right side. His mind froze. Someone had died between his and Cassie's tents. Who had died?

"Oh, my god! Is that blood?" Zayne exclaimed. "What happened? Whose blood is that?"

Henry kneeled beside her and grabbed Zayne by her shoulders. As he gently spun her to face him, her eyes remained locked on the pool of blood.

"Zayne. Zayne," he coaxed. Not receiving her attention, Henry shook her. "Zayne!"

Her eyes finally snapped over to him. As she tried to focus, her eyes rapidly darted back and forth between each of his. Henry was unsure how much she was really seeing.

"Zayne, I don't know any more than you do. It is blood, but I'm not sure whose," Henry paused, glancing at the surrounding destruction. "We need to be quick. I don't want to linger here any longer than we must. Grab what you need. You might want to grab a change of clothes as well."

"Ok," she said, "you won't leave me, will you?"

Henry winced, reminded of his earlier flight. "No. Of course not," he soothed. Henry's eyes drifted over to the meal tent. Unsure of how long it would take to make it to safety, he figured it might be prudent to grab some food. Henry struggled to his feet and took a step in that direction. Henry stopped as he felt a small hand latch itself to his.

"Where are you going?"

"I'm going to get some food."

"You said you wouldn't leave me!" Zayne exclaimed, grasping his hand tighter.

"I'm not leaving you; I'm just going..." Henry trailed off at the look of accusation in Zayne's eyes. "I'll wait for you right here. Then we can grab the supplies together. Ok?"

"Promise?" she pleaded. At his nod, her face relaxed considerably. Henry had barely even noticed the intense tension and anxiety written across her features until it drained away.

Zayne skirted around the blood, then slipped into her tent. She spun to shoot Henry one more furtive glance before she pulled the flaps closed. With the sound of Zayne rummaging around inside the tent, Henry shifted his attention away from the girl and let his gaze wander across the camp, alert for any threat.

Henry moved over to the pool of blood. It was a lot of blood. Too much blood. From the size of the pool, he knew there was no way whoever it belonged to had survived. As Henry's eyes swept the scene, he looked for any clue to the identity of the victim. There weren't any overt signs in the immediate vicinity. It could have belonged to anyone.

He caught sight of the axe lying on the ground not far away. By the look of the scene, it hadn't done its previous user any favors. Still, he figured it was better than nothing. As he knelt to pick up the axe, Henry's eyes flew over the area again. The cool, smooth wood of the axe's handle pressed against his palm as he snatched it off the ground.

His breath caught as a rustle behind him snatched his attention and brought him around. When Zayne emerged from the middle tent on the north side, Henry let out a deep sigh. She'd changed into a colorful, star print dress in hues of pink, blue, and purple. Beneath which, she wore a pair of skinny jeans and purple sneakers. It amazed him that after everything she'd been through, she still wanted to dress cute. Henry gave her a slight smile.

"You ready?"

"Yeah."

Henry adjusted his grip on the axe's shaft, then led them toward the food tent.

CHAPTER 31

Dr. Theodore Stone
1:27 pm

Dr. Stone had still found no sign of blood. His second search of the caves had been more thorough than his first panic-filled scan. He'd pushed himself up the incline and into the smaller cave Jordan had described. He got as far as the fault passage without seeing anyone. There were obvious signs of pursuit, but no blood.

If there was no blood, then they were most likely okay.

Maybe. The thought filled him with hope.

Zayne is okay, probably okay. When she'd left the cave, she hadn't been injured. *If she is still with Jamie, she has a better chance.* Stone gazed into the bright afternoon light. Where to go next? Would they have gone back to the van or the campsite? *What if they'd returned to the campsite right after we fled?* Did they meet up with the creature there?

Stone shook his head, trying to expel the doubts creeping in. No matter what happened, he wasn't leaving without his daughter. He'd sent two of his students for help. Stone glanced at his watch. They had to be getting close to the van by now. It would only be a matter of time before help arrived.

Stone stepped from the cave mouth into the mid-day sun. He stood just outside the entrance, peering around and wondering where to go. His eyes panned across the horizon. *Should I go to the campsite or the van?* Where would they have gone? He might have just missed them if they'd headed for the camp. Fleeing after the attack, he'd gone a completely different route to the caves. On the other hand, if they had gone straight for the van—

His mind protested; it wouldn't have made any sense to go to the van unless they were being chased. *Were they being chased?* God, he hoped not.

The woods were too vast. Walkie talkies, they should have brought walkie talkies. *No one could have foreseen this.* With that thought, he tried to ease his guilt. It didn't work. At all. One student dead, two more missing, plus his daughter. He could only hope Cassie and Jordan were nearing the van. If they could hurry up and get help, maybe no one else would die.

Stone turned toward the camp. He figured he should probably check it before heading to the road.

Fifteen minutes later, Dr. Stone crept toward the clearing. Stone had circled around the clearing to a vantage point on a hill to the northeast. Through the trees, he caught sight of the tents. He couldn't help but picture the scene he'd witnessed no more than an hour before. So much blood. From where he squatted, he could look down on the whole campsite. There was no sign of the beast. No sign of anyone. Neither Jamie and Zayne nor Henry were there.

Stone let out a sigh. He had hoped they'd be there. Perhaps it was stupid to think Henry would come back. Stone shot another glance around, then hefted himself up to his feet. Before leaving, he decided to comb the area. Stone made his way down the hill, half walking, half sliding. There was a possibility they were hiding in a tent. He doubted it, but he had to check.

As he swept around the northern row of tents, a scarlet stain that had once been Michael's lifeblood came into starker contrast. *That poor child.* He'd come at an ancient predator with an axe. Stone's eyes narrowed. He quickly scanned the surrounding ground. Where was the axe? Hope swelled again. The axe was gone. *Someone grabbed it.*

Stone strode to the first tent, Jamie's. Ducking down, he looked inside. Sunlight bathed the floor; the rear of the tent had been torn out. Jamie's clothes were strewn around the floor. The pack was still intact, so he wasn't sure if the sabre-tooth had made the mess, or Jamie herself. In truth, it didn't matter; she wasn't there. Stone looked across the aisle to Michael's tent. From his vantage point, he saw that it too was empty, having also been torn open.

Stone moved to the tent his daughter had shared with Jordan the night before. He squatted, whipped open the tent, and stuck his head inside. The acrid odor of urine assaulted his nose. Eyes roaming the inside, he caught the sight of two sleeping bags, two packs, as well as some dirty clothes. Stone snatched a pair of jeans from the floor. They were the ones Zayne had worn that morning and that shirt, that was the shirt she'd been wearing.

Stone let out a deep sigh of relief. His daughter was okay. *At least, she had been. No!* He mustn't think like that. *Of course, she was okay; she must be.* After whatever had happened at the caves, they'd come back here for a change of clothes. Why had they come back for a change of clothes? *Obviously, they didn't know that the beast had been here.* They had come for help. Come to find him.

Next, Stone gave a quick look into his tent. All was as he'd left it that morning. Stone yanked the flaps shut and hurriedly checked the two remaining tents, careful to skirt the blood pool. After failing to find any further signs, he strode over to the mess tent. It too had been left in chaos. After a swift look around, he noticed some food might have gone missing. *Smart girls.* They'd grabbed some supplies.

Stone considered his options and glanced at his watch. The girls were probably getting close to the van. Help would come soon. He'd never make it to them in time. After he found his daughter and Jamie, it would probably be best to hide. Hold up somewhere and wait for help to arrive. The cave was his best bet. It seemed safer than being out in the open, anyway. Too bad the road was so far away.

After a moment, he decided to grab some provisions. Theodore Stone grabbed a bag and stuffed it with a few bottles of water as well as some food. Just in case. Well, anything could happen. The prehistoric predator stalking them proved that.

CHAPTER 32

Cassie Byrne
1:46 pm

Heart racing as she stumbled through the undergrowth, Cassie threw yet another worried glance behind her and let her eyes scan the forest. As before, the only movement her eye caught belonged to Jordan. The last hour had to be just about the longest she'd ever endured. Sixty agonizingly slow minutes of suspense and terror. Cassie had been sure the beast would reappear to rip them to shreds. How could it not? The closer they got to the vehicle, the more worried she became. What if it was waiting near the van? What if it was some kind of game? Could the sabre-tooth be playing with them? Did they do that?

Cassie tightened her fist around the bundle of keys again, just to make sure she hadn't lost them. The hard metal pressed painfully into her palm. Cassie searched her memory. She couldn't recall exactly when, but at some point, she had pulled the keys from her pocket, figuring it would be quicker if the keys were already in hand. As she slowed her forward movement, Cassie lessened her grip around the keys. Pain throbbed in her hand. Confused, she opened her hand and surveyed her palm. The keys had dug deep into her skin, one key even breaking the skin.

Cassie's left shoulder brushed the trunk of a tree which snapped her attention back to the surrounding forest. She glanced back; Jordan was still right there behind her, not more than five feet away. She had to focus. Cassie slowed a little and peered around in front of her, then down at the map.

Somehow, they weren't far off from the same route the group used before. She'd managed to memorize several landmarks the first time they'd trekked to the cave. Still, Cassie was surprised she'd guided them so well without conscious thought. Or had she? She couldn't recall if she'd been focused on their destination the whole time.

The feeling was familiar. Sometimes when Cassie drove, especially during longer trips, she would zone out. Without meaning to, she'd set part of her brain to the task while letting the rest of her conscious mind wander. Before long, Cassie would find herself nearing her destination without remembering much of the details of the trip. Whenever she realized she was doing it, she would try to focus harder. It made her feel unsafe.

Another tree branch brushed against her scalp, jolting her mind back to her flight yet again. She rounded a bend, and the van came into view ahead of her. Breaking into a sprint, she rushed toward the vehicle. Once she escaped the tree cover, she slowed. Cassie refocused on the keys and realized she'd begun squeezing them again. She released the pressure and used her thumb to spin the key fob around. Cassie pressed the unlock button.

Nothing.

Confusion flowed over her as the expected chirp failed to sound. Brow crinkling, Cassie shifted her thumb as she looked down. Her eyes swept the key fob, making sure she'd pressed the right button. Cassie deliberately mashed the button again. Cassie's eyes darted at the van once more, expecting a chirp and the flash of lights.

Again, nothing happened. Worried, she pressed down once more as she jogged around the rear of the van. Still nothing. Had she grabbed the wrong keys? *These are the only keys,* she chided.

As Cassie arrived at the driver's door, she attempted to suppress a panic flooding into her chest and shifted the keys again. She stabbed the key into the lock and twisted her wrist. Once she felt the satisfying click of the lock releasing, some trepidation she'd been feeling lessened. She did have the right keys. Why hadn't the keyless entry worked? Could the fob be busted?

Further doubts evaporated as Cassie wrenched the door open. She grabbed the handle along the top of the door frame and hoisted herself into the driver's seat. Cassie clutched the wheel as she jammed the key into the ignition. A loud bang startled her. She jumped, a cry exploding from her lungs. To her right, the source of the noise peered at her through the passenger side window. Jordan, worried expression plastered to her face, knocked on the window impatiently. Cassie let out a deep breath. She'd forgotten all about Jordan. Cassie leaned over to press the unlock button on her door. At the thought of the open door, she pulled it shut.

Cassie switched her focus back to the steering column. On the other side of the van, Jordan wrenched her door open. Left hand holding the steering wheel in a death grip, Cassie grabbed the key again with her right. She gave her wrist a firm turn as she twisted the key in the ignition. The dash lights flickered, and the engine clicked.

The van shifted as Jordan plopped into the passenger seat.

Panic started building yet again. Cassie cranked the engine again.

Click. Click. Click.

"Come on!" Cassie yelled, "Start, you piece of junk." She twisted the key again. Still no joy. She slammed her hand into the dash, removed the key, and took a deep breath.

"Cassie," Jordan murmured.

Cassie inserted the key into the ignition and tried again.

Click. Click. Click.

"Cassie," Jordan said more urgently.

"What?" she hissed back, twisting her head to look at the other girl. Jordan was staring toward the rear of the van. Cassie followed Jordan's sightline toward the object of her focus. A dim glow still shone from the rear carriage light.

"Someone left a light on," Jordan stated dejectedly, her eyes meeting Cassie's. "The battery is dead."

Jordan Adler
2:00 pm

Jordan gazed blankly at the engine. She'd asked Cassie to pop the hood a bit earlier, in a vain effort to improve their situation. Jordan had hoped there was a loose connection, or else something easily identifiable. No such luck. Everything looked fine. No matter how much she fiddled with the wires, it wouldn't draw any more power from the failing battery.

She silently cursed the fool who'd left the light on. After seeing the look of defeat on Cassie's face, she hadn't had the heart to ask if she knew who it had been.

Jordan glanced to either side, then over her shoulder, eyes searching for any movement. Her mind went again to her friends. The professor had pleaded with her to go get help. She hadn't really considered the order. Followed blindly behind Cassie. Would she have really abandoned her friends? It wouldn't be abandonment if she'd gone for help.

Now though. Jordan sighed.

Miles from anywhere, it could take days to hike out of the area. Jordan couldn't do it, couldn't just leave them. She had to do something. She didn't know what, and she certainly didn't want to die. Jordan slammed the hood of the van. Through the windshield, she saw Cassie jump at the loud noise. Jordan winced; she hadn't intended to close it so roughly.

Wiping her hands on her shirt, Jordan scanned the area once again. A wary expression on Cassie's face, the other girl's gaze followed Jordan's progress as she stepped around to the driver's door. As she reached Cassie, Jordan considered her options. Tracks had been carved through the light coat of grime covering Cassie's cheeks where her tears had flowed. Jordan reached over and placed a hand on the side of Cassie's face. With her thumb,

Jordan stroked a stray tear from Cassie's cheek.

"I have to do something. I can't—"

"We can hold up in the van. It can't get in here," Cassie blurted.

Jordan gave a tremulous sigh. "I can't just sit here. I need to go back. I need to find the others," she breathed.

Cassie gave her a slight nod, muttering a solemn "Okay."

"Cassie, what do you want to do? Do you want to come with me?"

Cassie gave a timid shake of the head.

Jordan could almost feel Cassie's eyes follow her as she walked around to the rear of the van. Jordan scanned the whole area before turning. She pulled the handle to open one of the rear doors. On hands and knees, Jordan crawled to the stack of water bottles. She stuck her fingers into the hole to stretch the plastic wider. Then Jordan pulled out two fresh bottles and stowed them in the pocket of her cargo pants. As Jordan's head popped above the rear seat, Cassie's face appeared, hopelessness written in her expression. The older girl had spun around in the chair, knees on the seat; hand gripping the headrest.

"Please, don't go. It's not safe," Cassie begged.

Jordan put on her most reassuring smile. "I'll be fine," she lied; almost convincing herself.

Jordan crawled from the rear door and closed it behind her. Hands resting on the door, she closed her eyes. As she leaned her head against the cool metal, Jordan took two deep breaths. Some of her tension floated away. The true terror she had been experiencing had somehow faded into the background, leaving a surreal feeling. After a while, fear loses its bite.

Jordan circled to the front of the vehicle one last time. Cassie sat in the driver's seat, hand resting on the open door, a pleading look in her eyes. Jordan gave her a fractional shake of the head. Cassie slumped a bit in her chair.

"Just…" she exhaled with a long regretful sigh. "Just try to be careful, okay?" Cassie closed the door.

Jordan gave her as convincing a smile as she could muster, which couldn't have looked like anything more than a weak grimace. Jordan nodded and turned from the other girl. Eyes focused on the woods before her, Jordan heard the low click of the locks engaging to her rear.

CHAPTER 33

Dr. Miriam Segen
2:15 pm

Dr. Miriam Segen sat in the passenger seat of her beat-up pickup. A passenger van with the rest of her team was somewhere ahead of them. She sighed. *I really should get my truck checked.* Engine problems had delayed her departure from the University's Fayetteville campus, giving the other group a good ten to fifteen-minute head start. A couple of days before, Segen's reliable old truck had begun to emit a low grinding clatter.

Sighing again, Segen glanced at the dash.

Hours before she'd received a call from her colleague, Dr. Theodore Stone, claiming to have discovered a group of cave paintings that might rival Lascaux in complexity and importance. The single picture Dr. Stone had sent seemed to collaborate his claim. Painted in a rusty red pigment, with black outlines, the scene depicted a man aiming a spear at a giant ground sloth. The animal couldn't have been anything else. It towered over the humanoid shape.

Segen didn't know what to think. She'd known Professor Stone for years and he was highly respected, solid. If it were true, it would be the oldest example of cave art found in America, predating the rest by more than 6,000 years.

It didn't seem possible.

However, as soon as he'd asked, Segen knew she'd go. The fact that she owed him had barely figured into her calculations. Stone had extended many favors to her and others over the years. He always assisted people when he could and asked nothing in return.

As her mind wandered, her unfocused eyes took in the landscape flashing by.

The call had come at an opportune time. She'd been with one of her brightest grad students, discussing his dissertation. She glanced over to Neil Singh. His ebony hair was styled in a trendy cut. Prominent eyebrows and a large nose dominated his face. A couple of day's growth sprouted from chunky brown cheeks. Two inches shy of six feet, Neil carried about fifty extra pounds. After getting his bachelor's degree, he had joined the workforce, returning to school only the year before to get his doctorate. At thirty-four, Neil was older than many other grad students just beginning their Ph.D. programs.

After Stone's call, she'd scrambled to put together a small team willing to join her in surveying Stone's discovery. She'd had to pull in a few chits to get some of her associates on board without giving them too many details. Segen had wanted to invite the heads of both the Geology and Anthropology Departments. Unfortunately, both were unavailable, offering instead a member of their department. She had been able to get a few more members of the staff as well as a few students to join the party.

Segen had charged Neil and another of her grad students with preparing the supplies and arranging for their transportation. The bed of the truck was full of the group's equipment. In the limited time since the call Dr. Segen had—

A loud thunk snatched her attention. Steam poured from beneath the hood of her pickup. *What the hell was that?*

"What the hell was that?" Neil blurted beside her.

Segen's eyes darted to his face, then followed his gaze to the dash. The oil pressure indicator plummeted. Neil had removed his foot from the gas and let the vehicle continue to coast. Neil shot a glance over his shoulder and flicked the turn indicator with his thumb. He slid the vehicle past the empty lane to his right, then continued onto the shoulder. As he pulled the truck to a stop, she watched the steam billow from the engine.

"That can't be good," she moaned.

CHAPTER 34

Jordan Adler
2:20 pm

While Jordan drifted through the woods alone, her mind mulled over the decision she'd made to search for the others. Alone, of all things. While firm in her choice when she'd departed from the van, the plan had lost its luster quickly. A huge part of her wanted to run and hide. Jordan understood why Henry had run, and she forgave him for abandoning them.

Still, she had to try. She just had to. Jordan knew that if she survived, and that was a big if, she wouldn't be able to live with herself if something happened to the others without her even trying. *Sure, courage has its place, but when does courage turn into stupidity?* Jordan had a feeling she would find out.

Green pervaded her vision as Jordan wove through the thick collection of saplings and shrubbery that swept the forest floor. She'd decided to angle away from the route she and Cassie had just taken. She had no real experience with being hunted by a monster, but she figured that it might be smart not to travel the same ground twice. She had no clue how powerful the beast's sense of smell was.

She was heading into the wind, so that put her downwind of

the creature. Jordan narrowed her eyes. *That's right, isn't it?* She hadn't ever been in a situation to consider whether or not she needed to be upwind or downwind. She considered the problem logically, trying to think of it as just another math problem.

The last place they'd spotted the beast was the campsite. *Where Michael died.* She shook her head, trying to force that gruesome image out. *Math. Just math.* The wind was blowing out of the northeast. The campsite was to the northeast. That would put the campsite, and hopefully the beast, upwind of her current position. *Maybe the beast won't catch my scent. Yeah, right!*

To avoid poison ivy and insects, Jordan had tucked her pant legs into her boots. At the beginning of the trip, ticks had been a major concern for her. They'd dropped a few levels on her threat meter, but she didn't want to chance it. A friend of hers had gotten a disease from a tick that stopped her from being able to eat red meat, which sucked for the girl because she'd been an avid hunter. In the back of her mind, Jordan had wondered if it was nature's way of fighting back.

Is the sabre-monster nature fighting back as well? Now that was a scary thought.

Jordan moved much slower on her way back north. Attempting to help the others was one thing, rushing headlong into danger was another altogether. A sudden explosion of sound erupted somewhere to her right. Jordan dropped and skirted around some foliage. She huddled behind a tree, listening as it crashed through the woods. Afraid that it was the beast, Jordan peered around the trunk. Not glimpsing the source of the movement, she swung her head around to scour the surrounding woods. Being in such thick undergrowth made it easier to hide, but wreaked havoc with her visibility. She sighed when she realized it, whatever 'it' was, wasn't heading in her direction.

After several minutes without seeing anything further, she slowly rose to her feet. Eyes peeled for any sign of movement; Jordan crept further to the west, away from her previous route.

CHAPTER 35

Henry Blake
2:25 pm

Henry's eyes roved over the landscape ahead of them. He and Zayne followed a faint trail worn into the forest floor. Around them, massive trees cast shadows on the undergrowth as far as the eye could see. They'd made decent time. During the two trips the day before, he'd memorized the way.

He glanced down at his tiny companion; she was holding up much better than he would have at her age. And that whole wetting of the pants thing, understandable. *Hell, if I hadn't gone just before the attack, I might have been the one in need of a change of clothes.*

With his firm grip on the axe handle, Henry was prepared to fight back if needed. So far, neither Zayne nor he had glimpsed any animals. Predator nor prey. Not so much as a stray piece of fur. That hadn't stopped him from feeling as though he was being stalked. Henry could feel the beast out there. Where did that thing come from? Could it really be the same one from the paintings? It defied belief. Of course, a lot of things that day had defied belief. After his pathetic performance earlier, *I still can't believe I ran,* Henry swore to himself that he would do whatever it took to protect Zayne. Whatever it took.

As Henry rounded another bend, he caught sight of an old gnarled stump. He recognized it. The stump couldn't have been more than a couple hundred yards away from the van. He picked up his pace. Once they got to the van, they would have to figure out what to do next. Without a key, they wouldn't be able to leave, but that didn't mean the vehicle was useless to them. Henry could smash a window, *the small one in the rear*, and the two of them could hide. *Stick the girl inside and have her unlock the door.* The creature wouldn't be able to get through that tiny hole.

Of course, it was possible the others were there. Waiting. Surely, they wouldn't have left. The professor would have never left Zayne behind.

As they came over a rise, a gap in the thick row of trees lining the road revealed the van's white paneling. More of the vehicle appeared between the trees and Henry increased his pace. *So close. Almost there.* He wanted to be through with this nightmare. He could almost feel the safety radiating from the vehicle.

A sudden jerk on his left arm almost caused him to lose his balance. Zayne had been holding his hand on and off since he'd found her hidden between the boulders, so it was no surprise, looking down to see her clutching his arm. What surprised him was that she'd seemed to have lost her footing. No, she didn't trip; she was literally hanging from his arm. Zayne dragged her feet, trying to get him to stop, a look of pure terror on her face.

"What?" he grumbled, nonplused by her actions. They were almost to the van and now she was... what? Playing a game?

"Shhh!" she whispered emphatically. She covered her lips with her finger, then pointed toward the van.

Partially because of her demeanor, partially to pacify her, Henry lowered his voice. "What is it?" He hissed, adding a little edge to his words. "We're almost there."

Seeing tears leak from the corners of her eyes, he gave in to her jerks and allowed himself to be pulled to a crouching position next to the girl. What was wrong with him? Why was he so angry? *She's just a scared kid.* Shoulders raised and neck hunched, Zayne turned her head. As she lifted her finger to point again, Henry followed her sightline.

In the thin line between the undercarriage and the ground, Henry could see a small portion of what was happening on the other side of the van. Something moved from behind one tire, edging into view.

Henry squinted his eyes to lessen the glare reflecting off the white paint. What was that? Were those legs? As they moved, they looked like someone's feet, taking mincing little steps. *Is someone standing there?* Someone was just trying to get into the van. Dread filled his chest as he saw more feet come down. They slammed onto the dirt road, kicking up a small puff of dust. *Not feet. No, paws.*

The sabre-toothed beast prowled back and forth, just on the other side of the van. They were lucky Zayne had been paying attention. *I certainly wasn't.* Henry took a step back, edging away from the van. He placed a calming hand over both of Zayne's, still wrapped around his bicep, clutching his arm like a vise. She followed him as they shuffled away from the hope the van had once offered and the terror the beast evoked.

Together they continued to creep away as fast as possible. They were nearing a copse of trees, close to stepping out of direct sightline, when the sabre-tooth swept around the front of the vehicle, coming completely into view. The two of them froze, afraid to draw the creature's attention. However, with its entire focus aimed at the van, the sabre-tooth didn't even glance in their direction. It slunk along the side of the vehicle, curious. After a moment without turning their way, Henry and Zayne began to edge away again. Henry heard a loud clang and a rending tear as the beast swiped at the body of the van.

Out of sight, Henry decided they might be able to move faster. He and Zayne fled from the area.

The Beast
2:26 pm

She had figured that going to the group's camp would be the

best way to scare them off. And it had worked. When she'd slaughtered one of their number at the campsite, the others had run. She thought her task complete. That should have been it. They should have fled. But after storing the young man's remains, she'd rushed to the wide trail where the multitude of magical mobile dwellings had appeared the previous week. Anger had boiled within her; the group hadn't departed. They were still in her valley. Why were they still in her valley?

There was someone in the snow-colored, mobile dwelling, she was positive. At least one. However, she couldn't figure out how to get in. Her senses told her that two of the humans had been there recently. A scent trail led away from the object, indicating that someone had returned to her forest.

She let out a low growl. They should have left. She'd given them a chance to leave. She swung her powerful foreleg at the metal dwelling, rending another gash in the thin metal.

Cassie Byrne
2:29 pm

Cassie cowered on the van's floor, soaked and afraid. She couldn't recall ever being more terrified in her life. Earlier at the campsite was bad, but she hadn't been alone. *Alone!* Why hadn't Jordan stayed with her? *Why didn't I go with Jordan?* Watching the other girl disappear into the woods hadn't been easy, but the decision to search for the others was Jordan's to make. Cassie just hadn't been able to bring herself to go along. And she'd remained content with her decision to stay at the van until a few minutes before when the beast reappeared.

Cassie had been in the vehicle's rear, grabbing a bottled water. As she'd taken her first drink, a movement on the south side of the dirt road drew her eye. For a split-second, hope swelled within her. Cassie thought someone else had made it, that she wouldn't be alone. She should have known better. It was the wrong side of the road. The camp was in the other direction. Her hope turned sour as a shape slunk out from the foliage.

It had been the cat. The damnable sabre-toothed cat. The Wampus Cat. *Sabrewampus.* The thought almost made Cassie giggle, it sounded so strange in her head. *What is wrong with me?*

Cassie dove to the floor, landing on the water bottle. Stupid, so stupid. Had it seen her? The creature had trotted right up to the van, placing massive paws on a side panel. Claws gouged metal as its weight shifted. Huddled on the floor, Cassie had watched the beast's shadow move as the cat inched toward the rear of the van. When the cat dropped to the ground, the vehicle had rocked slightly, its weight shifting back into place. It had prowled outside. Every so often, the van would shake. Then came a loud rending noise from the opposite side of the van.

Cassie shifted her position, trying to see out of the window a little better. Somehow locking the doors earlier had helped her feel more secure. It was ridiculous to think a prehistoric beast would know how to open a car door.

There was another thump, and the van rocked a bit. Cassie scooted along the floor to the sliding door. She gasped as the van rocked again, an impact on the passenger door. What was the beast doing? Cassie raised her head just enough to peek at the passenger side mirror. The sight reflected in the mirror took her breath away. Cassie watched horrified, mesmerized, as the sabre-tooth used its jaw to pull at the door handle. Unable to open the door, the cat slammed its body into the door yet again.

Cassie slid down the wall, huddling as best she could on the floor. She found it hard to catch her breath. How did it know how to open the door? Did it? Or was it just random?

Wishing the thing would just go away, Cassie squeezed her eyes shut.

Cassie wasn't aware of how long she lay there before the beast left. She just slowly realized she hadn't heard it in a while. She took a deep breath and closed her eyes again. No need to move.

Zayne Stone
2:34 pm

Zayne just knew they were all going to die. Zayne let Henry drag her along as she played the day's events over in her mind. First Jamie in the cave, then whoever that bloodstain had belonged to at camp, *now this*. The van had still been there. The cave, the camp, and the van had all been attacked. Her father and the others were missing. Surely, if someone had been at the van when the beast attacked, they would have driven off. Where could Daddy be? *Is he even still alive?*

She didn't even know why Henry was so insistent to keep going. What was the point anyway? They were out in the middle of nowhere, running from a literal monster. Sure, after Henry had found her cowering—Hey, you would have hidden too. Don't deny it—Zayne had felt sure he would get her out of this mess. After the campsite, all that blood, she'd lost a bit of her certainty. But at least she wasn't alone. The long hike to the van, most of the time spent holding Henry's hand, had allowed some worry to dissipate.

They'd finally made it to the van, their only clear way out of the situation, only to be confronted with the beast they'd fled from before. Had it been up to her, Zayne might have found another cozy place to hide, possibly wait for help. Well, at least she wasn't alone.

As Henry tugged at her hand again, Zayne realized her pace had been flagging. She sped up, matching his pace. Zayne's gaze moved past his strong, shadowed jaw and focused on his eyes. Henry had such beautiful blue eyes. They were alert, taking in every minor thing in front of them. Every so often, he shot a look back, checking to make sure they weren't being hunted. Zayne followed his gaze; luckily there was no sign of pursuit.

"Where now?" she almost whimpered. Henry's eyes shot over, focusing on hers.

"Huh?" he asked. His eyes bouncing between both of hers, then scanning the horizon.

"What are we going to do now? Where can we go?" she said,

trying to fight back at the despair filling her.

"Hmm... I'm not sure. Let's put a little more distance between us and that—that thing first. Okay?" he asked.

CHAPTER 36

Dr. Theodore Stone
2:40 pm

As he rounded the last bend, Professor Stone's heart fell. Like a punch to the gut, he realized the van was still there. Why was the van still there? They should have left over an hour ago. Stone jogged along the path, fury building. *What are those fool girls playing at? Help could have—should have already been here. What a waste of time.*

Clouds parted, shifting the shadows cast on the van, which revealed a gash torn into the side panel. Stone's eyes widened at the sight; the cat had been here too. He kicked it up to a run. Was Zayne here at the time? Was his baby girl gone?

Stone emerged from the trees and rounded the rear of the vehicle. He slid to a halt near the edge of the dirt road. Neck on a swivel, he glanced right and left. His eyes scoured the area, looking for any sign of a struggle. Stone stepped to the van. Forehead to the window, hands blocking the sunlight from either side, he peered through the window. Stone scanned the inside of the vehicle. The quick glance through the window failed to produce anyone.

He spun and paced forward. His eyes roved over the craggy

dirt turnaround, past the overgrown grass, and followed the road to the nearest curve. *Thank God!* There was no sign of blood, or anything else for that matter.

None of the students were there. Zayne wasn't there. Mind racing, Stone tried to think where she could be. He spun to face the woods and stared into the shadows, trying to see something. Anything. The cave, the camp, and the van; everyone had disappeared. He'd lost all his students and his daughter. How could it be? He was in Oklahoma, not the Black Forest. There were populated areas nearby, well no more than three or four miles away. Yet there he stood, clueless what to do next. He glanced at the sky; the sun had passed the midway point a while ago, *so west*. He knew that was west; *I'm not the one who's lost.*

Without a cell or a radio, Stone couldn't see any possibility of getting help anytime soon. He couldn't leave his daughter, wouldn't. There was absolutely no way. Nor would he just leave his charges, with the possible exception of saving Zayne's life, and only then reluctantly. He'd have to go back; there was no other option. If he tried to hike out, unfamiliar terrain, poor health; If he even made it, it might take him all evening, or maybe all night.

Stone felt a bead of sweat run down his forehead. Mind whirring, he swiped a palm over his bald pate, feeling dampness transfer to his hand. Absentmindedly, he wiped the perspiration onto his shirtfront.

Where did the girls go? Flashes of injuries, blood, and claws flew through his mind. Had they gotten lost? Perhaps they were out in the woods, lost and alone. Huddling together behind a fallen tree, a bone sticking from a leg. *In a forest this thick, I could have passed within a hundred yards of them without realizing it. Their lifeless bodies, covered in brush, left to ripen in the elements.*

Stone slammed his palm into his forehead with a loud smack. *No! I mustn't think like that.*

Stone paced around the front of the vehicle, along the passenger side, and came to a stop by the sliding door. After a brief look into the forest, Stone spun and slammed the side of his fist against the glass. A stifled yelp surprised him. He peered down through the window, scouring the interior again. His second inspection of the van proved more fruitful than the first. Cassie lay on the vehicle's floor, cowered on her side in a near fetal position against the sliding door.

"Cassie! Cassie!" he yelled, slapping the window with a palm.

"Professor?" she said, voice quavering. Cassie shifted to peek over her shoulder. "Professor Stone! Oh, thank God," she croaked, pushing back a sob. Cassie rose to her knees, looking at him through the tinted glass. "It was here! The beast was here. It tried to get in."

Stone shot a glance around. "It's not here any longer. It must have gone."

"Are you sure?" She sniffed, peering around him from the window. Cassie looked around the professor, trying to see if the beast was out there.

"Cassie," the professor coaxed, drawing her attention with a smile, "Can you unlock the door?" he asked.

Her eyes widened when she realized that he was still locked out of the vehicle. She reached over and flicked the lock mechanism. Stone grabbed the handle and jerked the door aside, sending it sliding along its track. Cassie rose from the floor to plop onto a seat.

"What happened? Why haven't you left?" he asked, eyes scanning the interior. "Where's Jordan?"

"The battery is dead." His heart fell at the announcement, "Jordan, she, she left. She went to find the others," Cassie whimpered. "I tried to get her to stay, but she wouldn't."

"That's okay, it's okay," Stone soothed as his mind whirred, "it's not your fault. None of this is your fault. Have you seen any of the others?"

"No," she answered.

"You haven't seen Jamie or Zayne?"

Cassie hunched her shoulders and shook her head.

"There appears to have been an attack in the cave. I found signs of a struggle. However, there wasn't any blood, so I think they're okay; I hope so, at least," Stone couldn't share his doubts. Couldn't voice them, lest they become real.

"What do we do now?" Cassie implored. She had hope and fear written on her features.

Stone thought for a moment as he scanned the area. "I think you should stay here," he replied. "It might be best if you stayed here. If anyone else shows up, make them... implore them to stay with you in the van. There's enough water in here for days." Shoving his bag into her hands, he continued, "Here's some food. This should last a little while."

"You're not going to stay either?" she moaned.

"No, I have to find the others," he replied.

"Zayne," she mumbled.

"Yes, I have to find my daughter. But I have to look for Henry, Jamie, and Jordan as well. We can't leave any of them behind. Not after what happened to Michael." He saw Cassie's face fall. "Are you going to be okay here all alone?" She gave a slight shrug of her shoulders but nodded slightly. "You'll be okay. Just keep hiding. If it comes back, hide."

"It attacked the van," she stated dispassionately.

"I know. I saw claw marks in the metal," he confessed.

"It tried to open the door with its mouth. It actually pulled the handle," Cassie quavered.

"But it didn't get in. Lock it again. Hopefully, it won't come back, but if it does, hide."

"I just realized; the wound Michael gave it. You know when he hit it with the axe," Cassie paused, waiting for him to respond, so Stone gave her a curt nod. "It... It was almost fully healed."

Stone jerked his head back and narrowed his eyes. "Are you sure?" *That can't be right.* While the injury hadn't appeared serious, it would take much longer than two hours to heal.

His face must have shown his doubt. "I'm positive," she assured. "It was right there on its left flank. I saw the bloodstain, but the wound had already closed up. It barely even left a scratch."

Stone's eyes shot down to the road as he assimilated what Cassie told him. It was likely that she hadn't seen it right. But could the animal have some kind of rapid healing? While it sounded unlikely, Stone knew he couldn't just dismiss it. Could it have something to do with the magic that transformed a young woman into the beast? *Magic.* Here he was considering magic as if it were real; as if it had always been so. *The beast could be considered proof of the existence of magic thousands of years ago.* Stone shook his head forcefully, returning his gaze to Cassie. *Now isn't the time to consider the legitimacy of magic.*

"Just stay here. Segen's group will probably be here in the next couple of hours. Tell them exactly what's going on and get them to call the police and drive you to safety," he said.

"Everything?" she asked, looking bemused.

He knit his brow together. His mind whirred, confused by her question. "What do you mean, everything?"

"Am I supposed to tell them that a prehistoric, mythical creature with the appearance of a sabre-tooth tiger, with six legs is stalking the forest?" Cassie asked, finally calm enough to break into a wry smile.

"Ah," Stone replied, "that might not be the best way to put it."

"I'll think of something," Cassie said, breaking into a reluctant smile.

"Good, good," he replied, darting his eyes around the interior of the van. At the rear of the vehicle, he thought of something else. "Could you grab me a couple waters?"

Cassie scurried around the rear seat and plucked two bottles from the case, then returned to Stone. "Here," she said, passing him the water. "You're leaving?"

"Yeah. Don't forget to lock the door."

"Like I'd forget that little detail," she smirked. Cassie pulled the door halfway shut and then paused. She met his eye again, worry written on her features. "Stay safe," she ordered, then slammed the door shut.

Stone gave her a slight smile, then strode away from the van. His mind whirred as he headed back into the woods. *One student is safe.* Now he had to find the others. *I have to find my daughter. My Zayne.* What if something had happened to Zayne? What would he do?

He came to a sudden halt. Squeezing his eyes shut, Stone

grabbed his furthest thoughts. As he pictured the process in his mind, he cupped them in his hands and slowly, methodically squeezed all his thoughts into a little ball. When the ball reached the size of a golf ball, he dropped it. Just discarding it in the middle of the forest.

Mind much less frenzied, he reopened his eyes.

Stone set off, back the way he'd come.

CHAPTER 37

Amber Park
2:55 pm

Green swept by on both sides of the country road. The closer they got, the harder it was for Amber to contain her excitement. After Dr. Segen received the call, there had been a mad dash to prepare themselves for the expedition. The average expedition usually took much longer to plan and prepare. Her team had done several day's work in a few short hours. Professor Stone's team had already done a lot of the heavy lifting. Site selection, site prep, and camp setup; among other things.

Segen only invited those who had been around at the time. Several more senior members of the faculty and plenty of students were away for Labor Day weekend. *Their loss.* Amber might not have been asked to come along if everyone had been around. She was thrilled that her plans had fallen through. Aside from Amber, only a couple of students had been invited, and those were grad students. Being a sophomore, she knew her role in the expedition would be minimal; probably consigned to grunt work. After the briefing Segen had given, Amber was fine with that. Even a footnote in a discovery this significant would be enough for her.

At first, they'd received limited information, only that there had been a discovery nearby. They'd been told to show up and bring enough clothes for a few days. While two of her grad students went to the supermarket for food, Dr. Segen gathered the rest of those invited into a conference room. Before being briefed on the discovery, they'd all had to surrender their cell phones. Dr. Segen had wanted no leaks.

After the revelation, the excitement in the room had been palpable. There'd been much speculation on the meaning of the artwork, as well as the identity of the creators. Segen had split them up, assigning each group certain tasks. Much of their equipment had to be packed. There were packs and tents to collect, a vehicle to check out, and tools to bring. The university had recently bought several of the new box-shaped passenger vans. Amber wasn't a fan of the new design.

Amber glanced around her at the occupants of the van. She couldn't recall all their names, having just met some of them, but thought it was a good sampling of disciplines. Out of the nine people present in the vehicle, five were professors. KT Hollis, one of Segen's grad students, was behind the wheel. Raven black hair and sprays of freckles accented the pale skin of her beautiful face. Dr. Stein, an elderly professor of Anthropology, sat in the front passenger seat. He was clean-shaven, with a mop of thick white hair atop his head. Amber was taking a class from him. She didn't think he'd even recognized her. *I'll just have to make a favorable impression.*

Three professors, each in their mid-forties, populated the first row. If Amber remembered correctly, one was a geologist and another a paleontologist; she couldn't recall the specialty of the third. A woman with a mane of gray-streaked red hair sat in an animated conversation with an Asian professor. One of them was the geologist, she was almost sure. Mirrored on the window to his left, Dr. Walczak's spectacled face was visible as he eyed the landscape flying past. Or was it Wilczek? Slight in stature, the paleontologist's wavy black curls sprouted from the back half of his scalp.

Amber's eyes slid across to the reflection in her own window.

Soft-black hair framed her smooth, pale skin. Another of the grad students sat beside her in the second row. She'd forgotten the young man's name. The young blonde woman sitting across the aisle was an associate professor. A heavy grad student, by the name of Brian, had taken the last row. With no one else back there, he'd stretched out.

Amber shifted her gaze back to the window; they had to be getting close.

Cassie Byrne
3:00 pm

Cassie still lay on the vehicle's dirty floor. She'd tried to put on a brave face for the professor, but she hadn't felt it at all. Dr. Stone left some time ago, but she hadn't been able to bring herself to get up. About fifteen to twenty minutes after he'd gone, there had been the sound of movement outside. Not being sure of its source, she'd decided not to check. She would not let the sabre-tooth fool her. She feared it had come back. It was trying to trick her.

Cassie had only huddled tighter into her hiding spot, waiting for the noises to go away. A loud thump on the side of the van caused her to wet herself. It had only been a tiny squirt, *still mortifying*. Not long after, Cassie had heard the movement outside fade into the distance. She still hadn't been about to move far from her hiding spot, no matter how full her bladder.

Instead, she'd used an empty water bottle to drain her bladder, a skill she'd picked up years before on a dig.

She wasn't sure how long she'd lain there before she heard another noise, this one surely man-made. Cassie's eyes widened as she followed the sound. Over the low hum of an engine, she caught the crunching sound of tires as they ran over gravel and dispersed the small rocks spread along the dirt road.

Help! Help has finally come! Who was it? Cassie shook her head; it didn't matter who it was. Whoever it was would help. They had to. Cassie rose and took a furtive look out the window. She

211

shot an anxious glance around, looking for the beast. Not catching a hint of the animal, she scooted along the floor, moving behind the passenger seat. She caught her breath and then peeked around the seat. As Cassie peered through the windshield, she saw the source of the noise.

Coming toward her was another passenger van. They must be the colleagues the professor had invited. She hadn't expected them this early; she figured they wouldn't be on site until later. Cassie cleared her head with a shake. It didn't matter; they were here now.

Instead of circling the turnabout, the other driver veered left and pulled directly in front of her van. Cassie raised her head higher to get an unobstructed view. Through the windshield, she saw the van coast to a stop a few car lengths away.

Cassie moved closer to the door, ready to open it. As she glanced back toward the other vehicle, she saw the man in the passenger seat staring at her. There was a confused look on the older man's face. Cassie smiled at his bewilderment, he probably wondered why she'd been hiding. Her attention drifted back to the sliding door beside her. As she grasped the handle, Cassie's eyes narrowed. Had she just seen something moving at the edge of the windshield? She popped her head back up and slid across the floor before coming to rest between the front seats. Eyes wide, she searched the edge of the windshield for the source of the movement she'd seen. Thought she'd seen.

Cassie felt her eyes widen as she recognized the source. The sabre-toothed creature slid out of the trees and rushed toward the passenger side of the new van. Eyes shooting back to the old man, she hoped he would see her terror as she mouthed, "Lock the doors."

The man's eyes narrowed in confusion, then widened in, what she thought was, comprehension as he shifted his arm toward the door. She wouldn't ever be sure whether he had understood, because just as his hand touched the door, the beast reached the sliding door behind him.

Cassie watched in horror as the cat's lower jaw caught the door handle and lifted it. The electronics built into the door, meant for convenience, kicked in and pulled the sliding door open along its track. She doubted anyone had even seen the animal before it squeezed itself through the opening door. Cassie would never forget the terror etched on their faces. The van rocked; blood sprayed across the inside of the window.

It was just too much. Her vision blurred as blackness crept in from all sides. Cassie could feel her heart rate slow as she lost consciousness.

The Beast
3:12 pm

Why had more people shown up? Where had they all come from? She couldn't have that. She had to stop this. There were already more than enough, too many people, invading her territory. When this additional group had shown up, she realized that just scaring them off wouldn't be enough. She had to get rid of them. Slipping up on the object, she'd used her maw to enter. It has been simple. They hadn't stood a chance.

After that, she'd reentered the forest. She couldn't wait for the hidden one forever, stalking the metal thing; there were others to take care of. She had an idea where they were, some of them, at least. She'd find the others. She might even use them to find each other. Would it be easier that way? Let them run around the woods, trying to find each other?

CHAPTER 38

Cassie Byrne
3:27 pm

As awareness began to return, Cassie stirred, trying to find a more comfortable position. Rough carpet rubbed against her cheek as she shifted her head. Lightly brushing her fingers across the material, she tried to figure out where she was. Cassie slowly opened her eyes. As her eyes focused, she recognized the carpet lining the vehicle's floor. From where she lay, she had an excellent view of the dirty carpet under the seats.

Mind foggy, she had trouble understanding why she had woken up on the floor. Cassie lifted her torso and shifted her arm to rest her weight on an elbow. She winced at the slight friction burn she got as her skin drew against the rough carpet fibers. The pain focused her mind on her situation. She lay on the floor between the driver's chair and the first row of passenger seats.

The memory of the other van suddenly came back to her. The beast had slaughtered them. All those poor people. Cassie dragged herself to the nearest window. Fists clenched; she lifted her body so that her head was just below the window frame. She popped up and shot a glance outside. Cassie's eyes scanned the immediate area. After ducking below the window frame, she squeezed her eyes shut and mentally assessed the input. That thing hadn't been there. Cassie's eyes drifted open, and she peeked out the window again.

Cassie eyed the surrounding woods, taking longer to process the area this time. She spun to look out each of the windows in turn. She let out a long breath; there was no sign of the creature. Of course, it was probably hiding out there, as it had before, waiting to ambush the next unwary person to wander out of hiding.

How had Professor Stone survived? Why hadn't the beast mauled him?

Cocking her head to see it better, Cassie's eyes returned to the other van. She'd only allowed the vehicle a cursory glance before. But this time she studied it more closely, taking in the entire scene. As she ran a hand through her hair, Cassie felt her heart sink. The other van was no longer parked in front of hers. It appeared to have moved during the struggle. Passing her van by, it had run off the road, over a massive rock, and slammed into a tree. Front end lifted a few inches off the ground, the van rested on top of the rock. A trickle of fluid leaking from beneath the vehicle looked like a mixture of water and oil.

From where Cassie crouched, she could see an amber-colored light continually blinking, the left turn indicator. Disappointed at the wrecked vehicle, it took her a moment to realize its significance. *A battery.* The other van had a working battery. If she could get the other battery, she could figure out how to replace hers. She could get out of there, could get help. All she needed was that battery... *and tools.*

Cassie remembered seeing a small canvas bag of tools tucked into the corner by one of the rear doors. She stood, bent at the waist, and swung around the seats toward the rear of the van. Her eyes locked onto the rear passenger side corner. She failed to see the bag. Had someone brought it to the camp by accident? Cassie continued rearward and caught sight of the other rear corner. No bag. As she rounded the last seat, she swept her eyes along the floor on the driver's side. Tucked, almost fully hidden, behind the stacks of bottled water she spotted the bag. Cassie snatched it.

Cassie slumped to the floor, suddenly realizing the beast was still out there. Somewhere out there. Waiting. Watching. Mind racing, she tried to come up with a solution. In the end, it didn't matter. She knew she had to do something. *I can't just sit here, not again.*

Henry Blake
3:31 pm

A niche had formed in the stone beneath a natural rock overhang, giving them a great place to hide. Formations on three sides obscured them from view. Henry sat tucked on the ground, his back leaning against the stone. Zayne sat huddled into the crook of his arm, curled into a ball much like how he'd found her before. He gently stroked the young girl's hair, trying to calm her. After being thwarted in their flight to the van, whatever hope Zayne still grasped seemed to have slipped away. She was disconsolate. Her will to keep going had been ripped from her.

Henry welcomed the momentary respite. His head ached. He was exhausted. They had been going almost nonstop the whole day. They needed rest. He needed a chance to catch his breath. He needed time to think. Henry let his eyes drift closed. He had to come up with a plan. However, it seemed like nothing he thought of would work.

Zayne was his responsibility. His main concern. He had to do something, anything to keep her safe.

CHAPTER 39

Jamie Long
3:40 pm

As Jamie's eyes fluttered open, an intense throb of pain bloomed in her head. Confused, she scanned the area, taking in the pervading darkness. A dim light bounced off the rock far above her. Jamie ran her hands along the smooth surface of her helmet as she searched for something. What was it? What was she looking for? It took a moment for her thoughts to clear, then Jamie slid her hand forward and pressed the rubber-coated light switch.

Once. Click!

Twice. Click!

Thrice. Click!

No luck.

Discouraged, Jamie moved her right hand down and along her chin, following the strap to its buckle. She squeezed the release firmly and the plastic catches detached from each other. Jamie groaned as she attempted to struggle up to a sitting position. The ache in her head got sharper, forcing Jamie to pause before she'd reached the halfway point. Resting her weight on one elbow, she palmed the left side of her forehead and grimaced in pain.

"God, that hurts," Jamie mumbled, voice sounding blurry even to herself. *No wait, that's not right,* she thought, *not blurry, slurred.* She sounded drunk. Jamie shook her head, trying to clear it, and her universe drifted away. All thought was abruptly swept aside, then flowed back a few moments later, as if brought in by the tide. *That wasn't smart,* she chided. *You need to be smart.*

She lowered her body back to the cold stone and allowed the helmet's cushioned foam layers to cradle her head. Jamie closed her eyes, and she tried to rack her brain. What were her options? What did she have? What did she need?

Light!

Light should definitely be her first goal. If she had light, she could better assess the situation. The light on her helmet didn't work, it was more than likely broken. Jamie reached down with her left hand and groped around inside her pants pocket. She wrapped her fingers around the thin flashlight the professor had given her as a backup. As she slipped it out of the pocket, Jamie depressed the button on the end with her thumb. It clicked on and illuminated the surrounding area. She panned the light around the space.

From her position on the floor, all Jamie could see were the rough sides of the pit she'd fallen into. Rock walls rose at least eight feet on all sides. *How the hell did I end up here?* Jamie remembered the ledge she'd been scoping. She remembered falling and an impact shortly after. Had she slipped? That didn't seem right. She hadn't slipped, had she?

Jamie braced herself and tried to sit up once again. She pressed a palm against the rock floor to lever herself up into a sitting position. Fire blossomed across her stomach as her abs contracted, but at least her head didn't ache as bad. The fresh pain continued as Jamie scooted toward the nearest side of the pit. Once she came to rest against one of the rock walls, Jamie pushed the newer pain to the furthest reaches of her mind and focused on the injury that worried her the most. She felt a sharp pain as she grabbed her helmet and peeled it from her head. Jamie used her right hand to probe the back of her skull for injuries. Her fingers encountered a warm, sticky fluid mixed in with her hair. Jamie already suspected what the wetness was and reluctantly brought her hand back into the light. A deep crimson color brought a groan to her lips.

Jamie rubbed her thumb across her fingers, feeling the thickness of the blood. It was thicker than usual; it must have already started clotting. *How long have I been down here? Why did they leave me?* As Jamie laid her chin on her chest, she rested her eyes and she took deep breaths. When she reopened her eyes, Jamie wiped her soiled fingers on her shirt. That was when she noticed rips in the front of her shirt tinged in blood. Jamie brought her left hand up to her mouth, and she gripped the flashlight between her teeth. The pain exploded again as her right hand pressed gently around the wound. *How did that get there? It almost looks like claws.*

The beast! Oh God, that's why she'd fallen. She was trying to get away from that monster. *Zayne! What happened to Zayne?* Jamie whipped her head up and tried to catch a glimpse of anything. When that failed, she lowered her head and closed her eyes. Jamie let her ears scan the area for any sign of either the girl or the beast. Silence. There was nothing but the slight impact of dripping water. No screams. No whining. No movement. Nothing. At that moment, Jamie knew that she'd figure out what had happened to that poor girl, no matter what.

But to do that, she'd have to take care of herself first.

Using both hands, she gingerly lifted the cloth from her toned stomach. The clotting blood had caused the fabric to stick to her skin and required her to peel the shirt away. Jamie scrunched the cloth together and tucked it under her bust. She studied the area where the beast's claws raked her. There were four shallow gashes, claw marks, running most of the way across her abdomen. The blood had already clotted most of the way over. The wounds weren't life-threatening, but they would definitely leave scars. After she saw the claw marks, the stinging began in earnest.

Starting with her feet, Jamie methodically checked the rest of her body for injury. Aside from some areas that had already started to show signs of bruising, her injuries were surprisingly not too serious. It seemed that she'd partially landed on one shoulder, at least it felt that way. That would definitely be sore in the morning. Her hip was also throbbing something fierce, already beginning to swell. As Jamie turned her head, the flashlight illuminated her helmet and something in the shape caught her eye. She reached over and picked it up. As she flipped it over, she noticed a deep crack in the plastic along the back of the helmet. How hard had she hit the ground? Surprise swept over her. How had none of her bones snapped? She gently stretched her shirt back over the injuries. She'd have to clean it up once she got back to camp.

Something was wrong; they should have already come looking for her. She glanced up, out of the hole. Unless they had come looking and hadn't found her.

She hoped everyone at camp was all right.

Suddenly remembering her cellphone, Jamie reached into her back pocket to grab the device. She brought it out and shown the light over it. There were a series of spider webbing cracks across the entire screen. She pressed the power button, holding it for a few seconds, hoping it would still power up. No such luck. She tried again, nothing. As she flipped it over in her hand, she saw the thin plastic of the back panel also split open. She tossed it aside and heard it clatter on the stone floor. *I must have landed on the stupid thing,* she thought gloomily.

Head feeling clearer, she plucked the light from between her teeth. Pushing the pain aside, Jamie carefully got to her feet, wary of more pain. She scanned the ledge above with the light, searching for an easy way up. All the sides were about the same height, so she moved toward the closest. Jamie switched the light to her other hand, and she reached up. She could just barely wrap her fingers over the ledge.

She swept her light across the floor, looking for her helmet. As Jamie bent over, a wave of dizziness crashed over her. She paused to let the feeling pass. She'd have to watch that. It wouldn't do to pass out; especially as she was about to climb out of the hole.

Jamie scooped the helmet up from the floor. *I might still need this.* At the edge of the pit, she shoved the helmet up over the ledge. She took one last look around her, scanning for anything else she might need. The only object she saw on the cave floor was her now useless cell phone. Jamie sighed and spun to face the wall. What a shame; it had been expensive.

Jamie slipped the light back into her pocket, then reached up to grasp the ledge with both hands. Her muscles groaned in protest, but she started to pull herself up, pushing all her pain aside. As her elbows bent, she brought her feet up to press them firmly against the wall. Soles of her feet gripping against the wall, she pushed out with one leg as she pulled up. Her left arm cleared the edge, and she rested her forearm and palm against the cool stone. She pulled up again and pressed her other palm against the stone to lever herself up. As soon as she felt her waist clear the ledge, she brought her left leg up and planted the heel on the solid stone. Jamie pushed herself further with leg and arms. She rolled to the left, bringing her right leg around.

Lying on her back next to the pit, she took her flashlight out of her pocket and switched it on. *Now what?*

CHAPTER 40

Jamie Long
3:46 pm

After Jamie's climb from the pit, she scoped out the immediate area. She let her small light bathe the area as best it could, but it wasn't all that powerful. Jamie's eyes swept over the ten-foot-high cliff she'd tumbled from, then taken in two tunnels, and finally locked on the pit. The pit, which she had concluded was likely a massive driphole, had been cut into the bedrock a few feet in front of the cliff face. Near the edge of the pit, fresh marks on the ground showed where she had apparently bounced before dropping into the hole.

Jamie couldn't recall that part of her tumble. She didn't remember much. She remembered lunging away from the beast's claws. Pain. Then a powerful wave of vertigo as she tipped back. She remembered thinking she should try to curl her body, try to land on her back as much as possible. There was a moment, as she slammed into the stone incline, that she felt the air explode from her lungs. Then there was blackness. Her head must have slammed into the rock hard enough to knock her out, even with the helmet on. The helmet had probably saved her life, and going limp from the head injury had probably saved her from broken bones.

"Thank God, I was wearing the helmet," she murmured. Jamie figured that even if she didn't know whether she still believed, a whispered prayer couldn't hurt.

As she studied the wall, Jamie tried to spot a way back up the rock to the ledge she'd fallen from. She could not spot any decent hand or footholds. Jamie moved away from the stone wall to get a better view of what lay overhead, but the angle was just as bad below as it was above. While she may have been able to scale the wall, Jamie didn't like her chances. That last climb had been excruciating. And even if she somehow managed, she would have had to deal with that long smooth incline.

Jamie decided she needed to take a breather and plopped down onto the cold floor. She didn't know what happened to Zayne, and she felt guilty that she wasn't able to rush up to check. Part of her didn't want to know. A large part. Jamie didn't know if she could handle discovering that something had happened to the young girl. She wouldn't have been able to deal with Zayne's small, broken body. She shuttered at the thought and tried to push it to the furthest reaches of her mind.

Jamie jerked upright; she'd been letting her mind wander. She couldn't do that, couldn't allow that. She needed to get going. Jamie bounded to her feet, which brought on another wave of dizziness, and scanned the tunnels. There were two directions to choose from. A passage directly in front of the ledge canted downward at an angle and looked as if it led deeper into the cave system. It was the wider of the two tunnels. The other passage led to the east. Her brows narrowed as Jamie closed her eyes and wondered if that was right. She tried to picture the layout of the cave in her mind. The massive cavern, where she'd been attacked, was north of the Arrowhead. She couldn't be sure, but she thought it might be east or northeast.

Jamie chose the smaller passage, bent double, which incited a fresh wave of pain, and slipped inside. She aimed her small light down the passage, illuminating its stone walls. Rock jutted from the wall at random angles, mixing with the shadows cast by her light to resemble waves on a rough sea. The ceiling above her was lower than the other sections of the cave, which made her glad she'd brought her helmet along. It was still useful, even with the massive crack running along the back. Though her effort to slip it back on hadn't been easy. Her head still hurt like a bitch. She glanced back; was she making the right decision?

After a while, the ceiling sloped down, further lowering the clearance of the tunnel. Jamie tried to stoop over more, but it wasn't enough. She felt a sharp pain as a jagged piece of rock grazed her back. Jamie arched her back as she dropped to her knees and reached around to feel the tender spot. Her fingers swept over the sweat-damp cloth until coming to a tear in the shirt and a patch of exposed skin. She gingerly dragged the tips of her fingers over the spot and felt a scratch marring the otherwise smooth skin. Jamie brought her hand back around and shone the light on it. *No blood. That's good. I've already lost enough blood for one day.*

On hands and knees, she continued along the passage. It was slow going, flashlight in hand, she had to lean her weight on one elbow to shuffle forward. Her awkward posture brought fresh waves of pain, adding to what she'd been feeling. Maybe she should have taken the other tunnel. *At least then, I wouldn't have had to crawl.* Ahead of her the tunnel ended, opening into another chamber. Despite being used to caves, she had a healthy desire to exit the one she was in. She increased her speed, hobbling toward the opening.

After entering the next chamber, she rose to her feet and took a moment to sweep the caked dirt from her elbow. Then aimed the light down and dusted the knees of her tight pants. That would definitely stain. A shame, they were good pants. Her eyes moved up to her shirt; blood stains and rips also made it a total loss. This trip wouldn't reflect well on her clothes budget.

With a sigh, she closed her eyes and tilted her head back. *How can I think about clothes at a time like this?* She scolded herself. *The others are who knows where, and in who knows how much trouble. And I'm thinking about money and clothes. What is wrong with me?* Even as the thought drifted through her mind, she knew she wasn't being fair to herself; she couldn't control every single thought that popped into her head.

She grunted and forced herself to switch her focus to the task at hand. As she reopened her eyes, she took in the cave around her for the first time. Her breath caught in her chest as she absorbed the splendor of the cave. It was majestic. Eyes following the beam of her light, she studied the room. There were formations everywhere. Speleothems of every type spotted the ceiling, walls, and floor. Spread along the walls were massive columns, created over millennia. For the most part, evenly spaced, the columns circled the entire room, which gave the cavern an appearance similar to a Greek temple. Deposits of flowstone clung to the exposed portions of the walls, appearing to be curtains hanging between pillars. Above her, calcite sheets draped from the ceiling in wondrous patterns. Spread throughout the center of the room were several more massive columns, along with stalactites and stalagmites of various sizes and shapes. To her left, at the far end of the room, her light reflected off a pool of water with a couple of large columns growing from it.

Aiming her flashlight up, Jamie studied the patterns of the naturally formed plafond. There were tiny cracks running along the ornate ceiling, seeping water. Jamie moved forward to the nearest column and examined the top of the formation. She stepped back and spun around to scan the room again. Her light hit an odd shape that broke up the outline of the floor.

Squinting in the dim light, she stepped forward for a closer look. A human skeleton lay in a gap between two columns. Jamie took a few more steps toward the bones. From the sediment built up around its base, the skeleton appeared to have been there for a very long time. The ulna and radius of each arm were positioned across what had once been the ribcage. All the bones from the hands had separated from the end of each arm and fallen into the gaps between ribs. The area where the feet belonged was also a jumble of bone. The rest of the skeleton lay as if positioned for a funeral.

Between the next set of columns lay another skeleton. As Jamie scanned the room further, she spotted many more skeletons. Each body having been positioned with the utmost respect and care. She was in an ancient burial site. How had she missed that? She wondered how old the bodies were, how long they'd been there. She was also curious about what culture they represented.

Around most of the skeletons lay the scattered remnants of objects. Some items she easily recognized. There were stone tools and weapons. Arrowheads dotted the floor, some next to slivers of material once belonging to wooden arrows.

Aside from the weapons, other artifacts had been placed around the burial site. Along with the various examples of remarkably preserved earthenware and stoneware, were worn and cracked vessels, as well as potsherds. Scattered about was a mixture of ornaments and small statues. Figurines had been fashioned from bone or shaped from metal, carved from stone and cut from wood. Jamie saw examples of people and animals, mammals and birds. Native copper had been hammered into numerous shapes. A few of the wooden objects had fared better than others, depending on type and age. What remained were mostly indistinct wooden shapes, their features worn away by the ages.

Layers of sediment had flowed over several items as well, encasing them in stone. The coating around one bundle of arrows was so thin as to be transparent, leaving them to appear frozen in time.

CHAPTER 41

Jordan Adler
3:54 pm

Jordan scurried along the ground, crawling the remaining five feet to the crest of the hill, then up onto one of the boulders that dotted the landscape. Jordan hadn't been able to bring herself to head straight back to the camp, deciding to visit the cave first. Without a watch, she couldn't be sure how long the journey took, but she was certain it had taken her much longer to reach the cave this time than during her first trip. By her reckoning, the skulking and hiding along the way had tacked on nearly an hour, likely more.

She tightened her fist around her only weapon. If you could call it a weapon. At some point in her journey, Jordan had armed herself with a heavy stick. She'd figured if all else failed, she could use it as a cudgel. She knew it wouldn't have done much damage to the massive predator, but it made her feel better none the less. She broke into a wry smile. *I've found myself a wooden security blanket.*

From her perch, she peered down into the gully. Her gaze moved from the cave opening to the supply tent, then along both sides of the creek bed. There was no sign of the beast, or anyone else for that matter. Jordan couldn't help but wonder where the others were. Last she knew, Jamie and Zayne had been inside the cave. Surely, the professor would have fetched them. Had some ill befallen the professor and his daughter?

This whole trip had become a nightmare. What should have been a fun learning exercise had turned into a terrifying game of hide-and-seek. Jordan doubted whether any of them would make it.

Hunkered low on the boulder, her eyes darted back and forth. With no sign of the beast, Jordan slid to the edge of the boulder, still scouring the area. She rolled off the rock, got to her knees, then stood. Crouched to lower her profile, Jordan raced down the slope, careening off boulders on the way down.

As she reached level ground, Jordan sprinted across the dry creek bed and darted into the supply tent. She spun and moved just close enough to the opening to peek out with one eye. She studied the west side of the gully. Not seeing the beast bearing down on her, Jordan took a moment to catch her breath. Her heart thumped like a subwoofer. Surely, the beast could hear it from miles away.

Jordan poked her head from the flaps and shot a fleeting glance to the south before withdrawing back fully into the tent. With no sign of an immediate threat, Jordan stepped from the tent. As she inched along the canvas wall, her eyes flitted back and forth along the hilltop. Once Jordan reached the corner, she peeked around and scanned the eastern side of the gully. *Nothing.* Jordan let out a deep sigh and then crept back into the tent.

Feeling slightly safe for the moment, Jordan perused the equipment piled in the tent. She laid her stick atop one table and crouched to examine the contents of the bags. She tore through the bags, searching for something she'd seen earlier that day. "Where is it?" Jordan mumbled to herself. One case after another, she failed to find what she was looking for. She shunted another case to the side and reached down to open the final case. "Of course," she complained, "it would be in the last place I check."

Jordan plucked an old rock hammer from the bag. She hefted

it and checked its balance. It wasn't a great weapon, but it was better than the stick she had been lugging around. Now armed with a weapon of sorts, Jordan examined the contents of the bags for anything else she might need. She glanced through the transparent plastic section that served as the tent's window and considered the shadows forming outside. Though still hours away, time was flowing inexorably closer to sunset. She feared she couldn't stand being alone all night. Then again, she wouldn't have thought herself strong enough to weather all the difficulties she'd already been through that day. *No one really knows what they can endure until the situation arises.*

Jordan plucked a helmet from a bag and checked the batteries in its headlamp. Wary of how awful the whole situation would be with no light, she took a handful of spare batteries and stuffed them in a pocket. For backup, she also grabbed a pair of the smaller flashlights. She realized her collection of necessities would soon outgrow her pockets. As she shifted through the supplies, Jordan came across a nylon drawstring backpack and poured its contents in one case.

She scooted to an empty spot on the canvas floor. Jordan lay her new backpack on the ground along with the helmet, flashlights, and hammer. She emptied her pockets of the water bottles and batteries. She twisted the cap off one bottle and took a deep swallow, emptying the small amount of liquid that remained. Jordan wished she'd grabbed more water from the van. She was down to a single bottle. And a hollow feeling in her stomach made her realize she had eaten nothing since breakfast that morning. *Perhaps I should have swung by the campsite to grab some food and water.* A wave of fear rushed over her. *Maybe not.*

Jordan eyed her equipment, trying to figure out if she needed anything else. Not immediately thinking of anything, she stuffed most of her meager collection of supplies into the bag. She pulled the drawstring tight and swung it over a shoulder. All that remained on the floor was the helmet, a single flashlight, and the hammer. Jordan brought the helmet up and strapped it on, connecting the catch under her chin and pulling it tight. She plucked the flashlight off the ground and jammed it into her pocket. Jordan snatched the rock hammer, and she rose to her feet.

Jordan took one final glance outside, then flew from the tent. She rushed toward the opening in the cliff, scurried to the top of the rock, and entered the cave. A quick look from the cave confirmed that she was still alone. After switching her lamp on, she let her eyes follow the passageway.

Her shoulder brushed the rough stone as she prowled toward the artifact chamber. Jordan leaned forward to peer around a corner in the passage while letting her eyes scan ahead. Not spotting anything of risk, she proceeded cautiously into the chamber. A portable work light still lit the area, giving her a complete view of the room.

Jordan gazed covetously at the objects lying on the floor. Though some may have been valuable, she wasn't interested in any wealth she might gain from the artifacts. Jordan thought only to defend herself and the others. She stared at the small hammer clutched in her hand. Jordan had a hunch she might have a better chance if she used one of the weapons scattered along the cave floor.

Jordan tore her eyes from the artifacts and spun toward the interior of the cave.

Dr. Theodore Stone
3:58 pm

Frustrated, furious, and at his wit's end, Stone wondered how he would ever be able to find his daughter. She could be anywhere within a couple of square miles. With a prehistoric beast after them, he had no idea what to do next. He had searched the cave, camp, and van and had only managed to locate one of his charges. One of the five that remained, that were still alive. At least he knew where Cassie was. She was safe. Telling Cassie to remain in the van had been the right decision.

Part of him still wished he had brought her along. *At least then I wouldn't be alone.* It was wrong. He despised himself for letting the thought enter his mind. How could he even think of putting her in danger just to make himself feel better? He was responsible for the wellbeing of all his students. He'd botched the whole situation.

Now here he was, at the campsite again, with little to show for it. Stone approached from the southwest this time. As he surveyed the clearing, his eyes swept over the stream, past the prep tent, and around the campfire. The dead generator lay in the middle of the field, followed by six abandoned tents sitting in the shade on the far side of the clearing. The camp still appeared as deserted as it had been the last time he'd been there. He had hoped Jordan would have already arrived. He'd hoped somebody would have been there.

If Jordan isn't here, she must be at the cave. Part of his mind screamed for him to rush headlong for the cave. If Jordan was at the cave, then there was a chance Zayne was there as well. *My students have to be somewhere.* Why not the cave? He could understand why nobody had stayed at the campsite. There was nowhere secure to hide.

Stone hopped over the stream, and he darted to the kitchen tent. With a glance inside, he confirmed it was empty. Stone ducked under the aluminum poles that made up the tent's frame. The food remained untouched and the canvas walls were still pristine. He grabbed another drawstring bag, knelt, and started to stuff it with food and water. He packed the bag with plenty of food to feed a person for a few days. But left enough for anyone else that might show up.

Stone got to his feet and lifted the bag over his shoulder. He gave the tent another quick look before exiting. Stone swept his head around, scanning the clearing for movement. He rushed past the busted generator without a glance, moving toward the tents. Stone felt a pang as he passed the pool of blood. It was a painful reminder of what they'd already lost. A quick inspection of each tent confirmed the absence of occupants. With a sigh, he spun to the north and hustled toward the cliff.

Jordan Adler
4:01 pm

Jordan crept through the cave, wary of every bend and corner, on alert for the slightest noise or movement. Her tiny fault passage was clear, and the second cavern had been as empty as the first. She stalked into the third chamber, the hub. Jordan feared it unlikely she would find anyone. One foot in front of the other, she put her weight on the outside of her feet as she continued, sneaking.

The single light in each chamber, when mixed with the light shining from her headlamp, gave the cave an eerie visage. If she hadn't already been terrified most of the afternoon, the caves would have spooked her. As it was, a surreal feeling of fear and wonder were tied together.

Aiming her eyes and consequently her light at each of the tunnels, she looked for anything out of the ordinary. Anything that hadn't been there on her previous trip through. She hadn't paid much attention before. She'd only traveled through the room once, having taken her route through the narrow fault passage both times she'd gone to see the cave art. She remembered that the chamber with the artwork was through the passage directly in front of her but had no clue where the others led.

Jordan started on her right and investigated each of the tunnels. The first tunnel opened into a smallish chamber she hadn't seen before. There was another passage on the far side of the empty room that she decided to explore. As she snuck through the empty chamber, Jordan glanced around. She hadn't seen any sign of a struggle in the cave system so far. That boded well, at least. She peeked around the rock wall before entering the passage, then she slipped through the shallow tunnel. Jordan entered the cavern that led into the hall of art. She scurried through a tunnel and into the chamber full of artwork.

She took a moment to scan the ancient artwork before studying the entrance to her grotto. *That would be an excellent place to hide.* She wondered if anyone was in there. It would be just her luck to cross the entire chamber only to have the beast slip from the passage. She shut her eyes and took in a deep breath. Delaying the choice wouldn't suddenly make it any more appealing. Jordan reopened her eyes, let out a determined sigh, and strode purposefully for the small room on the opposite end of the chamber. Halfway through the cavern, Jordan shot a furtive glance over her shoulder. As she reached the passage to her grotto, she peered up the inclined tube eroded from the rock. Jordan took in the marks where the creature had gouged the rock. *Those weren't here before.* She let out another sigh and scampered up the incline. Jordan stuck her head over the lip, and she searched the beautiful cavern.

"Hello," she croaked. Jordan let out a cough to clear her throat and tried again. "Hello?" she asked, this time louder and much more clearly. After a minute without an answer, she slid back down the incline and her feet landed on the floor with a thump.

Jordan backtracked past the artwork and out into the next room. Then she strode across the room and entered the other passage that led back to the hub. As she reached the junction, Jordan glanced both ways before turning right. She crept along the passage to another room she'd never seen. Lit, like all the rest, by a single work light, the room had a few tunnels leading from it. There were tracks in the sediment where someone had set up the light. However, the footprints led right back out of the room. With no further evidence of exploration, she decided not to check out the passages yet. *Maybe later.*

Jordan skirted along the side of the tunnel, back into the hub. So far, her search through the cave system hadn't proved fruitful. If she didn't find anyone in the cave, she'd have to make her way back to the campsite. Jordan still wasn't sure how she felt about that. She wasn't thrilled. Could she go back to a place where she'd watched someone die? Not just die, get ravished by a beast. Torn apart.

After another quick check of the hub, she scurried to the last passage. Something that could have been a faint echo drifted through the caves. She paused. *What was that? Was that me? Is something else in here?* Light panning across the room, she examined the chamber. After a moment with no further sounds, Jordan stepped into the passage.

Jamie Long
4:08 pm

While discovering a hidden graveyard was wondrous, she dared not linger too long. Thirsty, hungry, and concerned for the others, Jamie decided to move on. She quickly re-scanned the room, giving each of the tunnels that led from the chamber a closer look. Jamie pulled the layout of the cave from her memory. She could see right away that two of them led to the north, away from the entrance. There were three tunnels that might lead toward the cave's entrance. Of those, one passage ran downward at a sharp angle. As she was lower than the rest of the cave system she'd previously explored, she crossed that one off the list too.

My options are dwindling swiftly right before my eyes. That left only two choices. It was possible for one of the passages to twist around or to lead out of the cave another way. With a pang of anxiety, she wondered if she had been too rash in her judgment. Jamie drew in a deep breath and attempted to push her mounting worry to the side. *It's not like I can't try again.* She had to remind herself she was just looking for the best guess.

She rescanned the final two passages. Her eyes danced back and forth between the two options. One way led to the southeast, the floor at the same level as the cavern she was in. Her gaze kept returning to the other option. Wedged into a corner of the ceiling more than a dozen feet off the cave floor, the passage that looked most promising was also the most difficult to reach. It might have just been her hope speaking, but the passage appeared to be about the same height she'd fallen earlier. In her mind, it increased the odds of the tunnel connecting to the front of the cave.

A mass of rock lay beneath the opening, in a heap rising two-thirds of the way to the passage. Jamie moved to the pile of rock, determined to mount it. She cautiously picked her way up the mass of stone. Smaller rocks hampered her progress as they became dislodged and tumbled from the mound. She tried to put most of her weight on the larger stones as she climbed. After she clambered to the top of the heap, she rose to her feet. Hands out at her sides for balance, she edged to the opening. Jamie pulled herself up onto the lip of the rock and wriggled into the passage.

Ahead of her, she caught the barest hint of diffused light bouncing off the rock wall. It was a different color temperature than her light. As she switched her flashlight off, the light radiating from the end of the tunnel became stronger. *Why didn't I think of that?* The lights they'd left in the rooms could have helped her decide quicker. It had been her idea to use them after all. Maybe she still wasn't thinking as clearly as she'd assumed. Was her head injury affecting her critical thinking?

Jamie shook her head and switched her light back on. She proceeded along the passage, following the tunnel around a bend and into the next room. The room was lit by one of their work lights, but it still took a minute after her eyes swept the cave for recognition to set in. After hours alone, she had finally hobbled into a part of the cave she recognized. *This cavern is near the Arrowhead.* Jamie rushed to the room's entrance. *Yeah, this tunnel splits; one direction leads toward the Exhibition Hall, the other to the Arrowhead.*

Now I can look for Zayne.

CHAPTER 42

Jordan Adler
4:15 pm

Jordan studied a hand-drawn map she'd stumbled upon while exploring the chamber. She was in the immense room above the—*what was it again?* Her finger traced the sheet of paper attached to the clipboard and found the chamber. The Arrowhead Cavern, that was a good name. Much better than the hub. Jordan scrutinized the drawing, trying to figure out who'd created it. It had to have been Zayne or Jamie.

Why had they left it hidden behind a boulder next to a crumpled-up jacket? Jordan ducked down and plucked the jacket off the cave floor. She shifted the jacket, letting the material catch the light. Studying it closely, she recognized it. It was Jamie's jacket; the same zip-up hoodie she'd worn earlier. That Jamie had left her hoodie concerned her much less than the abandoned map. The two girls must have put a lot of work into the drawing.

Eyes raking the chamber, Jordan looked for any clue as to what had happened. There were a few scuffs on the floor, but no overt sign of an attack. If someone had left the map and jacket behind, it suggested that they'd fled in a hurry. Perhaps they'd been spooked. At least the lack of blood was a promising sign. No bodies or body parts, a better one.

Jordan looked around the cavern, a shallow breath escaping from her lungs. Where had they gone? Had she missed something? She spun and swept the room again. As she considered her options, Jordan tapped two fingers against the clipboard. She hung onto it; the map it held might come in handy later. She bundled the jacket under her arm before setting off across the room, roaming the chamber aimlessly.

Jordan wasn't sure where she should go, nor was she looking forward to leaving the relative safety of the caves. She'd been out in the woods for hours; petrified of running across the animal. The beast. The campsite was on her agenda, but she'd hoped to have already found someone. Somehow, being alone seemed to make the whole mess worse. *I should have stayed with Cassie at the van.* She pushed the thought from her mind. She'd made the right decision, she had to keep going.

If the beast made an appearance or if she couldn't find anyone by nightfall, she would have to decide on the best place to hold up. The van was an ideal place to hide, but it was too far away. She'd have to slog back through the woods to reach it. The campsite wouldn't be nearly as secure as the caves. The clearing where they'd set up camp was open on all sides and had already proved to be dangerous. Though, if the creature popped up somewhere in the caves, she would still be in plenty of trouble. While the beast wouldn't be able to see her from as far off, it might still catch her scent.

If she was very lucky, she might outrun it for a short distance within the caves. Her eyes strayed to the passages leading from the room. Another option would be to disappear deeper into the cave. But if she wasn't careful, she might literally disappear. Blundering through an unknown cave system, at any hurried pace was a recipe for a broken neck or a tumble into a crevasse.

In her mind, the only place within the system with an ounce of safety was the narrow passage leading into her grotto, or as the mapmaker had labeled it; her gallery. She could hold up in the tiny passage indefinitely. Well, until she died of thirst. If she stretched out her remaining bottle of water, she might survive three or four days.

Swish. Thump.

Jordan whipped her head around. She could have sworn she'd heard something for sure that time. The noise came again. She hunched and darted to the nearest wall, then crouched against it. Jordan reached up and rapidly smashed the button on her headlamp twice. As the cave dimmed, she took a deep breath. Someone or something was creeping around inside the caves with her. *I should have left ages ago.* Jordan clung to the stone wall as she skirted the edge of the cavern. She came to a halt on one side of the tunnel opening.

Swish. Thump.

Concentrating intently on the noise, Jordan tried to figure out its source. She just couldn't quite get it. She squeezed her eyes tight, letting her ears follow the sound.

Swish. Thump.

It wasn't the beast. It couldn't be, could it? It didn't sound like any animal she'd ever heard. The creature had too many legs to make that sound. So, it wasn't the beast. Probably wasn't the beast.

Swish. Thump.

Could it mimic human sounds? She couldn't remember that being part of the tale. Supposedly it had once been human. Why was it hunting them? What had they ever done to it? Could it possibly know they'd found the story of its creation?

Swish. Thump.

It was getting closer. Jordan's heavy, rapid breathing seeped into her awareness. *Stop it, stop it! You're too loud, stop breathing so loud.* She fought to control her respiration. *Take deep silent breaths. Come on, girl. Calm down.*

Swish. Thump.

The noise became clearer as it moved closer. *Footsteps. They're footsteps;* she was almost sure. Someone was dragging their foot in a shuffling gait.

Swish. Thump.

Jordan peered around the corner. Through the passage, she

caught sight of a tall young woman. Head down, she held one hip and dragged one foot with every step. The woman had rips and bloodstains on her clothes, but Jordan recognized her right away. *Jamie, it's Jamie.*

"Jamie," she blurted, sweeping around the corner into view. "Oh my God, Jamie, are you alright?"

At the sound of her name, Jamie looked up. Her eyes widened a moment before she met Jordan's gaze. She let a small smile creep along her face. "Jordan," she murmured, "it's good to see you. I was afraid you guys had left me."

"Zayne?" At Jamie's slight shrug and grimace, Jordan continued, "Michael died."

Some strength left Jamie at the statement, and she slumped noticeably. "Ohh," she grunted, taking the words in as if they were a physical blow.

Jordan flipped the light back on and rushed to the other girl. Her eyes swept over Jamie's injuries, pausing briefly to examine the gashes on her stomach, then moving up to her face. Jamie flinched away as the light hit her eyes. Jordan rested a hand on the taller girl's cheek and studied her right eye. There was something wrong with it. Fully dilated, her pupil was as large as a saucer.

"Please get the light out of my eyes?" Jamie complained.

"Sorry," Jordan said, aiming her light away from Jamie's face. "Are you feeling ok?" she inquired with concern.

"I have a headache, a few bumps and bruises, and I've been used as a scratching post by a rather ginormous kitty cat, but overall I'm ok," she replied, voice turning raspy. Jamie let out a stifled cough into her fist.

"We need to get you cleaned up," Jordan worried.

Jamie waved the statement away with a flick of her wrist. "It's not that bad," she said, trying to dismiss Jordan's concern. "You wouldn't happen to have any water on you?"

Jordan took a step back and unslung her bag from around her shoulders, dropping the jacket in the process. "Sure, I have a bottle," she said, prying the bag open. Jordan reached inside, extracted the water, and passed it to her companion. Jordan wouldn't let Jamie's unconcerned attitude sway her, but she dropped the topic for the moment. There was a first aid kit in the supply tent, she'd grab it once they made it outside.

Jamie twisted the cap to open the bottle and brought it up to her lips. She took a long swallow before bringing the bottle down and replacing the cap. Jamie offered the bottle back to Jordan in an outstretched arm. "Thanks," she murmured.

"No, you keep it," Jordan declined, holding her arms up, palms out. "It's yours."

"Are you sure?" Jamie asked.

"Drink up," Jordan replied.

Jamie removed the cap and took another long swig while letting her eyes wander down to the fallen clothing. "Is that mine?" she asked, nodding her head toward the jacket. "It's a bit chilly in here."

Jordan leaned down and plucked the jacket from the cave floor. She whipped the jacket to dislodge all the dirt and dust from it. Jamie allowed Jordan to help her slip the hoodie on, offering one arm and then the other. As Jordan draped the cloth over her shoulders, the material fell against the blood, which transferred some to the jacket.

"Oops," she blurted, staring at the stain.

Jamie looked down and let a soft sigh slip out. She grabbed both sides of the material and held it out from her stomach. "Don't worry, we can go shopping when we get out of this," she promised, "and you can buy me a new one."

CHAPTER 43

Dr. Theodore Stone
4:25 pm

At a cautious pace, Stone followed the dry creek bed along the base of the cliff. He glanced behind him, then scanned the top of the slope. He kept an eye out for the supply tent and the beast. It had seemed a good idea when he'd chosen to take this route. Now he was having second thoughts. His logic had been sound. He had figured the trip straight through the woods to the cave could bring unwanted attention to him and anyone he came across. Jordan. Jordan had to be at the cave, she just had to. There was nowhere else she could be.

While the route offered a straight shot along the base of the cliff to the cave entrance, it provided little cover. At least in the woods, he could have slipped behind a tree or under a bush if the beast had shown up. Or if he'd heard something. Or at the slightest hint of movement. Or if there was a strong gust of wind.

Stone's return trip from the van had worn at his nerves, testing him. If he hadn't been trying to find Zayne and most of his students, he would have taken much longer to cover the distance. Hell, he would have stayed with Cassie in the van and waited for Miriam.

Head turning and eyes darting in all directions, he looked for any sign of pursuit. Stone was painfully aware of the hair on his neck standing up. The beast. A beast. Even after seeing the thing murder one of his students, he still couldn't quite believe it. Oh, he knew for a fact it had happened, it just didn't feel real. That couldn't happen again. Never again.

As it was, he'd thrown caution to the wind and plowed forward. He knew he'd made way too much noise but hadn't been able to bring himself to slow. He'd been hoping to find Jordan at the camp, waiting for him. Almost expecting it. Finding Henry, Jamie, and Zayne at the same time would have been ideal. Yet there had been no one. Not a single student.

Stone expected that was why he now put so much hope on the cave. He couldn't even contemplate, didn't even want to consider the possibility that no one was waiting for him at the cave either. In his low points, he couldn't help but imagine them all dead. His moods in the last several hours had been like a rollercoaster. Except they never went too high, remaining instead in the mid to low range. While his fear, on the other hand, seemed to careen all over the place like a pendulum.

As he advanced along the creek bed, Stone skirted rocks and boulders spread about. He tried to stay as close to the cliff as possible; as a consequence, the natural fluctuations in the path hampered his vision. He knew moving from the cliffside would allow him a better view of what awaited him, but he couldn't bring himself to take the chance. His steady pace seemed to take forever but brought him ever closer to the cave. The closer he got to the cave, the more hope he felt.

After he rounded another bend and the supply tent came into view Stone knew, he absolutely knew, that he was about to find someone. One of his students. The idea of not finding anyone was inconceivable.

Stone flew to the supply tent. When he ducked inside, he saw the disorder that somebody had left. Somebody had searched through their gear, leaving supplies and cases strewn around the tent. It hadn't looked like that the last time he'd been there, and it was too organized to be the beast. "Oh, thank God" he murmured. "Thank God." Someone was still alive. It had to be Jordan.

Stone darted to the boulder in front of the cave entrance and mounted it. He hefted himself up, stepped onto the lip of the rock, and entered the mouth of the cave. He rushed through the entry passage and broke into the first chamber. A quick look confirmed it empty. Upon entering the next tunnel, he stopped. He'd heard something. He held his breath and let his ears pick up whatever they could.

There was the sound of gravel crunching beneath feet and a murmured conversation. His heart leapt. He'd found someone. More than one person. At least two, maybe more. Could it be all of them? Could he be so lucky? After the dismal day he'd endured thus far, he deserved a little luck.

Stone shot around the bend in the passage. From the look on their faces, he feared he'd nearly scared the two girls to death. Jordan and Jamie had fallen back a step as he appeared. Their apprehension turned to relief as they recognized him.

"Professor," Jamie beamed. "You're ok."

"Yes, my dear," Stone agreed. His eyes shot around the young women, looking for any sign of his daughter. His heart fell. He'd been certain that he would find Jamie and Zayne together. Stone moved closer to the girls. "Zayne?" he choked, doing his best to hold back a sob.

Jamie's face fell as she sputtered. "She's... she's not with you?"

"I haven't found her yet," he moaned.

"When... when that thing came... I... I told her to run," she whimpered.

Stone nodded; he'd just have to keep looking.

His eyes darted between the two young women, taking in their appearance. Jordan looked about the same as the last time he'd laid eyes on her. She was still in her khaki cargo pants and a blue and gray t-shirt. There were stains and rips in the clothes, giving evidence of a rough trip through the woods.

Jamie appeared much the worse for wear. Muck was

spattered across her beige pants, and her knees were covered in dirt and grime. An arm was cradled across her stomach and one hand clutched both sides of her lightweight hoodie together. There appeared to be dark red stains soaking through the jacket and dried blood on her hands and neck. She moved toward him with a slight limp. A closer look into her face revealed a blown pupil.

"What about you, my dear? Are you alright?" Stone inquired, worry building.

With a slight shrug, Jamie released her hold on the fabric. Unzipped, the material parted on its own, revealing her torn and bloody tank top. And torn and bloody skin. Stone's eyes widened as he took in her injuries.

"I've been better," she murmured.

"My God," he mumbled, rushing to her. Bending over, Stone inspected the slashes.

"It's stopped bleeding," Jamie assured, "and it's not very deep."

"We need to clean that," he said. Eyes moving back to her face, Stone studied her right eye more closely. The pupil had expanded to almost the same size as the iris. Stone knew that a blown pupil could indicate a head injury. "We need to get you to the hospital."

"No, I'm fine." Jamie waved it off. "We need to find the others."

"No," Stone stated resolutely. "You two will stay here."

"But Prof—" Jordan complained.

"I want to—" Jamie sputtered.

"No. No buts," Stone interjected, cutting them off. "You are both going to stay here. I have been worried sick, traipsing back and forth across this valley, and I've just now found both of you. I need you to be safe, and I need to know where you are. I found Cassie alone, huddled in the van, scared out of her wits."

"She's ok?" Jordan interrupted.

"Yes, but I don't know what possessed you to go blundering around through the woods all alone. You should have stayed there."

"After finding the battery dead, and what happened with Michael…" Jordan trailed off.

Stone took a deep breath, running a hand through the hair on the side of his head. In truth, he understood why Jordan had gone looking for the others. He admired her decision, but it had been reckless, and he couldn't allow her to do it again. "I want you to promise me this time. Promise that you won't leave the cave until I come back. I want both of you to promise."

"We don't have any food or water, and I need to get the first aid kit for Jamie's wounds," Jordan objected.

Stone unslung his nylon bag and thrust it into Jordan's arms. "There's enough food and water in there for now, and I'll go grab the first aid kit."

"What if we need something else after you've gone?" she challenged.

"Fine, you can go to the supply tent if you need to, but just don't leave the area." Stone shot back. He didn't understand why Jordan was being so difficult. It wasn't like her.

Tears burbled from the corners of Jordan's eyes. "I jus… I just wan… wanted to help," she whimpered. "I couldn't stand it if any… anything happened to anyone else."

Stone took her in his arms. "I understand, I really do," he soothed, "but how do you think I'd feel if anything happened to either of you? I have been bouncing around the woods like a pinball since Michael died. In the last several hours, I haven't had a clue where any of you were. I brought five students and my daughter into a precarious situation. I need to know you're safe." He glanced over to Jamie, "both of you."

When he had begun the embrace, Jordan's arms had been straight down at her sides, her muscles rigid. As he continued to speak, Jordan had relaxed noticeably, finally enveloping him in her arms as he finished his explanation. Stone and Jordan were rocked as Jamie turned the embrace into a group hug.

CHAPTER 44

Cassie Byrne
4:35 pm

Cassie crouched at the rear door, ready to spring into action. It had to have been at least an hour since she had woken up; in that time there had been no sign of the creature. She'd decided to make a run for the other van. She needed to check for survivors, not that she expected to find any. After searching for anyone else, she would need to grab the battery as quickly as possible.

In an effort to prepare herself, Cassie closed her eyes and took long, deep breaths. She tried, as best she could, to push aside the panic filling her chest.

Ok, one... two...

She pulled the handle and slammed her shoulder into the door. With a grunt, she bounced off the door and fell to her butt. Sprawled on the floor of the van, Cassie reached over to cup her shoulder. "Ouch," she mumbled, shooting an accusing look at the door. She'd forgotten to unlock it.

Cassie rose to her knees and peeked from the window, attempting to find any movement that could be the beast. Her eyes swept the base of the trees. Cassie shifted her weight, getting back to her feet. She moved into position, shoulder against the door. "Ok, let's try this again," she breathed. One hand poised on the lever, this time she made sure to push the lock up as she leaned into the door. Cassie jerked the door handle toward her. After swinging the door open, she sprang from the rear of the van.

Her legs pumped as she darted for the other van. Cassie was painfully aware of the rubber soles of her shoes as they thudded against the dirt road. She didn't look around, couldn't look around. If by chance she'd seen the monster, she knew it would be over. The end. Cassie knew she would've frozen.

As Cassie swooped around the rear passenger side of the other van, she saw what she had hoped for, and dreaded. The sliding passenger door was still wide open. Purposefully ignoring anything inside of the van, Cassie leapt in through the open door. She grabbed the handle as she spun and smoothly slid the door shut. Cassie glanced down to the lock and watched her finger push it down. Her eyes shot back up. Gazing through the window, she searched for the beast. She had almost felt the animal breathing down her neck as she ran. Eyes darting back and forth she waited.

After some time, it could have been a minute or it could have been an hour, she couldn't be certain, she realized the beast hadn't shown itself. Cassie fought to control her breathing as she slowly took in a large lungful of air. She exhaled deeply, pushing the air from her chest. Cassie gazed through the window for another few minutes. What did it mean? Had the beast gone? Cassie slowly noticed a metallic smell. Through the corner of her eyes, the grizzly sight she had been trying to block faded into clarity. The scene that greeted her as she turned her head was ghastly.

All around her. Blood. Blood on the seats, the windows, along the floor and dripping from the ceiling. So much blood. More blood than she had ever seen. And the bodies. The bodies. Cassie squeezed her eyes shut as she tried to push the horror away. Turning to face the window once more, she realized that since the sliding door had been open; it hadn't been sprayed with blood. It was her safe place.

Cassie steeled her nerves to look around. She had to find out if anyone was still alive. She had to check. She swiveled to her left and inched forward on her knees. Cassie checked the front seats first. The small elderly man sat, eyes open wide in surprise, chest still. In the driver's seat, a young woman sprawled, turned around in the chair, back against the wheel. Cassie skirted her eyes around any major trauma. It appeared as if the young woman had bumped the gearshift in the struggle, causing the van to come to rest where it had. Cassie could hear the little click-click-click as the turn signal light flashed away. She reached past the poor girl and pulled the key from the ignition. *I can't let this battery die too.*

The three in the first passenger seat were also dead. She had to look away from the sight. She felt her stomach tighten. Cassie swiveled her body away from the carnage, turning herself to face the door again. She had to fight hard against the queasiness threatening to overwhelm her. Fists on the glass, Cassie stuck her head between her arms and leaned forward. *Don't throw up, don't throw up.* She took deep, shaky breaths.

A moan rose from behind Cassie and caused her to let out a stifled scream. Cassie spun, wide-eyed, in the noise's direction. She clasped her hands over her mouth while her eyes flew across the van, searching for its source. The final two rows were ever the vision of horror as the others had been. The person nearest the door hadn't even had time to unbuckle their seatbelt. The seat, separated from the other two in the row, held a young woman only slightly older than herself. Head tilted down, resting on her chest, her right arm was positioned across her body as if reaching for the seatbelt. Her other hand rested on her lap, palm up, covered in blood. It looked as though she had been trying to stifle a wound in her neck.

The next person Cassie saw was a heavy young man in the back seat. His chest gouged and his neck set at an unnatural angle. Cassie quickly averted her eyes, not even able to think about the poor man's suffering. She felt her stomach lurch. Cassie attempted to ignore her own reaction as her gaze swept forward to the middle row again. Two bodies lay in the space directly in front of the seat. A young man lay draped over a feebly stirring young woman.

The young woman was the source of the moaning. She was trying to push the body from atop her. Cassie grabbed the young man's shoulders. She hefted his upper body from the floor and pushed him toward the rear of the vehicle. Uncovered, Cassie was better able to assess the young woman's injuries. As soon as the man's weight had been shifted, the blood flow from several deep gashes along her upper leg had begun in earnest.

CHAPTER 45

Jordan Adler
4:55 pm

After the professor left, they'd ventured back through the cave system and holed up in her gallery, which was lit by several of the work lights. *Her gallery.* She broke into a smile at the thought. Jamie and Zayne had named the small chamber after her. *I hope Zayne and the Professor will be alright.* While she understood his plan to stake out the campsite, wait for his daughter, it seemed crazy.

After accompanying Jamie through the caves, Jordan had begun the process of cleaning her wounds. Unfortunately for Jamie, it hadn't been easy with the supplies she'd had on hand. Aside from giving them the food and water, the professor had fetched them a rudimentary first aid kit from the supply tent. While helpful, it hadn't been enough, and she'd longed for the more comprehensive kit back at the campsite. The professor had agreed to bring it on his next trip to the caves. Without it, Jordan had been compelled to squeeze through the thin passage to fetch a few more supplies.

Jordan had started by thoroughly cleaning the area around the wound. At Jamie's suggestion, she had next filled a plastic bag with clean water and poked a hole in the side. The hole in the bag let her expel the liquid out at a higher pressure, which allowed her to irrigate and debride the wound. Jordan then used a piece of sterile cotton from the first aid kit to scrub the wound. Next, she used a pair of tweezers to pick out any remaining debris. The process had elicited a few choice words from the injured girl, but remarkably, the gashes weren't too contaminated by dirt and particulates.

As she cleaned them, the wounds had bled again. The size of the claw marks had forced Jordan to improvise a bit with the bandages. She used gauze to cover the wounds and then used some duct tape she'd found to secure the gauze.

Jordan and Jamie sat together in the small chamber, relatively safe for the time being. While there were two ways to get in, only she and Zayne had been small enough to fit through one passage. The beast was too large to squeeze through. There was still danger from the other direction, but the beast would have to trek through the entire cave system to get at them that way. Hopefully, they would have ample warning.

The professor had bid them stay hidden in the cave. From there they were to keep an eye open for the others. Henry and Zayne were still unaccounted for. With night fast approaching, there was little they could do. It wouldn't help for any of them to stumble through the woods alone in the dark. They would be asking for the beast to take them. She only hoped they could find the others the next morning.

CHAPTER 46

Cassie Byrne
5:02 pm

After finding the young woman, Cassie had promptly banished the beast from her mind. She'd yanked a belt from the waist of one corpse. How had she done that? If it hadn't been for the woman's dire need, she wouldn't have ever thought herself capable of such a thing.

The young girl had passed out as Cassie strapped the belt just above the wound and yanked it tight around her leg. She had wound the cloth belt under the injured leg, letting the limb's weight hold it in place. Cassie had quickly scanned the inside of the van for a clean towel or shirt, something to help stop the bleeding. There were several small bags of clothes under the rear seat. Cassie had grabbed a random shirt from one bag and pressed it to the gash.

Weight resting on the girl's leg, Cassie leaned over the other girl and held the t-shirt firm against the wound. The gash in her leg was deep. Cassie knew first aid, but she'd never had to deal with anything so severe. She had only used her makeshift tourniquet to slow the bleeding. She understood that the longer a tourniquet was in place, the greater the chance of tissue damage.

With the worst of the bleeding slowed, Cassie traced the young woman's features with her gaze, looking for any further sign of injury. Her eyes swept over the young woman's short, straight black hair and her creamy pale skin. In her late teens, perhaps early twenties, epicanthic folds in the corners of her large eyes spoke of her Asian heritage. Her pointed face was splattered with blood. Cassie snatched another shirt from the bag and used it to wipe crimson liquid from the girl's face as she looked for its source. There were no lacerations or contusions on the girl's face, which indicated that the blood had likely come from the young man who'd been sprawled atop her.

Blood also drenched her cream-colored tank top and grey slacks. While the source of blood stains along her pants was readily visible, Cassie's brief examination of the young woman's torso failed to reveal further wounds. It appeared that the blood soaking her shirt belonged to the young man as well.

The poor girl stirred as she drifted back to consciousness.

As Cassie looked the young woman in the eye, she could see the pain induced fog lifting. "What's your name, hon?" Cassie asked.

"Amber," the other girl whimpered.

"Hold this for a second, Amber," Cassie said, moving the girl's hands over the cloth. Amber added pressure to the wound as Cassie spun to glance from the window. There was no sign of the creature, but that didn't mean much. Cassie glanced back at the other girl before sliding the door open. She slipped from the van and spun around toward Amber again. "I'll be right back." She held up a finger.

Cassie darted to the front of the vehicle. She still needed a battery. She had to get Amber to the hospital. She had to get help for the others.

Cassie's heart fell as she stepped around the front of the van. When the vehicle had slammed into the tree the hood had buckled. She studied the metal for a moment. It was bent, twisted at the impact site. She didn't think she'd be able to open it.

A moan from Amber pulled her attention away from the misshapen hood. *First things first,* she thought. *I need to help Amber, get her away from the bodies.* Cassie moved back to the open door. Another quick look around confirmed the absence of the beast. She returned her gaze to the girl. Amber gave her a pained grimace.

"Come on, we need to get back to my van," Cassie said. All she got from the other girl was a slight nod, but it was enough. She leaned into the van, reaching a hand toward the girl. As she grasped Amber's hand, Cassie assisted her as she wriggled toward the opening. When Amber got to the door, Cassie pulled her to her feet. Amber, balancing on one foot, allowed Cassie to duck under her arm. She reached down and snatched the bag of clothes from the vehicle floor.

They might come in handy.

Cassie supported the other girl's weight as she helped Amber hobble across the way to the other van. She kept an eye out for the beast as they crossed the distance. Not that it would help. Luckily, it didn't pop out from the trees. Cassie pulled the rear door open and helped Amber inside. Amber used her good leg to push herself further into the van. Cassie gave another quick look around before climbing in and shutting the doors.

CHAPTER 47

Henry Blake
Twilight

Henry held tight to the haft of the axe as he darted through the trees. He needed to put more distance between himself and the sabre-toothed monster. Sabre-tooth?! Bloody hell! Was he really being chased by a freaking sabre-toothed tiger? Not just any sabre-tooth, a Native American legend. Henry heard the heavy steps of the beast thudding behind him. He ran as if his life depended on it. Because, in fact, it did. Henry didn't know what had ever possessed him to attempt this mad folly. He could have stayed hidden, safe. Well, relatively safe anyway.

Henry glanced down to see his long, thin legs pumping and feet pounding through the layers of dead leaves, twigs, and vegetation. As he looked up, Henry was forced to dart around a bowl in the ground the size of a bathtub. He shifted his direction and shot to the right. Another low hanging tree limb forced him to duck again. He put on as much speed as he could manage.

After jumping over a wide, shallow stream, his foot landed in the damp earth along its banks and shot out from under him. Henry stumbled a few steps before he shot his hand out to steady himself on a nearby tree. His palm scraped along the rough bark. He looked down and saw the blood seep from the wound.

No time for that now.

The longer he ran, the more labored his breath became. Henry felt himself getting winded. His legs felt stiff. He just couldn't get away. Henry felt like he was running through quicksand. He couldn't keep this up for much longer. He was slowing. *Too slow.* It wouldn't be long before the beast caught him. Henry felt he had done pretty well, considering the obstacles in his path and the fact that he was being chased by a monster.

He bolted toward a particularly large, dense section of young trees, hoping to slow the oncoming storm. As he wound his way through the saplings, Henry could feel the thin branches snap under the weight of his body. The nursery thinned ahead of him.

He put on more speed.

Henry shot out of the trees into a clearing. He slowed as he reached the middle of the open space. Decayed leaves covered the ground around him. Two grand trees stood on either side of him, vast crowns casting shadows over the entire clearing. The steep hill in front of him bowed around, surrounding him on three sides. As he glanced to the right and left, he knew he would never make it up. Behind him, Henry could hear the beast forcing its way toward him. His luck, whatever luck he'd been running on, had just dried up.

He doubled over and tried to catch his breath.

Deep breath, in.

Long exhale, out.

Deep breath, in.

Where was Zayne? Hadn't she just been with him?

Movement in front of him pulled his focus back. Saplings bent under the weight of the beast. Henry straightened his spine, rising to his full height. He glanced at the axe in his right hand. It was better than nothing. His wrist tilted forward and brought the axe's shaft flush against the back of his arm, the heel of its handle at shoulder height. As he loosened his grip slightly, Henry let the handle slide through his hand. He felt the smooth wood of its haft sliding across his palm, the weight of the head pulling it toward the ground. Henry halted the movement of the axe as his hand reached its throat. He brought the axe handle up to his shoulder, its head even with his. Henry moved his left hand across his body and grasped the haft with both hands as if it were a baseball bat. He squared his body, preparing to swing.

The beast leapt forward, landing on all six feet with a thud. Six feet? Henry glanced around him. There was nowhere to run. The hills had even seemed to get steeper since his last look.

Where the hell is Zayne? Had he left her?

That didn't seem right.

The beast stalked ever nearer. Relentless in its pursuit, it slowly came for him. There was nothing he could do.

A breeze hit him, chilling him. Why had one side of his body suddenly gotten much cooler than the other? Henry shifted his stance. His arm wouldn't move right. He couldn't swing the axe if his arm didn't work.

The beast charged.

Henry Blake
7:02 pm

Henry's eyes flew open. His heart thudded as he leaned forward to search for the creature. It was nowhere to be seen. A soft moan brought his gaze to the shape beside him. Henry's mind whirred, trying to make sense of the situation. Zayne shifted her head against his chest, murmuring something lightly in her sleep.

He could have kicked himself; he'd fallen asleep. *How could I be so dumb?*

Zayne Stone
7:30 pm

The minuscule amount of light piercing the tree cover dimmed around her. As darkness inexorably fell, her level of panic spiked rapidly. Her heart nearly exploded from her chest with every rapid beat. She didn't understand how it had gotten so dark so quickly. Henry had awoken her from a blissful dream. She couldn't recall much of the dream, but she'd been with her mother and father, safe and happy.

Zayne had been young when she'd lost her mother. Too young. She only had vague recollections of her mom, being with her, holding her, talking to her, singing to her. A tear rolled down her cheek. If it weren't for the pictures her father kept around the house, she probably wouldn't know what her mother had looked like. As she grew up, there was a hole left behind by her mother's absence, but the love and attention she received from her father had done wonders to fill the void.

Another tear streaked down her face at the thought of her dad. He would be so worried about her. Where was he? Was he ok? She didn't think she'd be able to stand it if anything happened to him too.

Bumbling through the woods, Zayne didn't know how long it had been since they'd woken up. Why had they ever fallen asleep? They'd had hours and hours of daylight before, now they were down to mere minutes. If that. It was her fault. All her fault. She'd sensed Henry start to drift off. She hadn't meant to nod off too, she really hadn't, but she had been so comfortable. Sitting there with his arm around her, her head tucked against his shoulder; it had been the safest she'd felt in hours. Next thing she knew, Henry was shaking her awake. He said they'd been asleep for hours. He had even apologized. It wasn't his fault.

She didn't know where they were, nor could she remember where they were going. Had Henry told her? He must have. She hoped he wasn't leading them back to the van, the monster had been there, or the cave, it had been there as well. And there was the pool of blood at the camp. Nowhere was safe from the beast. Why was it chasing them? What had they ever done to it?

Zayne stumbled. As she slammed into the ground, she gashed her knee on a sharp rock and promptly burst into uncontrollable sobs. She couldn't do anything right, not even walk. And now she was lying on the ground, crying like a baby.

"Zayne, honey, are you ok?" Henry asked.

Zayne looked up and saw him kneeling on the ground right in front of her. She could see his eyes despite the glow of the headlamp, her headlamp. He had such kind eyes. *Why is he even bothering with me?* She was just slowing him down. She wanted to ask him, but was afraid that he would leave her. With short gasps, she tried to control her bawling. A pressure built in her chest and heat flooded her face. She was furious with herself, but mostly embarrassed. *I'm such a baby.*

"Zayne?" he asked again, not breaking eye contact with her.

She rolled onto her bottom. Keeping her injured knee elevated, she tucked the other leg underneath. Zayne unclasped her hands from around her knee and showed him the wound. Her pants were torn and there was a gash, about an inch long, on the inside of her knee. It was bleeding freely, and there was blood on her hands. Her sobs turned into a high-pitched mewling sound. There was so much blood.

"That's not so bad," he soothed, trying to calm her. "Look at this." Henry brought his arm up.

At first, she thought he was flexing his muscle, but he continued to bend his elbow until his fist rested under his jawline. She wiped her eyes with the side of her hand and blinked, trying to see what he was showing her. There was a large V-shaped scar on the back of his forearm, just in front of his elbow. Zayne gave a powerful sniff, bringing up a load of phlegm.

"What happened?" she whispered, reaching over to run a finger along his scar.

"I was in a bike wreck, years ago," he confided. "I was camping with my family. One day, my brother and I decided to do the bike tour the campground offered. It was my first time on a ten-speed, which was my first mistake. My second mistake came around the time I decided to ride the bike with a can of pop in my hand." She felt her eyes go wide as he paused, giving her a smile. "My final mistake occurred when I was going down the first hill and I tried to slow my bike down, with the wrong hand." Henry gave her a self-deprecating smile.

"Oh, no," she giggled.

"I remember seeing the ground, then the sky, then the ground, then the sky. I'm not sure how many times I flipped; it was all a blur. The bike was totaled, and I got forty-seven stitches. But that wasn't the worst of it," Henry sighed.

"What was worse than that?" she asked, rapt at the tale.

"Well, there were other kids on the tour, you see. So, when I took my tumble, two of them went to get help. They were in such a hurry they collided. One fell from his bike and the other ran over him, snapping his collarbone."

"Oh, no," she repeated. She winced, feeling a sharp pain on her knee as water flowed over her cut. Looking down, it surprised her to find that while Henry told his story, he had started to dress her wound. Her eyes took in the scene. He'd pulled a t-shirt from his bag and cut strips from it. A pocketknife lay extended on one scrap of cloth. Henry picked up one of the folded strips and pressed it over her knee, eliciting a slight gasp.

"Yep," he confirmed, "but you know what?"

"What," she asked, eager to concentrate on something other than her knee as he wrapped another strip around her leg.

"I found my can of pop," Henry continued, "some had spilled in the wreck, but I finished the rest."

"You did? Why?" she asked. Zayne felt another shooting pain as he tied the piece of cloth tightly over her knee. She flinched.

Henry lifted one shoulder in a slight shrug. "I didn't see any point in wasting it."

Knee bandaged; Henry helped her to her feet. She hadn't realized how much of her anxiety had drifted away.

CHAPTER 48

Dr. Miriam Segen
8:44 pm

As they wound along the dirt road at night, with only the headlamps to illuminate the way, Dr. Segen felt her excitement building. It had taken long enough. She glanced at the digital readout on her phone. Segen's eyes shifted back to the road as she sighed; it was almost 8:45. She wanted to hate her old truck so much right then, but she just couldn't manage any resentment at the moment. The truck hadn't ever failed her like this before.

AAA had taken more than an hour to reach them after she'd placed the call. After they'd arrived at the mechanic's shop, Miriam hadn't been able to convince the arrogant little man to move them up in the queue. He said he'd get to it when he got to it. Segen hadn't been thrilled with that answer.

Upon reflection, perhaps confiscating all the cell phones from her group had been a poor choice. She hadn't had any way to get ahold of her team to tell them of the delay. Neither had she been able to connect with Professor Stone. She had made several calls trying to arrange for them to get to the site quicker, but with the holiday weekend, waiting for her vehicle had proved the quickest course. The whole situation was a mess.

They had spent most of the rest of the day sitting around waiting. Much of the time they had waited for their turn. Then they'd had to wait for an employee to run to get several parts the shop didn't have in stock. Had the fool checked the truck when they'd arrived, he would have known he was missing parts and could have saved time by sending someone for them right away.

By the time everything was ready, it had been near closing time. The owner had been willing, after the promise of more money, to have one of his mechanics stay late to finish the job. He must have chosen the most amateur member of his staff to affect the repairs. The young man couldn't have been older than eighteen, and he didn't know exactly what to do. Neil had walked in on him watching a how-to video on his phone.

The young man had stuck it through, however, fixing the truck. Miriam Segen didn't know much about cars, so she hadn't paid much attention to what needed replacement. There'd been something about a water pump and some hoses, maybe a belt or two? Neil had agreed with the mechanic's assessment of the damage; that was good enough for her.

It had been almost dark by the time he'd completed the repairs and they'd gotten back on the road. The garage had been a little less than an hour away from the valley, and Neil had been a bit heavy-footed on the rest of the trip.

They still had a long walk to get to the campsite. They might even have to blunder back through the woods in the dark to get more supplies. She considered the problem more closely, and she concluded that tents and bedding were all they needed for the night. The rest of the supplies could wait until morning.

As she glanced back to the phone, she scanned the display again; 8:46. It had only been a minute? Her eyes wandering up to the corner, she read the battery percentage remaining; twenty-four percent. Segen realized she'd forgotten her charger. In the rush to get packed, it hadn't even crossed her mind. She would have to see if one of Stone's party had a charger compatible with her device.

Segen brought up Theodore Stone from her contacts list; she

might as well try to get ahold of him again. Her eyes moved to the signal strength indicator. As she watched, the indicator dropped from two bars to one. Segen pressed the call button, then placed the phone to her ear to listen as it tried to connect. The speaker suddenly came to life. "You have been forwarded..." Segen removed the phone from her ear and hit the disconnect icon. Her eyes strayed back to the battery readout. It had dropped to twenty-three percent.

Her attention shifted to Neil as he spoke, "Doctor, I think we're here."

Eyes focusing through the windshield, Miriam Segen scanned the parking area. The other team's passenger van was positioned along the side of the road ahead of them. It looked as if their own van had been parked in front of a clump of trees not far away. KT must have positioned it in the shade, smart.

Doctor Segen gestured toward the first van. "Park in front of them."

Miriam opened her door before Neil pulled the truck to a stop. She bolted from the vehicle, aiming for the truck bed. As he cut the engine, the clearing fell into darkness. Miriam snagged her light from her pocket and brought it up to illuminate their supplies. Neil joined her from the other side of the vehicle as she was taking inventory.

"Here," she said, handing him the light. Segen reached over the tailgate and grabbed one of the nylon bags. She unzipped the bag to check its contents. Not seeing what she'd been looking for, she re-zipped it and set it aside.

"What are you looking for?" Neil asked, following her movement with the light.

Segen stretched over the side of the truck, reaching for another bag. "I'm looking for the tents," she explained. As she lifted it, she could tell by the weight it was the wrong bag. "We don't need to bring everything with us tonight." She set the bag down and moved around Neil to the other side of the truck. She felt the cold metal through her shirt as she leaned into the back of the truck again. Miriam grabbed another bag, then dragged it to the wheel well.

As she pulled the zipper along the length of the bag, she revealed the tents she'd been looking for. Miriam Segen shot one more glance over the truck's bed, then turned to the north.

"Come on," she urged.

CHAPTER 49

Henry Blake
9:27 pm

The warm glow from the sun had vanished hours before, leaving Henry Blake lost, completely and utterly turned around. It was all they needed, to be roaming through the forest at night, with a creature stalking them. Henry spun, trying to take in his surroundings. His heart pounded as his eyes strained to spot any recognizable landmarks. Save for the headlamp, set at its lowest setting and hopefully dim enough to avoid notice, the surrounding woods were black. He'd been forced to choose between having visibility and being visible. Between seeing and being seen.

Their flight from the van earlier had led them to the northwest toward the river. It had been his intent, before their impromptu nap, to search for escape along the water. However, he'd had to adapt when he and Zayne had awoken so late in the day. The approaching darkness had reduced the likelihood of finding a way out along the river. *How could I have been so stupid, allowing us to fall asleep?* With dusk fast approaching, he'd attempted to lead them back to the van again. That had been the plan, anyway. It had been a good, solid plan.

Henry sighed… *the plans of mice and men.*

Unfortunately, it hadn't worked out as well as he would have liked. He had somehow missed the van completely as they'd crashed through the brush in the dwindling light. As far as he could figure, they'd gone too far to the east; he'd led them too far to the east. It was all his fault. He had this young girl, injured and hobbling, trusting him to get her to safety. Loyally following him as they traipsed through the woods. He couldn't fail her. Would not allow himself to fail.

As the last of the light faded, it had forced him to reevaluate his plans yet again. They might have still been able to reach the van, but the darkness lowered the odds markedly. Nor could they approach the van stealthily enough to recon the area and still be able to flee if necessary. There was the possibility that the creature would still be loitering around the vehicle. As it had been the last place they'd glimpsed the beast, his fear felt justified. He still might have chanced it if he'd known the precise location of the van.

At that point, the only other place he could think of, which might provide even the slimmest amount of safety, was the cave. Spending the night out in the open hadn't appealed to him, nor did he think it possible for them to survive. He'd headed north for the cliff. At least, he thought he'd headed north. Now he wasn't so sure. Several minutes after they'd turned north, clouds had rolled across the sky, making it impossible to continue to check the stars.

He'd continued to wander through the forest for what seemed like hours. It had to have been hours. Every direction appeared the same. Dark and foreboding, the woods were alive with the various sounds of the night. Nocturnal animals scurried through the forest and insects buzzed. Every new sound evoked images of the beast. He'd spent the last several hours positive that it would break from cover at any moment.

Henry looked back at Zayne. She was doing her best to keep up. He gave her a warm smile. She was such a trooper. He'd certainly underestimated her at the beginning of the trip. She was blindly following him. She must know he was lost, had to sense it, yet she didn't complain. Her injury slowed their pace. Which wasn't altogether a bad thing. Without an exact heading, speed was inconsequential. However, being in motion was the right call. But now he had to figure out where they were, as well as the direction they should travel.

He came to a stop and dropped to a knee, then switched off his light. Zayne plopped down next to him. Aside from wanting a break, Henry needed to figure out their next move. *North, we need to go north.* They were both his responsibility. He shut his eyes and filled his lungs with the clean forest air. He let the sounds of the forest wash over and through him. *I have to stop reacting. I need to come up with a plan.* Henry tried to think of a way. Knowing the direction moss grew had proved useless, he wished he'd had one of the compasses when he'd fled. *Ran away like a coward.* If the sky hadn't been overcast—

"That's the great bear," Zayne murmured beside him.

His eyes snapped open as he jerked his head toward the young girl. She was staring at the sky above them. The clouds had parted, revealing a glimpse of the exact stars they needed to see. Henry rose to his feet to get a closer look, prompting Zayne to rise as well. He traced the outside edge of the big dipper's bowl with his eyes, following the so-called 'pointer stars', Merak and Dubhe, toward the North Star. While the star itself wasn't visible through the cloud cover, it didn't matter. They now had a bearing on the northern cliffs, which would lead them to the cave.

He leaned over and kissed the top of Zayne's head. "You're brilliant," he praised. Henry flipped the headlamp back to its lowest setting. He ignored Zayne's look of wide-eyed surprise and led her to the north.

CHAPTER 50

Dr. Miriam Segen
9:41 pm

Miriam Segen led her grad student through the pitch-dark woods, a single light piercing the night. Her beam simultaneously sliced a corridor through the darkness ahead and killed her night vision, plunging the surrounding forest into deeper darkness. The contrast between the well-lit plant life ahead and the dim waves of green that radiated away created an eerie effect.

Spooky. Segen shuttered.

It had only been once they were well on their way when she'd realized she didn't know exactly where the campsite was. With everything that had gone on, between the car troubles and the rushed preparations, Segen hadn't thoroughly considered the problem before. As she drifted through the woods, she'd concluded that heading to the caves would be her best chance to find everyone.

Segen groaned and hit redial. She'd expected the other group to answer their cell phones. The call went to voicemail yet again, and she cursed. Why wasn't he answering? Was Teddy's phone broken, or dead? Did the cell service cut out deeper into the forest? Why had she taken her group's phones? It had seemed like such a marvelous idea at the time. All she'd wanted to do was avoid leaks. She hadn't wanted the site contaminated by two-bit treasure hunters. Or people that enjoyed unexplored caves. Or rival archaeologists. There was no telling what damage could have been done if the word had gotten out.

It doesn't matter, she sighed

During their conversation earlier, Professor Stone had suggested that Segen and her group ought to head straight for the caves once they arrived, and he'd sent her a digital image of a crude hand-drawn map. If it hadn't been for that map, she and Neil would have likely been forced to sleep by the vehicles. She glanced at the map on her phone. The dot indicating their progress through the woods was slowly approaching the edge of the valley and the spot she'd marked. As it was hand drawn, the map didn't show the exact location of the cave. If she'd read the map right, cliffs surround almost the whole valley. All she needed to do, was find and follow the northern cliff face. She knew she would come across the cave, eventually.

Hopefully, there would still be someone near the cave. Segen glanced at the time displayed on the phone. *At this late hour, that might be a forlorn hope.* Everyone should have already settled down for the night. Stone had planned to either be waiting at the cave himself, or at least have some of his students there. If all went as intended, her group had rendezvoused with his at the cave and been shown the way to the campsite. But that had been hours before, and she couldn't have expected them to wait around all night.

A rustling sound prompted Segen to pan the light to illuminate the surrounding woods again. She had been hearing movement emanating from just beyond the edge of her light. In the last few minutes, the noises had seemed to occur more often.

Jordan Adler
10:16 pm

A piercing scream drifted through the thin passage, snapping Jordan out of her reverie. As she whipped her head toward the source of the noise, she sprung to her feet. She snatched her hammer from the floor and stepped toward the fault passage. Jamie grabbed her arm, arresting her forward motion.

"Don't go," Jamie pleaded. "Please. It's not safe."

Jordan placed her free hand over her friend's and squeezed it. "I have to at least try," she replied, giving Jamie a resigned shrug. "I have to."

"Try to be careful then."

Jordan peeled Jamie's hand from her forearm.

With a determined sigh, Jordan squeezed her way into the fault passage and wormed her way toward the cave opening. After slipping from the tiny crack in the wall, Jordan sprinted into the Shrine. The objects scattered along the floor caught her attention once more. Called to her. Most of the weapons were incomplete, the dusting of spearheads and arrowheads outnumbered the selection of whole weapons. However, there were a few complete weapons to choose from. Jordan shot a quick look toward the entrance, then made a beeline for the collection of objects.

Knowing she shouldn't, Jordan plucked one item from the cave floor. It was a club carved from jawbone; its handle wrapped with old leather. She had to at least try to defend herself and the others. None of these artifacts would matter if they died; one object wouldn't be a great loss. It wasn't like she would break it or anything, *well not on purpose*. She had almost convinced herself that time. It was too late to change her mind, anyway; she was already moving for the cave entrance.

Jordan rushed through the passage. She reached the cave entrance at a run and leapt over the boulder to the ground. This was probably the stupidest thing she'd ever done, including the time she'd gotten her *Where's Waldo* tattoo. She landed with a grunt, pain shooting up her shins.

As her eyes took in the scene, Jordan saw two people she didn't recognize. Back to the cave, a woman in her mid-to-late fifties cradled a young man in one arm while holding off the beast with a stun gun clutched in her other hand. The guy, somewhere in his early thirties, had a gash along his arm which bled freely. The beast had been pacing in front of the pair, likely wondering what to make of the electronic device.

When she'd flown from the cave, the thing had stopped its pacing and shifted its attention to her. The beast hunkered lower to the ground and coiled its hind legs under its body, ready to pounce. Bathed in light from her headlamp, the beast displayed telltale signs of aggression. It studied Jordan for a moment, then returned its attention to the woman and her odd weapon. The woman shot a glance over her shoulder and scanned Jordan before snapping her eyes back to the creature.

"I fear I've only angered it," she warned.

Jordan aimed her light onto its face, into the animal's eyes. The animal let out a low growl. The light impeding its vision agitated the creature. Stiff ears lay flat on its head and its fur stood on end. Eyes narrowed and dilated; the beast's stiff whiskers angled back toward its face. The beast slunk back a few strides, then resumed its pacing. It strode back and forth in an arc in front of them.

Taking short, shallow breaths, Jordan inched closer to the duo, her eyes fixed on the predator. The beast flicked its gaze in her direction and then let out another low, menacing growl. Jordan tightened her fingers on the worn leather, shifting the club slightly in her hand. The creature's attention remained mostly focused on the older woman, more specifically the item in her hand. Jordan had a hunch that the animal would attack soon. Her mind whirred as she tried to figure out why she had rushed out into danger again.

Oh right, Jordan reminded herself, *it's the right thing to do.*

Her suspicions proved true, as the beast lunged. It launched itself forward and lifted its front two legs from the ground, extending its torso. With a sweep of its massive paw, the creature went for the stun gun. The woman jerked her arm back, trying

271

to avoid the blow, but she was too late. While she avoided most of the swat, the impact still sent the plastic weapon spinning away from them.

Seeing a chance, however slim, Jordan sprung forward. Elbow bent, she swung her weapon around behind her and up in a circular motion while stepping toward the beast. A move learned from many, many hours playing Wii tennis. The bone club lanced toward the beast as it shifted in preparation to strike out with another, and likely more fatal blow. At the last moment, the beast seemed to notice Jordan's intent, and the thing tried to dart away from the weapon's trajectory. It was fast, very fast. The creature almost avoided the blow entirely. But Jordan's bone club grazed the creature and tore into its hide.

Jordan watched in astonishment as the beast's skin began to smoke and then sizzle. Before her eyes, scorch marks appeared, running along the length of the wound and expanding a further inch to either side of the ripped skin. *What the hell?* The beast looked as surprised as Jordan felt as the thing let out a pained yowl and lunged away. The way the thing tucked in on itself, it appeared as if the beast might have been preparing to pounce. Jordan followed the creature's eyes with her own as they darted from the weapon, then to her, and back to the weapon. After a moment, a deafening roar escaped from the beast's throat and it sprang into action. *This is it; I'm going to die.*

Except she didn't die, nor had the beast charged. *It's running away. Why is it running away?* Mesmerized by what she'd just witnessed, Jordan stared after the beast as it flew up the hill, watching until it disappeared over the rise. What just happened? Jordan's eye fell to the weapon in her hand. Why did it run? What happened to its skin?

A moan escaped from the young man, drawing her attention. Jordan shifted her gaze to the two strangers for a moment before returning her eyes to the ancient bone club. *What just happened?*

"Is he ok?" Jordan asked distractedly.

"The creature got him good," the other woman responded.

After a moment, Jordan returned her gaze to the woman.

"Are you the associate, Professor Stone called this afternoon?"

"Yeah, I'm Dr. Miriam Segen and this is my teacher's assistant, Neil." Segen's eyes scanned the young man's wounds, evaluating their severity before looking in Jordan's direction.

"Where did you get that?" Dr. Segen asked with interest, eye resting on the implement in Jordan's hand.

She looked down at her weapon again. Eyes flicking from the club to Miriam and then back to the club. Jordan shrugged as she hooked a thumb over her shoulder and pointed back to the cave mouth. "In there," she murmured. Jordan's eyes raked the bone weapon. *What was that? How did my club burn that thing? Is it poisoned?*

Segen stood, drawing Jordan's attention once again. "It was in the cave?" Segen asked. Her eyes were unfocused, as if she were puzzling out a great mystery. "That's an authentic Native American war club. An actual artifact from the cave…"

Jordan felt a pang of guilt as the woman kept bringing up the fact that she'd disturbed the site. "I know I shouldn't have grabbed it, but I just thought…" she trailed off as the woman held up a hand. *She didn't have to shush me like that.*

Jordan watched a look of dawning comprehension filter into the other woman's eyes. "You misunderstand me, young lady," Segen said, excitement building in her voice. "Teddy said it was like a shrine," Miriam continued. *Teddy?* "A shrine to hunters, or for hunters. What constitutes a shrine?" she quizzed, ever the teacher.

"It's a holy place. A place where they might go to… to…" Jordan's eyes moved back and forth. Clarity snapped into focus. Jordan's mind summoned images of an old medicine man, fanning a feather over a burning bundle of sage. The smell of sacred herbs burning as the smoke billowed over the implements. A chanted blessing. More than that, a series of medicine men, over the centuries, consecrating the artifacts. Jordan's eyes widened. Over the years the objects were blessed, countless times, by many people. "To bless them," she finished with a murmur.

"Exactly!"

"And over the years, the centuries," Jordan speculated, with an encouraging nod from the other woman, "the blessings soaked into the objects... seeped into them?" she inquired.

"That would be my guess as well," Segen agreed.

A noise from behind her caused Jordan to swing around. Jamie appeared in the cave mouth, limping and out of breath.

"Oh, thank God! You're still alive," Jamie blurted, surprise evident in her voice.

CHAPTER 51

Jamie Long
10:37 pm

Jamie was having a difficult time wrapping her mind around what Jordan and Dr. Segen had told her. According to them, the artifacts in the sanctuary had somehow absorbed an undercurrent of energy from decades, or rather centuries, of prayers and rituals. Jamie wasn't sure that she could believe in the power of ancient rituals, or the power of prayer.

After years of Sunday morning sermons and Wednesday night lessons, years of being preached at and lectured, it was difficult to reconcile her beliefs. It would be comforting to believe that some supreme being could love her unconditionally; had formed her to be unique. It was a nice thought, and part of her had always wanted to trust it.

While there was a certain longing in her soul to have faith, there were certain things she couldn't balance. So many horrible things had been done in the name of religion, from people claiming to speak for this god or that. Wars had been raged; innocents slaughtered. The poor had been fed and clothed, orphans housed; there was so much good too. Followers from this faith or that, spewing hate or spreading love. Her new friend

Jordan, who she now trusted implicitly, could be condemned for her preferences, or else embraced for her generosity of spirit. It varied from church to church, person to person.

The earth itself added to her doubt. Throughout her years, she'd been exposed to sermons and debates arguing for or against both creationism and evolution. She never understood those individuals that argued that the earth was created only six thousand years ago. Their argument, based on the literal six days of creation, followed by the genealogy and other events in Genesis. That couldn't be right. Could it?

From all the evidence, the planet had been formed some four billion years ago. She had studied rock strata dating back hundreds of millions of years. She'd examined cave formations that would have taken millennia to form, fossils that supported the theory of evolution, as well as plants and animals so beautiful, so majestic that they could have never been formed by mistake or random chance.

To be a believer, did you have to believe everything? Was that even possible?

Jamie gave her head a sudden shake, snapping her focus back to the moment. She couldn't know all the answers and was far from figuring out the mysteries of the universe. Her eyes shot over to the new arrivals. Neil's wounds were deeper than hers; the creature got him good. Jordan and Jamie had helped them into the cave, and Dr. Segen had treated the young man's injuries. Dr. Segen had dressed wounds in the field before and stopped the bleeding quickly. After cleaning his wounds, she'd fetched two shirts from his bag, ripping one into strips to bind his slashes and snugging the other around that.

She lifted her new shirt and eyed her own duct tape covered injuries. Jordan had done an impressive job, but Jamie wished they'd had some clean cloths with them when they'd dressed her wounds. She released the cloth and let it resettle on her abdomen. Jamie had shucked her torn and bloody tank top when Dr. Segen had given her a tee that matched her own. *Pink? Really?* Not just pink, hot pink.

The group hadn't ventured all the way back into Jordan's

Gallery, choosing instead to hole up in the Shrine. Jordan alone had nipped through the tiny passage to snatch their supplies and spread the work lights around the Shrine. With the artifacts supposedly imbued with power, she understood the other's desire to be near them, but she couldn't deny that she'd felt safer before. If they were in Jordan's Gallery, then the beast would be forced to stalk through the whole cave before it got to them. Jamie sighed. As it was… *What if they're wrong?*

Jamie glanced over to the cave entrance again. Jordan had gone to grab something from the supply tent. After recognizing the power infused in the artifacts, they'd been discussing the best ways to create more weapons. In the middle of the conversation, Jordan had jumped to her feet and just shot toward the opening, tossing back an 'I'll be right back.' Jordan should've known better, *that's definitely not something you wanna say in this kind of situation.* Maybe Jamie should have accompanied her. What if something happened? What did Jordan need so badly, anyway?

Just as Jamie was about to leap to her feet and head outside, Jordan appeared in the passageway. Still clutching her bone club in one hand, Jordan carried a duffle bag.

"What took you so long?" Jamie grumbled. "I was getting worried."

Jordan narrowed her eyes. "I was only gone like three minutes," she said.

"No, it was much longer than that," Jamie argued.

Jordan strode across the room, then slipped the strap from her shoulder. "Really? It didn't seem—"

"It had to have been at least four, maybe five," Jamie countered.

The bag fell with a clunk. "Oh, five whole minutes, huh?" Jordan said, breaking into a smile.

"Yeah." Jamie nodded.

"Well, I didn't mean to worry you. I didn't realize I'd been out of your sight for so long," Jordan beamed.

Jamie tilted her head. "Just, don't let it happen again."

Smile still lighting her face, Jordan shook her head as she bent over and extracted another work light from the bag. She aimed the light at the artifacts and flipped the switch.

As the objects were bathed in more light, Jordan turned to Jamie. "What type of weapon do you want?"

The Beast
10:40 pm

A new couple had shown up in the black of the night, hand-held torches throwing light that cut through the darkness. Just like the bright lights in the cave. How could they do that? How did they have that much power? What kind of magic did they possess?

She'd watched from a distance as the duo waded through the woods. Until she realized where they were going. As they approached the cave, she attacked. She'd gone for the man first, him being the biggest, the most dangerous to get. But it had been the woman and the magic lightning box that had driven her away. When it'd zapped her, she hadn't known what to make of it. It hurt more than anything she'd experienced, including all the injuries she had earlier that day. The shock had flowed through her.

As if that wasn't enough, one of the young ones flew from the cave, armed with a sunbeam that blinded her and the young woman had held one of the ancient weapons. She had thought it would be easy to take them, but when she attacked, she felt pain like no other. Worse even than the arrow and the axe and the electric box.

How had the girl done that? What powers did she have? She had to retreat; to try to figure it out. They wouldn't go anywhere, not at night. She wouldn't let them. She conceded the cave to them, for now; it would always be there. She had to figure out how to get them away from the weapons. It would be simple enough, lure them out alone. Take them down one by one.

CHAPTER 52

Henry Blake
10:56 pm

The beast was out there, prowling through the forest, just out of sight. Henry could feel it watching them. Tracking them. Stalking them. It had shown up several times in the last little while and appeared in a different location each time. The creature was taunting them, waiting for the right moment to strike. The night had brought with it a sense of anxiety more severe than he'd ever experienced.

All day long, he'd kept his senses on high alert for any sign of the beast. His mind had been cognizant of the possibility that the creature could be on the other side of a swath of trees, or just over the next rise, painfully aware that it might simply pop up out of nowhere. From his first sight of the animal at the campsite, he'd felt and heard it everywhere. The day had been a nightmare of half-heard noises and partially seen movement.

However, this was different; both Zayne and he had glimpsed the animal, the monster, in the last several minutes. While before, the sounds of brush shifting and limbs breaking had been in his head, Henry was now positive that the creature was actively hunting them. Pursuing them. Sometimes materializing in front or behind, to the left or right, it never seemed to show up in the same place twice. It shadowed them, keeping to the edges of their vision. Staying just outside the range of his light.

Why hadn't it attacked yet? It knew where they were.

He'd toggled the light to full power some time ago. There had been a vain hope that the light would frighten the beast away. No such luck. It wasn't afraid of the light; he'd illuminated the beast a few times without reaction. The creature kept showing up, but it always kept its distance. Could it be afraid of the axe for some reason? Did that make any sense? For the life of him, he couldn't figure why that would be. It couldn't be the axe. *It's just an axe.* Whoever had died at the camp had been holding the thing. It didn't make sense.

A part of his mind screamed for him to take Zayne and just make a run for it. A mad dash to safety, or at the very least cover. His rational mind, however, knew that would be a mistake. While the creature's current method of stalking them put him on edge, he didn't want to risk it. *If we run, we won't make it far.* Eons of predatory instinct would drive the animal to attack. To see them as prey. Countless hours of Animal Planet had taught him that much at least. On the other hand, you're not supposed to turn your back to a cat either, are you? He gave a jerk of his head; it didn't matter. Continuing was their only real choice.

The creature appeared on Henry's left. His heart skipped a beat. *God, not again.* It was closer this time, prompting them to shift further to the right. Every time the beast showed itself, they had changed their course to avoid it. His eyes widened with sudden understanding. The beast was herding them. The thing would materialize to get them to change course, then disappear again.

Oh God, it's leading us exactly where it wants us to be, and there's nothing I can do about it. His mind spun, trying to come up with options, any options. Nothing came to mind, however. He was certain they wouldn't be able to outrun the creature. And trying to find a place to hide when it was so close was pointless.

Zayne Stone
11:12 pm

With the beast continuously prowling around them, popping up and vanishing, Zayne Stone should have been paralyzed with dread. Her whole day had been filled with waves of panic. Though still absolutely terrified, she had Henry. Henry Blake was holding her hand, protecting her, leading her to safety. With him beside her, she still had hope that they might survive. He wouldn't let anything happen to her. He had the axe. He'd cut the monster in half if it came too close.

Ever since he'd found her hiding in the woods, he had tried to keep her calm, to soothe her frayed nerves. And he had been so kind. Henry was so chill; at least he had been, anyway. In the last several minutes, she had detected a difference in his expressions and mannerisms. Where before, despite knowing he was tense, Henry had suppressed much of his fear. Now, however, the fear was seeping out.

Trampling through the thick woods was much more difficult at night. While the larger trees were easy to avoid, the dense undergrowth caught at her ankles and feet, making it feel as if the very plants were against her. The small beam of light emanating from the headlamp atop Henry's head only cut a narrow path through the darkness in front of them. As the beam traveled further from its source, the light dissipated to the sides, leaving only the barest hint of illumination to the right and left. She could just barely make out his features most of the time. Occasionally, the light would reflect off a section of leaves or a clump of bushes and highlight his face.

Zayne shot a furtive glance to Henry's face. Agitated, his eyes were wide and darted to every fresh sound or movement. Why was he getting so scared? What could he see that she couldn't?

Had he seen something? Noticed something?

As the beast again appeared in front of them, Henry clutched tighter to her hand and pulled her further to the right.

Was that it? Had Henry figured out what the creature was doing? It hadn't attacked them, hadn't even come close to them.

It must be afraid of the light or the axe. Surely it didn't want to get hit with the axe. That had to be it. *Right?*

Then why had Henry become so afraid? She was missing something. There was some part of the picture she just couldn't see. Fear prevented her from voicing any questions.

The surrounding forest began to sprout various rock formations. At first, it was just the occasional boulder, big and small, laying atop the soil. There was also the odd outcrop of rock jutting from the earth. The further they traveled, the more frequently boulders and rock outcrops sprouted from the ground. Before long, they were forced to weave over and around an increasing amount of the formations.

They came to a massive stone outcropping. Taller than Henry, it stretched over the earth in both directions for several hundred feet. As he glanced left and right, scanning its natural structure, Henry's light panned across the uneven surface of the rock. Tears of frustration leaked from the corners of Zayne's eyes. *Why can't we ever catch a break?*

Henry Blake
11:18 pm

His eyes darted back and forth as he bit his lip. Henry's mind spun while he examined their options. The two obvious choices would be left or right. With the beast herding them, he'd lost his sense of direction again, so either way would be a gamble. He shot a look to the heavens. Clouds blotted out most of the sky again; he'd get no help there.

"Which way should we go?" Zayne blurted beside him, jerking his mind back to the moment. "Left, or right?"

Henry's eyes darted back and forth again, then he cocked his head up. "Neither," he responded, pointing to the top of the rock outcrop, "let's go over." It was as good a direction as any, and there was a chance, no matter how slim, it would foil the beast's plans for them. He moved forward to the edge of the cliff and waved for her to join him. "Come on," he urged.

"Ok," Zayne agreed, stepping toward him.

He leaned the axe against the stone outcropping and prepared to help Zayne over the obstacle. He could easily boost the girl to the top of the ledge and then climb over. Henry lowered his center of gravity and brought his hands together. Then intertwined his fingers, ready to give Zayne a boost.

Zayne let out a stifled scream and stumbled back. His head whipped around, and he saw that the creature had materialized atop the ledge. Henry ducked down and lost his balance. He slid against the stone wall and landed with a jolt on one knee. Henry snatched the axe and lurched away from the beast. He slid in beside Zayne and clutched her hand in one of his. Henry lifted the axe higher with his right hand, which caused the beast to settle its weight onto its haunches and elicited a slight growl.

When she shot a look to his face, the light from his headlamp made it easy to see the panic flooding Zayne's eyes. He took in the beast on the ledge, allowed his gaze to dart to the left and right, then snap back to the beast. Henry knew that the axe wouldn't do them much good, but he wasn't in a hurry to prove it to the animal. It was important to keep every advantage they had. He tried in vain to calculate the next move. Any move really. Was this it? Was this where the beast had been leading them?

It hadn't attacked yet, and while they were still alive there was hope, so he had to make a choice. Should they go left, or right? With a sudden jolt, he realized there was a third direction; back. He doubted they'd be allowed to head back the way they came, but it might be worth a shot. The decision was yanked from his grasp as the beast leapt down. It landed to their right side, a good fifteen feet from the rock outcrop, simultaneously snatching two of their options. Henry took it as a sign and tugged Zayne in the opposite direction.

Clutching Zayne's hand, Henry led them along the side of the rock face. The beast had shown up, yet again, to drive them where it wanted. Herding them like sheep to the slaughter. Henry wasn't keen to be shepherded by the beast, but couldn't see any other alternatives at the moment. He had to protect

Zayne.

Henry decided to test the theory. As they continued in their flight, he subtly angled away from the cliff. Just as he'd expected, the beast took shape to their left, yet again forcing them to change direction. Damn, the creature was patient, calculating.

Henry shifted their course back toward the outcropping as he considered their limited options. They could continue to follow the beast's instructions, and while not yet hazardous, they would eventually arrive exactly where it wanted them to be. Henry had a strong hunch that wherever it was leading them wouldn't be all rainbows and puppies. They could try to make a break for it. But even if they split up, which he was loath to do, neither of them was likely to make it far.

The final of the terrible choices would be to stand and fight. He might be able to hold the beast off for a few minutes, *long enough for Zayne to escape,* but he doubted it. The beast would rip him in two, just like it did the previous owner of the axe, leaving it free to pursue Zayne. Part of him longed to make a stand, but it just didn't seem likely to work, and he had to protect Zayne. As it was, with the creature leading them exactly where it liked, Henry didn't see any point in resisting just yet. There would come a time when he'd have to, *probably sooner rather than later.*

What was he going to do? Zayne, he had to protect Zayne. He couldn't let anything happen to her, wouldn't. Henry squeezed her hand in his. He would figure something out. *No matter what, no matter the cost, I have to save this little girl.*

CHAPTER 53

Henry Blake
11:47 pm

The beast had continued to herd them along for a while until the stone outcrop split. A natural slope had been cut between the two sides of the outcrop, which allowed the creature to force them up a slight hill. It appeared to be leading them in a direct course now. The thing showed up each time he tried to veer to either side, always driving them back. The beast would also show up behind them every time their pace started to lag. Tired of the animal continually popping up, he resolved to see where it wanted them to go.

They came to another outcrop, jutting up from the ground. This one had a fissure split into the rock, which formed a narrow tunnel. Henry came to an abrupt halt, jerking Zayne to a stop beside him.

"Ow," Zayne murmured.

Henry's eyes raked the outcrop to either side, then returned to the narrow passage. A cave. The beast's lair. It had been leading them to its lair this whole time.

"A cave," Zayne revealed.

"Yeah," Henry agreed. *Why was it leading us to its lair? Stupid question.*

Henry released the girl's hand and swung the axe across his chest, gripping it in both hands. He let his eyes drift around the whole area.

"Do we go inside?" Zayne asked.

That wouldn't be my first choice. "Dunno," Henry replied. *Can't scare the girl.* "Maybe."

No, he was absolutely positive he didn't want to go inside.

But where else was there? Where could they go?

A movement behind him brought Henry spinning around to find the beast to their rear once more. "Damn it all to hell," he mumbled. When he shifted the axe in his hands it elicited another low growl from the animal. Though wary of the weapon, the creature failed to retreat. *Dammit, what now?* It started to pace back and forth, slowly getting closer with each pass, wanting them to enter the cave.

Again, Henry saw no pleasant options. It was obviously a trap, but what else could they do? They couldn't run, nor could they fight. That left hiding. They might be able to find a place to hide in the cave. He doubted it, but anything was possible. While he was still alive, as long as he had breath, he would keep trying.

"Yeah, go inside."

Henry lifted one hand from the axe and used it to nudge Zayne toward the opening in the rock face. Though reluctant, she moved to the tunnel and dropped to her knees. Henry snatched the light from his head and handed it to the girl. After she slipped the lamp onto her head, Zayne scurried into the passage while he kept an eye on the beast.

Zayne let out a startled squeak a few moments later. "What is it?" he called, glancing into the opening, then returning his gaze to the beast. "Zayne are you ok?" he choked after a moment without an answer. Had something happened? Had the trap sprung sooner than he'd imagined?

"I... I found Michael," she quavered, "he's... well, he's dead."

Henry let out a groan. That explained the bloodstain in the camp. If Michael was dead, what happened to the others? Could other members of the expedition be injured or, God forbid, dead? Henry attempted to push the growing panic from his mind. He was only partially successful. There was no time to mourn, no time to worry.

Henry Blake glanced back into the hole, then dropped to the ground and darted into the passage on hands and knees. As he wriggled through the small opening, he expected a sharp pain in his legs at any time. It never came. The tunnel angled downward and was shallower than he'd expected, so it only took him a few seconds to clear the passage.

He only took a fleeting look at the cave around him before he spun back to its entrance. The beast was peering in from the opening of the cave, barely visible in the dim light of the moon. He shuddered, that was creepy, it was just staring at him. After a moment it slunk away. His ears strained to follow its movements. And he caught the slight sound of it, pacing right outside the cave.

As the beast seemed to be leaving them alone for the moment, Henry turned to examine the rest of the cave. Zayne was standing off to the side, staring down at what remained of Michael's body. The light washed over the corpse, highlighting a gash in its torso where his organs had been removed. Henry stepped over to the girl and spun her away from the morbid scene, pulling her into a swift embrace. There was no reason for her to see that.

She didn't try to look back around as he slipped the lamp from her head and snugged the elastic strap around his own. He grabbed her shoulders and pulled her further away from the body. As they moved, Henry's eyes darted around, studying the chamber. The ceiling above only rose a few inches over his head and stayed at the same level throughout most of the room. From the narrow passage, both sides of the room spread wide, and the floor tilted down slightly for a couple of yards before coming to a drop-off. On either side of that ledge, natural ramps led down into the rest of the cavern.

Henry shot a quick look back to the entrance before he stepped over to the ledge, Zayne in tow. Down each ramp and along the sides of the cavern, the sedimentary rock matched the walls and ceiling. Directly below the drop-off, in the middle of the room, was a swimming pool-sized area of darker sediment and chunks of, what appeared to be, asphalt. There were massive fissures and clefts in the darker stone. It looked as if something had burst out, or perhaps clawed its way out.

Eyes darting back and forth, he tried to process the new information. It had to have been the animal, the beast. This is where it had come from. It had to be. Henry shuffled Zayne down one slope, coming to a stop next to the fractured asphalt. He stooped to grab a chunk of the fragmented stone. Henry brought the stone to his nose and gave it a deep sniff. It was asphalt, all right. His eyes danced over the shattered stone as he took in every detail. It had to have been—

"There's another body," Zayne blurted, breaking his train of thought.

Henry spun, his gaze darted to the young girl, and then followed her line of sight. Zayne was looking in the opposite direction. He studied the remains. The body was that of a woman. She had long black hair and a pale brown skin tone. Dressed in olive-colored pants, her tan shirt had a yellow badge embroidered onto the left breast. The name sewn onto the right side read 'Hernandez'. She too was missing her organs. While he couldn't tell how long she'd been there, he assumed it was longer than Michael. The cooler temperature of the cave along with the missing organs must have slowed her body's decomposition.

He spun Zayne away from the body and bent down in front of her. "I think I know where the Wampus Cat came from," Henry exclaimed, attempting to divert her attention.

"Huh?" she murmured. Zayne's eyes drifted to him as she tried to regain focus.

"The Wampus Cat, I think I know where it came from."

"Where?" Zayne asked, turning her head to gaze over her shoulder.

"No, look here," Henry urged, bringing her attention back to himself. Her eyes met his, then followed the handle of the axe as he pointed it toward his revelation. "It's asphalt."

"Like a road?" she inquired, clearly confused. "How did a road get down here?"

"Well, yes and no," he stated.

"Huh?" she asked again. By the deepening look of confusion on her face, he could tell he'd obviously cleared everything up.

"They do sometimes make roads from crushed asphalt, but this isn't a road. I think it is what's left of a tar pit," he explained.

"Like in Los Angeles?" she asked.

"Exactly, the tar bubbled up from deep in the earth and into this cave. Thousands of years ago, someone lured the creature here and trapped it. At least that appears to be what happened, according to the last part of the story we found. In the intervening time, the tar pit must have dried out."

"But how is it still alive?" she contested. "If it got stuck, it would have died like all the fossils they've found at La Brea."

"Ok, well, I'm not sure, but I think it was the magic that made her," he guessed.

Zayne got a stubborn look on her face. "Magic isn't real. It's—"

"Is it?" Henry cut in. "After what we've been through today, do you still believe that?"

Zayne scrunched her nose and brought her lips to the corner of her mouth. "I guess not," she wavered, "but how did it get out?"

Henry thought for a moment before replying, "My guess would be time, or maybe an earthquake, but I can't be sure."

A rumbling from the cave's entrance drew his attention. He stared across the room only to see gravel shift as the beast slid into the cave. *Not again!* He cursed, bolted to his feet, and brought Zayne behind him.

CHAPTER 54

Jordan Adler
Sunday, September 2nd
12:05 am

Once she scaled the lip of the gulley, Jordan sprinted for cover. As she dropped into a crouch behind an old oak, she extinguished her light with a press of a button. Jordan strained to pick up any sign of movement in the low light as her eyes tried to sweep the trees around her. Despite the feeling of a massive hand gripping her heart, her pulse raced. In search of materials for their weapons, they'd been forced to leave the relative security of the caves.

While her eyes proved useless in the limited visibility, her ears strained to identify any movement in the dense woods. Aside from uneven respiration from Jamie and herself, all she detected was a chorus of chirps and screeches expected in the night. After several minutes, Jordan switched her headlamp to its lowest setting and glanced at her companion.

With Jamie beside her, she felt just a bit safer. At a little over six feet tall, Jamie cut an imposing figure, regardless of her injury. Elbow tucked into her side; her hand cradled her injured abdomen. Jamie still hobbled around in a shuffling gait, painfully aware of her right hip.

Blade covered in rust and pitted from age; the antique tomahawk clutched in Jamie's hand was a temporary measure until they could construct her a decent weapon. Many of the artifacts had once been sturdy weapons, but years of neglect had weakened them. What little metal there was had oxidized, which left dull edges and coats of rust. While some objects still had their wooden handles, the time had weakened the material or else worn away their bindings. They would need proper weapons if the beast reappeared. Otherwise, they'd risk a broken tool in the middle of an attack.

Jordan examined the growth around them for a suitable tree or branch. The woods in front of her lacked the thick vegetation present in many other places. In the light from her headlamp, she could make out a similar mix of brown and gray spreading throughout the whole of the woods. A jumble of decayed leaves, broken branches, acorn husks, and stones spread out to the edges of her light.

Jamie had opted to construct a spear from one of the large spearheads. With a longer reach, it would contrast well with Jordan's bone club. Her eyes raked the weapon for what had to be the hundredth time. Made from a solid piece of jawbone, likely from a horse or buffalo, the club was a little over two feet long. The strips of worn leather wrapped around the handle almost seemed to disintegrate in her hand. Her inner archaeologist screamed for her to return the artifact, cursed her for disturbing the site, and railed at her for the desecration. One quick glimpse at her companion silenced most of her inner turmoil.

She hadn't taken it for monetary gain or even comfort. Only the threat of imminent harm had spurred her to wield it. Jordan had taken it to protect people and kept it for the same reason. *Nothing bad will happen to anyone else on this cursed nightmare of a trip.* Her hand tightened around the weapon.

"What do you think?" Jamie asked.

With a start, Jordan realized she'd missed what the other girl had been saying. "Sorry, what do I think about what?" she asked.

Jamie broke into a slight smile as her eyes lit up. "Oh nothing, I was just over here trying to figure out a way for us to survive," she smirked.

Jordan flashed her a contrite look. "Come up with anything good?"

"My grand plan so far is—" Jamie gave it a beat as she brought up both hands for the big reveal. "Are you ready for this?" At Jordan's nod, she went on. "Don't die."

A slight chuckle escaped her lips as Jordan blinked and shook her head. "Solid plan," she praised. "Any idea how we'd accomplish that?"

Jamie returned a muted shrug. "It's still in the early stages," she admitted as she gave Jordan an airy wave.

"What was it you were saying earlier?" she coaxed.

"I was wondering what you thought of using a sapling's trunk for my spear shaft, instead of scouring the woods for a branch of the right size," Jamie proposed. "Besides, I really don't want to climb any trees right now." This time her shrug was minuscule as she slightly rotated her open palm and flicked her thumb out.

Jordan considered the idea as her eyes lost focus. Questions popped into her mind about the durability of the younger wood. She knew saplings were terrible to use as firewood, but other than that she'd always overlooked them. They'd seen tons of saplings spread throughout the woods. Unfortunately, none were present. But Jordan thought she remembered a grove of the young trees nearby. It couldn't hurt to check it out.

"It's worth a shot," she conceded, "we can take a look." She cocked her head to the side and mashed her lips into a thin line. "If it does work, I think we should grab a few spares. It would be nice to have extra spears, just in case."

"That sounds good," Jamie agreed.

Side by side they crept through the forest. On the way, the crunch of leaves and twigs beneath their feet sounded as if fireworks were exploding around them. Jordan kept a constant eye peeled for any movement at the edges of the light.

Before long, they arrived at the spot she'd remembered. A massive oak tree had split at its base and fallen aside long before.

With the renewed source of sunlight, dozens of younger trees had popped up and vied for dominance. Some were still small, but others stretched well over Jamie's head.

Jordan grasped the trunk of a thin sapling with one hand. Her thumb and forefinger barely brushed together as they met around the wood. Satisfied with the diameter, she brought her other hand up and wrapped it around. With a grunt, Jordan tried to flex the wood and only gave the sapling a slight bend. She dropped to her knees in front of the tree and dug in her pants for the small knife Neil loaned her. As soon as Jordan pulled the black pocketknife out, she flicked a catch on one side, which expelled the blade to click into place. Jordan gazed at the metal for a moment. Serrated halfway down the blade, it should work well to cut the wood. It was a nice knife.

Jordan dragged the knife back and forth along the base of the tree, sawing through the young wood with its serrated edge. It took a bit of effort to cut through the sapling, but it was doable.

As the weight of the tree caused it to tip over, Jordan popped her head up and gazed at all the other trees around her. It looked like the perfect place to find what they needed. For once, luck seemed to be on their side.

Neil Singh
12:20 am

The sharp pain pulsing from Neil's upper arm kept his mind focused. Where he sat, between the cache of artifacts and the cave's first passage, he had an unrestricted view of the entry tunnel. Head against the wall, Neil kept an eye trained on the entryway. He gingerly cradled his injured limb against his chest, careful not to jostle it.

After Dr. Segen had dressed the wound, with the help of the two J's, Neil hadn't been in the best frame of mind to remember their names, she'd given him three Ibuprofen tablets. Not until a fresh pain blossomed in his chest, did he remember that

Ibuprofen gave him heartburn. *Just my luck.*

By that time, the two young ladies had left on their mission to gather supplies. More weapons would be essential; however, he wasn't sure how he felt about them going off on their own. Not that he'd wanted to join them. Nor was he given a say in the matter. Dr. Segen had seemed okay with it.

Armed with a small, stone dagger, Neil doubted he'd be any use in a fight anyhow. Injured as he was, he would be a burden, *a liability.* The doctor had grabbed an ancient wooden war club. Ragged as it was, the club appeared as if it might break at first impact, but he supposed it was better than nothing. Once the others got back, he would feel much better.

It was hard to believe that a Native American legend had actually slashed him. The beast. He could still see it in his mind, would likely never forget it. Not that he wouldn't try. He also saw many strong drinks in his future.

That creature had just popped up out of nowhere. So many legs. There had only been a slight rustle before the beast sprang from behind cover. If he hadn't lurched back as it slashed his arm, it might have killed him. Would have killed him. If Miriam hadn't been spooked enough to be clutching her stun gun, they would also both be dead. As it was, she'd been able to hold the monster off until that crazy girl had come flying from the cave.

He should have continued teaching middle school. *At least those little monsters are predictable, mostly. But no, I decided to go back and get my degree.* He'd met Professor Segen and become one of her grad students.

KT Hollis. Neil's mind jumped to his friend and colleague. She and the rest of their group were unaccounted for. Dr. Segen had inquired after them first thing, but neither of the J's knew anything. He didn't want to think about what might have happened.

The van had just sat there with no sign of them. He and Miriam should have taken a look. *Why didn't we look?* He cursed. *How were we to know something was wrong?*

And the two J's were afraid for their friend. *What was her name? Cassie.* Yeah, her name was Cassie. What happened to her?

Why hadn't she stopped them? She was likely dead as well. He knew for certain that the other group had already lost one of their number. *How many have we lost?*

Lost in his thoughts, it took him longer than it should have to notice a shuffle come from the entryway. The noise prompted him to raise his knife. As the two young women rounded the corner, Neil let out a deep sigh and lowered his knife.

The young women each carried several pieces of long, straight wood, bundled under an arm. The short one ducked over a vinyl bag she'd brought in earlier and shoved her club inside. After that, she snatched the bag from the floor and moved toward him; or rather, the artifacts.

Jordan Adler
12:25 am

Jordan strode over toward Neil. He looked much better than he had before. Some color had returned to his face. She was glad. There for a while, he had seemed to be on the brink of shock. Professor Segen had made him take slow sips from a bottle of water. It appeared to have helped.

For some reason, she'd thought you weren't supposed to give food or drink to someone in shock. She inwardly shrugged.

Once she set the bag down, she crouched and placed her bundle of wood on the ground. Jordan popped up and spun to Jamie, and she relieved the other girl of her burden. As Jordan lay the wood next to her own, her eyes darted from the artifacts to the poles and then to the bag.

"Any sign?" Segen asked from across the room.

Jordan wasn't sure who the professor was asking about. *Her group, our group, or the beast?*

"No," Jamie quickly replied. She walked over and gently lay the tomahawk in its previous position.

Jordan plopped down to the stone floor and crossed her legs. With her left hand, she reached out for one stick and dragged it toward her. From her pocket, Jordan withdrew Neil's knife and flipped the blade out.

"Did you get everything you need?" Segen inquired, breaking her concentration.

Jordan slowly nodded. "I think so." She attempted to picture the best way to make a spear. "Jamie, can you hand me a spearhead?" After a moment she added, "Maybe one of the notched kind, but not an older one, no need to risk those."

Jordan heard footfalls as Dr. Segen ambled closer. A tingle shot up her spine as she felt the other woman stop and hover over her. She hated it when people watched over her shoulder. After a moment, Jordan lifted her butt from the floor and shifted so that her back was away from the doctor.

Jamie hobbled over and eased down beside her. One artifact, a spearhead, rested in Jamie's extended palm. Made of slate, it had a triangular shape. Longer than it was wide, its two sharpened stone sides were even, while the other was thinner. Below its horizontal shoulders, the neck thinned, then tapered out again. The spearhead's base was rounded.

Jordan estimated the thickness of the arrowhead, then pulled the pole across her lap. It extended several inches past her leg. With her body in the way, the branch stuck out too far to the right. She wouldn't have a good angle to cut into the wood. Next, Jordan tilted the trunk back across her lap, so it rested on her other thigh. Positioned like that, it wasn't secure enough to cut. Finally, she swung the wood under her thigh and wedged it between her leg and foot. The tip extended six inches from the edge of her shoe.

As Jordan dragged the blade across its tip, she gouged deep into its rings. Fibers flaked away as she sawed, and wood chips peppered the cave floor. It was fast work to cut the groove. Before long, the gap stretched a quarter of an inch wide and an inch deep.

"How are you thinking about attaching it?" Segen asked.

"I was thinking," she murmured, "zip ties."

A dubious expression crossed Dr. Segen's face. "Zip ties?"

"Yeah, watch," Jordan assured.

Instead of hemp rope or strips of leather, neither of which

they had, she was forced to improvise. Jordan dug into the bag and tugged a package from the depths. With her teeth, she ripped the thin plastic package open. She slipped three of the grooved plastic strips from the baggy. After plucking the artifact from Jamie's hand, she slipped the spearhead into the divot. She wrapped one zip tie around the spearhead's neck. A string of clicks burst out as Jordan snugged it. The second, she wrapped around one side of the blade and its opposite shoulder. Across that, she placed the final tie, set diagonally across the second.

Finally, Jordan clipped the tails from the ties. Slate head now secured to the pole, she held the spear up.

CHAPTER 55

Zayne Stone
12:44 am

Zayne's mind whirred, she'd done it again. She'd just run; just left someone else to die. The light of her headlamp bobbed up and down as she sprinted away from another failure. It was all her fault. She'd left them both to die. They'd saved her, protected her, and she'd just left them to die. First Jamie and now Henry.

When the beast slunk from the passage, Henry stepped in front of her. It was on top of the ledge, higher than they were. Henry had scooted her back, away from the creature. He held up the axe to delay the animal. She'd watched the light shift to the second corpse they'd found, then back at the beast as Henry looked between them. He'd suddenly darted away from her, which had elicited a startled squeak from her throat. A wild part of her mind thought he was finally leaving her.

But that hadn't been it at all. Henry rushed to the body and pulled the gun from the holster. Zayne hadn't even noticed the gun. After he'd grabbed the weapon, Henry flew back to her side. The beast prowled toward them. Henry took her hand again and then led her to the rear of the cavern. They'd chosen a random passage, though now that she thought about it, it could have just been the first passage they'd come to. Either way, they'd gone deeper into the cave.

The beast was behind them, always behind them. The long tunnel split into two passages, forcing Henry to pause a moment before he chose the left fork. They'd heard the creature behind them, following them. The tunnel had opened into a small chamber about the size of Jordan's Gallery. It wasn't as beautiful as Jordan's had been, but what they'd seen in the room's corner had definitely made up for it.

Oh God, I miss Jordan. Is she even still alive?

Zayne let out a sob as she stumbled over a tree root. After regaining her balance, she sped up again. *North.* She was headed north, just like Henry told her. It was the last thing he'd told her. She'd never forget that. *Never.* She remembered the feeling of joy that swept over her as she'd seen the skylight. But her joy had quickly turned bitter.

At first, they hadn't realized what it was. It had just been a dark spot on the far side of the cave's ceiling. As they'd passed underneath the spot, they'd both checked it out. The moon, she'd seen the moon. That beautiful silver orb. The ceiling was a foot or two above Henry's head, and the skylight ran up through the rock almost vertically. It had to have been fifteen to twenty feet high.

Henry had jammed the gun into a pocket and waved her over. "Come on." He'd urged her forward, keeping an eye on the passage where the beast hovered. After pulling his headlamp off, Henry slipped it over the crown of her head.

He'd stuffed the axe under his armpit before bending down. Still eyeing the creature, he brought his hands together, giving her a platform to step on. As she'd stepped up onto his palms, the beast let out a warning roar. Before the animal could react, Henry had quickly stuffed her into the tube.

She still hadn't understood. She might have argued if she'd realized what he was doing.

As she grasped the edges of the shaft and lifted herself in, she'd seen a second light flick on below her. She'd climbed shafts before, at one of those indoor playgrounds, so she knew to spread her arms and legs to press against both sides. To stabilize her weight, Zayne kept her knees slightly bent as she'd moved one hand up while increasing the pressure on her other three limbs. Next, she'd brought the opposite foot up. She'd continued to alternate, hand to foot, then the opposite as she climbed up the narrow tunnel. She'd tried to move as fast as she could to make room for Henry.

After shimmying several feet, Zayne had paused, resting her back against one wall and pressing her feet against the other. Peering down, she'd seen Henry just standing there. He was shifting his small light between her and the beast; he hadn't yet started to climb. She'd been confused as to why he wasn't following her. When she asked, his answer had horrified Zayne.

"It's too high. Besides, I doubt the beast would let me. I don't think I can make it."

Her eyes had gone round at the statement. Thoughts had flown through her head as she'd tried to understand what he meant. She hadn't understood why he would want her to go without him, or why he had even considered letting her climb out if he couldn't follow. She'd urged him, begged him to try. When he'd finally relented, Henry wanted her to grab the axe. She didn't know why he was so worried about it; he could have left it behind. But she hadn't argued. She was just so glad he'd decided to join her. As she'd reached down for the tool, the beast let out a deafening roar and Henry had taken two quick steps back, brandishing the axe toward the animal.

When she asked what happened he'd explained, "It definitely didn't like that. It rushed forward. I think it only stopped because I warded it off with the axe. For some reason, it really hates this thing." Zayne started to head back down the shaft, only to be halted as he snapped at her. She hadn't understood why he was yelling at her. He told her to keep climbing, that he'd try to find another way out. She'd ascended another several feet before pausing once more.

She hadn't wanted to keep going, not without him. When she'd tried to explain, he'd told her the thing wouldn't let him and kept insisting she climb. He promised once again to find another way out. As Zayne climbed, Henry kept up a constant stream of encouragement. Whenever she paused, he'd urged her to keep going. She'd begged to be allowed to stay with him. He wouldn't hear of it. She remembered wondering why he didn't want her anymore. *I wasn't that bad, was I? I tried to keep up.*

She'd continued to scale the shaft, tears leaking from her eyes, shooting looks down at him every couple of minutes. She kept begging him to join her. Pleaded with him to at least try. At some point he'd pulled out the gun and was aiming it at the beast, holding it off.

As she'd neared the top, he told her to go north, to head north to the cliffs.

Zayne had no clue where north was, and she told him as much.

"Find the Big Dipper," he'd patiently guided.

"The what?" she'd whined, only partially paying attention. How could she leave him?

"The Great Bear. Find the Great Bear and follow the two stars on the outside. You'll see the Little Dipper, the Little Bear. The very tip of the Little Dipper's handle is the North Star, which will guide you north, just keep going north."

She glanced back up at the stars, re-located the North Star, and adjusted her course slightly. In truth, she'd known that the North Star was part of the Little Dipper, but in all the excitement it had slipped her mind.

After climbing out of the shaft, she'd peered down at him and once again begged him to join her. He said he couldn't chance it with the beast already so angry and repeated his plan to find another way out, then once again prompted her to go north. The light originating atop her head just barely illuminated his face enough for her to see his expression. He had been smiling; he had tears on his face, but he was smiling. Why had he been smiling?

That had been the last time she'd seen Henry Blake. She would never forget that smile.

CHAPTER 56

Dr. Theodore Stone
1:03 am

Head resting against the vinyl fabric, Theodore Stone sat on the thin sleeping pad, peering from the mesh window of his tent. Since help had not yet arrived, Stone assumed the other group had delayed their departure. His mind ruminated on the day's decisions. Every time he replayed the events, he couldn't discern any better choices. He'd left his daughter alone with one of his most responsible students. It had been an easy decision to make; there had been no uncertainty. Now, his daughter was missing, and Jamie was injured; that blown pupil could be a sign of a much more severe brain trauma. At least she had Jordan with her. He'd insisted they stay there.

His decision to send the girls for help had also been sound. Stone had to admit, he was still a little upset at Jordan. It had been foolish for her to trek through the woods all by herself. Cassie was hopefully still safe at the van, though all alone. Stone hadn't wanted her, nor had she seemed remotely willing, to accompany him back into the forest. Michael was dead, and he couldn't think of a thing he could have done differently. At that moment, there had been no way of saving the boy. Henry was missing. He'd run off. Could he have gone for help?

Stone squeezed his eyes shut and let the cool night air invade his chest. The breath burst from his lungs in a sigh. As he reached up to massage an ache blossoming in his right temple, Stone hefted his eyelids open. Nothing had changed, the area was just as silent and lifeless as before. Eyes flicking up to the stars, he considered the long night ahead. At least the clouds had moved on.

His remaining hope lay in the possibility that Zayne or Henry would try to rejoin the group, or else circle back to familiar territory. With Cassie at the van, Jordan and Jamie in the cave, and himself at the camp, which was by far the most exposed, they were well-positioned to spot them. There was a good chance one of his missing charges would try to find safety in one of the three locations. It was all he could think to do until morning.

If neither his daughter nor Henry had shown up by morning, he would have to reevaluate his options. He was loath to leave them, but he had three other students to take care of. He had to find a way to get them to safety.

His best bet might be to grab as many supplies as he could carry before swinging by the cave and getting Jordan and Jamie. Together, they could venture down to the van, pick up Cassie, then head to the river. Once his students were safely away, he would resume the search for his daughter.

The more he thought of it, the more appealing the river became.

Starting in the mountains of Arkansas, the Illinois River followed a meandering course as it descended in elevation, flowing north, then east, and finally to the south into the Arkansas River. Between this cursed valley and the Arkansas River lay Lake Tenkiller. There were several populated areas along the banks of the river they would come across before they reached the lake. Surely, they could find help along the way.

Zayne Stone
1:16 am

As Zayne bent over, she clutched a handful of fabric in each hand and rested her weight just above her knees. Zayne took deep lungfuls of air, trying to calm her ragged breathing. She'd been stumbling through the dark woods, scared and alone, for a while. It was horrible. A stinging throb pulsed from her injured knee, and she could feel prickling coming from several fresh scrapes on her arms and face. Apparently, she hadn't done a very good job of dodging the trees.

In truth, Zayne couldn't recall much from the last several minutes. Her mind didn't seem to work right. She was having a hard time paying attention. After abandoning Henry in her second cowardly flight, Zayne seemed to recall being in a daze. She'd been wandering through the woods, only occasionally peering at the stars. *Why was I so interested in the stars?*

As her body snapped straight, Zayne's head whipped up and her eyes flew to the sky. Zayne took small, uneven steps as she spun around, desperately searching for the Little Dipper. North, she had to keep going north. Henry had told her to go north. Her eyes bounced from star to star. Constellation to constellation.

There it is! She let out a sigh, gazing at the bright, tiny, beautiful star. *If that way is north, then*—Zayne jerked her head from side to side. She tried to spot the direction she'd come from. Had she even been going north before? She couldn't recall. Her eyes danced from tree to tree, glancing at each. Every direction looked exactly the same.

She gave a shake of her head. It didn't matter.

Her eyes reacquired the star; she oriented herself and set off.

Dr. Theodore Stone
1:32 am

Stone's eyes widened as they locked onto a glimmer of light, bobbing up and down through the trees to the east. Someone was out there. Stone ripped the tent flaps apart as he bolted from the shelter. Thumb mashing against the rubber switch, a beam shot from his small flashlight as he set off in a waddling run. Who was it? Whoever it was, they were coming from the south. That crossed Jordan and Jamie from the list, and he seriously doubted Cassie would roam through the forest at night. That left either Henry or Zayne. *God, I hope it's Zayne*, he prayed, *God, please let it be Zayne.* He didn't know if he could handle it being anyone else but Zayne.

He meant no offense to Henry; he liked the boy well enough, but Zayne was his daughter.

Stone shoved everything from his mind but the light as he slipped from the clearing into the tree cover. The light was further away than he'd first thought. Eyes tracking the floating glow, Stone tried to estimate its distance. It had to be at least two or three hundred meters away. *Distance doesn't matter, exhaustion is irrelevant, I have to reach them.* Stone ducked under and dodged around most of the tree limbs and foliage. It didn't always work out, and he failed to avoid some obstacles.

The glow bobbed through the woods at a constant pace, strobing as it passed behind trees. Stone altered his course again, so he was on an intersecting path. *Who is it? Could it be Zayne? It doesn't matter who it is*, he reminded himself. *Please let it be Zayne.* He had to reach them. Be it Henry, his daughter, or a stranger, he had to get to them before that creature did; get them to safety. *Please let it be Zayne.*

The light was getting closer, ever closer. As he staggered through the dense forest, Stone pushed through or trod over the smaller vegetation while sweeping by or between saplings and shrubbery. With each new course correction, he could feel his energy seeping away. Not until that day, did he realize how right Zayne was about him needing to exercise more. For him it wouldn't be about weight loss, as he'd always been content with his body, Stone needed more stamina.

As he got within a hundred yards of the light, the runner skidded to a halt. The beam of light spun toward him as he increased his pace. Stone could only make out a silhouette of the person, but they appeared to be small in stature. His heart skipped a beat, then quickened. *They are small, could it be—*

"Who's that?" A tremulous voice croaked out. No matter the situation, he'd have recognized that voice in an instant.

"Zayne!" he exploded. A wave of immense relief flooded over him. His daughter was alive. *Zayne is alive.*

"Dad?" she quavered. "Daddy!" she called out as she sprinted to him.

Time seemed to slow while they rushed toward each other.

Zayne slammed into him, wrapping her arms around him and looking up into his face.

"Oh, Daddy, it was so horrible there was a monster—I was so scared. It got Jamie, it killed her and I ran and ran and ran," she babbled breathlessly. With tears flowing down her cheeks, she fought to maintain her composure. "Then Henry found me hiding—we went to the camp and there was a pool of blood—who died? Was it Michael? Where are the others? We couldn't find anyone so we tried to go to the van to find everyone, but it was there—we snuck away and hid. And oh, Daddy it's all my fault—I let us fall asleep. It was almost dark when we woke up and we got lost. The monster showed up again—it followed us for a long time."

As she spoke, her tears fell with greater intensity and her words ran together. Hands resting on her head, Stone used his thumbs to brush the hair from her face. "It kept following us—it wouldn't leave us alone. We found a cave and Michael's body—Henry said it was the beast's lair. There was another body—a girl—I didn't know her." Her breaths were coming in short gasps as she fought sobs. "It appeared again and chased us deeper into the cave. There was a hole in the roof—Henry lifted me up and I climbed—but Henry wouldn't come; I begged him to come—but he wouldn't. I left him like I left Jamie—it's all my fault, they're dead because of me." Zayne's last few words were a high-pitched whine, then she buried her face into his chest, sobbing uncontrollably.

"No, no, none of this is your fault," Stone soothed, stroking her head, "none of it. And Jamie is still alive, she's hurt but alive."

Her head whipped back, and her eyes shot to his. "Really? She's ok? You promise?"

"Yes, my dear, I promise."

Stone wanted to ask if she'd actually seen Henry die, but couldn't bring himself to utter the question. He wanted to spare his daughter any further emotional trauma, but he had to admit, even if it was only to himself, part of him didn't want to know. It could wait.

CHAPTER 57

Zayne Stone
1:54 am

Zayne shuffled along behind her father. They'd snuck through the forest and followed the cliff line to the cave. That was probably Henry's plan too. The thought brought with it a pang of guilt. No matter what her father said, she knew it was her fault.

Her mind shifted to the other person she'd abandoned. *How will Jamie react when she sees me?* There was a pressure in her chest as she thought about it. She hoped Jamie wouldn't be mad. Despite the worry, she couldn't wait to see Jamie. *And Jordan is there.* She missed Jordan. When she'd found out Jordan, Jamie, and Cassie were all ok, she had been exhilarated. Oh, it would have been so awful if something happened to them too. A pang of sorrow shot through her heart as Henry flashed into her mind.

They'd loaded the remaining food and water into their packs. Zayne reached up to adjust one of her straps; it was heavy. Not only did he have his own pack, but her father was also lugging the first-aid kit.

As they rounded the last bend, Zayne spotted the cave's

entrance. A brilliant light reflected off the interior wall of the fissure, making it easy to see. Her father broke into a trot at the sight of it, forcing her to match his pace. As she got closer, Zayne saw they'd moved one of the powerful lights into the entry. She and her dad scaled the boulder and slipped through the entrance. The bright light momentarily robbed them of their night vision.

They stepped around the light and continued along the passage. As Zayne rounded the bend, she was confronted with an odd sight. Jordan and Jamie stood at the end of the tunnel, both brandishing spears. *Where did they get spears? Did they make them? Can I have one?* At the sight of them, both girls lifted the stone tips and set the spears aside.

"Oh, Zayne, you're ok," Jamie bellowed, rushing toward her then enveloping Zayne in her arms. Jamie let out a sharp gasp but hugged Zayne even tighter. "You're ok! I was so worried," she cried.

"I thought it got you."

"It did get me a bit," Jamie confessed.

"I'm sorry I left you," she whimpered. Lip quivering, tears leaked from her eyes.

"Oh, honey, it's not your fault," Jamie consoled. "I begged you to run, remember?"

"But I—"

"No, no buts," Jamie bulled over her. "You did exactly what you were supposed to."

"I got lost," Zayne whined.

"Nobody's perfect," Jordan broke in, kneeling beside her.

Jamie released her hold and Zayne jumped into Jordan's arms. "Oh, Jordan, I missed you."

"Me too, kid," Jordan agreed.

Zayne felt her dad squeeze around their group, and she tracked him with her eyes, turning her head to watch him walk further into the cave. Her eyes jumped to someone she hadn't seen before. *Is that—*

"Miriam? You're here," Stone murmured, thunderstruck.

"Oh, Teddy, have you seen any of my students or anyone

from my group?"

"No," Stone muttered. A wan expression swept over the older woman's face. "How did you get here? Is help coming?" Zayne couldn't recall Segen ever having such a dire look. It scared her a bit.

"We didn't know anything was wrong. Neil and I didn't get here until after dark. We saw our van parked at the edge of the clearing," she explained mechanically.

"Cassie?" he worried, shooting another look toward the entrance.

"We didn't see your student, but to tell the truth, we weren't really paying attention. We were in such a hurry to get here," she finished lamely, lifting her arms to indicate the cavern.

Dr. Theodore Stone
3:00 am

The night was a mixture of anxiety, sorrow, and relief. Stone wanted to hear everything. Despite already knowing much of what happened, he had them review it none the less. In turn, each of them related their personal journey. He listened intently throughout the retellings. Like a sponge, he soaked in every detail.

All afternoon they'd been fleeing from the prehistoric myth, the legend. *The Wampus Cat.* From the sound of it, each had a harrowing day. Even Miriam Segen and Neil's trip had been eventful, though not as bloody until the end.

The events of the day wove together like a tapestry.

Stone sought to track the beast's progress from the moment the creature had first shown up. Either with Jamie's tumble and Zayne's flight, or his and Jordan's dash from the camp. Unable to place either accurately in the sequence, he lumped the two events together. Regardless, the creature had shown up around mid-day and dogged them ever since. What could have made it so aggressive? By his reckoning, the creature had been in the area at least since the attacks the week before. *So why didn't the thing attack yesterday? It doesn't make sense.*

His mind strayed to Henry's theory of the beast's reappearance, as relayed through Zayne's heartbreaking story. Could it have been trapped in the muck for millennia? That would explain much. Stone squeezed his eyes shut. His daughter had been through so much in the last several hours. *Too much.*

Henry's willingness to sacrifice himself for Zayne weighed at Stone's heart. Jordan and Jamie had expressed a desire to search for Henry and Cassie right away, but he'd been forced to reject the suggestion. Part of him longed to go out and look for the kids too. To rush headlong into danger to rescue his students. But he couldn't, not in the black of night. Even with Jordan's discovery, it was too dangerous.

Though amazed that the ancient artifacts could cause such severe harm to the creature, oddly, it made logical sense. The objects could have been imbued with the same sort of magic that created the Wampus Cat. Here he was, comparing magic with logic. Only this situation could have ever joined the two.

Zayne's description of the cat avoiding Henry's axe also followed. After Jordan hit it with her weapon, the thing had obviously associated the two items. That gave Stone hope that Henry could still be alive.

Stone looked to his side. Snuggled up as close as she could, Zayne clung to his arm. Soon after they'd arrived in the cave, he'd noticed she'd glued herself to his side. Since then, Zayne had not allowed him to take more than a few steps without accompanying him. Not that he minded. He did vaguely wonder if she'd allow him to relieve himself. Stone took a deep breath; he'd deal with that later.

Eyes staring at nothing and everything, she followed every movement and noise. His fatherly insight told him she was exhausted. Still, he couldn't blame her for not wanting to close her eyes. He was reluctant as well. The events of the day had been too much for him to be able to calm himself.

Even with Jordan and Jamie planted at the mouth of the tunnel, Stone couldn't relax. Spears in hand, they were ready if the beast reentered the cave. Impressed with the ingenuity they'd shown when making the weapons, he'd told them as much. For once, he'd felt no sense of loss when he'd discovered the site had been disturbed.

Jordan and Jamie had been in a whispered conversation, almost continuously, since the last account was told. Fear of them doing something impetuous had driven him to make them each swear they wouldn't leave the cave until morning. Keen to find their missing classmates, they ran through ideas for the morning. Not knowing what had become of both Cassie and Henry weighed on all of them.

However, no one was as distraught as Dr. Miriam Segen. Shrouded in misery, she sat, back against the cave wall, and fought back tears. Missing so many members of her party must have been devastating. Segen had held out hope that some of them made it to the campsite. When he'd only returned with Zayne, Stone had seen a piece of her soul crumble along with the hope. A spark in her eyes had been snuffed out.

CHAPTER 58

Alan Harris
7:11 am

Alan Harris arrived at his office on Sunday morning a bit late. As he looked around, he failed to see his colleague, Myranda Hernandez. It wasn't like her to be late. According to the itinerary she'd given him, she should have been back to the states the day before.

Harris ducked his head into his co-worker's office. "Hey, Owen, have you heard from Myranda this morning?"

"No," Owen said, with some hesitation. "Is she supposed to be back yet?" he asked, shifting his chair toward his large desk calendar. Owen started at the written notation of the previous Sunday and then ran his finger along the final week of August. At the 31st, he glanced down at his wristwatch, checking the digital numbers. "Hmm," Owen grunted. He grasped the bottom right-hand edge of the calendar page and yanked it up and to the left. Just like that, he ripped the month of August away.

Alan Harris knew better than to interrupt Owen. He had his own way of doing things. At 63, he was by far the most senior man in the wildlife service. Consigned to desk duty, he'd refused to retire years before.

Finger poised over September 1st, Owen read his handwritten notation, Hernandez returns from vacation. "You're right. She should have been back yesterday. Perhaps she's just running late?" Owen half inquired; half stated.

"It's not like her to forget to call in."

"Is aught amiss?"

"Nah, I doubt it. I'll give her a call," Harris intoned.

Owen nodded as he turned back to his computer monitor. "Ok, well let me know either way," Owen said offhandedly, already immersed in something else.

Harris extracted his mobile phone from his pocket as he walked back to his desk. He scrolled through his contacts and found the entry for Myranda Hernandez. After plopping down onto his swivel chair, Harris selected the call option under her name. As he brought the phone up to his ear, Harris heard the high-pitched trill that indicated the call was trying to connect. A recorded voice burst onto the line. "You have been forwarded to an automated voicemail system..." Harris pulled the phone from his ear for a moment and glanced at the screen. He double-checked her name before he returned the phone to his ear. "... 376 is not available. At the tone, please rec—"

Harris brought the phone down and tapped the red disconnect icon to end the call before placing his phone face down on the top of his desk. That was odd. *Her phone must be off.* Something didn't feel right.

Harris heaved his bulk from his chair. He made his way to the coffeepot. Harris reached over with one hand and absentmindedly grabbed a foam cup. With his other, he lifted the pot off the burner. He couldn't push past the feeling that something was wrong. In the several years he'd known Hernandez, Harris couldn't recall a time she'd ever had her phone off.

Scalding hot liquid poured into his cup as he tipped the pot. While placing the glass orb back in its niche, he thought about all the possibilities. Watching the steam rise above his cup, Harris realized he wouldn't be able to let it go. It wasn't his style.

With a sigh, he shifted his weight and picked up a plastic to-go lid. He pressed firmly around the edges to secure the lid onto his cup.

Harris strode back across the room and ducked his head into Owen's office.

"I'm going to step out for a bit," Harris said. *Maybe run by Myranda's house,* he added silently. "I've got to head to Tenkiller," he finished.

Alan Harris
7:20 am

On his way out of town, Harris swung by Myranda Hernandez's place. The beams of his headlights swept over Myranda's small house as he pulled his service truck into her driveway. Built in the thirties or forties, the outside was ornamented with irregular slabs of sandstone. Each chunk had a unique mixture of colors that ran the gamut of hues. Within the stones were shades of tan, brown, yellow, gray, red, and black. Each slab was secured into place by thick white mortar. Harris had always adored the look of the so-called 'giraffe' houses.

He pulled to a stop at the end of the driveway next to Hernandez's service truck. Like his, it was a black Chevy Silverado. In front of him, built in the same style as the house, a tiny one-car garage set detached from the main building. His eyes roamed the neighborhood as he exited the truck. Her small house stood out from those around it. Even in the quiet of the predawn Sunday morning, he could tell it was a nice neighborhood.

He slipped around the front of his truck and peered into the garage. Through one of the small windows, Harris caught sight of her car. Had she gotten a ride to the airport? Was that her plan? He couldn't recall if she'd mentioned it.

Harris moved away from the window and swung around the side of the building. Drawn curtains greeted him on all the visible windows as he strode to the front door. Though not surprising on a normal Sunday morning, she had been scheduled to work. The absence of any sign of life worried him. It appeared that she hadn't come back. When he lifted the lid, Harris was discouraged to see the mailbox crammed full.

Harris slammed a fist repeatedly against the door.

Now Harris was truly worried.

After a couple of minutes banging on Hernandez's front door, Harris dove for a massive chunk of rock. Kept in a groove cut into the heavy slab of sandstone, the spare key allowed him access to the front door. He swung the door open and strode into the living room.

His quick search of the small house proved fruitless. Hernandez wasn't home. Evidence of her absence lay all around. In the kitchen, a stench of spoiled food rose from the trash can, and unwashed dishes clogged the sink. An opened suitcase sat in the corner of the first bedroom, clothes neatly folded inside. The bathroom held a musty scent from a coiled towel strewn on the floor. Hernandez's second bedroom, turned home office, held the most disquieting sign yet. There on the desk next to her computer were her tickets and passport.

Not only was the house empty, it now appeared she hadn't left. Harris tried to push the anxiety back down. Had something happened to her? There could be other explanations. She might have met a guy; a whirlwind romance would account for the evidence. He shook his head; that just wasn't her.

CHAPTER 59

Jamie Long
7:25 am

As the first hint of soft morning light crept into the cave's mouth, Jamie and Jordan were away. Though eager to set off much earlier, they had reluctantly promised the professor they'd wait until morning. And while they had obeyed his words, the spirit of the promise had been shattered. Both Jordan and Jamie knew what the professor had meant when he asked for their vow. Now, against all better judgment, they scrambled up the side of the gulley. Their only aim, to find Henry.

When they reached the tip of the incline, they peeked over. Light from the new sun pierced a morning fog, creating a thick, soupy mist. Beams of light pierced the veil, shooting through the thinly spread trees.

Jamie peered through the fog for any hint of movement. The night had been one of the longest she'd ever had to endure. Not capable of sleep and unable to do anything else, the two of them had kept watch on the cave's entrance. Necessity demanded someone must. Armed with her spear, she felt safer than she had in days. She'd used the same process to make her spear as Jordan had to make the first. Jamie's, however, was longer and thicker, and the stone spearhead, bigger.

With Jordan beside her, covering her with that bone club of hers, Jamie knew they could, at the very least, hold the thing off. If they were lucky, they might even be able to kill it.

Yeah right.

The night before, as they told their stories, they'd learned that Henry might still be alive. She'd listened with rapt attention to every detail that came from Zayne. By that time, she'd already decided to go after him. Jamie had seen a burning intensity flood over Jordan's features too. She wasn't sure why Jordan came, nor had she asked. It didn't matter. Much of Jamie's desire sprung from the fact that she had slumbered while everyone else was in peril.

Her mind rationalized it, claimed it wasn't her fault, told her that Henry could be dead, and begged her not to venture from the safety of the larger group. But her heart, that was what she listened to now. Henry was a decent guy and if by any chance he was still alive, she would never forgive herself if she refused to even try.

When Zayne had finished her tale, Jamie and Jordan had asked the girl pointed questions. They tried to get as many clues as they could until Professor Stone had realized what they were up to. After that, he'd pestered them to make a promise not to venture out until daylight. While they weren't happy about the restriction, they understood. Besides, the night was a horrible time to wander through the woods. As witnessed by Henry and Zayne's rambling trek.

Once Stone drifted off, they'd pulled Zayne aside and asked even more questions. The more information they had, the better the chances of locating Henry. Poor Zayne, she hadn't realized what they were up to until it was much too late. When she had, her eyes went wide and filled with panic. She'd begged them not to leave her, not again. They had reminded the girl of the promise they'd made to her father and swore they wouldn't break it. And they hadn't, not technically.

They'd discussed the matter all night. Neither of them had wanted to leave the others undefended, so right before they left

Jordan had woken Neil. By the look on his face when Jordan informed him of their quest, Neil didn't think much of the plan. Though he had reluctantly stayed quiet as they departed.

After a time, Jordan sprung up and turned east into the rising sun, toward camp, Jamie following close behind her.

Neil Singh
7:27 am

Lounged against the wall, he'd watched the two girls leave. He couldn't help but wonder if he'd ever see them again. *Chances are I won't.* Neil could hardly believe they'd do something so impetuous. *Call a duck a duck*, something so stupid. Sure, he understood the drive. And had Henry been his friend, and he'd been uninjured, he might have considered joining them. *Maybe.* To top it off, he would have to be the one to tell everyone they'd gone.

Neil's eyes roved from Stone and his daughter, to Dr. Segen, and then back to the cave mouth. Their sleep, like his, had been fitful, they'd drifted in and out all night. He was loath to wake them for such poor tidings but figured he ought to. Stone's plan had been to travel as a group to the truck, then get help. Neil had no clue what the professor would insist on doing. Would he get the four of them to safety, or would he go after his three wayward students? There was only one way to find out.

"Professor," he croaked in a voice only barely audible. Neil let out a strong cough to clear his throat. "Professor," he called, his deep voice much stronger.

All three of them started awake. Stone jerked his head up from his chest, where it had been resting, Zayne gave out a startled squeak, and Segen peered around the room bleary-eyed.

"Professor," he said once more to get their attention. All eyes focused on him.

"Yes?" Dr. Segen intoned.

"Well, I have some good news and some bad news," Neil paused for effect. "The good news is we survived until morning.

The bad news is—"

"Where's Jordan and Jamie?" Zayne squeaked.

"Yeah, that would be the bad news. They waited 'til morning, like they promised, then set off in search of your missing student." He addressed the last part to Dr. Stone.

Stone let out a defeated sigh and lowered his head. "Henry," he surmised.

Neil felt sorry for the man as he affirmed the statement with a nod. After spending most of the day yesterday trying to find his students, they had disappeared again. And poor Zayne had tears leaking copiously from her eyes.

"I can't say I'm surprised," Stone commented wearily.

Zayne burst into racking sobs. "It's all my fault," she moaned, only barely intelligible. "They kept asking questions." She took deep gasping breaths. "I didn't understand." Zayne dissolved into tears again.

"Honey, none of this, not a single bad thing that's happened could ever be your fault," Stone insisted sharply. From the expression shadowing his face after the outburst, he must have figured it was too sharp. When he continued, it was in a much more soothing tone. "Sweetie, they made their own decisions. Besides, if anyone is to blame, it's me."

"No, Teddy," Segen cut in, "you're not at fault either. There was no way for you to know the trip would become this nightmare."

Fredrick Delacroix
7:45 am

"Fredrick Delacroix? This is Alan Harris, with the O.D.W.C., we met last weekend," the man greeted.

"Right, you're Hernandez's partner," he recalled. "What can I do for ya?"

"Yeah, I have a quick question."

"Shoot," Fredrick coaxed.

"Did you happen to see Hernandez leave last week?" Harris

inquired.

"How do you mean?" Fredrick shot up in his chair. "I assumed she rode with you."

"I left early," Harris explained, "not long after I killed the mountain lion. Hernandez told me she'd catch a ride back into town."

"A week ago, though?"

"She was supposed to be on vacation, scheduled to leave last Sunday and return yesterday. She didn't show up to work today." Harris paused, increasing Fredrick's alarm. "I can't find anyone who has seen her since the search. Besides, that whole business with the mountain lion last week left me with an odd feeling."

"How so?" Fredrick felt the dread swarming over him. Did Harris have any of the same doubts he'd been struggling with all week?

"It's hard to explain. Just some actions were atypical for a mountain lion. If it weren't for the way I found the thing, I would have said it wasn't the culprit. Have we heard back on the DNA test yet?"

Fredrick started. As he'd scanned the subject tags in his inbox earlier, Fredrick had glimpsed something from the lab. "Just a sec." Fredrick dragged his mouse across the screen to select his email. The screen flashed as it swapped programs. "I got an email," Fredrick muttered. His eyes flowed across the words and soaked them in.

"The DNA isn't back yet," Fredrick summarized. "However, they do have some preliminary results from the necropsy." Fredrick's eyes widened. "My God."

"What's wrong," Harris shot back.

"The contents of the mountain lion's stomach—"

"What about them," Harris cut in. "It was eating the girl's arm."

"Yes, there were human remains inside the digestive tract, but it was a single blood type—"

"One—" Harris tried to cut in.

"And female," Fredrick finished. His final words brought a ringing silence to the phone line.

After several moments, a new wave of dread flowed over Fredrick. He let out a groan. "My God," he mumbled again. How had he forgotten? *The kids, the college kids. The archaeology survey.* His eyes closed as his head smacked against his chair. "My God," he murmured again.

CHAPTER 60

Dr. Theodore Stone
8:02 am

Theodore Stone fumed; he was livid. Shocked, the girls had chosen to do something so reckless, so dangerous. Of course, he was more worried by the thought of what might happen to them. And the danger the girls, his students, were so rashly blundering into. How could they have been so foolish as to wander through the forest on their own? *Again.* And to seek the beast at its lair. *Madness.*

Stone gave a shake of the head and groaned. As much as it pained him, he knew he couldn't afford to focus on them at the moment. He had to concentrate on his own group. He had three people counting on him, including his daughter.

There was also Cassie to think of. She had still been in the van the last time he'd seen her. And for the life of him, he couldn't think of a reason she would have moved. Perhaps she'd just fallen asleep. That was the best-case scenario. He hoped that was all. Hoped she'd been asleep when Miriam and Neil had pulled up. *If not—*

He pushed the thought from his mind.

For the last 30 minutes, they'd plowed south through the

forest, on course for the van. And by extension, Miriam's truck. As far as he knew, it was the only working vehicle they had. He could stuff as many people as possible into and on top of the thing and bolt. In the first town, they would call for help, or perhaps the National Guard.

He focused again on the spear in his hands. Jordan and Jamie had done an excellent job assembling them. At just over five feet long, his was one of the shortest. But with his slight stature, it fit him well. Zayne's was smaller than his; the girls had made it with her in mind. While she was still missing, they had gone ahead and constructed a weapon just for her. They, like himself, had refused to accept the possibility that something bad had happened to his baby girl.

There was a deep pit forming under his heart. *Am I making a mistake, choosing not to go after them right away? No!* No, the best thing he could do would be to get his small group to safety and then come back for them.

A sidelong gaze at his daughter caused that notion to crumble. As much as he might want to look for the others, he knew he couldn't leave his daughter to search for his wayward students. After his frantic search the day before, Stone had thought he'd been fortunate to find the four girls. To get them safe, at least. It wasn't until arriving back at the cave with his Zayne that he found out Cassie might not be where he left her.

First Michael, then Henry, one dead, the other missing. Now the girls; Jamie and Jordan had run off, and there was no telling what had happened to Cassie. He had to be the worst teacher ever. God, it was like a nightmare, except he couldn't, wouldn't wake up. His mind ran in circles as they rushed through the trees. What ifs flashed like lightning through his mind. No matter how hard he tried, he couldn't stop them, so he stopped trying.

The massive creature bounded out from nowhere and thudded in front of them. The sudden appearance of the beast brought the group to a halt. As one, they lowered their spears to ward off the attack. It didn't seem afraid. Positioning itself in front of the group, the creature cut off their ability to continue forward. Crouched on its haunches, it settled its weight as if prepared to spring.

Spear held at the ready, Segen a half a meter to his side, Stone studied the animal in front of him. This was only his second glimpse of the beast. It was beautiful as such deadly creatures sometimes were. Face scrunched up in a ferocious scowl, its eyes, *her eyes*, floated between his group as she examined them. He had to remember; according to the legend, it had once been a young woman cursed to roam the earth like this forever. Muscles coiled; her body shifted slightly as she tucked her legs beneath her.

She was preparing to spring. Stone's mind reeled as he tried to come up with options. All the carefully planned scenarios he'd considered had fled at the first sign of the beast.

Distracted by Stone and Segen, the beast didn't notice Zayne dart forward until she was upon it. Spear lowered, fear and pain etched on her face, Zayne howled and plunged the stone tip toward the beast's colorful hide. While the thing avoided most of the thrust, by darting to the side, the stone tip raked across its hide as Zayne attempted to track the creature's movement. The furrow gouged in its coat began to sizzle and smoke with the brief contact from the blessed weapon.

As the beast let out a high-pitched yowl, it swung one of her enormous paws in an arc toward the young girl. The massive claws would have gouged deep into his baby's skin, had Neil not sprung forward and yanked the girl back. Zayne stumbled back and fell on her behind with an "Umph".

I owe that man a beer.

The beast let off a low growl and darted away, losing itself in the brush.

CHAPTER 61

Fredrick Delacroix
8:12 am

Bright morning light burst through the windshield and momentarily blinded Fredrick as the sun drifted into his sightline. A smooth shift of the wheel sent the sun back behind the right-hand visor where it belonged. Outside, small stones popped and crackled as his tires briefly engulfed them. Thick trees on either side of the dirt road blocked sightlines in front of him. Fredrick navigated the dirt road as quickly as was safe. In his rear-view mirror, he spotted Harris's black Silverado following close behind.

Harris's call had filled him with equal parts of purpose and dread. Fredrick needed to go out to check on the group his information had led into harm's way. He'd asked Harris to meet him out there and was surprised by the other man's quick ascent. After he hung up, he'd known there wasn't enough evidence to drag anyone else out to the middle of nowhere. It was just a hunch, after all. Still, Fredrick had popped into the sheriff's office and gave him a quick overview of his concerns.

Fredrick tightened the side of his mouth into a half-smile. While the sheriff hadn't been convinced of danger, he'd still supported Fredrick's request to drive out and have a look. It was nice to have a supportive boss.

As he followed the gentle curve of the road, the trees opened into an oval-shaped clearing where the road ended in a loop. Three vehicles sat around the clearing. Two parked on the north side of the turnaround, and one against the trees to the east. With the sun and the tinted windows on both vans, he didn't see anything unusual at first.

Things came into view as he followed the road and circled toward the furthest van, one of the newer, box-shaped Fords. Fredrick swept his eyes along the van. Clashing against the white paint of the van, reddish-brown streaks radiated out from around the sliding door's handle. A more thorough scan revealed spatters of dried blood on the windshield and passenger window, as well as a still shape in the passenger seat.

Fredrick slammed on the brakes, shifted the car into park, and opened the door in one fluid motion. From the gun rack mounted next to his seat, he pulled his matte black, pump-action shotgun. His eyes swept the other two vehicles as he bolted from his cruiser. There were more swipes of dried blood by the handle on the rear door of the other van. The truck didn't appear to have any bloodstains, but it was a dark brown color already, so he couldn't be sure.

The sound of a door slamming behind him brought his head whipping around. Harris stood next to his vehicle holding an M4 Carbine assault rifle. It seemed a much better choice than the bolt action both he and Hernandez had used the week before. At a nod from the other man, Fredrick strode toward the Ford. Behind him, he heard the crunch of rocks under Harris's feet added to his own. Shotgun held firmly in his grip; he scanned the vehicle.

Aside from the blood he'd previously spotted, there were more subtle signs of damage. He'd missed the slight space between tire and ground, caused by the vehicle's precarious position on a boulder, and the dark fluid staining the rock and soil beneath the engine. As he circled around toward the front of the van, the crumpled front end wedged against the tree became clear. How had he missed that?

Through the passenger window, he spotted two still forms slumped in the front seats.

"Movement." Several feet away, Harris lifted his rifle and pointed it at the other van.

Fredrick shifted direction. As he advanced toward the rear of the vehicle, he let his eyes shift over and briefly study the other windows. Black tinted glass concealed much of the van's interior behind the front seats, but he could distinguish vague shapes inside the van and on the inside of the windows. He wasn't able to see through to the other van until he swung around the rear of the Ford.

Peering along the barrel of the shotgun, Fredrick took in the second van. It was a Chevy. White like the other, this one didn't look to be in horrible shape. A shadow in the shape of a head peeked out from the tinted window.

"It's a girl," Harris murmured.

Fredrick brought his hand up from the trigger and motioned for Harris to lower his barrel while doing the same with his shotgun. It wouldn't look good if they accidentally shot a survivor. As their barrels lowered, the girl's head lifted. Fredrick's eyes darted around the clearing; with a wave, he motioned for the girl to come out. He saw a quick movement of the head, then the shape started moving to the rear of the van.

The rear door of the Chevy swung open about a foot. Scared brown eyes peered out at him through the gap. Her square face was lined in worry as the eyes darted between them. "Is 'it' out there?"

Unsure what 'it' was, he shot another look around before answering, "No, nothing out here but us." He gestured toward Harris beside him. "What's your name?"

"I'm Cassie. Cassie Byrne." The young woman swung the door wider and stepped out. From the knees down, dried blood soaked the front of her pants. And there were further bloodstains on her thighs and shirt front. "She's hurt. We need your help."

"Who?" Harris asked.

She pointed into the van. "Amber, she's hurt." Cassie Byrne turned and stared over her shoulder into the woods. "The rest of my group is missing. I don't know where they are."

Harris zipped in front of Fredrick and then circled around the girl. Weapon still at the ready, he glanced into the rear door. Harris caught Fredrick's eyes, nodded, then lowered his rifle butt-first to the ground and leaned it against the van. He crawled into the rear door as Fredrick moved toward Cassie.

Fredrick jerked his head toward the other van. "What happened?"

As she brought her head back toward him, she caught sight of the old pickup. Dazed, the girl studied the truck and took a moment to answer. "Somehow 'it' knew how to open the door. 'It' got them just as they showed up," she murmured.

"What did this," Frederick asked. "What was 'It'?"

Her eyes drifted back over to meet his. "You won't believe me," Cassie warned.

"Try me."

"Well, it was either an ancient Indian myth or else a genetic mutation or cloning experiment gone wrong..."

Frederick's eyes narrowed, but he nodded for her to continue.

"It—well it looked like a sabre-tooth tiger—I know how that sounds. But that's not the weirdest part. It had six legs. Two pairs in the front, fully functional, and a pair in the back," Cassie explained.

Seeing the look on Frederick's face, Cassie opined, "See, I told you, you wouldn't believe me."

"It's not that—well... I'm not sure if I do believe you, but I don't think you're lying."

"Oh great, so I'm just crazy," Cassie mumbled as her eyes strayed to the vehicles behind him, then swept back to the pickup. "Whose is that?"

"I don't know. It's not part of your group?" Fredrick was confused. "You didn't come together?" He'd assumed they had.

"No, it wasn't until yesterday the other group got here," she answered, pointing vaguely in the direction of the Ford. Cassie was still staring openly at the pickup. "When did that get here? Amber, did you see them arrive?"

From inside the van, a soft voice drifted out, "No, but I know whose truck it is. It's Dr. Segen's."

Dr. Miriam Segen
8:27 am

We must be getting close to the parking area now. Dr. Miriam Segen followed Stone as he led them through the forest. She hadn't a clue where the vehicles were parked. And truthfully, she dreaded what she might find when she got there.

"We're almost there," Stone called as he put on a burst of speed.

He trotted along the narrow game trail, thick brush on either side of them. The rest of them shadowed him. Before long, they rounded a bend in the trail and the glossy white paint of a van came into view. Stone hastened toward the vehicle, breaking from the trees.

Gashes, torn into the van's thin metal skin, marred the white paint. How had they missed that? If they'd only glanced at the van the night before, they would have seen it. Why hadn't they looked?

Stone faltered as a tall bald man swung around the rear of the van, rifle in hand. As the man eyed them, the barrel of his gun drifted to the ground. Segen darted past Stone and the man, the officer. As she flashed by, her eyes raked the man. The embroidered badge on his sleeve identified him as a game warden. Assault rifle in hand, his eyes tracked her as she passed.

Segen's gaze swept the clearing as she rounded Stone's van. Her eyes paused briefly on the pale, blood-soaked young woman and the black sheriff's deputy before they shot to her van. It didn't look so bad. She proceeded toward it until the deputy stepped forward and cut her off.

"You don't want to look in there," he cautioned, holding up both hands.

Tears clouded her sight as her worst fears seemed confirmed. "They're my colleagues, my students," Segen pleaded.

"Ma'am, I'm sorry," he replied.

She halted, staring into the young man's eyes. "All of them?"

Before he could answer, a soft voice floated from behind her. "Dr. Segen?"

She jerked around, searching for the voice. Eyes squinting into Stone's van, Segen tried to make out the shape sitting inside. She lurched for the open door. As she got closer, Segen recognized Amber scooting into the light. Miriam Segen took the young woman in her arms and wept.

Eyes squeezed shut, she thanked God that she hadn't lost them all. Still, of the eleven people in her party yesterday, only three remained alive.

Dr. Theodore Stone
8:32 am

Stone watched Harris attach both the positive and negative clamps to Segen's truck battery. Though he had never jumped a car himself, he knew that wasn't how they told you to do it. His eyes followed Harris as the man straightened the jumper cables. The black clamp at the opposite end of the cable had been clinched onto the cable itself so the two ends wouldn't meet and create a spark. Harris unclipped it and held it to the side as he attached the red clamp to the positive side. He swept his hand over the drained battery as if shooing a fly, then nonchalantly attached the final black clamp directly to the battery.

Harris stepped around the front of the truck and nodded for Segen to start her engine. The engine in the old pickup roared to life. Cassie turned the van's key.

Click. Click. Click.

After the string of clicks, she waited a moment before trying again. Cassie twisted the key again and the van's engine coughed to life.

According to the officers, backup was on the way. That

331

hadn't made Stone's group feel any better about sticking around, however. Without knowing where the creature was, even with the two officers and their guns, Stone hadn't felt safe. The officers hadn't put up a fuss when he'd suggested they be allowed to leave. They had decided Stone should drive everyone to the hospital in Tahlequah while Harris and Frederick stayed behind. They were determined to wait for backup before starting the search.

Three possible missing students and the creature. Stone could tell the two officers didn't fully buy his explanation of the creature or the sequence of events. Not that they thought he was lying; it was just a hard story to swallow.

CHAPTER 62

Jordan Adler
8:35 am

From the cave, they'd trekked east toward the campsite. Jordan and Jamie had flown past their abandoned camp, barely glancing at the ruined and empty tents. Neither of them had any desire to revisit the spot. According to Dr. Stone, Zayne had careened north through the trees the night before, until they'd reunited two or three hundred yards east of the clearing. Propelled by purpose, they'd slowed only when they neared the area Stone had described, then turned south.

Jordan and Jamie slid through dense trees at a brisk pace, on the lookout for the few landmarks Zayne described. As the girl had only given them a general account of the area, Jordan wasn't sure exactly what they were looking for. According to Zayne, the terrain became rockier as she and Henry had approached the entrance to the beast's lair, which was cut into the side of a rock outcrop.

Only an occasional muted conversation escaped their lips. Neither of them wanted to draw the beast's attention. Even if everything went as planned, they would likely have to confront it at some point. Jordan preferred any confrontation come later rather than sooner.

If they were lucky, they might even be able to sneak in and slip out without being noticed. That was her hope anyway. There was also a concern they might overshoot the whole area and get lost in the woods. Without an exact layout of the area, it was a distinct possibility. But they had to at least make an attempt, they owed Henry that much.

Once they found Henry, she and Jamie would have to find the van; which could also be an issue. In case they happened to get lost, they could always swing around and head for the river. If they curved far enough to the south, they would come to the road. Then all they would have to do was follow it northeast to the van or south to civilization.

After a while, individual stones had peeked from the soil. Not long after that, stone outcrops of all different sizes burst from the ground. Unsure exactly where the cave lay, Jordan and Jamie had wandered around to see the distribution of the rocks. Since the beast had been steering Henry and Zayne, she hadn't known which way they'd traveled.

Between the trees, rocks spread as far as the eye could see. After they followed a rambling course around the perimeter, they'd begun to see a pattern. The outcrops grew as they headed to the northeast and shrunk to the south, west, and the southeast. If this was the place Zayne had described, the cave should be where the stone outcrops turned into small bluffs. Jordan led the two as they prowled toward what they hoped was the beast's lair. *Hope?*

Even in her own mind, that sounded mad. How could anyone willingly seek such a perilous destination? If it weren't for the slim possibility that Henry was still alive, she would have bolted, run in the opposite direction as fast as her feet could carry her. There was a piece of her mind insisting she do just that.

Before long, the two of them came to the exact types of outcrops Zayne had described. It took them a further twenty to thirty minutes to locate the cave mouth.

Jamie stood at the entrance, studying it. A deep sigh

exploded from her lungs.

"What is it?" Jordan worried.

"Hmm? Ohh, it just looks to be unstable," she paused. "That's all."

"Oh? Is that all? I feared we might be rushing into danger or something," she chuckled.

"Rushing? No, not rushing. It's more like a brisk walk," Jamie mused.

Jordan gazed at the other girl. "So, whatever happened to your grand plan?"

"You mean the one where we don't die?" Jamie lifted an eyebrow.

"That's the one," Jordan said as she snapped her fingers and pointed at the other girl.

"Well, my idiotic, new best friend decided to try a foolhardy rescue attempt. I couldn't just let her go alone. Good friends are hard to come by," she mused.

"Idiotic, new best friend, huh?" Jordan questioned.

"Yup."

Jordan shot a quick look around. "When are they getting here? We could use some backup."

Jamie shot her an annoyed glare through squinted eyes and brought her lips to the corner of her mouth.

"What? It was funny." Jordan shrugged.

"No," Jamie deadpanned, "not even a little."

Jordan shrugged and turned back to the entrance. She eyed it carefully. Part of her had feared that the beast would come rushing out to greet them. But now, they had to venture into its lair with no clue to the beast's whereabouts.

Jordan spun back to Jamie. "You ready for this?"

Jamie sighed. "Nope." Nonetheless, she stepped forward.

"Why don't I go first," Jordan offered. "You stand here and watch our backs while I see if the coast is clear."

"Sounds like a plan. Not a great plan, but a plan," Jamie joked.

Jordan strode to the opening before she turned. "Not everyone can be a great thinker," she paused, "but I still love

335

you." She gave a quick wink, then slid into the fissure.

From above, she heard light laughter.

As her feet slid from the inclined tunnel, Jordan reached up to flick her headlamp on. Her eyes darted around the room. They first landed on Michael's body, then whizzed to either side of the room to scan the ramps. The beast wasn't in sight. Jordan shot to her feet and brought her bone club up. Her eyes darted around the chamber once more, then she stepped forward to the ledge.

She took in the entire scene. "Huh," she grunted. It did appear as if the creature burst from the stone in the center of the floor. Her eyes danced around the room once again before she spun to the passage. "All clear," she called.

A moment later, Jamie emerged from the tunnel, the massive spear in hand. She too flipped her light on and shot a look around the room. Face illuminated by the boundaries of Jordan's light; Jamie let out an involuntary gasp as her gaze fell on Michael. Her eyes squeezed shut. Jordan knew that even though Jamie hadn't been fond of him, she wouldn't have wished him dead.

After a minute, Jamie reopened her eyes. "I was half hoping you were wrong, that Zayne had imagined it."

A slight nod was all Jordan could think to do.

"Right," Jamie croaked. She cleared her throat and began again. "Right, we need to find Henry."

Jordan's eyes followed Jamie's light to the rear of the chamber. "Which one?"

They both gazed at a few tunnels worn into the limestone. Zayne hadn't been sure which one they'd fled through. However, she mentioned that it might be near another body.

"You go that way, I'll go this way."

Jordan split to the left and followed the ramp down to the lower level. She glanced to the far side of the cave. Jamie was prowling down the opposite ramp. Before, she'd leaned heavily on her staff as she'd hobbled through the woods. Now, the spear was at chest level, ready to strike.

Jordan turned and quickly scanned her side of the room.

There was nothing of note along the rock wall. *The body must be on Jamie's side.*

Sure enough, Jamie called out, "I found her!"

Jordan zipped around the floor of shattered asphalt and edged next to Jamie. It was a young woman. Mud and blood merged over the patch on her breast, obscuring it. Dressed in tan and green, she must have been some kind of law enforcement officer. They continued to stare at the body for a moment before Jamie turned to the first passage.

"What do you think?" she gestured.

Jordan eyed the other two, then shrugged before she answered. "As good a choice as any. After you," she said, sweeping an arm in front of her.

"Oh no, after you, I insist." Jamie smiled and repeated the gesture.

"Not falling for it, huh?" Jordan returned the smile.

Jordan aimed for the nearest tunnel and snuck in. The passage reminded her of their cave. Also made from limestone, this cave might have been formed around the same time. It would take testing to determine when it was created. She wondered if the two cave systems connected at some point. *How likely is it to have two different cave systems this close?*

They came to a split in the passage, one way angled right and the other left. Jordan paused at the junction to listen. Her eyes swayed between the tunnels. *Which way now?*

For some reason she couldn't fully comprehend, she chose the left fork. Jordan led them along the passage for several minutes, still creeping. As the tunnel widened into another chamber, they came across a ghastly sight.

Henry lay, splayed out across the floor, in a pool of his own blood. The axe, its tip covered in blood, rested next to his outstretched left hand. Brass casings, ejected from the pistol in his other hand, sprinkled the cave floor. Some lay in the blood pool, mired with the red liquid, while others were arranged haphazardly near the body. The gun's slide was locked in an open position. He'd emptied the thing.

Knees weak and speechless with horror, Jordan let her eyes

wander as tears flowed. The room was the same one Zayne had described. Above his body, the tube ran up through the solid rock. By the look of it, he hadn't survived long after Zayne left. Mere minutes at most.

Poor Henry.

Beside her, Jamie collapsed to her knees and sobbed. Jordan crouched down and rubbed her friend's back. She tried in vain to soothe the other girl.

A sudden, mighty roar drifted through the cave behind them. Both girls jerked their heads around, twisting their necks to find the source.

CHAPTER 63

Jordan Adler
8:47 am

With her arm under Jamie's, Jordan shot to her feet, dragging the other girl up with her. *The creature. The beast is here. Somewhere.* Jordan's head spun to each side as she reevaluated their position. They'd been stupid. They had traipsed into the beast's lair on a fool's errand. How had they possibly expected Henry to still be alive? *It was ridiculous. Of course, the beast would have slain him.*

Now she and Jamie were in dire trouble with nothing to show for their effort. Jordan couldn't tell which direction the roar had come from. It could have been the way they'd come, or through the opposite passage. Jordan's eyes shot to the tube Zayne had used to shimmy out.

Still holding tight to Jamie's arm, Jordan dragged her friend toward the chute. Jamie seemed to realize her intention and accompanied her. Just as they reached the natural chimney, they heard the thud of paws hitting the stone floor. The sounds came from the tunnel they'd used.

Jamie's head swept to the passage, then back to the chute. "No time," she decided.

Jordan dragged the other girl toward the opening. "Maybe you can—"

"No!" Jamie cut in. As she stared down at the shorter girl, Jamie shook her head firmly. "Whatever we do, we do together."

Jordan's eyes danced between Jamie's as she took a moment to consider her words. She finally gave a curt nod and released her grip on Jamie's arm. In truth, she felt better with the decision. Though she would have tried to buy time for her friend, Jordan didn't relish the idea of dying alone in some cave. *At least this way we'll be together.*

They each shot another glance to the passage, then darted into the unknown. As they slid around corners, from passage to passage, they heard the thumping of the creature's paws steadily behind them. Jordan knew the beast could have easily caught up to them. She didn't understand why it hadn't. Was it that afraid of their weapons? Or could it be herding them like it had done to Zayne and Henry the night before?

Jamie led them through the cave, always taking a left-hand turn when it came. Jordan thought for sure they'd get lost or wander off a cliff. But they didn't. Jamie must have known what she was doing. Before long, they'd popped out of one of the other passages, into the first large chamber.

Not a few seconds later, before they'd really processed their location, the beast loped from the tunnel behind them. The beast kept its eye trained on the girls as it edged in front of them. Jordan threw an arm in front of Jamie, and the two girls inched away from the animal.

The creature was as terrifying as ever. It's four powerful forelegs tensed, the muscles flexed and relaxed as it studied them. The animal shifted its torso and brought up its two front legs. Mouth open menacingly, it stared at them. Jordan tightened her grip around the handle of her weapon.

She felt a pressure on her left arm as Jamie pushed it down, out of her way. As she brought up her spear, the beast let out a low snarl. The beast's gaze swept between Jordan's club and Jamie's spear.

Jamie Long
8:52 am

With a sudden movement, the creature rushed forward. In a flash, the thing swept her left paw toward the pair, which backhanded Jordan, sending her flying. The creature's sudden motion had prompted Jamie to whip the spear in front of her to block its strike. The other front paw, aimed for the pole directly between Jamie's hands, swept down and snapped it cleanly in half. When the spear snapped, the force pushed Jamie back, which caused the left paw to miss her as the creature brought it back around. The sharp claws swept inches in front of her face.

In her peripheral vision, Jamie saw Jordan sprawled on the floor as she backpedaled. Jamie held tight to the business end of the weapon, letting the other end of the pole fall away. As she slammed into the wall behind her, Jamie's air exploded from her lungs and she slid down the wall. Just as Jamie's butt thumped the floor, Jordan sprang to her feet and stumbled toward the beast. The bone club swept in an arc toward the creature. It leapt away from the weapon as it got close to impact.

The motion brought Jordan closer to the creature than Jamie would have liked. Sure enough, as Jordan stepped within the beast's range, it brought around its massive paw and cuffed her along the ribcage under her outstretched right arm. The force of the blow sent her flying into the chamber's rear wall.

Jamie heard a sickening snap as Jordan's arm crashed into the stone wall. The jawbone club slipped from her hand as she shifted her body and fell to the floor. The bone tool clattered out of reach. Broken arm cradled in front of her, Jordan twisted her body to face the beast. The right side of Jordan's ribcage was bloody where the beast's claws had pierced the skin. Luckily, the claws hadn't raked her as they'd done to Jamie earlier. Defiant look plastered to her face; Jordan scowled at the thing. Body coiled tight; the beast inched toward her.

Jamie knew if she didn't act, the beast would savage Jordan, then her. Jamie thrust a hand against the cold stone floor to push herself up while clutching what remained of her spear with her other hand. The sudden movement as she attempted to rise drew the beast's attention away from Jordan. The thing took a step back and crouched. Just as it prepared to lunge at her, its head jerked to the side and it took several quick steps back, crouching even further.

Taking advantage of the creature's odd behavior, Jordan tried to regain her feet. Injured arm held securely against her side, she popped up. She came up too quickly and stumbled, losing her balance. As the girl careened toward her, Jamie caught her friend's arm to steady her. Once steadied, Jordan lunged for her club, almost losing her balance again. She swept the weapon from the ground and spun back toward the beast.

Jamie was amazed; the beast was paying them no attention. Hunched low to the ground, its eyes darted around as it backpedaled. Its head jerked back and forth and around as if trying to locate a threat. Jamie and Jordan's eyes met, each puzzled by the beast's behavior. With sudden clarity, Jamie realized she couldn't have cared less why the creature was acting so strangely. It had almost killed them both just moments ago. And she wanted to leave. Would it let th—

The rock below her feet shifted. *Earthquake. It sensed the earthquake.*

As the quake got stronger, a chunk of the ceiling across the chamber plummeted to the floor.

"Run," Jordan called as they lurched toward the ramp. She stumbled again, but Jamie caught her under the arm. Left hand wedged into the other girl's armpit, Jamie half-dragged, half-carried the smaller girl toward the exit.

At their sudden movement, the beast snapped out of its trance with a roar. Already halfway up the incline, they wisely ignored the petulant creature. Around them, chunks of stone were falling from the ceiling and walls. They dodged the falling rock as best they could as they swept up the final few steps of the ramp and sprinted for the cave mouth. The beast appeared, rushing up the opposite ramp. A large rock clipped Jamie's shoulder as it tumbled from above. A numbness spread down the length of her right arm at the impact, almost causing her to drop the spear.

Jamie shoved Jordan toward the opening and brought the spear up, pointing it at the beast. Through the corner of her eye, Jamie watched Jordan scramble up the incline. More stones were falling throughout the cave, crashing down all around her.

"Come on! Hurry up!" Jordan bellowed as she dropped to her knees just outside the cave.

After one last look at the beast, Jamie darted for the tunnel. Her eyes locked on Jordan's extended hand as she careened off the sides of the passage. Behind her, she heard larger rocks slam into the ground. It felt like the stones followed her through the tunnel, falling at her heels. Would she make it? A cloud of dust shot up the passage and obscured her sight as she dove for the exit.

Jordan Adler
8:55 am

Jordan sat back on her legs and peered into the dust. She swept her good arm around, trying to clear it. Deep coughs boomed from her lungs, a result of the dust that invaded her nostrils and mouth. A moment ago, Jamie had barreled up the tunnel toward her. Then, poof, she'd disappeared.

"Ouch," Jamie murmured, hidden from view.

Jordan sighed. *At least she's alive.*

As the stone dust dissipated, Jordan caught sight of the other girl. Covered in stone dust, Jamie lay on her belly. *She's ok.* Jordan shifted her weight and brought her legs out from under her, then she sprawled onto her back. Her chest heaved as she tried to catch her breath. Faces only a couple of feet apart, Jordan stared at Jamie.

Jamie arched her back and lifted her shoulders. As she brought her arms forward, her weight settled on her elbows. Head resting on one palm, she let out a soft grunt.

"What's wrong," Jordan muttered.

Mouth curled into a pout and nose scrunched up, Jamie

glowered at her. "I'm stuck," she grumbled.

Jordan shifted her gaze to Jamie's legs. Only the heel of her right shoe protruded from the pile of rocks now blocking the cave entrance. Jamie gave her leg a few quick tugs, then moaned.

"Well, it's been nice knowing you." Jordan shrugged impassively. A slight grin spread across her face at the glare the other girl shot her.

"That's not funny," Jamie grumbled.

"A little bit." Jordan held her thumb and forefinger barely apart and peered at Jamie through the gap.

CHAPTER 64

Fredrick Delacroix
One Month Later
10:34 am

Fredrick Delacroix stood at the ready, behind the heavy equipment. Armed with an M4 of his own, Fredrick was prepared for the so-called beast, if it were to attack. A pair of inexpensive earplugs dampened most of the racket emanating from the industrial hydraulic hammer as it shattered the chunks of rock into smaller pieces. As the breaker's arm moved aside, he watched a massive earthmover scoop a load of soil and rock. Small bits of earth fell from the edges of the bucket as it shifted to dump its load.

A month before, not long after Professor Stone had driven his handful of survivors away, Fredrick Delacroix and Alan Harris had been surprised to experience an earthquake. With a magnitude of 3.8, the earthquake had been nowhere near the largest in the state, nor was it as large as the one the week before. With the earthquake, a rockfall had collapsed the cave's entryway and the instability of the cave system had made it difficult to uncover the spot where the girls had last seen the 'creature' as they called it. Aside from the necessity of confirming the status of the animal, it was imperative they recover the bodies reported to be in the cave.

For nearly a month, the recovery process had been delayed as the Corps of Engineers attempted to bring in excavation equipment to dig out the cave-in and was further hindered by the need to clear a route to the cave. Luckily, the massive cave system to the north, where he'd found the Native American artifacts and later the professor, and his students, found the prehistoric artwork, had been spared any serious damage. Researchers were already clamoring to study the find, demanding access to the site, despite the danger of a bloodthirsty predator. So far, the authorities had been able to keep the scientists away with claims that the area may still be unsafe. But, as the weeks passed without any further sign of animal attacks, nor even a hint of a big cat, the scientists were becoming more insistent. Hopefully, when they cleared the cave, they would be able to confirm the danger had passed.

He still didn't know if he believed that an ancient mythical creature was responsible for the carnage, or that it had chased the group through the forest. But, with the story in his mind, waiting with the corpses of eight people had been disquieting. A closer inspection of the deceased's wounds had convinced Frederick that something had attacked them, and it hadn't been human. Each story had been similar, yet different enough, that they hadn't sounded rehearsed. He'd come to a decision that day, which he would likely never admit to a living soul, if anything had come out of the surrounding woods on more than two legs, he would have shot it. Squirrel, deer, or giant cat. Luckily, he hadn't been forced to kill any wildlife.

He felt the same about the cave now.

An immense wave of relief had swept over him last month when the surge of emergency personnel flooded the area. They had still been in the preliminary stages of the search when two young women had been spotted shuffling toward them. They'd come up the road from the southwest. There had been general confusion. According to the little girl's information, the two had been assumed to be somewhere off to the east. Though, it had been a sight to see, an incredibly tall girl with lacerations across her torso, a blown pupil, a limp, and one missing shoe, had been leaning heavily on a much shorter, petite girl carrying a Native American bone weapon and cradling a broken left arm. The uniform coat of stone dust covering them was broken up by strokes of deepest crimson where both girls had received scrapes and gashes.

Things became clearer as the two young women, Jordan and Jamie, had shared their story. According to them, the earthquake had buried the creature in its lair, along with the bodies of their classmates. With the appearance of the last known survivors, the search had shifted from search and rescue to recovery. For most, the news of the animal's confinement had come as a relief. However, not everyone was convinced the danger had passed, Fredrick and Harris among them. Though, with the threat the animal posed seeming to have vanished, the search for the cave had begun. It seemed the girls had left a signpost at the entrance of the collapsed cave. The discovery of Jamie's right shoe sticking from between the fallen rocks had allowed the searchers to make a positive identification of the collapsed entry. From there it was a waiting game. Several of the searchers had tried to begin excavation, but it had proved too difficult. The section of rock that caught the edge of Jamie's shoe had been so big, so heavy, that Fredrick was amazed the girl hadn't lost her foot. If she had been a breath slower, she would have, at the very least, lost several toes.

It hadn't been until a week after the incident that searchers found a hunter's body in the woods to the northwest. The coroner had determined he'd died the same day as all the others. The man's brother was still missing, and it was assumed he was somewhere in the caves, though none of the girls had seen him. They had unfortunately identified Myranda Hernandez, much to Harris' dismay. All three of the young women had seen Michael Redfern, and the older two had come across Henry Blake deeper in the cave. From what he'd heard of the young man, Fredrick was deeply impressed. Keeping that young girl safe had been an astounding accomplishment.

Around Fredrick, the search and rescue personnel had begun to shift as if in anticipation. His gaze swept up from the spot of earth he'd been focusing on and scanned the nearby faces. Without knowing it, Fredrick had let his attention wander from the excavation. Lost in his thoughts, he'd failed to realize how close they were to clearing the tunnel. Each face he scanned was a mixture of apprehension and relief. His gaze drifted back to the opening as the excavator's boom arm angled away, its bucket carrying one last load of stone and debris.

Both Fredrick and Harris had volunteered to go in ahead of the first wave of SAR personnel, so they moved up to the newly opened entryway.

"Are you ready for this?" Harris murmured.

Fredrick shrugged and inched the rifle's bolt back while turning the M4 to the side, making sure the first round was in the chamber. He'd checked his rifle several times during the wait, but still took a moment to double-check. For the first time, he wondered whether the animal could be hurt by bullets. At the time, he'd considered the protestations about the creature being immune to anything except the blessed weapons to have been panic. Now he wasn't as certain. With the flick of a switch, a lance of bright light shot out from the flashlight, mounted on the right side of the rifle and illuminated the cave's entrance.

"I guess," Fredrick replied.

At a nod from Alan Harris, both men rushed into the opening, one after another. Upon entering the cavern, Fredrick broke to the left. Keeping his focus locked just beyond his front sight, he shifted the rifle's barrel across the room. A powerful beam of light followed the movement of his weapon, its cone illuminating the cave floor. The worst of the rockfall seemed to be centered around the entry tunnel, but large rocks, small to medium-sized boulders really, lay strewn about the floor in his line of sight. *It's a wonder the young ladies made it out.*

In the illumination, he failed to notice any sign of the creature as the light arched from the middle of the cavern to the wall to his left. Nor did he catch sight of either body said to be in the cave.

"Clear," Harris called as he completed the sweep of his side of the room.

"Clear," Fredrick responded.

He shifted his gaze toward the other man. Harris stood in a niche at the bottom of the right-hand slope, peering at a bloodstain that had seeped into the rock floor. From the information they'd received from the girls, it should have been where they'd last seen the body of Myranda Hernandez. Absent too was the mortal remains of Michael Redfern. Another stain was all that marked the space where he'd lain.

By all appearances, the creature, or whatever it was, had survived the cave-in. Fredrick brought the barrel of his rifle around to aim it at the entryways to the three tunnels leading further into the cave system.

"Harris." After a moment without receiving the other man's attention, Fredrick tried again, "Allen."

That got the other man's attention, and he whirled to gaze at Fredrick. As the first wave of the rescue personnel swarmed into the cave, accompanied by another armed deputy, the lights they carried better illuminated Harris. Etched on Harris' face was a look of grief Fredrick hadn't been prepared for. Tears threatened to burst from the other man's eyes.

"I can't do this," Harris lamented. "I'm sorry, I thought I could, but I can't."

More sheriff's deputies and other armed law enforcement personnel were flooding into the cave system.

Making sure to keep his weapon trained toward each of the three tunnels, in turn, Fredrick stepped over to his new friend. A month of being in each other's company, be it meetings, reports, or a beer after work had cemented their bond.

"It's ok," Fredrick soothed. "Come on, let's go back up. We'll leave this to the others."

"I thought once I'd seen her body…" Harris trailed off, turning back to the space Hernandez should have lain. "But now she's missing all over again."

During their many talks, Harris had implied that he believed seeing Hernandez's body would give him some of the closure he hoped for. Fredrick hadn't been convinced, but how was he to know. But for Harris, finding his young protégé missing, yet again, must have been tough.

Fredrick gave the tunnels one more fleeting glance before he led Harris out of the cave system and back to the sheriff's mobile command tent.

Once they reached the command center, all they could do was wait. Scores of people had swamped the caves to search for the bodies and the animal. Along with the deputies were officers from the nearby towns, EMS personnel, firefighters, animal control officers, caving experts, and even several hunters.

About an hour after the search began, news came back to them that the remains of three bodies had been discovered deep within the system. From the descriptions, it appeared to be Henry Blake, Myranda Hernandez, and Michael Redfern. Though saddened, Harris took the news well.

As the hours stretched, the searchers still hadn't come across the animal, dead or alive. It wasn't until almost evening that a group of searchers found a narrow passage of freshly dug soil and rock, which led from the cave system. Overlapping footprints left in the dried mud near the newly discovered exit suggested that the animal had escaped sometime during the previous month.

Jamison Roberts

A fan of horror, Jamison Roberts particularly enjoys the monster movie, the creature feature. In *Cherokee Sabre*, his first foray into writing, Jamison shares his love of the genre with this adaptation of a Cherokee legend. A proud member of the Cherokee Nation, Jamison is a native of Tulsa, OK, and attended Tulsa Community College, where he studied videography, photography, and graphic design.

JamisonRobertsBooks.com